THE LIBRARY BOOK

THE LIBRARY BOOK

by
John Fiske

Black Spruce Media
Prides Crossing, Massachusetts

In Memory of my Godfather

George J. (Jay) Hill III
1932–1999

"A tongue-tied Yankee"

Cover photograph: *New York Public Library*, © Jason Speros and
BigStockPhoto.com
Title and end page photograph: *New York Public Library* (front and back)
courtesy of the New York Public Library
Cover & Interior Design: Mark Jewett, Appingo Publishing Services,
www.appingo.com

Distributed by Black Spruce Media, www.blacksprucemedia.com

Library of Congress Cataloging-in-Publication Data is available.

Printed at Versa Press in the United States of America.
Printed on recycled paper (30% PCW and FSC-certified) using soy-content inks.

10 9 8 7 6 5 4 3 2 1

Author's Note

The idea for this book lurched unexpectedly into my brain one evening as I sat on our sofa reading *The Man in the Iron Mask* by Alexandre Dumas. My wife and I had recently seen the movie starring Leonardo DiCaprio, and I was reading the book because I wanted to find out what really happened.

I had been doing a lot of scuba diving in Vermont. Most people associate Vermont with the Green Mountains, skiing, maple syrup, and quaintness in general. Not I. I think of Vermont as home of an extinct industry: marble quarrying. A hundred years ago, marble was Vermont's biggest industry, and quarries operated the entire length of the state from south to north, but principally near Dorset, West Rutland, and Proctor. Therefore, today the landscape is pockmarked by hundreds of abandoned water-filled quarries. To me, each one represents a dive opportunity.

It has been great fun tramping through Vermont's Central Valley looking for now-forgotten quarries. Many are overgrown and set back hundreds of yards from a road. Sometimes a quarry is accessible enough to warrant a dive.

As I read *The Man in the Iron Mask* that evening in June 1998, scuba diving in Vermont was on my mind: I had just been there. At the same time I was reading Dumas's convoluted story, I was wondering where all that quarried marble had gone. I also noted that Dumas seemed not to be in control of his story as he wrote it. Why was Dumas out of control? I set the book down and said, "I have to find out why he's out of control." All I knew was that somehow the marble would be part of my investigation.

I found out rather easily where the marble had gone: headstones, mantels, churches, libraries, courthouses, zoos, academic buildings, and the like. Exploring the creative relationship, however, proved to be much tougher. I spoke with artists I knew, read books by scholars of the human mind, and tried my own hand at watercolor painting. Most of those I interviewed thought I wanted to know about the creative *process*.

"No," I said, "the creative *relationship*." One portrait artist refused to discuss it with me, saying that it was too personal. Other artists nodded knowingly as I spoke, but were unable to find the words to describe it. The one man who could was my uncle, Francis Fiske. He's a musician and composer with an excellent ability to construct just the phrases I needed. Those phrases form the backbone of the creative relationship discussion in this book.

I found through my research that the marble used to construct The New York Public Library had come from Vermont. The Library was sufficiently monumental as the subject of my emerging story. And there was a tragedy that would give the story an appropriate ending. Therefore, rather quickly, I settled on the design and construction of The New York Public Library as context for the story. The architectural firm that had designed the Library was Carrère & Hastings, well known in its day although now largely forgotten.

Here I must acknowledge that two of the vignettes in this book are not fiction of my creating but actual events. The story of Charles McKim and Thomas Hastings — the picture of the bench and the nude—was told by William Adams Delano, who had known Thomas Hastings personally. The tale appears in *The Century*, the 100th anniversary book on the Century Club (1946). I found the tale about John Carrère, John Mitchell, and George Cable in Carrère's own diary, which is in the Library of Congress in Washington, DC.

I must thank Professor Alden Gordon for tipping me off to Channing Blake's dissertation on the architecture of Carrère & Hastings in the Avery Library at Columbia University. Marthe Aimée, my longtime art teacher, taught me about negative space in the context of art. As you'll read, you'll discover that I had a lot of fun with the concept.

Lisa Colt read a horrid early draft, and I thank her for doing so. Kay Bourne has lovingly encouraged me to write since I was an adolescent. Mary, my wife, has quietly and patiently supported this endeavor. And my son Alex knows more about Beaux-Arts architecture (and bad public art) than any nine-year-old in America.

Prelude

On a perfect October Saturday in 1997, my friend Gil and I arrived at the side of an old marble quarry nestled in a flat valley in central Vermont. Occasional white and gray clouds loitered overhead, while all around the quarry, yellow leaves fell from white birch trees. Under my feet lay an exposed slab of gray granite: the solid earth. I studied the black water in the old quarry. The water rippled clear, and pure, and oh-so-suitable for a dive. We knew little about the place except that the quarry extended far underground, forming a cave. Prudence and caution told us not to go in, but there would be a lot to see, and I was excited.

I stood on a granite ledge that rose about four feet from the water. Here and there, rusted iron rods and rings embedded into the stone, spoke of the old operation that had taken marble from the earth, leaving this pit. At my feet I saw no reflection, only clear water, and opportunity. I could see the muted shape of a vehicle, lying upside down. What else waited down there? My excitement mounted.

Moments later we were in the water, attired in neoprene wetsuits to protect us from the anticipated cold, and a thousand dollars' worth of scuba equipment. That car was to be our first waypoint, we agreed, and then we'd see what we'd find. In fifteen feet of water, we encountered a Jeep Cherokee missing all four wheels. How did it get here with no wheels? A wrecked dirt bike lay nearby. Just beyond, the water deepened dramatically. Gil and I adjusted our gear so that we neither floated nor sank, but swam across that intriguing depth. We released a small amount of air from our buoyancy vests and slipped downward into a space that reminded me of a cathedral. Neatly chiseled walls on all four sides grew farther apart as we descended. Gil slowly angled away from me, suspended with nothing between us except clear, frigid, motionless water. His underwater lights threw sharp yellow beams like the light sabers in *Star Wars*. I examined my gauges and found that the water was only forty-two degrees Fahrenheit. The roaring noise of my exhaust bubbles came close, louder and more noticeable: I knew I was swimming at a depth of about one hundred feet. The bottom was still twenty feet below me. I shined my light saber onto the tire of a giant earth-moving vehicle and a wooden rowboat. Then I studied Gil's bubbles, which rose inexorably like ever-expanding mushroom caps gleaming in the yellow beam from my light. Far above, where the walls of this great stone cathedral came almost together, I saw a very small, blue, bright square—the surface. I turned round, surveying the rock walls in three quadrants. They defined the experience and this space. The fourth side was a black cave. That place's space made me wonder: how could this extraordinary place exist? Only divers came here. And yet, it was there because something real had happened, long ago. There was no marble to be seen—it had been cut out and taken away. As I swam in that old quarry I was puzzled: what do you *call* this kind of place?

Part One

Design

Sequence

At lunch Monday, I stole a few minutes in our firm's library to find out what I could about Vermont marble. I had been working at a small architectural firm, Simcoe + Verbridge, for about a year, and I had not really explored the library. Of course, I was well acquainted with the Avery Library at Columbia, where I had studied architecture and urban planning, but while there I had never looked up marble. There were quite a few marble buildings in New York, but I had never wondered where the material came from. Now I had a vague idea—a marble quarry, of course.

The library at the firm wasn't much, just a few dozen books randomly shelved in the hall at the top of the stairs leading to the third floor. Most of the books were engineering texts; one book was a photo collection of Walter Gropius's work, and several others dealt with urban designs. One book, *Drafting Room Practice*, had a bookplate indicating that the book belonged to one Roy W. Burger of Santa Barbara, California, 1937. My mother was born that year. How did that book get here?

How did *I* get here, a young architect at a firm in the still-gritty former mill town of Manchester, the largest city in New Hampshire? I had loved New York's excitement, its social possibilities, and of course, its varied architecture (except the endless brownstones). But I didn't want a crowded or fast life. I wanted clean air and to be able to see the stars at night. So I came home and found Simcoe +Verbridge. In the interviews, Alan Simcoe and Jayne Verbridge said that they were delighted to find someone with Big City credentials. Within a week I was at work in Manchester.

We were located on the second and third floors of an old mill building in Manchester, New Hampshire. Outside was the Merrimack River; the Amoskeag hydroelectric dam upstream to the right in my view. Paralleling the other side of the river was Interstate 293. My job there was pretty typical for a small-city architect. I designed houses, additions, and from time to time I worked on municipal projects like parking garages or fire stations. I was not a "celebrity architect," and I didn't want to be one either.

As I crouched to look at the books on the bottom shelf, Jayne stepped in behind me and asked if she could help me find something.

"I'm looking for some information about marble as a building material," I said quietly.

Jayne said nothing.

"There are marble buildings all across the country." I looked up at the forty-year-old partner. I didn't know much about her except that she was a very talented designer and a part-time rock 'n' roller with a band in Portsmouth. "The Supreme Court in Washington is one." I said thinking out loud as Jayne stood by. "How can I find out where a building's marble came from?"

"You should be able to look that up."

"At the Avery Library, not here," I said, instantly regretting that I had left New York.

"I have something that might help. Come with me to my office and I'll show you." Jayne flipped her long dyed-black hair from her left shoulder to her right. "But tell me, why the interest?"

I described scuba diving in the quarry. "Isn't that dangerous?" she asked, pulling a slim paperback from the shelves along the wall.

"We know what we're doing."

Jayne thumbed through the book, replaced it, and took out another. " I still have one of my father's books. It could be helpful, if I remember right."

"Why would you have that?" I asked. "You do interior designs."

"My dad gave it to me a long time ago before he died."

"Oh, I'm sorry," I stammered.

"It's okay. He was killed in a motorcycle accident when I was in college, more than twenty years ago. He was a structural engineer. He thought this book might interest me. Ah! Here it is. I'd never part with it."

Jayne handed me the book with a tan cover, about eight by ten inches, two inches thick, matte pages. "I think there's a chapter near the beginning on structural marble," she said. "Why don't you take it home?"

"This book's precious to you. I can study it here."

"Wherever you like," Jayne said softly. "Just, when you're done, please tell me what you find."

Jayne's book was filled with information I never knew about marble. According to the first chapter:

"In the warm, shallow Ordovician sea, primitive life abounded. Five million cen-

turies ago, trilobites, corals, mollusks and other animals colonized the sea floor. After each tiny animal died, its hard shell fell to the sea floor. Over the course of seventy thousand centuries, the shells accumulated. The shells reached astonishing depths: thousands and thousands of feet in some regions of the sea floor.

"The land was forbiddingly stark, barren rock supporting no life. There was no ice anywhere on the planet either. In the vast, desolate expanses of time, storms eroded the land, bit by bit, little by little. Minerals, sand and silt washed into the sea, and settled onto the shells layered on the bottom of the ocean.

"While life thrived and evolved in the sea, the Earth's surface, too, changed. Its large sections moved slowly, ever so slowly, in such a way as to cause the warm shallow sea, swarming with life, to be displaced by land. As the sea and its life gradually disappeared, the shells eventually solidified into limestone.

"Over the next ten thousand centuries, the planet's crust shifted, broke and sheared. Some rock was buried under miles of surface material. Mountains were built up and gradually eroded. Rock layers folded. Newer rock was shoved beneath older rock. Rocks buried deep in mountains now called the Taconics recrystallized. Heat and pressure metamorphosed the rock. The limestone became marble."

I set the book down on my desk and stared out the window toward the Merrimack. How many quarries were there, I asked myself. I looked at the book's cover. Who wrote this? Strange sea animals metamorphosed into limestone and then marble. New Hampshire was the Granite State. Maybe Vermont should have been the Marble State. And Manchester would be the brick city, because all the mill buildings along the river were brick.

Chapter three explained some of the challenges of marble as a building material, as well as things I had never heard of in rock—grain, cutters, cracks, coloration, and so on. There were also pen-and-ink sketches of the Supreme Court building in Washington and the New York Public Library. I had seen and studied both, I realized, but I did not know they were Vermont marble. What if the stone had came from the quarry we dove last weekend?

I burst into Jayne's office without knocking. She was on the phone and putting on lipstick at the same time. I tried not to notice that she must have been going out after work.

"That was fast," Jayne said, hanging up.

I threw the book down on her uncluttered desk, open to the sketches. "These buildings," I spluttered excitedly. "I spent quite a lot of time at the New York Public Library when I was at Columbia. If I'd only known."

"Only known what?" The white straw sticking out of Jayne's can of Pepsi had red lipstick on it.

"Um, if the—marble, the library," I actually didn't have any idea.

My girlfriend, Peri, and I had been planning to go to New York to see some graduate school friends, so it was a perfect opportunity for me to see what I could find. She went to nursing school at NYU and lived in Brooklyn. We had met at our church, the Fourth Universalist. An old girlfriend had gotten me involved there. It wasn't near Columbia, and I liked the rector and the welcoming congregation. Peri and I both were in the choir. After a while I realized I was wasting my time with Lyn and I really wanted to be with Peri. So I sent Lyn packing, and before long Peri and I had been together for three years.

She was more eager than I was to return to New York, but once there I made a quick trip to Columbia's Avery Library of Architecture. I knew that there I would find some answers about the New York Public Library and its marble. After all, I had spent many graduate school hours there, so I knew what I would find. I bent over to kiss Peri—at six-three I stood a foot taller than Peri—and assured her that I'd be only a few hours.

As a New Hampshire architect designing additions and fire stations, I didn't really feel entitled to the regal treatment I received when I darkened the Avery's doorstep. The librarians recognized me! I was merely one of the hundreds of architecture students that pass through Columbia. "Henry Peabody, what brings you here? It seems like yesterday that you graduated," Priscilla Sukoski, the librarian, greeted me.

I must have blushed because I felt my face get hot. I took a seat at her desk in the same chair I had used when I was a graduate student. "It's only been a little more than a year since I graduated," I protested mildly.

"Are you still with that nice girl?"

"Yes, and we live in Manchester, New Hampshire. Peri found a job in the hospital there, and I joined a local firm. We might get married someday."

"Oh, I knew everything would turn out okay for you," Mrs. Sukoski said, leaning toward me. "But you didn't come here just to see me."

"I wish I could say that, but I'm actually looking for some information." I had brought only a legal pad and a mechanical pencil with me. "I want to look at a dissertation by C. Channing Blake on the architecture of Carrère & Hastings—you know, the architects who designed the New York Public Library."

"Yes, I remember Channing Blake," the librarian smiled. "I can get that for you." Mrs. Sukoski efficiently bustled out of the carpeted room to get what I hoped would tell me where the quarry's marble went.

I read on pages 233 and 234 of Channing Blake's dissertation that the New York Public Library's marble had come from The Norcross-West Quarry in Dorset, Vermont, and not from the quarry Gil and that I dove. But when I read the dissertation, I realized I wanted to know more about Carrère. I called Jayne to let her know I'd be in New York another day. Peri worked three twelve-hour days a week and wasn't conflicted by another day in the Large Apple.

The next day, I went to the New York Public Library's archives to study some very obscure manuscript diaries of some of Carrère & Hastings's employees. The archives had interesting stuff, and I learned about Carrère, but not much about Hastings. It seems that John Carrère had wanted to write a book about the New York Public Library, but never did.

As an undergraduate I had briefly studied classical architecture, but had never thought about it again. At Columbia, I learned about Walter Gropius, Le Corbusier, and the other fantastic modernist architects who changed the world. And then, deep within the New York Public Library, I read about columns and pilasters, vaults and capitals. It was like a new language to me, and I rubbed my eyes.

Peri's Kia was an inexpensive, lightweight shell of a car. Even when I put the seat all the way back, there wasn't enough room for my long legs. She drove carefully, often too slowly, in the Merritt Parkway's right lane. We were passed all the time by expensive new BMWs and Saabs. The Kia, though, got great gas mileage, and I didn't complain.

"You were in the library for a long time," she said.

Peri hadn't ever been to the New York Public Library, so I tried to explain what it was like. "I went to the archives, a room with several large tables off the main reading room. They bring the materials to you."

"You must have found something; you're kinda quiet." She looked quickly at me, and then glanced in the rearview mirror.

I waited a few minutes before addressing this. Peri shifted to the left lane to pass an old, slow-moving Cadillac. I clasped my hands behind my head. "I think I'm onto something very important."

Peri whipped me a glance. "How can you know it's important?"

"Well, you see, there were two architects, Thomas Hastings and John Carrère. Carrère & Hastings was their firm."

"I thought you were trying to find out about the marble quarry," Peri interrupted.

"Well, that turned out to be easy. Marble was taken from different parts of Vermont, not just the quarry Gil and I had visited. I went to the library, since it's of Vermont marble, to see if there was anything else." Peri washed the windshield; the wipers oscillated back and forth. "There must be more, and I'll just have to see where it leads." I put my hands in my lap, feeling satisfied for now. As the Kia whined back to New Hampshire, I fell asleep.

Months passed. I thought marble and libraries whenever I could. Jayne was a dedicated boss. She hectored me to produce, produce, produce—drawings, engineering information, and ideas. I sometimes envied Peri's job, even though her hours at the hospital were very scattered. She certainly didn't have such a demanding employer.

Gradually, I started to think about Carrère's book. I wanted to know more about the marble and why Carrère wanted to write a book. What was it going to be about? Why didn't he finish, or even start? What were Hastings's methods, and did they provoke Carrère somehow? I learned that the Library of Congress in Washington, DC was in possession of Carrère's diaries, so I went there to read them. The Library of Congress had only two volumes out of the eleven Carrère had supposedly written. Perhaps there were clues to the unwritten book in the missing volumes.

At the Library of Congress, red carpet stretched in front of me for miles and miles along a corridor leading toward discovery and accomplishment. Building additions and fire stations somehow weren't so interesting anymore. I looked into Carrère's family history. He had had three daughters. One died an infant; one lived into her twenties; and the other, Anna, had never married but lived to about eighty. There was only one living descendant of John Carrère, but he knew nothing about his ancestor the architect.

Carrère was one of three brothers, as was I. Only one survived him, and in 1949, that brother's house had burned down. I wondered whether the missing diaries had gone up with the house. I'd never know. I took back what I had just said about fire stations.

Back in New Hampshire, I was awakened early one morning in May by the vernal songs of robins and chickadees outside our bedroom window. I had never heard spring songbirds in New York. Peri rolled over. Before I let her go back to sleep, I whispered, "I've started writing Carrère's book."

"When?" she sleepily asked.

"Every day, all the time," I said, sitting up, dazzled by the early morning sunlight streaming through the crack between the window shade and the casing. Little did I know how one thing would lead to another, and to another.

Peri nodded off again saying, "That's fine, honey."

Carrère

Carrère waited as his partner, Thomas Hastings, made another change to the drawings for a client's country house. It was time for lunch. "One more thing here. Another thing here and here," Hastings bubbled. He furiously erased, drew, erased, and drew again. His eyes seemed to pop out of his head; his every nerve was on fire. And as Carrère watched, he wondered: Does Hastings own the drawing, or is it the other way around?

"Let's go to lunch," Carrère finally suggested. "Aren't you done yet?"

Hastings agreed, "There's one more thing, though. I've got… to…" He was reluctant to stop what he was doing. "It's good for now. I can always change it later, if I want."

They bounded down the stairs to Broadway. "Compare New York to Paris," Carrère barked as they jostled their way through the crowd. Unbroken lines of men dodged and weaved in and out like runners on a football field, crowding the sidewalk, each man in pursuit of an objective. Carrère was 39, making a living as an architect in New York. Before that he had studied architecture at the Ecole des Beaux-Arts in Paris. Born in Rio to American parents, he lived in Lausanne as an adolescent. "Paris has a monument in every public square," said Carrère. A gentleman stopped abruptly in front of him to gaze into a shop window and Carrère bumped into him. " 'scuse me," he said.

It was almost noon on that bright late April day in 1897. "The Arc de Triomphe is one," agreed Hastings, who was two years younger than Carrère. A stooped man walking head-down nearly collided with him. The partners ducked down the three steps into their usual lunch spot at 163 Broadway. The pale yellow sign hanging out front proclaimed "Homemade" in black letters. The small café was dark; it always took a moment for their eyes to adjust.

"Will it be the usual?" called out Vincent, the counter clerk, upon seeing the architects. Vincent was an older man with bushy, graying eyebrows reminiscent of an amiable cobbler Carrère had visited one summer long ago while vacationing with his grandmother in Dieppe. Gran had brought him to Maurice's shoe repair shop because the heel of one of his shoes had started to fall off. Maurice had given the young Carrère a chocolate candy.

"Soup and crackers for me," Carrère called out to Vincent.

"Minestrone?"

Carrère nodded.

Vincent reached for a plate and two bowls. "What about you, Mister Hastings?"

"Tomato and celery soup and rye crackers," said Hastings, ready with his reply.

Hastings and Carrère made themselves comfortable at the counter side-by-side on wooden stools. Carrère leaned on the counter and studied Hastings. All he saw was clear, unalloyed ambition—nothing to suggest anything like what had happened to Carrère's friend Horace Avery.

Hastings shook his head slowly, then smiled, "The Arc de Triomphe at the head of the Champs-Elysses. I love Paris."

Carrère's thoughts turned back to his sick friend. It seemed like a very long time ago that Horace Avery, the prolific portrait artist, had gone into the hospital.

He had simply vanished, disappearing from Carrère's life, from society. Horace had gone crazy; Carrère wanted to know why.

They had become friends at a farm stand in Staten Island. Carrère loved telling the tale: a bin of summer squash at a farmer's market tipped over and dumped its contents on a woman whose arms were already full of vegetables. They both had rushed to assist the woman. In the commotion Horace and Carrère had become acquainted, and by chance discovered they were in related professions. Within a couple of months they were dining together, discussing art, each enjoying the company of the other introspective artist.

Carrère thought of his first visit with Avery in the hospital. "Horace, it's me—your friend, John Carrère," he announced cautiously. In the air hung a faint medicinal odor, which reminded him of the infirmary at school in France, when he was young. It was not an infirmary, though. It was a place for people who are sick of mind. Horace had been there for a few months.

Avery was seated toward the window, back to the door, in a brown wicker chair, his shoulders covered with a white blanket. At first Carrère could see only the top of Horace's head. He walked slowly around to see his artist-friend, whose white angular hands were folded on his lap. Avery's blue hospital gown was open at the neck; his collarbones protruded unnaturally, plainly revealing how much weight he had lost. His once-thick mop of brown hair was now thin, tangled, and substantially gray. Carrère was stunned at the change in his friend's appearance: Horace was only 31.

A half-empty glass of water sat on a table beside the chair. The dirty window was open a few inches. Spring breezes drifted into Avery's room, carrying vernal aromas of life and hope. Alas, Horace appeared hopeless, and his condition made Carrère uneasy. "It's a nice day to be outside, Horace."

Horace's sunken eyes were gray and lifeless. Not a flicker of recognition—not even a shrug—indicated he was aware of Carrère's presence. Carrère looked around the room for another chair. He found a steel one near the porcelain sink, carefully moved it near Horace's, and sat. "Horace," he repeated in a strong, clear voice, "it's John Carrère here to see you. Miss Bough told me you were here."

Horace stirred, shifting his weight in the chair, and looked at Carrère, this time with recognition. He mumbled something unintelligible. A rotund, well-endowed nurse entered carrying a tray with an apple and a fresh glass of water. She wore the customary white nurse's dress, white cap, and round-toed white shoes. Seeing Carrère, she demanded to know who he was and with whose permission he was there.

"My name is John Carrère, and I am visiting my friend, ma'am," he said. "I want to see if there's any way I can help to make him well again."

"Oh, I don't think you can," the haughty nurse said. "He's going to be here a long time, and you shouldn't be here at all."

With the nurse's arrival, Horace became agitated. "I wish you would leave," he growled at the nurse. He spit into a bowl reserved for the purpose.

"That's the first thing he has said all day," the nurse sneered. "He's not well. Anyone can see that."

Carrère waited, not knowing what to say or do. This was the first time he had ever visited a mental hospital. Miss Bough, his secretary at work, had warned him that there might be some tension between Horace and the nurses. Then the fat nurse said, "You have fifteen minutes." She placed the apple and glass of water on a bedstand beyond Avery's reach and abruptly left.

"I hate her," Horace said in a low voice. "I hate this place." It was an unusual pronouncement from him. Carrère had always known him to keep his opinions to himself. Horace Avery, the fine portrait artist, communicated with a paintbrush. He was a master of visual detail, always finding a unique way of expressing something. And he usually let his paintings express himself rather than words, of all things.

"I can see why," Carrère agreed. "She's harsh. I wouldn't want to see her every morning."

"It's worse that that," Avery explained, straightening in the chair again. "She's taken away my pencils and books. She won't let me do anything. I can't even draw. What's the point?"

Carrère leaned forward, elbows on his knees, recognizing his friend's lost, forbidden activity, "This nurse is a witch. I see why you hate her, especially after Miss Bough. Did you know Miss Bough came to us after you came here? You lost a lot more than your freedom, I'd say."

Avery stroked a scraggly beard on his chin, and said, "I loved her—her sweet smile, the way she organized my things, her love of all the things I did—but my work! It was everything, my whole life, until—"

"I know." Carrère slid backward in his chair and looked at Horace again. He remembered how Horace had begun to lose weight, couldn't do his work anymore because, as he complained, he wasn't sleeping well. He babbled incessantly about Poe's pit, a pit with high steel walls. He wondered if there were some connection between his friend's artistic sensibilities and his deteriorating state of mind. If this ever happened to his partner, an exuberant artist himself, the firm would be ruined, because most of the creative energy would be lost.

Carrère crossed his legs, "You know, Horace, New York is going to build a public library, and we're going to bid the job."

"A library?"

"That's right, a library," Carrère adjusted a cuff-link. "We haven't built one before. We'll have to work hard and not let anything get in our way if we are going to win this commission."

"How are you going to make sure of that?" Avery sank a little deeper in his chair.

The nurse reappeared, this time with a clipboard and a thermometer. "Time to take your temperature," she called out.

Avery sipped from the glass of water. His voice concealed and low, he said, "At least she takes it from my mouth. It used to be from my ass." He trembled with rage at the thought. "I wish I could get out of here."

"You must leave now, Mister Carrère," the nurse instructed.

Carrère stood to move out of the nurse's way. She's a brute, he thought. "I'll update you if we win the commission. Please—" he said as Horace's figure huddled pathetically in the chair.

"Oh, I'll be okay," Horace said in a clarion voice, as if to annoy the nurse. "I want to see this library when it's done."

The drafting room at Carrère & Hastings was a chaotic place. It was filled with boxes of supplies and shelves full of both English and French architectural reference books. The flat-white walls were festooned with elevations and plans from other projects. The space was too small for the number of men who worked there, and often the room was crowded. The never-ending bustle of vendors hawking their wares, carriage traffic, and pedestrians—New York City—in the streets outside the window heightened the excitement within. Hastings and Carrère studied a map of Manhattan. Carrère pointed. "Fifth Avenue and 42nd Street is the proposed location for the Library."

"What about the reservoir?" Hastings said. "What's its name anyway?" There was a large, above-ground stonework reservoir on the site.

"The Croton Reservoir, I think. No, it's the Croton Distributing Reservoir," Carrère said, dredging his memory for the correct name. "It's going to be torn down."

"Won't that affect the city's water supply?" Hastings looked concerned.

"It hasn't been used in years... probably ten years." Carrère looked at the map again.

"That'll make the area nicer," said Hastings. "It's still mainly residential there, even with all the new shops moving in."

"I kind of like the Egyptian look of the reservoir. But a library will be a great improvement."

Hastings nodded vigorously. "Whatever is built, whoever designs it, the library will beautify Fifth Avenue. Well, that section of it, at least. " Hastings traced his finger along the avenue in the map. "There are only two excellent buildings here. Both are up at Central Park, and one isn't even finished!"

"You mean Dick Hunt's Metropolitan Museum of Art."

"And the Lenox Library."

Afternoon sunlight poured through the window onto one of the faded blueprints tacked to the wall. Hastings's carefully combed dark blond hair needed a trim. He wore a dark suit. His white shirt was crisply pressed, his tie straight and black.

Carrère continued. "Nothing can make New York into another Paris, but more buildings like Hunt's, or McKim, Mead & White's will help. Fifth and 42nd is the best place for the new library. It's a prominent spot, next to Bryant Park. Hunt's museum up here in Central Park—that's *country*. Even where the Lenox Library is, too." Carrère tapped the map with the end of a ruler. "70th Street. But down here at 42nd Street it's *city*."

"Also, a library at 42nd Street will interrupt the horrid parallelism of Fifth Avenue," Hastings glared, "Brownstones are just so tiresome, their interminable lack of interruption." Hastings thumped his fist on the table for emphasis.

Carrère took the gesture in stride, as he knew how emotional Hastings could get. Actually, Carrère liked it when Hastings expressed himself so strongly. It reminded him of those wonderful years studying at the Ecole des Beaux-Arts in Paris. The intellectual vigor, the criticisms, the creativity—it was so exciting to be part of it. Hastings was a creative dynamo.

Miss Bough, the secretary, swept into the room carrying the day's mail. Hastings added even more seriously, if possible, "This building could be a major contribution to better public art in New York and a major step toward beautifying the city." Miss Bough, fairly new to the firm, stayed to listen.

Carrère tucked in his shirt and said, "The library, therefore, should be bold, daring, revolutionary—"

"—American architecture suffers from anemia and ignorance," added Hastings with calm authority. He spun a spool of tape around and around on this finger, then tossed it on the table.

"I think so," Carrère agreed as they left the drafting room and walked across the hall to Hastings's office. A clock chimed in the anteroom. "An open competition will get an honest design. The Beaux-Arts movement is alive and well in this city." The bespectacled Hastings settled into a comfortable chair, lit his pipe.

Carrère reclined in another armchair. "Our design will look to classical motifs for inspiration, true to Beaux-Arts aesthetic theory."

"Yes!" Hastings's eyes widened. "Rich materials, frescoes, acanthus leaves everywhere! Rams', eagles', lions' heads—all the embellishments. What fun this will be!"

Sunlight angled into the room through a side window. It made Carrère think of the spring day when he last saw Horace Avery as a healthy man. They had gone for a walk in the park, the sun slanting through the trees creating wonderful patterns of light and shadow on the sidewalk. Nothing is ever simply dark and white, Carrère thought, as the sun's steady light fell onto the floor. Horace seemed to be in a dark world now.

"Steel! We'll use new materials, too, like steel," Hastings enthused, snapping Carrère back to the present. "The Romans didn't have it, but we do, and we'll use it!" He stood, and polished his glasses.

"Many of the older men in our profession have lost their inspiration," Hastings continued boldly. "When a young man comes back from Europe, he's got a thick sketchbook filled with pictures and ideas. He's got intellectual force, with the power to feel as well as to see."

"You mean that Charley McKim and Stanford White are without inspiration?" Carrère said testily. Carrère admired their former employers, but he felt that at times Hastings had too much inspiration. It was not a bad thing to have, of course, but Hastings never knew when to stop.

"All I am saying is that we can win this competition because we are younger."

"And better," Miss Bough added quietly from the doorway.

Carrère liked Miss Bough's confidence. "I think we are in a good place to compete," he said. Carrère noticed several cobwebs high in the corners of the ceiling. Somebody should get rid of them, he thought. The place was a cluttered mess, as well. Dozens of old drawings lay rolled up on top of an overflowing bookcase. Stacks and stacks of old magazines rose in a corner. "We are not as old as Charley and Stanford, yet we have been here awhile and have done some good work."

"Nothing as big as the Library," Hastings said. He locked his fingers together. He did that sometimes.

"True, but we are established," Carrère said.

Miss Bough, the first woman to work at Carrère & Hastings, moved further into Hastings's office and said, "I think you have many good men." Her auburn hair was fashioned in a tight bun, and she was dressed in her usual way, wearing a plaid floor-length skirt, dark flat-heeled shoes, and a brocade shawl about her shoulders. She did not wear any jewelry.

Hastings nodded, "They *are* good. I'll bet several will start their own firms. Barber is very sharp. Magonigle, too." He tapped out his pipe in a ceramic ashtray on the table next to his chair.

"You're a betting man now?" Carrère joked. Hastings grew up in the family of a prominent Presbyterian minister.

Miss Bough hastened to his defense. "He's never placed a bet in his life."

"Thank you Miss Bough." Hastings smiled, knowing that Carrère's ribbing was just fun. "We want to keep Barber and Magonigle around as long as possible. Ward too. They're good men who'll help us win the commission."

"You, gentlemen, are in the people-business," the ever-observant Miss Bough said, her focus shifting from Carrère to Hastings and back. "Make sure you keep your men happy."

"We need you to tell us who's happy and who isn't," Carrère said.

"They'll all be happy if you win the commission," she said with a twinkle.

"And if we keep the paychecks coming."

"We'll make a good design. It's in our training and our schooling." Hastings changed direction. He never concerned himself with the firm's finances. "You know what? Every new work is claimed to be a piece of art. But that's wrong," he said, his fingers drumming on the table. "So much of the new work out there is worthless because it comes from an impulse neither spontaneous nor deep," he concluded. "Our design is going to be revolutionary and perfect."

Hastings sometimes produced big ideas that made Carrère think. This was one of those times. Carrère's awareness of Hastings and Miss Bough faded. If the work is neither spontaneous nor deep, where does it come from? Is creativity spontaneous? Deep? Or both? But then Carrère's attention snapped back to the conversation as Hastings continued.

"We have to propose a functional, classic building for the New York Public Library." Hastings put his pipe in a jacket pocket. "The library we design will be formed by all our experience and love. We'll be John Keats in three dimensions." He moved over to the window, looked down upon peripatetic masses on Broadway, and noticed that the carriages weren't moving at all. He finally turned to face Miss Bough and Carrère, rubbing his palms together. "They'll call our work fresh and genuine, with a close connection to the wide-awake emotions and thoughts of two men who have youth and enthusiasm."

"We haven't won the commission yet," Carrère warned.

One of the things Carrère had to do every day was to sign correspondence Miss Bough typed for him. He then returned the letters to her desk, where she was engrossed with preparing other correspondence. Several of Hastings's sketches lay flat on a table next to her desk. Carrère asked, "Why are these here?"

Miss Bough explained, "He wants me to send them to Mister Geoffrey Harris." Harris was a client Hastings had been working with.

Carrère slipped behind Miss Bough's small wooden desk to look at the sketches. Miss Bough stood to look at the drawings with him. He leaned on the table;

she folded her hands in front of her. "Are these good drawings?" she asked, innocently enough.

"They are adequate preliminary drawings," Carrère said, "sufficient to illustrate the initial idea to the client." And Carrère thought, "Is the original intent of a new building the force that drives Hastings, or does Hastings himself force the building to become what it's going to become? What if he stopped working on the project now?"

"What if the client doesn't like them?"

"Well, Hastings would have to go back to the drawingboard. It's hard to be a designer for someone else because you can't always know what he wants."

"Have you designed your own house?"

"No, not yet," Carrère turned to face Miss Bough, and enjoyed her round, forty-four-year-old dimpled face. "Someday I'd like to."

"So, would it be easier to work for yourself than for a difficult client?"

"I don't know." Carrère picked up one of the sketches and thought of his schooling in Paris so long ago. The Seine River, Notre Dame Cathedral, the bakeries, the entertainment, the other students at the Ecole des Beaux-Arts. Hastings had focused on his studies and hadn't soak up Paris nearly as much as his peers. But his hard work in Paris was yielding superior designs all these years later. Hastings was devoted to his work, but at the expense of what? He'd always preferred to revise than revel. He was so serious about his work. Some things hadn't changed. Carrère dropped the sketch on the others.

"Hastings is a different kind of designer from you."

"Oh yes, very different. He can't stop sometimes and, well, I've pretty much stopped altogether."

"Does that frustrate you?" Miss Bough asked.

Carrère stiffened momentarily, then exhaled. "Not really. What bothers me is that sometimes he ruins a perfectly good design by working on it too much."

"I saw Horace do that a few times, too," Miss Bough said. "I hated what that did to him." She returned to her chair.

"Horace?" Carrère was incredulous.

Miss Bough nodded. "I think when he ruined a painting, he lost a bit of himself, and—"

"You're saying that this could happen to Hastings, then?" Carrère ran both hands through his hair.

"I'm not saying that." Miss Bough tried to calm him with soothing words. "Horace was a gifted man who had a hard time. I just wonder if there's a connection."

"I'm going to keep an eye on Hastings now, because he's the creative power here, and I don't want him to go crazy." Carrère looked up at the ceiling. Horace Avery was in a hospital. What if Thomas Hastings ended up there, too?

"What gives you the idea that he might?

"One time when we were at McKim, Mead & White, Hastings became angry, even irrational, when something he was working on didn't work out. He was sweating, his eyes bulged out. He went around the room shouting that it was unfair, and—"

"That sounds like a temper tantrum to me," Miss Bough said.

"Well, it was pretty scary, Miss Bough," Carrère said.

"Has he had a tantrum here?"

"No," Carrère said. "Not yet, anyway. We can't have outbursts and craziness if we're going to win the Library competition.

Interlude

Since I had been the most recently hired employee at Simcoe +Verbridge, I wasn't involved with the bid procedure on the renovation and expansion of the Farms Library, located in a nearby town. Alan and Jayne had developed the preliminary design proposal, determined the costs, and made the presentations. It surprised me that Jayne was the one who made presentations. Apparently, her manner put future clients at ease. Alan, not so much in contrast but in support, evidently embodied strength, permanence, character, and credibility. Here in the office, I hadn't seen how the Alan-and-Jayne show worked, but it did. Simcoe +Verbridge won the job.

The existing Farms Library was a small building, only a few thousand square feet. It was designed by a local architect, Mr. Augustus Loring, and completed in 1911. Its brick and terra cotta façade had deteriorated, the roof leaked, the heating plant was unreliable, and there was no handicapped access. Many of the exterior decorative details had disappeared. The project was to be funded by an architectural preservation grant from the state, the town, and by private donors.

We didn't design a new library; rather we renewed it in something of the same vintage as the New York Public Library. This was exciting to me: to be immersed in the period art and beauty of early Twentieth Century municipal libraries. The Farms wasn't the New York Public Library, but I was hopeful that the project would both transport me into an era I couldn't imagine and inform me as I wrote Carrère's book.

To that end, I covered the tiny dining room table in our little apartment with the rare books on Beaux-Arts architecture, Stanford White, and others from the period. I spent most evenings poring over them.

The one thing I didn't have was ready access to the New York Public Library's architectural drawings, but I found I didn't need them. In fact, I had in my office the original drawings for the Farms Library, and those drawings, made in the same fashion as the New York Library drawings, let me imagine what it was like to draw in the old days on linen.

Carrère's book started to affect my work at the office. It made it difficult to separate the New York Public Library from the Farms Library. I taped a postcard of the New York Public Library to the top edge of my computer screen; The New York Public Library was therefore in my face all the time. A couple of times, I made sketches for the Farms while thinking about New York. I had to shake my head clear and check the drawing to make sure it was what it was supposed to be.

After a routine design meeting one day, Jayne suggested we get lunch at a coffee shop across the street. I usually brought lunch, but agreed nonetheless. "Sure," I said.

I wasn't familiar with the place. Jayne, though, apparently was. She set her black leather purse on a table and quickly ordered a cinnamon-raisin bagel and Diet Pepsi. "You bring your lunch every day," she observed.

"Saves money and I get what I like," I replied. My lunch was usually two big roast beef sandwiches and a bag of chips. "I didn't get this big by eating bean sprouts all the way through college."

"I can see that," Jayne smiled. You studied architecture in New York. What's your favorite building there?" Jayne reached for a single-serving container of peanut butter and carefully peeled the foil top off of it.

"From which era?"

"Any era," Jayne picked up a white plastic knife.

I had to think for a minute. I had always loved the twin towers of the World Trade Center, how each tower stretched from the sidewalk to the sky without any interruptions. Now, though, I was learning about the New York Public Library, and I was totally fascinated. "I don't know," I said. "I've always been taken with the World Trade Center Towers. They're so high, and there are no step backs."

"That surprises me," Jayne said, "I don't know anyone who liked those towers. I'd have thought you were a Classical guy. You're so keen on the New York Public Library." She spread peanut butter on her bagel.

"I think it could be time for another Classical revival," I said, looking Jayne directly in the eye.

"I don't think Manchester, New Hampshire is the place for a

Classical revival," Jayne said. "I mean look at this town." She spread her hands and swiveled her head.

"I'm working on a Classically designed library near here," I said. "I'm focused, and I think there's something that people might be missing. We've got to spread the word."

Jayne slathered more peanut butter on her bagel. "How would you do that? What do you mean that people are missing something?"

"I can't say, but I think there is something else; and it's becoming my intellectual duty to find it and explain it. Carrère's book is going to show me the way." I ran one hand through my hair.

"You mean the book you're working on about the New York Public Library. You stuck a picture of it to your computer."

"That's right," I said.

"Instead of Carrère 's book, why don't you call it *The Library Book*?" Jayne suggested.

Carrère

Carrère carefully slit the manila envelope containing the competition circular dated May 21, 1897 with a pocketknife he carried everywhere he went. It was his favorite knife. It reminded him of the time he had watched a man clean a fish he'd caught. Somehow he knocked his knife into the water. It disappeared forever. The man, whom he never saw again, said aloud, "I can't believe I just lost my knife. That was my favorite knife." He stood, leaving the gutted fish alone for a few minutes. He looked into the sky. "Stupid man. Stupid man," he said. Then he returned to the fish. Carrère had never seen such a display of self-control anywhere.

"The library board is going to have two design competitions. But we're not in the first one." Carrère read aloud, "The first competition is for anonymous sketch plans and general designs. It is open to any architect practicing in greater New York."

"Well, that includes us," Hastings deadpanned.

"But in the letter addressed to our firm," Miss Bough said. "It's explained that when the second competition is held, we'll be asked to submit a design." She handed the letter to Carrère.

Carrère wondered how Hastings could be so calm over the possibility of designing a major building. He wasn't normally calm; he was usually high-strung.

"When do we have to submit our design?" Hastings asked. He sat and rested an ankle on a knee.

"It says here that the second competition will be in August," said Miss Bough, looking at the partners.

Twenty-six-year-old Donn Barber entered the room. He was a square-built architect who had graduated from the Ecole des Beaux-Arts in Paris that year. "What have we here?" he asked, smoothing his slicked dark hair.

"We've received the competition circular for the new library," Carrère explained to the younger man. "This line drawing is a rendering of a sketch Billings made." With his toe he pushed out the chair next to his and motioned for Barber to sit.

"Who's Billings?" asked Barber. He sat in the wooden chair.

"Doctor John Billings, the Director of the New York Public Library," Carrère said.

"I didn't know there was a New York Public Library," Barber said quietly.

"Well, there is and there isn't," Hastings said, still seated comfortably. "There's no building *yet,* but there's an organization."

"Where's the organization? Who's in it?"

"You'll learn your way around this city, my friend. The Lenox Library, the Astor Library, and the Tilden Trust all combined to form the New York Public Library," Carrère said. "When did they do that Tommy?"

"A couple of years ago, I think," Hastings said. "They hired Billings to construct a central building." He flipped through the two-page prospectus of the building. "Hmm. Two inner courtyards... It will be four hundred feet by two hundred twenty-five feet. The two courts will be separated by a center axis block."

"The courts would bring light into the interior," Barber said as he settled back into his chair.

"I think we should be able to do a lot with them," Hastings stated, his face aglow with excitement. He passed the prospectus to Carrère. "The main entrance will face Fifth Avenue. That's no surprise. Smaller doorways on Fortieth and 42nd Streets."

"Where do they want specialized rooms?" Barber asked.

"The Patent, Children's, Periodical, Public Documents, Lecture, and Accession Rooms are to occupy the first floor perimeter," Carrère said as Hastings searched for some aspect of the proposed building that would be a true design challenge.

"What about the bathrooms?" asked Hastings.

"It doesn't say anything about bathrooms," Carrère said without looking up. "It is a public building though. They'll have to be somewhere."

"Where're the service rooms going to be?" Hastings asked with a little shortness. Still seated cross-legged, he began doodling on blank paper with a newly sharpened pencil. He didn't sketch buildings. Carrère noticed that Hastings drew a cartoon dog—a hound, a puppy, a mutt, a cur—it was impossible to say for certain.

Barber again leaned forward to have a closer look at the library rendering. His shirt collar was buttoned down but flipped up in back. "The roof of the boiler house would be in the south courtyard," he said.

Carrère felt this was sensible, and he could see on Hastings's face that he felt about the same way.

Hastings, tired of waiting for the information to be read to him, uncrossed his legs and leaned forward, reaching for the sketch. He surveyed it for a few minutes. "There really isn't much here," he said. "That means we can do whatever we want." Frank Ward, newly employed at Carrère & Hastings, quietly slipped into the office. Hastings acknowledged Ward with a brief nod and a grunt; his attention remained focused on the library. "The rendering shows the main staircases behind the entry hall, blocking the exhibition room. What if we do it differently?"

Barber asked, "What do you mean by 'differently'?"

"Oh, I don't know yet. We just want to look at all the possibilities." He made eye contact with both Barber and Carrère as if seeking their approval.

"They want the reading room on the third floor," Carrère said.

"That's unusual," said Barber.

"Only because there've been very few large public libraries built in the United States," said Hastings.

Barber pressed for more, "It was Doctor Billings's idea, wasn't it?"

"It was," Carrère said. "He went to Europe earlier this year to look at libraries. He most assuredly liked the Bibliotheque Saint Genevieve in Paris."

"You must know the Bibliotheque, too," Barber said, grooming his mustache.

Hastings said, "Oh yes. Anybody who studies architecture in Paris studies the Bibliotheque."

"Can you describe it?" Ward asked.

"It was designed by Henri Labrouste and built in eighteen-fifty," Hastings said. "The lower floor's occupied by stacks." He spread his arms wide. "The upper floor is an immense reading room." Hastings then drew a line in the air, extending his palm away from his face. "Down the middle of the reading room is a spine of slender cast iron columns that support barrel vaults over each aisle."

"It was," Carrère said, anticipating the question, "the first use of iron in a prominent, visible way in a cultural building."

"A modern building," Hastings added, looking at Carrère.

"All buildings are modern for their times, as long as they're not copies."

"What Billings probably liked so much was the reading room above the stacks," Hastings continued. "He saw that the stacks directly beneath the reading room are more accessible. I would agree."

Ward appeared glad he had asked. Carrère noticed how he seemed at ease, slouched in his chair.

The discussion turned to the stacks as Carrère read aloud: "The stacks were planned to run from the first through the second floor, at the rear, westward toward Sixth Avenue." He paused and began to paraphrase. "The Library trustees expect the stacks to... grow to house more than... a million volumes in the next twenty-five years." Then he stated, "This could be a major innovation in American libraries, the placement of the reading rooms above the book stacks at the back of the building."

Great commotion suddenly rose from Broadway outside the offices, and Hastings leapt to the window to see what was going on. "Fire wagons headed uptown," he reported.

Carrère, whose attention remained on the project, thought it was interesting how the circular only offered the plan as a suggestion. He recalled how so often at the Ecole in Paris he would submit several designs for each assignment. His portfolio in Paris always contained several drawings for each project. As a teenager that one summer in Dieppe when he had discovered his interest in architecture, he liked to draw his favorite buildings again and again. "It says here that competitors are asked to submit a second design with the reading room on the first floor. I'm not sure we'll have to do that, since we're only participating in the second competition."

"It sounds like the Board is hoping to get new ideas from the various submissions," Hastings mused as he returned to his seat and polished his perfectly clean glasses with a handkerchief. "An interesting tactic. We'll begin work on our design now." Hastings drummed his fingers on the table.

"Agreed," Carrère nodded. "Even though you are fast, Tom, I'm not sure your best work emerges after all the revising you do." Carrère once hid a drawing Hastings was working on just to get him to stop.

"That's an understatement, John," laughed Hastings, poking some fun at himself.

"Also, the two competitions stir up public interest and support. Public support is essential, I think," Ward said.

"Right," Carrère said. "Are we ready for some long days and nights?"

Interlude

The task of bringing new Classical architecture to Manchester had to be done in baby steps. First, there was no interest in architectural art in the city. Second, there were no examples of Classical architecture, nor the perceived need for it in Manchester. It was a mill town straddling the Merrimack. The city was built by making socks.

I decided that to raise awareness of the "new Classical," as I called it, there would have to be a new, high-profile building that everyone would notice, one that would attract media attention. In moments of self-doubt I glumly stared at the picture of the New York Public Library taped to my computer. Jayne saw me in my funk one day and said, "Can't you think of something besides the New York Public Library?"

"I'm not thinking about it," I protested. "I'm searching for the kind of magic that those men had. Architecture today is so empty."

Jayne sat in a chair across from my desk. I had to look past the picture of the New York Public Library to see her. "No, it's not empty," Jayne said. "A lot of exciting stuff is going on everywhere."

"Not here, not in Manchester," I said.

"The architecture isn't the problem, Henry. It's your head that's the problem. Your brain. You've gotten yourself all twisted around antiquated designs that no one builds anymore."

I leaned back in my swiveling chair. "But I think people *should* build these things."

"Well then, you'll have to build them yourself," Jayne said. There was something of the facetious in her voice. One part dared me, another said, "Don't be silly."

"You'd have better luck building the Twin Towers right over there." She pointed out the window across the river. "At least people would be opposed."

"You don't even know what I'm going to build."

"Do you?"

"Not yet," I said. "I just need a media event to get things started."

Carrère

A few days later, Hastings and Carrère visited the site where the new library was to be built. Fifth Avenue was as busy as ever with carriage traffic; the sidewalk was populated with elegantly dressed ladies and gentlemen. The Croton Reservoir's familiar if imposing wall rose some sixty feet above the sidewalk. The empty sky above Fifth Avenue and the reservoir made Carrère feel small.

"How long's it been here?" Hastings asked

"It was built in the thirties or forties," Carrère said, adjusting his necktie. He wore a light topcoat because it was a bit chilly and breezy. A sudden sharp exchange between two men behind them caused Carrère to turn to look. A tall, well-dressed man argued with a taxi driver over his fare. The horse stood there idly, completely unaware of the dispute. Beyond the taxi, across Fifth Avenue and two blocks to the north, the new Delmonico building, a limestone Renaissance palazzo, was nearly complete. It was a fine new example of Beaux-Arts construction. Across Fifth Avenue from Delmonico's was the different, but equally delicious Sherry building with its multiple cornices.

They walked slowly side by side on the Fifth Avenue sidewalk along the Reservoir wall. "The trustees said they want not only a convenient storehouse but a great monument to the city," Hastings said.

"Not mutually exclusive goals," Carrère said, stepping over some debris on the sidewalk. A florist's cart passed by, and at a point closest to the architects, an earthen flowerpot fell off and shattered. The driver was unaware and kept going. There was junk in the road and on the sidewalk, not to mention all the horse manure. Carrère thought how nice it would be if the city were cleaned up.

"The new building can be both," Hastings agreed. They had reached 42nd Street. "What d'you think it will take to knock this thing down?" Hastings glared at the reservoir wall looming in front of him.

"Oh, I couldn't guess. I don't know how it's built." Carrère shaded his eyes and looked up to the top of the rampart. "It's pretty heavy, though."

"Once the Reservoir is gone, we will be able to see from Fifth Avenue across to Sixth," Hastings said. "It's an eyesore." He grimaced at the wall. Passersby on the sidewalk, though, seemed not to notice it. "I envision an ornate façade," continued Hastings, outlining imaginary figures in the air with his finger. "It'll extend along the two blocks from 40th Street to 42nd Street." He gestured toward 40th street with an outstretched arm. "It'll be ornamented with statues and animal figures," he continued with expectation in his voice.

"Three stories tall," Carrère added, pointing into empty space above the reservoir to indicate how tall the new building would be. "What else, partner?"

"It should be white marble," Hastings said, adding to their excitement.

"Ooh, marble!" They shook hands. "It'll be so good!"

They continued quickly south along Fifth Avenue. When they rounded the corner of the reservoir at 40th Street, a sharp gust nearly took Carrère's black top hat, which was just a little too large for him anyway. They stopped so Carrère could adjust it, and he said, "The building will be about two hundred feet, front to back. The rest of the land in back of the Library all the way to Sixth, is Bryant Park."

"We'll design a monumental building, just what the trustees want." Then Hastings's hat was nearly carried away by the wind. "It'll suggest its own importance," he said.

"There's more, I think," Carrère said.

"It has to be for the people, a democratic place," Hastings said. "Not a royal place. It's a *public* library."

"It has to be usable for the librarians too," Carrère said, framing the space along 40th Street with his outstretched hands.

Hastings suddenly realized something important and clapped Carrère on the back with much enthusiasm. "If we stick to the principles we learned in Paris, and yet are creative, we'll win this commission!"

"I think you're right," Carrère said, looking Hastings in the eye. "This will be our big break." Carrère brimmed with confidence and bounced on the balls of his feet. He was certain that they—he and Thomas Hastings—could bring the Beaux-Arts aesthetic into the most important area of architecture: the public building.

They returned by taxi to the office on Broadway and were soon ready to head home. Miss Bough was still there. She'd become indispensable, keeping order amid ambition and chaos. She maintained Carrère's calendar (she didn't keep Tom Hastings's), typed all of the firm's correspondence, and welcomed visitors.

"I am surprised you're still here," Carrère said politely as he stopped at her desk, coat still on.

"I wanted to finish the proposals for the Durban house," she said, "and to hear about the Library." She smoothed her skirt with her hands.

"We walked around the site," Carrère explained. "We know the basic dimensions and that the reading room will be on the third floor, but we will come up with the rest."

"I can't think of anything more fun for you than this," Miss Bough said.

"Fun? Some of it will be fun, but there's bound to be a lot of arguing and delay. Hastings will be in charge of the design. I'll be in charge of the administration. That's the way it is around here." Carrère looked at Miss Bough and saw empathy written on her face.

"You and Mister Hastings are always so sure of yourselves," she said.

"For the next few months we have to concentrate on a design. That'll be the fun part. Who knows after that," Carrère sighed.

Hastings stopped in Carrère's office on his way out the door. He had the competition materials tucked under his arm. "See you Monday," he said cheerily.

"See you Monday. I imagine you'll already have some sketches to show me?" Carrère had many times previously witnessed his partner generate sketches very rapidly.

"I think I will. I might skip church Sunday to get started. But that's not hard for me," Hastings's eyes twinkled.

"I've noticed that—"

"You're observant," Hastings said. "See you Monday."

Hastings left, hailing a taxi to bring him to 11 East 41st Street and his home. Carrère spoke briefly with Miss Bough about the weekend. He was looking forward to relaxing at home and maybe playing tennis if the weather cooperated. He lived in Staten Island. He knew Thomas would spend the entire weekend walking around the reservoir and sketching.

Carrère decided to have another look at the Reservoir. He went there over the weekend, and a few people were out. He carried his coat over his arm because it had warmed up. He approached the great stone structure from the south on Fifth Avenue and turned left on 40th Street. Walking west now, the sun was in his face. Carrère had to wonder, "How was this monstrosity, the Reservoir ever approved?" He guessed that the City needed the water. A library will be a better use of the site. He tried to estimate the chances of winning. Could they win?

He stopped, his hands thrust deep into the pockets of his trousers. Instinct! That was it. They would just have to follow their instincts… not try too hard… if they tried to make it something it's not… just let it happen, and they would get the job. That's what he thought. After they got the job, then they could work on the details

He started walking more briskly, turned right onto Sixth Avenue past the park to 42nd Street, where he turned right again. With the sun at his back, he approached the granite reservoir and looked up to the top of the wall. It did have an Egyptian look. But they were going to replace it with a French-Eclectic, Beaux-Arts, modern American masterpiece. Hah! *They just had to get the job.*

He pressed his hand against the cold rough stone. Then he kicked it. "It's a good building site," he said to no one. It was nice, flat land here beside Fifth Avenue, the finest street in New York. When the Reservoir came down, it would be easy to foresee a new Beaux-Arts building here. It was the perfect location.

Carrère walked back to Fifth Avenue, crossed and turned south again toward 41st Street. The reservoir cast a deep shadow most of the way across the avenue. He reckoned how good it would be to get rid of it and replace it with something useful.

Carrère

Carrère was down early, as he used to say, at the office that next Monday, May 24th, hoping to take care of some details on other projects. Since he was almost always the first to arrive each morning, he was startled to find the door unlocked. Nothing unnerved him more than an unlocked door when it was supposed to be locked. His first thought was that there might have been an intruder. Carefully, he tiptoed up the stairs and around the corner into the anteroom. It was as quiet as ever, but then he heard a loud thump, the dead, heavy smack of a book landing on the floor. It came from Hastings's office. Mystery solved: Hastings, the designer extraordinaire, had beaten him to the office that day. And he could barely contain his enthusiasm. There was no "good morning." Tom grinned and announced, "I've had some fun since I last saw you."

"I can see that, Tom, but when did you get here? It's 7:30 now."

"Oh, around five o'clock," said Hastings, who was not a morning person.

Carrère nodded, realizing that although Hastings was at work early that day, it would not be a permanent change. "You've made some rough sketches." He shouldn't have been amazed at the number of sketches Hastings produced, but he was. There were spontaneous, rough freehand studies drawn with a soft pencil on small pieces of paper. There was a carefully executed elevation drawing showing the Fifth Avenue façade replete with windows, pediments, and columns. Lying on top of all else was a perspective watercolor of the northeast corner from a position across Fifth Avenue. "Tom, I see you didn't go to church yesterday," Carrère gently chided his partner.

"I was unable to go yesterday, but the rest of the family did," Hastings grinned. "But I think I had a religious day anyway."

"It certainly looks that way," Carrère said, holding up the watercolor. "This is something special." Hastings smiled in a way that made Carrère aware that Hastings knew something but wasn't telling. They worked side by side at McKim, Mead & White for two years and had come to know each other's ways.

Carrère picked up a sketch. Hastings was a talent! He had followed the Beaux-Arts system exactly. The plan came first; the façade expressed the plan. It was already so perfectly done. He examined several more sketches. None of them showed any detail, but he liked what he saw and nodded imperceptibly. This was the best work Hastings had ever done. "You were thinking about symmetry and axial organization," Carrère probed, seeing the evidence in the drawing.

"Truthfully, I wasn't thinking about anything. I was just doing it."

"You were?"

"Yes sir, it was so natural and easy. I felt as if the work was being transmitted to me by an especially gifted architectural student at the Ecole." Hastings looked up at Carrère with sincerity and humility filling his eyes. "The student died some two to five years before my birth, was frustrated as hell at not being able to draw, and had become someone who taunts and pushes me, and—"

"What kind of person?" Carrère asked doubtfully.

"Well, he can be a know-it-all, too."

They both were quiet for a moment. Then Carrère began perspiring noticeably, as a recollection from their days in Paris came to his mind. There was a mousy student, Pierre, who always seemed in league with their teacher, the *atelier*, and who liked to challenge his peers. He was a know-it-all whose insouciance was annoying, especially when he was playing the critic. Carrère wondered if Hastings had ever bumped into this fellow. He looked at Hastings closely and asked, "Taunts you?"

"Well, yeah, and he's almost always there." Hastings raised his eyebrows and shrugged his shoulders.

It was nine o'clock. Miss Bough glided into the room with the day's mail and the *Tribune*. "Gentlemen," she said, "Today is the children's parade in Central Park."

"How could I forget?" Carrère exclaimed. Marion and the girls were going to be there. He and Marion had been married for more than ten years. The girls, Anna and Dell, were nine and six. "Dell's birthday was Saturday."

"And Anna's is in two weeks," the ever-capable secretary added.

Carrère reached for the newspaper and scanned the front page absently, hoping for something to jump out and give him an excuse not to go to the children's parade. "What time is the parade?" He traced an index finger along the engraved image of workers and thinkers between the words *York* and *Tribune* at the top of the page.

"Three-thirty," Miss Bough folded her hands.

Carrère nodded. "I'll go to the parade."

"A good idea for a beautiful day," Miss Bough said agreeably.

"I think so, too," Hastings said. Carrère might have detected a tone in his voice that he wanted him out of the office.

Miss Bough returned to her duties, preparing the outgoing mail. Hastings leafed through a half dozen sketches and explained, "I visited the site looking for some vital quality, and I studied the renderings." The thin paper rattled and crinkled as Hastings searched the drawings. "I wanted to find some life principle for the design."

Carrère leaned his elbows on the table and rested his chin in his hands, nodding in agreement. This was the intellectual Hastings he knew from their days at McKim, Mead & White. "I see that you're past the beginning of the project already."

Hastings found the drawing he was looking for and gave it to Carrère. It showed the Fifth Avenue façade in concept only. "Definitely. I want an easily understood combination of masses in the façade," he pointed to the drawing. His blocks, pavilions, and colonnades were not detailed, yet were already pleasing to the eye.

When Hastings employed his considerable intellect, Carrère realized, anything was possible. "Keep going, sir, and maybe we'll win a commission."

"It's too early to talk about that," Hastings said. "We have a lot of work to do."

"I know that, and I'm leaving most of it to you. In fact I'm going to Central Park in a little while."

"You could help me," Hastings's little admission of fallibility caught Carrère off guard. "When you head up town, swing by the Reservoir and let me know what you think or see."

"I walked around it over the weekend, but I'll try for another perspective." Carrère hastened down the stairs to a hail a taxi. The first one he beckoned stopped, and after a noisy twenty-minute trip uptown over the Belgian-cobbles that paved New York's streets, the stone reservoir rose in his view. He asked the taxi driver to wait at the corner of Fifth and 42nd Street. A pleasant doorman held the door to the Hotel Bristol, the aristocratic and elegant house across 42nd Street from the Reservoir. Carrère wanted to look *down* upon the site instead of looking *up* at the great masonry walls. From a tenth floor window that needed to be washed, he saw that the reservoir was nearly empty. The water in the bottom was stagnant and greenish. Not desirable to drink, he swiftly concluded. His gaze settled on a young couple walking arm-in-arm south on the sidewalk along the reservoir-side of Fifth Avenue. They reminded him of courting Marion. How could so much time have passed? What would it be like to fall in love all over again? The wall towered above them, out of scale, place, and out of proportion to the human needs of the city and its people. A modern library set several feet back from the sidewalk would allow this young couple-in-love to feel like they were important and not just *pedestrians*. The Reservoir was a tired landmark. Time to replace it!

Fifth Avenue was the most famous road in America, and 42nd Street was at the avenue's thriving midsection. There really was no better location to place a great library than the center of Manhattan. Carrère saw his taxi waiting for him far below. He checked his gold pocket watch. Two forty-five. The watch was five minutes fast, but he nevertheless hurried down the stairs and made his way to Central Park. Several dozen children waited expectantly; their voices filled the air. Marion, wearing a spring hat, stood behind Anna and Dell. "Hi, darling Missus Carrère," he said softly into her ear, attempting to surprise her.

She was surprised! "I didn't know you were coming." Her voice was a rich alto. She used to sing in the church choir. He had heard her once in performance. Her voice was marvelous—one of the things that had attracted him to her.

"It's a nice day, and Hastings wanted me out of the office. Miss Bough reminded me that today was the children's parade."

"Where would you be without Miss Bough?" The clowns and animals were getting ready. "Anna, Dell. Daddy came to see the parade." Anna was dressed for spring in a long skirt, white blouse, and a *very* grown-up-looking hat, Dell was similarly dressed but had no hat.

"Hastings wanted you out of the office?" Marion asked.

"I think Hastings likes to be left alone when he's in a creative moment. You should see what he's done."

"The library?"

The parade started. Shrieks of glee burst from the children. Six clowns—one dressed as a little toy soldier—approached. A donkey pulled along a cart full of toys.

"You should see what he's done. It's brilliant."

Marion nodded as she watched the parade. "I know you admire his talent," she said.

The clowns started clapping miniature brass cymbals together in a marching cadence. "He suggested I look at the library's site, so I did."

The donkey and the cart were now directly in front of Anna and Dell. Sparrows hopped around on the sidewalk; robins came and went. One of the clowns stopped and gave Dell a balloon. The other clowns twirled around on exaggerated black shoes. Yellow and blue lilies populated a new flowerbed lining the other side of the path. It was a perfect spring childhood moment.

"Anyway, I wanted him to have as much space and uncluttered time as possible. So I came."

"So you're not going back after the parade?"

"No, Hastings is busy and Miss Bough there. They don't need me." Carrère drew her hand into his and gave it a gentle squeeze.

Interlude

I began planning the event to reintroduce Classical architecture to Manchester, and the world, by studying the events listing in the *Manchester Union Leader*, our daily newspaper. There were lectures, fundraisers, classes, concerts, and performances of all types. I examined the listings every week for a couple of months, but there was never anything remotely similar to what I had in mind.

The problem was that what I had in mind and the grotesque reality of the situation were quite different. My dream was a staged presentation at a prominent location with local dignitaries: a public awareness campaign celebrating a forgotten style of architecture. The reality was that I had nothing except a silly dream and about fifty manuscript pages of a book that had never been written.

A media event! Even if it were nothing more, it would be an event on TV and the Internet. That's what it would be! I was so pleased with my revelation that I couldn't stop circling our dining room table, pacing with excitement, even though I had no idea how to begin. I decided I should issue a press release, contact the Mayor's office, solicit newspaper articles, and get local radio and TV coverage.

"All for what?" Peri asked, skepticism coloring her words.

"The world has to know about Classical architecture to understand Carrère's book."

"Aren't you calling it *The Library Book* now?"

"That's what Jayne thinks I should call it."

"So which is more important? The architecture, the event, or the book?"

I stammered, "Um, ahh, the, er, book. *The Library Book* by John Merven Carrère."

"No," Peri corrected, "by Henry Peabody, AIA."

I laughed, then sat down in a chair at the dining room table. "I'm not going to put American Institute of Architects after my name on the cover of the book."

"It might promote the book." Peri was clearly having fun with me.

"It's not done yet!"

"Why not? Are you doing your job, planning a ridiculous media bash, or writing the book?" Peri stood with her hands planted on her hips.

"The book comes first."

Carrère

During the summer of 1897, they debated, discussed, and compromised. At times their conversations were heated, and the July swelter certainly contributed. Hastings led the design effort. He made preliminary large-scale drawings and then asked the men to clarify the details with smaller-scale work. He engaged in a dialogue with each man in turn, the two drawing simultaneously on the same sheet of paper before he moved onto the next man. "Try *this*," Hastings said encouragingly, reaching across to sketch an idea. The men, leaning intently over their work, concentrated and delivered endless permutations of plan and elevation. Sometimes a sheet of paper became a cacophony of lines, the visual equivalent of a roomful of parrots squawking all at once. Nonetheless, he conveyed his idea to the draftsman, who would set out again on a fresh sheet. The conversations turned in time to the stacks, the reading room, and modern materials such as steel. Despite the intense effort, they were in no particular rush to finish any design, because they knew that Carrère & Hastings would enter the second competition, which began in August.

The Boston Public Library came up once in conversation, with Hastings pointing out its problems. He stood with his back to an open window in his office. The sash was propped open with a sawed-off broom handle. "See, Charley McKim didn't consult with the librarians." Criticizing his former boss and mentor, Hastings continued, "The result is a beautiful Florentine Renaissance palace, but—"

Carrère couldn't believe his ears. "This is a first! You've never criticized Charley before."

"I've always felt this way about the Boston library," Hastings said. "True, it's very agreeable to the eyes and it expresses the grandeur of the building's purpose." He had found a print of the Copley Square façade so that the assembled drafts-men could see. Most had never been to Boston. He made a quick sketch of the Boston Public Library's floor plans as best he could. His memory was excellent and he *could* draw plans from memory.

"One thing I do not want is the monumental staircase in the center of the entry hall. There has to be a better solution." He pointed to the staircase in the plan. The draftsmen nodded approvingly.

Carrère continued, "Billings wants a top floor reading room. McKim did that in Boston. But where are the stacks?" He pointed to Hastings's plan. "They're not convenient to the reading room, that's for sure."

"Anyone have a different or better idea?" Hastings asked.

Only Ward spoke up. "Why didn't McKim build a more practical building?"

Hastings and Carrère looked at each other. Hastings answered, "The trend today is to erect monuments modeled after the Roman-Renaissance masterpieces in Europe. These buildings are aesthetically excellent—just go to Copley Square." Hastings squared his shoulders after closing the magazine and tossing it into the center of the drafting table. "But a library, or a hospital or a museum, has specific functions that we can't afford to ignore." He cleared his throat and spoke with great strength and conviction. "To win this competition, we have to find the right way to express Classical beauty within the limits imposed by the uses of the building." Carrère wanted to applaud but didn't. Hastings bored ahead. "This drawing, you know, Ware's rendering—" he held it up for everyone to see, "in the circular is noth-ing more than a verbal description made diagrammatically." He gestured toward the rendering and then laid it on the table. "This plan helps solve the problem from a utilitarian point of view." He looked around the table to make sure everyone under-stood what he was saying. "But it makes the artistic problem only more difficult."

"It makes the artistic problem more difficult?" Ward repeated.

"Certainly does," Hastings said. "This plan shows only function. The build-ing's artistic quality is built upon the plan."

"That's why we will have to spend so many months studying the plan," Carrère said, hoping that everyone understood what Hastings was saying.

Hastings continued. "In a building of this monumental character, the plan is of the most vital importance from the artistic point of view." He looked at Carrère for approval, who nodded in agreement.

Ward, always with a lot of questions, asked, "What about steel? Will there be any in our design?"

"I like how you call it *our* design," Hastings smiled. "It'll take all of us to put it together." He referred the question to the firm's engineer, Owen Brainard, a square-built redheaded man who attended all the design meetings.

"We use steel only as a substitute for wood," Brainard said, his voice the baritone of an older man. "Steel is a new material, and in my judgment, it's theoretically only an improved wood. It won't be used anywhere to support the walls."

Ward asked further, "How will the walls be supported?"

Hastings answered, "There will be a brick masonry foundation with marble veneer." He adjusted his shirtsleeves and then rested his forearms on the table.

With Ward temporarily satisfied, Carrère asked Hastings to talk about the reading room. Carrère knew that his partner already had some strong feelings about it.

"Billings wants to divide the reading room in two. His ideas are only utilitarian. He has no concept of beauty," Hastings said emphatically.

"Are you contradicting what you said about the Boston Library?" Carrère asked rhetorically.

Hastings paused for a moment. "Not at all. See, Billings wants to divide the room in order to save on heat and light. He's being too frugal. This library—Charley's design is beautiful, but it just isn't useful. We can have both." He slid off the stool and stalked around the table. We can't allow Billings to defeat beauty with utility!"

"A thing of beauty is a joy forever," Carrère said.

Hastings continued his rant. "We'll have a battle royal if we win this commission. I'm not going to let the greatest room in America be ruined for lowly, practical, utilitarian purposes when it could be *très magnifique* if allowed to stand as one room!" He waved his arms around wildly making quite a scene.

Just then Donn Barber joined the meeting. He was nearly twenty years younger than Hastings but he was highly regarded for his original design ideas and his commitment to Beaux-Arts principles. "Remember, Billings designed the hospital in Philadelphia," he said.

"That's the problem," Hastings roared. "Billings is a doctor, a scientist, not an artist. He can't see what I—um, *we* can see."

"Not so fast," Carrère interjected. "Negotiation is the best approach. Let's find out what he's thinking."

"Yes, you're right, Mister Carrère. I just have strong feelings about art."

"We all know *that*."

The next day Carrère found on Hastings's desk several drawings of the New York Public Library. They were typical examples of Hastings's craftsmanship and talent. Beneath a couple of thin sheets of tracing paper sporting details of baluster types was a detailed floor plan. In it, Hastings had experimented with the graphic problems of solid and void by coloring black, small irregular shapes which represented solid piers, walls, or columns. The shapes outlined rooms and located passages and doorways. At this early stage in the design, Carrère knew, such effort was not yet necessary. Hastings apparently wanted clarity and so had begun shaping the interior spaces. The drawing—in ink on the waxy linen usually reserved for final drawings—was very carefully done, without a superfluous mark. Why did Hastings go to such length when there was so much yet to be determined? The stair location, for example, or even the basic shape of the portico—was he wasting time, or couldn't he wait? Or was he out of control—what was it? A door slammed somewhere in the building, jarring Carrère from his observations. He decided that Hastings wanted to let the white spaces on the paper become part of the plan. Carrère held the drawing closer to the window for better light and appreciated how Hastings had created the *effect* of a line by allowing the white paper to show between the rendered areas—by "reserving" the white of the paper in these places. Hastings used negative spaces so well and so subtly, and with such interesting results.

Carrère turned and found Miss Bough waiting for him. She moved around the office so quietly, *cat-quiet*, that she could turn up without one being aware.

"You need to sign paychecks today," she said. Carrère slumped his shoulders. They had had some trouble making payroll recently. "The checks are ready on your desk."

"Thank you, Miss Bough," Carrère said. "I'll do that in a little while." Then Carrère asked, "Have you heard any news about Horace?"

"He's still in the same room at the hospital," said the well-informed secretary. "His condition remains the same."

"Is there anything we can do to help him?"

"His doctors say he suffers from melancholy." Miss Bough rubbed her palms together slowly back and forth. "They want to keep him quiet."

"Horace was a quiet man to begin with," Carrère said.

"You are right. I'm not sure what good it does to keep a quiet man quiet. But the doctors must know what they're doing."

"They may not. Their patient is a talented but mercurial artist," Carrère said. "What could be more unpredictable?"

They strolled over to his office and sat. He offered her a an oatmeal-raisin muffin he had brought from home. "Nothing," said Miss Bough, shaking her head to decline the offer.

Carrère helped himself to one, nibbled thoughtfully, and said, "I don't trust the doctors, but there isn't much we can do but pray for him."

Miss Bough agreed. "I think Horace is in a good place. If I may say, tormented artists are not exactly a rare thing. Keep an eye on Thomas Hastings."

Carrère leaned sharply forward. "Why do you say that?"

"Because he's the volatile artist around here."

Carrère sighed, "I don't know if I can, or what I would do if anything happened."

Miss Bough stood, "You just have to. And sign those paychecks, too." She slipped from his office, leaving Carrère with more on his mind than he cared for.

Interlude

"There's got to be an easier way," I said. I was panting a bit, trying to catch my breath. Peri and I were on a day-hike at Mount Washington in New Hampshire. It was a fine early June day: the leaves on the trees at lower elevations were still tender green, indicative of their recent emergence for the summer season. The streams were still pretty full, the soil soft underfoot, and the air fragrant. Everything was new.

"You could exercise more," Peri said, "and be in better shape."

"I *am* in good enough shape," I protested. "There's got to be an easier way to write the book."

Peri bit off the end of a chewy granola bar. "You're doing fine on that. That's what I see."

"But you don't see everything," I said. "I struggle a lot. I spend hours and hours trying to imagine what Carrère must have thought or done, but I just don't have a clear image of him. Nobody has ever heard of him, except for those who have written dissertations about the firm." I turned to see if we were high enough up the trail for a view. I could just barely see the Carter Range through the trees. "So little of the book is clear. I just want there to be an obvious path, like this trail, to some kind of conclusion."

Peri said, "When you begin designing a building, you start with nothing, don't you? Just a blank sheet of paper, right?"

"Oh, not true! We have measurements, site descriptions, building requirements, and so on. This damned book, there are no require-ments, no landscape, no nothing. And there's so little known about Carrère. I just wish—"

"What about your idea of a media event?"

"I junked that. Seems like a wrong-headed approach to selling a book that's not done yet," I said.

Peri finished the granola bar. "So what are you going to do?"

"Write the book," I said. "But there's got to be an easier way. It's just so slow. Am I supposed to be John Carrère, or what?"

Peri was ready to get back on the trail and appeared impatient as she waited for me. "Well, he's dead. No one knows. So it has to be you."

"Why me?"

"Don't be a baby! You got yourself into it. Let's get going!"

Carrère

A week after they began Hastings announced that he had generated renderings to sell his ideas to the Library's Board of Directors.

"You're jumping the gun," Carrère said. "We don't even know which spaces in the library are the most important," he paused before adding, "or the most important for whom."

"You're right. I just like making an artistic presentation," Hastings said looking down at several drawings.

"I know you like to make art, Thomas." Carrère seldom called Hastings by his full first name. He wanted him to take notice of what he was saying. "But we have to be theoretical first. You know that."

Without further comment Hastings searched his pockets for a pencil. Finding one, he inspected the tip and laid out a new sheet of paper. Using a T-square, he made a rectangle about a foot by a foot-and-a-half representing a floor in the library.

Barber, entering the room, said, "The library has to be equally functional for patrons and librarians."

Carrère said in a clear voice, "The reading room was stipulated to be on the top or third floor. The stacks should be directly beneath. There will have to be a dumbwaiter to bring the books to the reading room. The Bibliotheque Ste. Genevieve is configured this way."

"The suggested plan in the circular shows two courtyards," Hastings said as he drew two squares within the rectangle. "You might think the reading room is the most important room in the building. But I am not so sure about that. Patrons need to request a book before using it in the reading room. They need to find the call number in the catalog." He looked first at Carrère, then at Barber. "The reading room will be back here on the west side of the building."

"The catalog room should be the passageway into the reading room," Carrère suggested.

"That's what I'm thinking," Hastings tapped the point of his pencil on the space between the two courtyards. "This area here could be the catalog room and the only way into the reading room."

"Elevates the significance of the catalog room," Barber said.

A loud crash on the street prompted Carrère to move to the window to see what was going on, but he couldn't determine what had happened.

Hastings asked Ward, who was wearing a white shirt and dark trousers and had grown a good-sized mustache, to get a new sheet of tracing paper from the supplies cabinet. Ward obliged. Hastings laid the paper over the first sketch, not bothering to align the corners of the new sheet with those of the old. He roughed in the outline of the building and the courtyards and said, "This is where the stacks are going to be."

"In the space directly beneath the reading room," Carrère said without looking.

"The stacks should be convenient to the reading room. If the reading room is on the top floor, the stacks should be directly beneath. A dumbwaiter will make the delivery of the requested books a simple matter." Hastings stretched his arms over his head.

Carrère examined his watch. "It's eleven forty-five," he said. "Is anyone ready for lunch?"

"Let's go," Hastings decided for the group.

Hastings, Ward, Barber, and Carrère tumbled out onto Broadway and paraded four abreast the short distance to the usual lunch counter. Carrère was now able to determine the cause of that loud crash: some movers had dropped a bureau on the sidewalk right below the office window.

Vincent saw them coming. "You've brought the whole firm today."

"Yep," Hastings said stepping up to the counter. Gesturing grandly, he added, "This is the firm that's going to design the New York—"

"Hush, we don't want to jinx our chances." Carrère nudged Hastings's foot with his.

"I know what you want, Mister Hastings, and you, Mister Carrère. What about the other gentlemen?" Vincent beamed.

"Ward wants a sausage roll, and Barber a hot turkey sandwich," Hastings said without consulting them.

A fat man rolled in and took a seat at a counter stool. His trousers hung from red and black suspenders and his shirt was coming untucked. Carrère had never seen him before.

"Get a table in back," Vincent called out to the group. He jerked his head in the direction of the rear of the shop. "I'll be right over with your lunch." Hastings led the party to an empty table and the design conversation resumed.

"Our plan requires everyone using the reading room to pass through the catalog room, and the room is right in the middle of the building." Hastings was perspiring a little. He removed his glasses and cleaned them with a handkerchief.

He looked around the table and the confined restaurant. "We've decided that the catalog room is the most important room in the library, haven't we?"

Vincent approached carrying a large round tray with the lunches. His white apron was stained with food and his dark trousers were rolled up at the cuff. His heavy eyebrows complemented his bushy but receding hair.

"Thank you, Vincent," Carrère said as the waiter-chef-owner deposited the bowls, plates, rolls, napkins, and silverware.

"My pleasure," Vincent said loudly.

"Its location is perfectly obvious," Hastings said. "Between the courtyards on the same floor as the reading room! Natural light can enter the catalog room from the courtyards." He shrugged. "And the space is a perfect passageway into the reading room."

Carrère shuttled the proper plate or bowl to the correct person and distributed the silverware.

Hastings reached for a pencil in a pocket and a paper napkin lying halfway across the table. "The catalog room becomes a crucial space. It separates the reader from the public. You can't get a book to read without having chosen one from the catalog," Hastings continued. "And look at the room's dimensions. It'll be a cube. The four sides all the same length and height."

Ward, a stringbean of a man, was puzzled. The inexperienced man could not yet see what the others understood. Hastings drew a third floor plan on the napkin.

"When you're looking for an item in the catalog, you feel like the most important person the room. You are standing, not sitting or lying down. You are concentrating on finding the card. The cube is an envelope for what you are doing."

Hastings pushed his bowl of soup out of the way. The men looked at the sketch while trying to eat. "Since we've determined the two most important spaces in the library, the next step is to get library patrons to those spaces. I want your input. How would you move people up to the catalog and reading room, if that's where they were planning to go?" He reached for his soup and let the others think about it while he ate.

"Hey, this place is pretty good," Ward burst out. His sandwich was gone and he was enjoying a cup of coffee. "I like the food."

"We haven't been coming here for nothing. It says *home-made* on the sign," Carrère pointed out.

Hastings was quiet, obviously lost in thought. He finished his soup quickly and announced that he was going back to the drafting table at once. It was twelve-thirty. He stuffed the napkin sketch into his pocket and disappeared, leaving the others behind.

"What's that all about?" Ward asked.

"Not surprising really," Carrère said. "He's driven, that's all." Thinking of Horace Avery though, Carrère made mental note of his partner's intensity. Had Horace been like this? He would have to ask Miss Bough.

Barber brought a napkin to his face and sneezed. " 'Scuse me," he said. "He *is* driven. It's a good thing. But I've wondered how he can draw and redraw everything with no end."

"Not long ago," Carrère said, sipping a cup of coffee, "Hastings told me that when he draws sometimes, it's as if some poor dead architectural student from the Ecole were doing the drawing for him."

Ward lurched. "So what's he mean?" he spluttered.

Carrère shrugged. "It's—you know, his spirit guide. Don't forget, Hastings is an artist of the first rate."

"He's an artist who is not always in control," Barber added having finished his sandwich.

"That's for sure," Carrère said looking squarely at Barber. Carrère thought for an instant, *that is the danger.* "He never knows when to stop."

"Does he seek perfection?" Ward asked.

"Every time. He's always looking for the next step. It's a good thing, I suppose," Carrère said.

"So what about this guru of his?" Ward wanted to know.

"That's Hastings's way of saying that this voice, or whatever it is—" Carrère sighed heavily, "—goads him into something more and better."

"It's what drives him," Barber added.

"Yep, that's it," Carrère agreed pushing back from the table. "Let's head back and see what Tom has done."

When they returned from lunch, a heavily marked up sheet of paper was on the blond oak table. Hastings was giddy. "Oh, I'm just playing around." He fired a rubber band across the room. "And did I ever say it feels like someone else is doing the drawing for me?"

Carrère

Days stretched into weeks. A few weeks slipped by. New York sweltered in the summer humidity and heat. Design meetings were continuous and endless. Hastings was focused and intense without a pause. Carrère liked to get out and away from Hastings at least once a day.

One day Carrère decided to investigate Crouch & Fitzgerald's luggage shop next to Vincent's lunch counter. He and Marion planned to sail to Southhampton in the fall, and they needed a new trunk. The old one's hinges were pulling away, the bottom was cracked, and the lock didn't work well.

Carrère browsed the selection. He noted that the better ones had brass locks and stronger joinery at the corners. He liked running his hand back and forth on the warm, smooth pine top. A large black cat rubbed against his leg.

The shopkeeper asked him if he needed help. "Just browsing," Carrère said. "I need one big enough—" Something stopped his thought. It had to be big enough for what? Hastings's ego? Perhaps. Seven hundred working drawings if they win? No, They were going to Europe for a couple of months. Big enough for that.

He opened the top of one, noting that the hinges were well fastened. The light was fairly dim in the shop, and it was quite dark within the trunk. Carrère lifted out the tray, inspected it, and noted that the interior was lined with paper. It was just right. The corners were square, with the joints between the sides falling straight to the rectangular bottom. Such nice craftsmanship, he noted.

He closed the lid, patted the cat and rubbed its ears, and prepared to leave the shop. But instead, he suddenly impulsively looked inside another trunk. He thought of the many different objects you could store in a trunk—papers, clothes, treasure, artifacts, a loved one's ashes, memories, perhaps? You could fill it up. Or what if you left it empty? He stood straight holding up the lid with his right hand. There was an empty trunk in the attic of the family's house in Lausanne when he was young. It was never used for anything. It just sat there empty for as long as he knew. He and his brothers used to play games in that attic with that trunk. It was great fun making up rules to the games and changing them at will for hours and hours. As an adult though, he abided by rules. He didn't make up new architectural rules. When they designed a building, they carved out the space as it was to be—a library, or theater, or hotel, or whatever it was they were building. One kind of empty space was not the same as every other, Carrère noted, looking into the empty trunk.

He gently closed the lid and left the store in a pensive mood. Broadway's customary hustle and bustle returned him to the present, however, and he bounded up the steps to the office. There he found Hastings mumbling about how to get the people to different parts of the Library.

"Most people would think the likely approach would be stairs opposite the main entry. The Boston Public Library is set up that way."

Barber, seated with his feet on another chair, challenged, "This library will have to exceed McKim's library in Boston or else librarians will consider it a failure."

"They might," Hastings said. "The problem I have with stairs opposite the entry is that they cut you off from the central part of the building." He paused, cleaned his glasses, and shifted forward in his chair. "Since we're thinking hierarchically, the importance of the space on the first floor beneath the catalog room would be right up there." He looked around. "Wouldn't it? What's going to be in that space?"

Carrère pulled up a chair and noticed Hastings's momentary lack of confidence. "The competition circular calls for the patent, children's, periodical, public documents, lecture, and accession rooms to occupy the first floor perimeter, while service rooms will fill the inside areas,"

Frank Ward spoke up. "That central space on the first floor could be very important and should be easily accessible."

"What if that space were a lecture hall or exhibition room?" suggested Barber.

"That's a good idea," said Hastings, who liked to hear every idea from every man around the table. "If I recall, the competition circular suggested an exhibition hall on the third floor. It could be on the first floor instead."

"And," Carrère added, "those patrons who wish to see an exhibition could do so without having to go up to the third floor and the reading room area."

"It would keep the two functions—exhibits and reading—separate," Barber said.

Ward pressed for a consensus on the exhibition hall. "Some patrons will come to the Library only to visit the exhibition space. Shouldn't it be visible and easy to get to?" Then he suggested that the stairs be located at the sides of the entry hall.

Hastings said, "I have thought of that. But I fear the arrangement would be confusing to patrons. It would not be immediately clear where the reading and catalog rooms are."

Barber saw what was coming. "We will have to decide what we want. Either the stairs facing the entrance and blocking the center of the first floor, or the stairs moving to the sides. It's subjective. Either way can work. It depends on our priorities."

"The configuration of the stairs could determine whether or not we get the commission," Hastings said.

Carrère fidgeted, realizing that there was now some pressure. He cracked his knuckles and pressed his fingertips together. "Not so fast," he said at length. "We're just at the beginning."

Hastings backed off. "A first floor exhibition space gives the library an added purpose for the public. Is this a feature the library needs or wants?"

"The exhibition hall should, in my opinion, receive a strong position in the building," said Barber.

Carrère looked at Hastings, who studied Barber. Barber was the type of man who would start his own firm someday. It was standard practice: Hastings and Carrère had worked at McKim, Mead, and White for a few years after returning from Paris. Then they had started their own firm. A man with Barber's talent would do very well.

Barber said, "An exhibition space belongs on the first floor in this great building." He pointed at the first floor plan on the table while continuing. "If this building is going to be civically useful, it should have the capability to serve many functions."

"I think you're right, Barber," said Hastings as he pushed his chair back and stood. "But I am not convinced this is the right thing to do. If there's a first floor exhibition space, it should be accessible and prominent. If it is located directly beneath the catalog room, its hierarchical significance becomes nearly equal to that of the room above."

"You have made a case for the stairs on the sides of the entry hall, and you have even said that the space below the catalog room would be more or less equal. You've also made a case for a central staircase. Where does that leave us?" Carrère asked. They all looked at Hastings, who showed his indecision by licking his lips. Hastings walked to a window and pushed it open. The street below was noisy as usual.

"There are many decisions we have to make," Hastings said as he turned from the window. Hot summer air filled the room. "There will be many design challenges we cannot anticipate. We can leave this decision alone for now. But we need to move forward with the plan for the rest of the first floor and the third floor. And the second floor, too. Has anyone even thought about the second floor?"

Carrère rested his head in his hands, elbows on the table. "The second floor will hold stacks."

"The stacks will be in the rear half of the building," Barber said.

"And the offices, too." Carrère mumbled, reminding the others what the competition circular specified. He had had enough and wanted to call it a day.

"Let's leave it here for now. We need to concentrate on the first and third floors," Hastings said. In truth, Hastings wasn't very interested in the second floor. Then he returned to the table and leafed through sketches of the entry hall and the third floor, removing any possibility that *he* was going to stop for the day.

Interlude

I sat every evening after work at our dining room table. That table was my home office, where my laptop was set up. There was a stack of books about New York City, McKim, Mead, and White, the New York Public Library, and other things on the floor. As I sat there, little came out of my head. So I sat on my hands, waiting and waiting... and waiting for an easy stroll into glory as the author of Carrère's book. But night after night nothing happened, or so it seemed. This was beginning to become a problem, I thought.

Peri agreed. "Why don't you take a break? You sit here every night hoping for the Great Pumpkin or something. Give it some rest."

"Then it won't get done."

"It will, but it might take longer, that's all."

"Yeah, Jayne at work would be happier if I set the book aside for a while. I think she thinks all I think about is the book and the New York Public Library."

"You do." Peri looked at me firmly. "You have a job, too."

"I can step away for a little while but not too long. I don't want to forget everything."

I heard Peri mutter something like, "Oh, for Christ's sake." She stalked away. "You're not going to forget everything. You've written sixty-eight pages and you have a mountain of books."

Carrère

In a quiet moment one afternoon in mid-August, Carrère approached Miss Bough at the top of the stairs. "I'm still worried about Horace. He's just not getting any better."

"His sister," Miss Bough said rubbing her palms together. She rubbed her hands together often, even when they were damp with perspiration in the summer's heat.

"Margaret?"

"That's right. I see her frequently—she's quite open and talks about him whenever I ask," Miss Bough said with gravitas.

"How's he doing?"

"Only okay, I guess," she said. "He's going to be at the hospital for a long time."

Carrère slowly shook his head thinking of how quickly their friendship had taken off. They were about the same age but he had never learned exactly how old Horace was. They hadn't seen each other all that often, but when they did, they always had a good time. "Who's going to help him? He's not married."

Miss Bough looked down shaking her head, then into Carrère's eyes. "I don't know. I was just his secretary. But I loved him."

"You what?"

"I was his secretary, yes, and I did more. I took care of him so that he could do his work. I loved his work, too." Miss Bough brushed away a tear.

Carrère helped Miss Bough into a chair. "I think I understand. I am losing a friend. It's sad and hard. He wasn't your friend—he was your—uh, employer. It can't be easy for you either."

"It's awful," Miss Bough said. "I have some paintings of his that may help you understand why he went insane."

"Paintings?" Carrère knitted his eyebrows.

"You will have to come to my place to see them. I'm not going to say anymore about them because they're a secret."

Carrère's breath shortened. A secret? What could these paintings be?

Carrère

August was muggy and hot with little air moving. The men worked with their sleeves rolled up and their collars open. The gaping windows allowed the sounds of Broadway to cascade in. One vendor below hawked newspapers in a loud nasally voice. In competition with him, another voice shouted the price and quality of fresh cucumbers. Two men quarreled over ownership of a horse. A jingling bell on a bicycle joined the cacophony.

Carrère announced, "The first competition ended." Eighty-eight entries were submitted in the first competition. Twelve entries were selected, and each entrant was paid four hundred dollars.

Barber, sweating in the heat and fanning himself with a folded piece of paper, asked, "What happens next?"

"I am not done explaining what has happened so far," Carrère said. "The jury selected six. Before anyone asks, the jury consisted of Dr. Billings, William Ware, and Bernard Green, an engineer." Barber, for some reason, made a note of this information. "The six were invited to join the second competition, which was announced yesterday."

"Are there going to be any changes in the second competition circular?" Hastings inquired.

Carrère held the circular up for everyone to see. "Haven't you seen it yet?"

"I looked at it this morning but I was distracted by another task," Hastings confessed.

"You were taken away from the design for the New York Public Library?"

"Well, I made a brief visit to the cobbler downstairs, and when I returned, someone had taken the circular from my desk," Hastings said. "Then I saw a sketch that needed a revision and I did that, and then we had this meeting. Things are just crazy around here sometimes."

"Okay, okay. There are changes. Third floor reading rooms are to total four thousand eight hundred square feet. They want ceilings as low as possible for aesthetic purposes. They want partitions in order to close off part of a room to save on heating expenses."

"I don't like those things. They will not be in our proposal," Hastings said. Anyone could see that he was not going to yield on this issue.

Carrère continued, "We must submit plans of the first and third floors, Fifth

Avenue and west façade elevations, and perspective drawings from the northeast and southeast."

Barber, sitting to Hastings's right, whispered audibly to Hastings, "We still don't have to think about the second floor." Hastings grinned and nodded.

Carrère mopped his brow. The humidity made paper soggy. Several flies buzzed against the glass of the open windows. No one bothered to swat them. "We are among the six firms invited to join the second competition. The date for submission is November first," Carrère said.

"Which firm is our main competition?" Ward asked. He tipped a pencil point down onto the table and spun it between his palms making a black smudge on the table.

Carrère explained, "None of the firms from the first competition. They were all pretty inexperienced. In the second group, our main rival is McKim, Mead, and White. "They built the Boston Public Library and Columbia University's library."

Hastings added, "We used to work for them. We know pretty much what they will do." He hesitated for a second. "We just have to do better."

Again, Carrère noticed the deliberateness of Hastings's voice and looked at him for some sign of how, exactly, they would compete against the titans of the architectural world. He would have to make imaginative use of the Beaux-Arts architectural elements. He had to stick to Billings's program, too.

Hastings added, "We're not afraid of them." He stuck his chin out as if looking for a fight. The men in the room all cheered. "We can win this competition!" Hastings exclaimed. The assembled architects and draftsmen buzzed with excitement.

"I'm not going to tonight's meeting at the Club," Carrère told Hastings late in the day.

Hastings, as Carrère predicted, thought nothing of it. Carrère usually went to only every other meeting. "Are you going home?" Hastings asked.

"A little later. Miss Bough has some of Horace Avery's paintings she wants me to see."

Hastings looked up from the book he was browsing, "Avery?"

"You know, my friend who's in the hospital."

Hastings returned to the book. "I remember now. I've heard you and Miss Bough talking about him."

"I'll see you in the morning," Carrère shrugged, and slipped down the stairs. He had never been to Miss Bough's street, even though it was an easy walk from the Broadway office. He checked his pocket watch—it was 5:45 and not as hot on the street as it was in the office. He quickened his pace. In twenty-five minutes he arrived at the secretary's doorway and knocked softly.

"That was fast," Miss Bough smiled. "Please come in. I've got the paintings out."

Carrère set his hat on a table in the front hall, where there was an oriental rug and an oil portrait of an old woman. She brought Carrère into the dining room, where Carrère found painting after painting of Miss Bough in the nude lined up along one wall. He immediately blushed and turned to leave the room. "Why— he started to ask. Then he looked again and noticed that they were all the same. Miss Bough had posed for each of the large paintings, and she was nude, and attractive. He shifted his gaze from the paintings to Miss Bough and back again, and back *again*, making sure that it was the same person in the paintings. It was. Carrère should have felt a surge of excitement, a breathlessness, when he saw the nudes but there was something wrong. The paintings were all the same. And he wondered, "Why is she in the same chair, in the same pose, with the same light and the same appurtenances in each painting?" None of the paintings exhibited any flair, vibrancy, desire, or love. It was very odd.

"Miss Bough, they are the all same. How many are there?"

"Forty-six in all," Miss Bough said.

"You posed for each one?" Carrère's disbelief grew with each passing moment. "I did."

"How long did each one take?"

"The early ones were slow, an hour or so, and the later ones much quicker," Miss Bough pointed to the paintings.

Carrère wondered if this dalliance between Avery and Miss Bough had been professional—was she a prostitute? Or if it was an early sign of Horace's madness. "When did you say he made these?"

"These were the last things he did before he stopped working and went into the hospital," Miss Bough explained. "I thought you should see them because they might explain why he went insane."

"He painted forty-six nearly identical pictures of you in the nude," Carrère summarized. "He must have been madly in love with you. His perception of you on canvas was permanently fixed. Try though he might, he couldn't ever alter, edit or revise his impression of you."

"So he could not control his art," Miss Bough said removing a knit sweater.

"You're not getting undressed are you?"

"Oh, no, of course not. I did that for Horace because he was an artist."

Interlude

One evening when I had gone out to pick up a quart of milk at the nearby convenience store, there was a power failure. All the streetlights were out, and familiar roads suddenly became unfamiliar. The streets glistened from the thunderstorm's rain; the car's headlights were the only ones to be seen. I thought, "You don't realize how useful store signs are as landmarks until they aren't there." I felt like a fugitive; I appreciated my anonymity in the night's ultrablackness.

I decided to wait in the parking lot a few minutes. Maybe the power would be restored. I leaned against a guardrail in front of the store simply listening and watching. The place was completely deserted. A dog howled nearby. A car went past, its tires hissing across the wet pavement. The car turned around and entered the parking lot, and then it peeled off again. "What was that all about?" I wondered. Still, I waited, getting a bit impatient. Was this darkness similar to the dark of a theater before the lights came up? What if a playwright liked Carrère's story and turned it into a theater production? Up there on the stage would be Carrère, played by— who on Broadway would play Carrère?—and Hastings, and everyone else. The program would state that it was a play based on the book by Henry Peabody. What would they call the play? It couldn't be *Carrère's Book* or *The Library Book* because it was a *play* not a book.

In the dark night, headlights seemed to me like the spotlights in a theater. The hissing of tires on the wet pavement sounded like distant applause. Yes, applause. The audience loved Carrère's story. How great it would be to have an audience love Carrère's story! And then they'd know about the man, John Merven Carrère, and the story of the New York Public Library. And then maybe, just maybe, they might wonder with the teensiest bit of curiosity where the marble came from. And I knew then what I'd really like to tell people about. The quarry!

Most people will never know what the inside of an old marble quarry is like. What a shame! There's so much drama, especially in the quarry Gil and I dove in. It's not derelict, rather it's inspiring. But you just can't pump all that water out and charge admission—or not. Nor could you expect people to learn how to scuba dive just to dive in a marble quarry. Most people want to dive in the tropics with the pretty fish, and yet there is something equally special, if unconventional, about diving in a space created by humans.

What if a playwright wanted to expose the drama in an old marble quarry? The stage set would be, well, unusual. A marble quarry set might be more successfully created in the movies. After all, digital special effects can achieve anything. I hoped someone would want to turn the book into a screenplay when I finished. Got to write the book. Got to write the book, I told myself.

The power suddenly came on and the blackness was lost, and so was the mysteriousness of the night. Suddenly there was light, and also sound, when the lifeless ice machine outside the store powered up again. I found myself longing for the darkness and the fantasy it held for me. The book, though, was not a fantasy.

Carrère

Later that day, Hastings, Barber, and Carrère studied the details in the circular more closely. The hot weather in New York persisted and there was no relief in the office. Barber sipped water. Hastings fanned himself. Hastings remarked that Carrère enjoyed the heat because he was born in Rio de Janeiro.

"I was born in Rio, but I don't like the heat anymore than you do," Carrère shot back. Then he changed the subject. "In the first circular, a book delivery room was on the first floor where we think there should be an exhibition room. The second circular specifies an exhibition room on the first floor."

"I wonder who leaked our idea to the Trustees," Hastings huffed.

It's a good thing they're going to hire an architect to solve these spatial problems, Carrère thought. Imagine laymen trying to figure out this puzzle. "They want the catalog in the reading room near the delivery desk. We've already decided the catalog room will be located between the two courtyards."

Ward quietly entered the office and Carrère recommended that they relocate to a bigger room. As the discussion turned to the reading room, the mahogany grandfather clock in the waiting area chimed two o'clock. "The reading room," Hastings explained, "is going to be a grand room running the entire length of the building, covering a third of the width front-to-back, with a delivery desk in the center of the room."

"The circular suggests a low ceiling," Barber said.

"A very high ceiling would give the room greater significance to the readers," Hastings said. "What's more, the decorated ceiling could be divided into three panels with murals.

Carrère agreed. "If the Sistine Chapel ceiling were low, would it be as impressive?"

"Are we going to do something like that in the reading room?" asked Ward.

"Of course not," laughed Hastings. "No painter in America is a Michelangelo—though a low ceiling would be against the monumental character of the building."

When Hastings mentioned *painter*, Carrère thought of Henry Avery. He was a painter but no Michelangelo. He was a real artist nonetheless. He wondered if Michelangelo had been in or out of control when he painted the Sistine Chapel. He certainly wasn't looking at Miss Bough. "That's right," Carrère said. "The reading room is the library's zenith. A low ceiling would be contrary to that spirit." Carrère read further from the circular. "Indiana limestone."

Hastings immediately interjected, "Limestone is too coarsely grained and isn't very strong."

"The librarian regards brick as best from a practical point of view," Carrère said. "They just want something stately and less expensive than marble."

Hastings said, "Marble is more durable than most other stones, and it carves fairly easily."

"The color characteristics of marble are superior as well," Carrère said. "Limestone looks best when it is new but ages poorly. Marble improves with age but costs more. That's the only drawback."

A breeze blew in through the open window, rustling loose papers on the large pine table and briefly providing relief from the heat. Hastings polished his glasses. Ward drew on his pipe and Barber patted his brow with a handkerchief. Carrère noticed quiet conversation from a separate conference room as two younger draftsmen discussed the heating system of a house they had been commissioned to design. He liked hearing the men solving problems.

Hastings started to talk about their two quick years with McKim, Mead, and White. "Charley McKim is a talented man with a fun streak," Hastings began. Carrère enjoyed the memories of the happy days working there and loved it when Hastings told tales. "Several years ago McKim was much in love with a lady who had a place in the Berkshires. I forget her name, but he talked about her all the time." Hastings gesticulated to illustrate the lady's shapely beauty. "She asked him to design a bench for her garden, and he was more than happy to oblige. Some weeks later he found a photograph of a bench somewhere, and he knew this was just the thing. But there was a problem."

Carrère had witnessed these events at McKim, Mead, and White and knew the story. He smiled inwardly with the recollection. The other men listened carefully as Hastings continued.

"There was a very naked lady on the bench! What to do? Charley asked me to touch up the photograph with some gouache to conceal the nude, and I did. Charley made a special trip to deliver the picture to his lady friend to show her the bench he had in mind. I wish I could remember her name." Hastings paused again to look at his now expectant audience. "The lady was so taken with the picture that she decided to put it in her scrapbook. To do so, she first soaked the picture in water, at which time the hidden nude magically reappeared!"

The men roared as Hastings finished the tale. "Charley returned to the offices with an ashen look. I don't think he saw his fancy again. Poor Charley!"

Carrère grinned, "Well done, Tom." McKim, Mead, and White had been such a serious, intense place. No one had ever told funny stories in the middle of a workday. He hoped that the jury would prefer a fun, happy firm when they chose the winner of the library commission.

Over the weekend Carrère played tennis in a tournament at the West Side Club in Central Park. He enjoyed outdoor athletics in the company of fine gentlemen, and tennis was intriguing to him. When viewed from above, a tennis court looked to him something like an architectural plan. Its boxes and rectangles, slender alleys flanking the sides, reminded Carrère of the buildings they designed at the office. Tennis is a Beaux-Arts game relying on the plan for its beauty. His studies at the Ecole in Paris taught him the primacy of the plan; all else, including a building's beauty was derived from the plan. And anytime he played, he could easily envision himself hitting a tennis ball within the lines as ordained by a different plan, different lines, shapes, and rules. What fun that could be!

Carrère's first opponent on Saturday was Bertram Howard, and he dispatched him quite easily. Carrère moved about the court well and placed his serves in the box consistently. Sunday was another matter, though. Carrère had had hopes of bringing Saturday's success to the next round in the tournament, but instead he struggled. The grass surface was good, but his opponent's serves were always out of reach. Carrère tried to blame his racquet. Alas, whether it was his racquet's fault or not, he was bounced from the tournament.

Afterward Carrère shared a drink on the clubhouse porch with his opponent, James Kidd. Kidd was a surgeon and a very active tennis player. "It was a good match, sir," Carrère toasted his lanky opponent.

"Well played, Mister Architect. It's good you came out." Carrère was well known around the club, as his profession attracted much attention.

"I don't think about work when I play, Mister *Doctor*,"

"Of course you don't," Kidd said. "You're a good sport."

"And you, too." The glasses clinked again.

A rising gust of wind whipped the flags and pennants at the club. A sudden summer maelstrom caused everyone to scurry for shelter. Carrère glanced upward and saw a terrible black cloud coming lower and closer to the ground. Soon fat raindrops and pebble-sized hail hurtled toward him. The hail bounced and scattered on the stone-paved patio. The howling and shrieking wind threw wooden lawn chairs around and tipped over the tasseled sunshade umbrellas. A booming clap of thunder shook the thin walls of the clubhouse. Carrère was glad Marion was at home. The squall would have frightened her.

Once the squall had passed, Carrère readied to depart. He hung his wooden racquet on a hook, changed from his long tennis whites back to city clothes, including a bowler hat, and cast another glance at the sky—it looked okay. He said goodbye to Dr. Kidd, walked briskly toward Fifth Avenue and hailed a taxi for the Staten Island Ferry terminal.

Marion was waiting for him when he got home. "Miss Bough telephoned a few hours ago," she said.

"That's odd. She's never called before." Carrère hung his hat in the closet.

"She called to give you the news that Horace Avery is dead. He hanged himself."

Carrère stood motionless for a minute as if his feet were cemented to the floor. He felt numbness creeping through his limbs, even his face. "Hanged? Himself?" After several minutes he sagged into a chair in the parlor. Then he began to wonder why, why, and why again. Horace didn't have to throw it all away. In the hospital he would have gotten well and life would have gone on as it had before. Poor soul. What tormented him? Carrère had to find out. But he was dead. The only person who might have known was Miss Bough.

Interlude

At a Fourth of July party I met a retired copy editor from the *Boston Globe*, the major daily newspaper in Boston. One thing led to another, and soon enough he and I were talking about Carrère's book. The editor, Bill Phinney, suggested I talk with literary agents. He gave me the names of several he knew, including that of Joe Coover, and suggested I use his name when I called.

"You're writing the book of a dead architect about a library that's in an architectural style nobody builds anymore." Joe Coover summarized my explanation when I called him from the office one morning. "Kind of interesting. But you'll have to send me the first chapter."

"I can do that," I said. It was a very exciting moment. An agent, someone who knows people in the publishing industry, was willing to read the first chapter. Immediately I had visions of literary success, a review in the *New York Times,* being on the Today Show. The red carpet was for real.

Jayne rapped on my office door and practically shouted, "Are you coming? The Library Board of Trustees is here to review the design. *It's your design.*" It was a few minutes after ten and the meeting had slipped my mind.

Shit, I groaned. I held two fingers aloft to indicate to Jayne that I'd be there in two minutes. My attention back with Joe Coover, I said into the phone, "Yeah, I'll send you the first chapter." Joe Coover didn't need to know that I'd written only one chapter.

"Joe," I said. "I've gotta go. Got a design meeting. Can I call you back? Answer your question later?"

"What kind of design meeting?"

"I'm an architect and we're renovating the library in your town," I said.

"Wait a sec," Joe Coover said. "I gotta know one more thing. Is this book your story or his story? If it's going to be your story, how do you know that it's yours and not his, or his and not yours? Do you know what you're getting into?"

I sagged into my chair no longer wanting to go to the meeting. *How could he know?*

"What if your story is controlled by that dead architect?" Joe Coover's voice hurtled out of the phone receiver impacting my brain with savage blows. "Call me later and we'll sort this out. Sounds like an ambitious project, and I want to be there for you when it's done!" He sounded like an insurance salesman.

Ugh, the key words *when it's done* should have been revised to *if it's done*. I hung up. I decided then and there not to call him again. The library needed my attention.

Carrère

Carrère stayed late one evening in September. It was not his custom to do so, but that particular evening he got caught up with some busy work. It was after seven o'clock and quiet in the drafting room. He found Barber hunched over an elevation within an illuminated circle around him cast by a bare light bulb hanging overhead. Electric light was a great improvement over those smoky oil lamps they used to use. "Why don't you stop for the evening, Donn?"

Barber carefully set his pencil down beside the drawing, pointing away from him and parallel to the edge of the paper. "I'm having a hard time with the light," he said. It's easier in the daytime with natural light coming in the window. I'll stop for now. I know you're thinking about your friend, Mister Avery." Barber was always good at knowing what was on Carrère's mind. "Probably nothing could have saved him."

"I don't know," Carrère said. "I wish there were a way of regulating an artist so that he stays within his limits."

Barber said, "I find that I go in and out of my work. Sometimes I concentrate, sometimes I don't."

"You can draw without concentrating?" Carrère was incredulous. He tugged at his tie.

"Sure. But that only lasts for a few seconds. I don't want to make too many mistakes!"

Carrère was speechless. A new thought tugged at him: what if they didn't finish the competition drawings by November? Drawing without concentrating. He pulled up a stool. "Do other men work that way?"

"How am I supposed to know?" Barber scratched his chin. "I can imagine it's different for everybody. How is it for you?"

"Well it has been a few years since I have drawn anything," Carrère said, almost ashamed to admit that this architect had stopped drawing, "Tom does the design, and I handle the clients. So I don't draw."

"What about when you were at the Ecole?" Barber probed.

"Oh, that was so long ago I don't remember. Plus I was just a glib student." Carrère smiled weakly, "I didn't know anything. So do you think Tom can draw without concentrating?" A fat brown mouse scooted across the floor squeaking as it went and interrupting the quiet in the drafting room. Carrère was shocked. "Did you see that mouse?"

"There are mice in here every night," Barber replied, suggesting that he stayed late quite often. "And I do think Hastings can draw without concentrating, especially if he is someone else's surrogate."

"You mean the guru?"

Barber smiled the smile that tells you he has known something for a long time.

Carrère looked after the mouse but it had scurried out of sight. "Maybe we should have a cat?" Carrère suggested, feeling a bit wan.

"The mice don't bother me. Perhaps you should observe a cat doing its job, too." Barber shrugged "You know, is someone else controlling the cat when it hunts?"

"I don't think so," Carrère doubted this quite strongly. "It's instinct for them."

"But it's not instinct when we draw." Barber said.

"No it can't be because we have to learn how. If we didn't, we couldn't do it." He glanced at his silver pocket watch.

"But maybe for some people it is instinct—people like Tom Hastings or Stanford White. Maybe they can't help it." Barber felt sure of himself.

"I think it can be controlled." But if it can't be... Carrère wondered. Was Horace in control of the Miss Bough nudes or was it the other way around? "Is the artist or the art in control?"

Barber said, "You'd better get going if you're going to get the ferry."

"You're right." Carrère jumped off the stool. "Does any of this make sense?"

"Sure it does. Just keep your eyes open around here and you'll see for yourself." Barber waved as Carrère rushed out the door.

"There's one more painting you didn't see," Miss Bough said in Carrère's office a few days later. "It was the first painting Horace did of me, and I have my clothes on."

Carrère looked up from the papers on his desk and then stood. "How else is it different?"

"You'll have to see it. It might help you figure out more of Horace's madness. He was still himself when he painted this one."

"Himself? You mean lucid, talkative, in control of his work?"

"That's it," Miss Bough said. She sat on a wooden chair, her ankles crossed.

Carrère returned to the chair behind his desk more puzzled than ever. He adjusted his tie and studied Miss Bough. He was unsure of what she was telling him. Was she admitting that Horace's illness was her fault? What if she enjoyed posing—was it fun? She did reveal that Horace had stopped being himself after he had started the nudes. Was Horace transfixed by his naked secretary? Carrère thought of the paintings, all forty-six of them. It was easy to see how he could have been. "So he painted forty-six identical paintings after that one. Why did you pose nude?"

"He asked me to," Miss Bough said. "He was such a gentleman, and I thought I'd try it."

"So it seems you liked it, and he went insane, and now he's dead." Carrère didn't intend to cast blame.

She glared at him. "Not so, not so," she insisted, her eyes blazing. "He liked having me nude!"

Carrère was stunned. "I didn't mean it that way. I meant—I don't know what I meant, except that you're very attractive—anyone can see that—and he's gone."

Miss Bough's eyes narrowed. "Horace couldn't handle me." Carrère rocked his chair back slowly, pondering what this new secretary of theirs was going to be. He hadn't known how strong she was when he had hired her. Someone was going to have to keep her happy. "I didn't see you at his funeral."

"I was in the back," Miss Bough explained, "and I left quickly. I saw you though."

"There weren't many people. He wasn't well known, I guess."

"He had few friends, his parents were gone, and there were no siblings," Miss Bough explained.

"Perhaps that's why you were important to him," Carrère said.

"I've never thought of that," Miss Bough slowly nodded. "Maybe..."

"And that affected his art?" Carrère wondered aloud. "Maybe you were a threat to his art. Which did he love more?"

Miss Bough stood, turned on her heel, and abruptly left Carrère's office.

Carrère

One day, Carrère wanted to see who was working on what. There were thirty large pine tables in the drafting room all covered with rolls of paper. Hanging electric lights, as well as large windows, illuminated the tables. On a typical day, one draftsman worked at each table. On this particular morning, seventeen men were present. All were wearing white shirts and dark trousers.

He noted several men copying designs from books kept in the firm's library. It was accepted practice to rely heavily on the past and to copy as needed. With three thousand years of architectural precedent, there was no need to invent a new architectural language. Whenever an existing design fit a proposed need, it was freely borrowed. Carrère noted the amazing accuracy with which Magonigle copied and drew balusters. He had a good eye and a steady hand.

Hastings and Brainard discussed construction methods and materials. Carrère heard Hastings explaining, "The Library will have all the classical decorations that have been proven for centuries." Later, Carrère heard Brainard's voice: "All the floor joists will be steel."

Later, several men gathered in Hastings's office. Hastings wore the usual white shirt with wing collar, silk tie, dark trousers, and black leather shoes. He had new glasses, with which he fiddled frequently, attempting to make them more comfortable. Brainard was similarly attired but didn't wear glasses. Weak sunlight filtered into the room through a dirty window. The lower sash was propped open with a thick book. Carrère said, "You've delegated the work, Tom."

"I've decided I can't do it all," Hastings replied. "We have a lot of good men here, might as well use them." Carrère used to think of the firm as an architectural version of the painting studio of Peter Paul Rubens, the seventeenth century artist in Antwerp, who would lay out a *cartoon* of one of his paintings and delegate the work on the large canvases to his trained assistants.

"I make an original sketch of an idea," Hastings said, "then give portions of it to the job captains, who have their draftsmen execute detailed drawings." A satisfied grin spread across his face. He knew a large project such as the Library would require a lot of draftsmen with a strong organization within the firm. "Aldrich is working on cornices of the Fifth Avenue façade. Magonigle is also working on the façade but in very small scale, and Ward is busy with the entry hall stair."

Carrère leaned toward Hastings in his chair. "Why are the men working on details we don't have to provide for the competition? We haven't even decided on the entry hall stairs yet."

"You know we have to study every detail many times over," Hastings said.

"We have not even won yet." Carrère wanted to make the point that they shouldn't get ahead of themselves.

"I want to be ready." Hastings used a gruff voice, which actually wasn't very imposing. He was a tenor and a lightly built man.

The next day Hastings hurried out to get a taxi. He was going uptown to see his friend and former employer, Charley McKim. It was a productive time at the firm, with the library drawings advancing well. Hastings and McKim regularly lunched at the Century Club up on 43rd Street. It was likely Hastings wouldn't be returning to the office afterward.

Barber and Carrère ducked out for lunch at Vincent's. Broadway was the usual mass of humanity. Traffic was stalled for some reason, but they hardly noticed. Just another day in the city. Carrère got his usual minestrone and crackers, while Barber deliberated for several minutes before ordering pork and beans.

"We're in good shape right now," Carrère remarked. "The Library, new business. I have a good feeling."

"I have that feeling, too. Hope it keeps going." Barber looked at the water in his glass. He was about to say something, and often when he did, it was completely unrelated to what he had just been talking about. Sure enough he asked, "Did you do any swimming last summer?"

"Only once, at the beach." Carrère said, not sure where Barber was headed with this one.

"I was thinking that if that reservoir at Fifth and Forty-second were a pool, it could be a tremendous Midtown recreational resource." It was a suggestion out of the blue sky.

"You haven't seen in it," Carrère said, recalling the time he had looked into the Croton Reservoir from the Hotel Bristol. "The water is foul, Donn. It would never be a good place for a swim."

Barber sliced his pork. "They could refill it with clean water."

"They can't! There's going to be a library there instead. Not a swimming pool. Where have you been?"

"I know there's going to be a library there, but I love to swim, and I was just thinking how great it would be to convert the reservoir into a pool." Barber chewed, then sipped some water. "I wish there were some apple sauce to go with this pork."

"Ask Vincent for some."

Barber went up to the counter but came back without any. "He didn't make any 'cause he ran out of apples. When I was younger, we used to swim in the lake behind my grandma's house everyday all summer long. I miss it, and living in the city makes me miss it even more."

"Well, we used to fly kites at my granny's in France in the summer. We used to make colorful kites with long tails and fly them so high they were tiny specks in the sky." Carrère loved France with its beautiful green fields. Two men and two younger women took seats at the next table. Could they have been on a double date? At lunch?

"Did you and Hastings meet in France?" Barber had noticed the party at the next table, too.

"No, we were in different ateliers. We met here in New York at McKim, Mead, and White. After a year or two, we started our own firm. Hastings and McKim became good friends. I was friendlier with Stanford White than McKim. I never worked on any of Bill Mead's projects, so I didn't get to know him too well."

They heard some giggling coming from the next table. Barber asked, "Did you understudy White?

"In a small way," Carrère said. "He didn't attend architectural school, and of course I did. So I had academic training. I learned from his practical experience, I would say."

"What was their reputation when you worked for them?" Barber asked.

"Oh, they were well established already. It was my first job working for them. Hastings's, too. We knew it was a good place to work because they were already the best."

"Tell me more about Stanford. I've heard he was unstoppable."

More customers. Vincent's little lunch counter was getting crowded. Carrère didn't mind though. "He really was a force. He almost always got his way in every matter. He was opinionated, demanding, and exceptionally talented. I admired those qualities but couldn't ever hope to equal them. Charley McKim was quieter, less flamboyant, didn't attract so much attention to himself." Carrère folded his napkin and set it on the table.

More giggling and some deep whispers came from that table. "Say, are you finished?" Barber whispered. "These love birds are driving me crazy. Brings back too many memories. Let's get out of here."

"Memories? Sure," Carrère said. "Speaking of love birds, Paris was the place.

When spring came to Paris, it was all love and lust in the air. I sort of expected it because I had spent summers in Europe, but Tommy Hastings must have been lost. You know, his church background." They thanked Vincent and soon were back in the Broadway crowd.

"You don't have to tell me about Paris." Barber's eyes brightened considerably. "The ladies were great. Everytime."

Carrère tried to look at Barber, astonished as he was, but he couldn't. Too many other people around. All he could say was, "Paris? Where?"

"Everywhere," he said walking with his chin held high. "Young girls, the boulevards and cafes. You should have been there!"

"But I was in Paris studying every minute of every day!" I protested. "Did you study at the Ecole, or did you—?"

Barber just smiled that same smile he gave when he knew something. He said no more.

Carrère

I"Less than two months until we submit our design," Hastings warned one morning. The windows had been washed, and the view from the 44 Broadway building was fresh and clear, as was the late summer air. Several of the men had cups of coffee or tea but Hastings did not. The men crowded around the table to hear him speak. "The façade is the first impression you have of the Library. It needs to say everything and to be orderly." A warm breeze from an open window stirred the papers. Someone found a paperweight to hold the drawings in place. "We have to submit our design proposal November first," he continued with urgency.

Barber held up one of Hastings's cartoons for the others to see. "This is a standard Beaux-Arts façade," he said. The thin paper crinkled noisily in his grasp. Hastings liked not having to do all the explaining, and sat back in his chair to watch. Barber continued, "It's a triple-arcaded entry flanked by sculpture niches, long ranges of arcades to the north and south, concluded by end pavilions. As you can see, we have the basic ideas. You have to hit the books and find the best elements for execution of Hastings's idea."

Hastings spoke up, "I think the stairs should be at the sides." He looked around for approval. "The exhibition hall should be centrally located and easily accessible. And that means the stairs are to the sides of the foyer."

Ward asked, "How are the staircases to be reflected on the façade?"

"They'll be located behind the sculpture niches on each side of the central portico." Hastings showed how it would work by spreading his sketch of the façade over a sketch of the entry foyer. The niches on the outside lined up with the stairs on the inside.

Magonigle, a young, skinny draftsman, frowned at the columns parading along the façade and inquired, "Excuse me, Mister Hastings, what do these columns express?"

Hastings, eager to teach, explained that the columns were to reflect the reading rooms behind them. "You see, there we have six engaged columns between each sculpture niche and the pavilion at the end of the façade. They evoke the room behind them."

"The pavilions express another room, is that correct?" Magonigle guessed.

"Yes, that's correct. The façade has three parts—the entry portico, the engaged columns framing the arched windows, and the pavilions.

Satisfied, Magonigle backed away from the table. "Thank you, sir."

Carrère

IA large part of Carrère's job was to meet with prospective clients. One day in October, he had lunch with someone who wanted to erect a summer house on Long Island. What this gentleman had in mind was interesting, and he certainly had the money for the project. Carrère assured him that they could design what he was looking for. It was raining when Carrère returned to the office. Puddles had formed everywhere on the sidewalk. In fact, there were more puddles than dry areas. Or so it seemed. They added an extra dimension to the pedestrians' usual swerving. As soon as he returned, Miss Bough handed him several things to be signed. She was so efficient; everything was always done. "Thank you, Miss Bough," he said. "I'll sign them this afternoon."

"No, we need to mail them, so sign them now," Miss Bough commanded. Carrère obliged and signed the eleven letters while Miss Bough waited. "Good, thank you, sir. I'll bring them to the post office."

"Miss Bough," Carrère called after her as she departed his office. "Can you please pick up some pastries at the bakery downstairs when you return? I meant to but forgot."

"I'd be happy to," she said brightly and disappeared down the stairs.

Hastings's voice for some reason was loud and strong. He was hunched over Ward's desk. The dark intensity on Hastings's face gave Carrère pause.

"One thing has led to another and you have gone too far," Hastings said. Hastings gestured at Ward's detail drawing of acanthus leaves and opened a book on the table.

Carrère recognized the book as the volume on La Place de la Concorde from the firm's library. How could Hastings accuse the draftsman of going too far? If only Hastings could practice what he taught—restraint. Carrère shook his head in disbelief.

"Mister Hastings," Ward protested, "I don't understand what you mean."

"I don't want *that*," Hastings retorted, tapping on Ward's drawing. "I just want you to find out what you can do. I think your best work has still yet to come out."

Barber, who was drafting a third floor plan, asked Hastings for an opinion. "There's balance," Hastings said, "in the relationship between the rear of the building, and the front works well." Several other draftsmen stopped what they were doing. "I like how the plan is rationally composed around the courtyards, with the catalog room being the only access to the reading room." There was a ripple of excitement among the assembled draftsmen.

"I knew this is what you would want," Barber said.

"It looks fine to me," Ward said.

Miss Bough swished into the room with a tray full of pastries. There were turnovers, croissants, and muffins. It was a good selection. "Thank you, Miss Bough," Carrère said.

"You're welcome," she said. "Is there anything else?"

"Not right now. We're in good shape." Actually, Carrère sighed inwardly, discretely. Ward was correct. No matter how detailed or artistically perfect the drawings were, Carrère knew the drawings would fall victim to the thick-thumbed bureaucrats at the Library. He wished he could save the junior draftsmen the heartache of having their inspirations torn apart for financial or tedious practical reasons. If they wanted a chance at winning the contract, however, the draftsmen had to proceed full speed ahead with their enthusiasm intact. Only the pure thrill of creation fueled their imaginations, and Carrère wasn't going to rob them of that. That excitement would yield the best drawings. Carrère warned them anyway. "Remember this is only a competition drawing. If we win the commission, the Library will want to change everything."

They were at Vincent's again. Hastings said, "So far, our design is functional, which is of utmost importance to Billings." He cleaned his glasses again with his handkerchief.

"What's going to make it special?" Barber asked.

"We are going to give them more than the librarians require," Hastings said.

The electric lights in the restaurant flickered unsteadily. Carrère hoped they would not go dark. "There must be some problem with the current," he said. The flickering lights reminded him of the subject of illumination in the Library's reading room. "There'll be chandeliers, and lamps on each table."

"Large windows will bring afternoon light into the reading room," Hastings said.

"We will design the lamps," Hastings said. "Vertical windows in the west façade will evoke the stacks." He drew a series of parallel lines with his finger on the table.

"What about the pavilions at the ends?" Barber asked

"They suggest interior rooms which won't be used for stacks," Hastings said. Vincent brought the lunches to the table. "Same as on the Fifth Avenue façade."

Barber nodded in agreement, "This is obvious now."

Carrère suggested, "Above each vertical window, between the nine reading room windows, there ought to be a doorway just above the frieze."

Hastings sketched the ideas on a napkin. He was able to follow Carrère's thoughts easily. "The doorways will add to the composition of the façade." Hastings tipped his head back, luxuriating in his favorite medium—Beaux-Arts architecture. "The doorways will be elements from the Beaux-Arts language, which is a language with origins in antiquity." Carrère loved it when Hastings spoke this way. "Look at any great building—the White House, the Metropolitan Museum of Art—and you will find details that make the whole thing more interesting."

"Architects are artists, you know," Carrère said. "We express ourselves with the language we have inherited."

Interlude

Late one afternoon, I visited the Farms Library. The old building was still serviceable but clearly it had been neglected. The original terra cotta ornamentation had been removed long ago. Mortar was falling out from between the bricks. The windows were intact—that is, not broken—but they were old and not effective in keeping the cold out during the winter. The building needed restoration, and the town also wanted to expand it.

I liked visiting a construction site "in secret" by myself, before anything started. I considered the possibilities, fantasized about the outcome. It was a few minutes of pure escape, a secure trip before the interactions with fussy clients and office personalities began to cloud the dream. And for the first time in recent weeks, I was able to get away from the book. After what Joe Coover, the agent I talked with on the phone, had said, I was ready for a break.

The site was level and big enough to double the library's size. I stood next to the existing building on the land that would be excavated. First, I looked at the windows with their peeling paint. Then, I examined the ground. Firm soil, no evidence of rocks or ledge. The empty space above my head filled my imagination with thoughts of a new reading room and new stacks. I envisioned vertical windows to express the stacks. Instead of recreating the terra cotta cornice on the addition, I thought we could fabricate a metal device that would echo the original.

The next day, Jayne led me to the conference room, where she had spread on the table the preliminary drawings of the library. The entry-way was still undetermined and was therefore not illustrated. She said, "That book project is taking too much of your time. You're on the phone a lot and we need more of you here."

This was fine with me. "Look, I've decided to shelve it for a while."

Jayne stood straight, erect with surprise. "Not what I thought I'd hear. You thought you could do *that* and *this* at the same time." She first jerked a thumb over her shoulder, then gestured toward the drawing.

"I can do both," I said. "But after what Joe Coover said, question-ing whether Carrère's book is or could be my book, or vice versa—or whatever he meant—I realized I had to take a break and let everything sort itself out."

"Who's Joe Coover?" Jayne asked.

I told her and added, "I'm not going to let him influence Carrère's book. Only Carrère will, and that's the way it's meant to be."

"So," Jayne said, "as you write *The Library Book*, Carrère will have a hand in it?"

"Oh, absolutely," I said.

Carrère

Carrère enjoyed the brisk autumn air on the ferry from Staten Island. He always tried to stand on the deck as much of the journey as possible, allowing the rising breeze to whip across his face, and watching sea gulls swarm a trawler. The ferry plowed through a swell. The spray hit the lower deck windows.

Carrère wondered what had motivated Miss Bough to work for Horace Avery. And about Horace Avery—why did he ask Miss Bough to pose nude? Did he have a guru, a guru like Tom's French student? It must have been a particularly malev-olent one. How could it drive Horace to paint the same work forty-six times?

November the first arrived, the day of the competition deadline. It had been a busy time at Carrère & Hastings, with the men putting on the final touches, making sure everything was perfect in the drawings and supporting arguments. Carrère suggested, "I think we should deliver the design ourselves—you and me, Tom, just to make a statement."

"Yeah, I think so, too," Hastings agreed.

They assembled a single portfolio with four drawings, a perspective rendering, and a folder with several pages of explanations Miss Bough had typed. They beckoned a cab to bring them to the Astor Library at Lafayette Place, where Billings's office was located. The carriage swayed as its wooden wheels clattered on Broadway's rough cobbles. The driver said little to the tawny horse. The slightly ragged top kept the weak November sun off the occupants. When the carriage stopped at the Astor's entry, Carrère asked Hastings, "Do you think it will be fair?"

"What, the competition?" Hastings replied, looking surprised.

"The jury, the competition."

"It won't be after they look at our design," Hastings said. He was always so confident, never betraying any doubt.

They ascended the granite exterior steps and pushed open the front door. Someone must have oiled the hinges because the door swung more easily than the last time Carrère was there.

"Hi there, John. Hi Tom. What a pleasure to see you," Charley McKim said, surprising them. Carrère hesitated for a moment, surprised and not surprised to see his competitor leaving the Astor Library. "I think I know what brings you here," he smiled and stepped back to hold the door for the younger men.

"Your hunch is correct, Charley," Hastings said. He and McKim shook hands warmly. "Is Doctor Billings upstairs?" Their voices echoed slightly in the entry hall.

"He's there," McKim assured us. "Happy to see me and our proposal."

"Was anyone else with Billings?" Carrère asked. What he really wanted was an early hint of when the designs would be reviewed.

"Only his assistant," McKim replied.

At the top of the broad stairs, Billings, the Library director, awaited the men. A large man, he cut an imposing figure as Hasting and Carrère ascended the stairs. Carrère shifted the portfolio from his right hand to his left, and then held out his free hand to greet Dr. Billings.

"We decided to bring the proposal ourselves," Carrère said. "This design is what you are looking for."

"I sure do hope so," Billings said warmly. "Please come into my office." The office, not an especially large room, was filled with medical texts, and framed diplomas and certificates, as well as architectural drawings from Billings's past endeavors. He motioned the architects toward sturdy wooden chairs. "I need you to sign this document here," Billings said as he slid a single sheet across his desk. "This will ensure that you are paid for your effort."

"Oh, yes, I nearly forgot about that," Carrère said. Billings offered the fountain pen on his desk and Carrère signed the form. He printed the words *for Carrère & Hastings* beneath. "When is the jury going to meet?"

"We will meet in the morning. And I am sure we'll have a decision in a few days."

Carrère nodded, wishing he could say something, anything, to advance their cause. But he knew the decision was out of their hands. "We look forward to hearing from you very soon."

"You will hear from us." Not a hint. . . not a hint.

Even though they were busy with other projects, the suspense overtook them all. Each morning as Carrère rode the ferry, he wondered what the jury was talking about. He found himself pacing the deck, unable to stay calm. He couldn't even enjoy the Statue of Liberty—its French origin always fascinated him.

There was palpable anxiety in the air at the office. Hastings was busy as usual with drawings and designs of other projects, but he seemed a bit agitated. He wasn't as focused as he usually was. Miss Bough was immune to the atmosphere. She conducted herself efficiently, attending to the many details that presented themselves in the course of a day's business.

As the days passed, they seemed to go by more and more slowly, to the point that time itself felt suspended. What could be taking so long? Didn't they have any questions? Carrère became more unfocused as the days dragged on. He spent longer and longer hours at the office in the hope that his extra hours would expedite the jury somehow. Miss Bough even suggested he take a day off.

"What? Are you crazy? I want to be here when the news arrives."

Miss Bough said, "All this pacing and worrying is going to wear you down. You should go home at least."

On Friday, word came from Billings that the jury was deadlocked between two designs. "Which two?" Hastings demanded. His face was red, sweat broke on his brow.

"How am I supposed to know?" Carrère said. "That's just what I heard."

"Where did you hear it?"

"At the Club. Stanford White told me." Stanford, Charley McKim's business partner, had his nose in everybody's business. And what Stanford knew and heard was probably accurate.

"Well, I guess that leaves us in the same place we were on Monday. They have to decide." Hastings checked his pocket watch. "Let's call it a week."

Carrère reluctantly agreed, calculating that it was doubtful they would miss anything over the weekend. "Okay. We'll send everyone home now. All we can do is wait."

"Good morning," Miss Bough announced each morning the next week, striving to keep spirits up. On Wednesday, Hastings showed up at about nine and said, "Stanford told me last night that the jury has made its recommendation to the trustees, but he said he didn't know who won."

"Are you sure he was telling the truth?" Barber asked.

"I'm sure," Hastings defended himself. "McKim was there, too, and he shrugged his shoulders. I could tell."

"Okay, then. We should hear something today." Carrère left Hastings's office and tried to busy himself with a letter to a prospective client. It was pointless, though. All he could do was sit in his black wooden chair and stare into the empty space above his desk. He couldn't rid himself of the possibilities that would be open to them if they won. A major public commission. . .everybody would know them. . .they'd be as established as McKim and Company. Then he heard footfalls come up the wooden stairs. It was Ward, late to work. The minutes crawled by, then some hours. Carrère thought for a moment to go outside for a few minutes, just to stretch his legs. But what if the phone call came when he was out? So he stayed and straightened up his desk. Then he had a conversation with one of the draftsmen about the fights. Carrère loved boxing. Hastings, Carrère could see, was quite busy drafting the porch to a cottage, oblivious to Carrère's nerves. A few minutes after the noon hour, the telephone rang. Miss Bough answered. Carrère's heart skipped a beat as he rushed out of his office to listen.

"It's John Bigelow," Miss Bough said. Bigelow was the president of the trustees of the New York Public Library. Carrère hurried to the telephone. Hastings came, too. He took the black earpiece from Miss Bough and spoke clearly into the black mouthpiece. "This is John Carrère." His eyebrows lifted. "I see," he said. "Yes, sir." Hastings tried to get his partner's attention but Carrère was concentrating on his phone conversation. "Yes, that'll be fine," Carrère said into the phone. "Thank you very much. Goodbye." Carrère gave the mouthpiece to Miss Bough, who returned it to the telephone. He counted to ten silently just to heighten the suspense before shouting, "WE WON!"

Cheers erupted from all parts of the drafting room. Someone opened a bottle of champagne. Miss Bough found enough glasses for everyone.

Hastings shouted with glee, "It's beautiful, isn't it!" He danced jubilantly with Ward as his partner, round and round.

Carrère stood on a chair. "Hastings, will you let Ward go. He has to get more champagne."

"I didn't know we had any."

"Stop dancing and raise a glass!" Carrère commanded.

Hastings complied. "What did he tell you? Why'd we win?" He asked breathlessly.

"You should know why!" he barked. "It's your design."

"Not true, not true," Hastings demurred. "It was all of us." He raised his glass and recognized everyone in the room.

"They said our design was functional and dignified, expressive and monumental." Carrère felt his legs become weak, the result of the relief and congratulation. "WE WON!"

"Anything else?" Hastings asked.

"They're going to send us a letter tomorrow."

"What about McKim?"

"Oh," said Carrère, "how could I forget? They were third. Howard and Cauldwell second." He shook Hastings by the shoulders in his excitement.

Hastings proclaimed at the top of his voice, "We've done it. We have beaten McKim for the first time!"

Carrère wished he could have seen the faces of McKim and Stanford at that moment. He wondered what they are thinking? Good sense took over: "But we must not gloat. We have a lot of work to do."

"Of course we do," Hastings said. "That's what we are here for. For now we can celebrate. Is Ward back yet?"

"Here I am," Ward called from the doorway bearing several bottles of champagne in a carton. Sobriety ended for the day. "I'll be right back with more!"

Interlude

"I'm home," I announced after my "secret" visit to the Farms Library. Peri sat at our modest dining room table looking at something on my laptop. I kept one at home separate from work, and I did all my *Library Book* research and writing on it. She sometimes used it to look up something on the Internet. She wore a white terry cloth bathrobe , and judging by her wet-looking hair, she had recently taken a shower. Her legs were crossed, her feet bare. I suspected she wore nothing beneath that robe. The apartment was quiet, not a sound, except for the tiny whir of the fan in the computer. She only used one light when at home by herself, so the place was dark. There was a faint smell of potato chips and I saw why. There was an empty bag on the counter in the kitchen. I put down the canvas tote bag I carried to and from the office.

Peri stood and reached around me for an embrace, at the same time letting her robe fall open. The dream that began at the Farms Library, with the fantasy of the stacks and the cornices, continued. She radiated warmth: she had actually taken a bath. My eyes followed her contours from her eyes, down the bridge of her nose, down to her breasts. My eyes darted from left to right, exploring the gap, the space between. She aggressively planted her lips on mine and pressed herself against me. My clothes were in the way. I couldn't feel her warmth, nor anything else so desirable... and I tossed my shirt over the back of a kitchen chair...the sofa was closest... it was just long enough for me—remember I'm six-foot-three... and Peri was all over me… It was quite a ride for her, I bet! After Peri had fallen asleep, I stealthily returned to the laptop and tried to write Carrère's book.

It was after midnight and the inspiration was brimming, about to gush over the sides of the glass. It had to be Carrère's book, I thought, as my hands hesitated above the keyboard. Some damn little monkey sitting on my shoulder chirped into my ear, "It can't be, you idiot, because he's dead." I looked wildly around trying to find that bugger. Nowhere to be seen in the darkened room. So I started again, and my hands hesitated, and the monkey taunted, "What's it gonna be? Can't you do it?" I turned on the light above the table hoping to see more clearly. No monkey anywhere. Okay, here we go, I said, almost audibly. I typed into the computer, "*The Library Book*. By Henry Peabody." That did it. It was my book, not Carrère's, and it was going to be The Library Book, Jayne's suggestion. Then I wrote a sentence: "The New York Public Library is located at Fifth Avenue and 42nd Street on the site of an old reservoir."

I saved my work, feeling pretty good about the start I had made. I shut off the lights, got a drink of milk from the kitchen, and fell into bed thoroughly exhausted. The clock on my bedside table read 1:15. At least I had started.

Carrère

"We got the job," Carrère announced in the front hall when he arrived home. We beat McKim!"

Marion greeted him at her usual stately pace with a kiss on the cheek. "That's wonderful, darling." Marion stood with one hand holding the other, listening to her husband's account of the day's events.

Carrère hung his hat and coat in the closet. "We couldn't be happier. We opened a bottle of champagne and sent Ward to get some more. Several of the younger men got quite tipsy."

"You had a party," she said.

"Hastings and I talked about what comes next, you know, signing the contract and stuff like that, but mostly we enjoyed having everyone celebrate."

"I haven't seen the library site yet," Marion said. "I'd like to."

"Well, actually, you have," Carrère said. "Most people wouldn't bother to notice the granite reservoir, and perhaps you haven't. But it's there, right on Fifth Avenue."

"Reservoir?"

"You know, the Croton. It'll be torn down to make room for the library."

After a while they settled into deep chairs that faced each other in the parlor.

Anna and Dell came in quietly. Marion instructed them to find books to read or to get ready for their baths. The girls obeyed and disappeared upstairs.

"This is our great opportunity, and everyone will know us when this project is done," Carrère said.

Marion liked what she heard. "Then we'll be able to afford a nice place to live in Manhattan, won't we?"

"I hope so." Carrère was thinking of not having to use the ferry every day.

Marion smiled, approving of the firm's rising fortunes. "How long do you think it'll take?" she asked.

Carrère began some mental calculations. "Next thing, we sign the contract. The Reservoir has to be demolished. That'll take some time, maybe a year." Carrère looked up then back to his hands. "Then the foundation, the walls, roof and interior. Oh, I'd estimate five years if there aren't labor problems, supply problems, the weather issues, legal complications, and everyone stays healthy."

"Those are a lot of things to worry about," Marion remarked.

"And I get to solve them. Hastings, secure in his little design world, will hardly ever know. We've got to keep him healthy."

"We'll keep you healthy, too," Marion said, rising from the chair. "That's important to me and the firm, too. Don't forget."

Carrère stood also. "I think we'll be fine. Just have a lot to do to build this Library."

A few days later, as Miss Bough was opening the mail, Carrère said, "Excuse me, Miss Bough—sorry to interrupt. Was there a letter from the Blake family today?" They had designed a summer cottage for the Blakes, and Carrère was awaiting final payment.

"Yes, there is a letter," Miss Bough handed it to him. As usual, she was cheery, her sunny disposition always a bright spot in that arduous business.

Carrère peeked in the envelope and saw that there was a check. Satisfied, he gave it back to Miss Bough. She would deposit the check later when she went to the bank, as she did every day. "I hope we receive timely payment from New York City," he said.

"That's one way everyone will stay healthy," Miss Bough said. Carrère's head bobbed when she said this. How could both his wife and secretary be thinking about the same thing? "To stay healthy, we have to put food on the table, certainly, but we also have to keep the air clean and fresh." She looked so serious.

"I'm not sure what you mean."

"We can't allow polluted air to suffocate our creative men," Miss Bough said.

Carrère, still puzzled, said with conviction, "We've got to keep Hastings and his team going."

"If someone makes it impossible to get the work done," Miss Bough said. "Would you fire him?"

"I'd have to."

"What if Hastings creates his own dangerous environment?" Miss Bough pressed.

"I just don't know," Carrère realized that she was thinking about Horace. "I hope we don't get there."

The next day, Hastings and Carrère met with John Billings at his office in the Astor Library. The Astor was a plain brick structure, a bit taller than neighboring buildings, with deeply recessed arched doors and windows. They climbed the familiar thirty-six broad marble steps to the second floor and Billings's office.

"Congratulations," Billings said with a warm smile as he greeted the architects. "Did you see this article in the *Herald*?" Billings produced a copy of the newspaper. He read the headline aloud, "Hail to the New York Public Library. It will be a world beater" and gave the paper to Hastings.

"We've seen it," Hastings smiled. "But, thank you." Hastings always liked the first meeting with a new client. There were no disagreements yet, and everybody was still happy. And of course, he *always* had to appease the disgruntled clients.

"You liked the Bibliotheque Ste. Genevieve," Carrère said.

"We know the library very well," Hastings added.

"I know you studied in Paris," Billings said, "but why would you have studied the Bibliotheque?" Hastings glanced toward Carrère, trying to conceal his astonishment.

"Henri Labrouste, who designed it, was a Grand Prix winner at the Ecole," Carrère said.

"What's that mean?" Billings asked.

"He won first prize in the design competitions at the Ecole de Beaux-Arts, and won the right to study in Rome for five years," Hastings said.

"Did you ever meet him?" Billings asked.

"No, he died in eighteen seventy-five, before we came to Paris," Hastings said.

"So he was well known," Billings said.

"Oh, absolutely," Hastings said with reverence. "That library is a great cultural institution in Paris. It took two years to build. The iron superstructure in the reading room is a great thing."

"I liked how the columns divide the room into twin aisles," added Billings.

"The columns were necessary because Labrouste did not have steel beams that could support the whole roof," Hastings explained. "We envision unobstructed space in our reading room."

"I am not sure we will always need all that space. We might want to be able to close off half of the room." Billings, an administrator, was concerned with both efficiency and heating expenses.

Hastings frowned. It was terrible idea. The firm wanted a monumental building. The space inside should be grand, too. He didn't want to carve it up. Carrère said with as much diplomacy as he could generate, "We are used to strict regulations. We will solve any problems we encounter creatively."

"I am not sure what that means." Billings shifted his large frame in his wooden chair. "I would hope the new library would be equal to the Ste. Genevieve."

"It will be," Carrère assured him.

Carrère signed the contract with Billings and John Cadwalader, who represented the Board of Trustees. Carrère felt it was a good contract; the city was being quite fair. It was December ninth.

Hastings asked, "What about the engineering fees?"

"Not out of our pocket. The city pays even if he's our man," Carrère explained.

"Good," Hastings said. "What about the exterior?"

"It says that the exterior may be either Indiana limestone or marble." Carrère knew this would only partially please his partner.

"We will have to find high quality marble at low enough cost," Hastings said, his face momentarily twisted with worry. "This library must be marble. Billings wants brick."

"It'll be marble. The issue probably will never come up. Plus, the choice of marble has to meet with our favor." Hastings's expression lifted.

"What about our fee?" Hastings asked.

Carrère usually had to spoon-feed the financial details of every project to Hastings. "It is five percent of the total cost of the building, as I said the other day, or four hundred fifty thousand dollars. Remember?"

"Including furniture?"

"Excluding furniture we don't design," Carrère said.

"That makes sense," Hastings said almost under his breath.

"The fee includes *all fixtures necessary to render the building fit for occupation*," Carrère said, recalling the exact the language in the contract. "But it doesn't spe-cify the extent of the details we add as we go along." Carrère noticed the delight in Hastings's blue eyes.

"That means there's no limit to what we do," Hastings said as satisfaction spread across his face.

"This contract is fair and good," Carrère said again.

Interlude

Peri said, "Why don't you go to New York and spend some time at the

Library. That might get you started."

We were at a furniture store looking for a better couch, even though I thought the one we had was perfectly fine. Rolling on the couch was pretty good on it. Did we really need a new one? I had to make sure it was at least six-foot-three. I noticed some lamps that looked a lot like the lamps on the tables in the reading room. I remarked that they were bad copies, and then I said something about the book being a bad copy of Carrère's unfinished book.

"No," I said. "It's not about the Library. I mean, I don't need to see it. The book is about something else, I think." I stuck my hands in my back pockets.

"What about this one?" Peri asked. It was a purple sofa with thick upholstery.

I measured it with the tape measure I had brought. "Seventy-eight inches. It's long enough."

"What do you think the book is about then?" Peri asked. She sat on another sofa that was clearly not long enough. "If it's not about the Library, what could it—?"

I had moved to a different part of the showroom, too far for a conversation. "Over here!" I called. "Look at this. It's exactly seventy-five inches between the arms. What do you think?" There were three cushions. Peri sat and crossed her legs.

"I think I like it but I'm not sure about the leather."

I sat at the other end of the sofa. "I don't know, I just don't know. This book is less about the Library than it is about Carrère, I think. So I don't need to go to New York. But I would like to see Carrère's grave."

"Where's that?"

"Staten Island, I think." I stood and lifted a cushion. Then I crouched to look under the sofa, wanting to determine how well its frame was built. I couldn't see anything. A salesman asked if he could help. Peri refused the offer and we kept looking. "You know," I said after a few minutes, "Except for that leather one back there, most of the stuff in here is crap."

"I'd agree with that," Peri said. "Let's go." In Peri's Kia she asked, "A book about Carrère? A biography?"

"No, he said he wanted to write a monograph. But that would be kind of dull, I think. How many bricks, tons of marble, workers, you know. Maybe there was something else going on. I just have to find it."

"Only you can do that," Peri said. She started the engine and turned onto the I-93 on-ramp. "The trouble for you, I think, is that the book won't be about architecture, and that's what you know best. You might get into trouble."

"Not possible," I said. I reclined the seat. "The book is a side project, no more. It's kind of neat that the Farms Library and the New York Public Library were built around the same time. Working on the Farms helps me understand—"

"Carrère?"

"No, not Carrère. The building, the times, the prevailing styles at the time. I've got a miniature New York Public Library right here in my backyard, and I'm renovating it. Pretty cool, huh?"

"Pretty cool," She looked at me for an instant. "Pret-ty cool."

Part Two

Revision

Carrère

It was beastly cold in early January 1898. Maybe it was the frigid weather, maybe it was something else that caused Carrère to grumble, "You just watch, politics are going to slow everything down." He knocked snow from his boots and hung up his heavy winter coat in the coat closet.

Miss Bough changed out of her boots. "You should try to be optimistic."

"We're only at the beginning," Carrère said, gently closing the closet door. He trapped a sleeve in the jamb and the door wouldn't close all the way. The floorboards creaked. The floors in the Library never would, he thought. They'll be stone or tile.

Miss Bough asked, "Why the sour grapes so early in the morning?"

"Because on a municipal building such as this, everyone will want to make changes. We've already received a letter from the Executive Committee."

"I saw it. What did they want?"

They walked by Hastings's office. Hastings was busily rearranging his desk.

"Good morning," Hastings called out cheerily.

"Good morning," Carrère replied not so cheerily. "Did you see the letter from the Executive Committee yesterday?"

"No, what's it about?"

"They want more light in the reading room by increasing the window area as much as possible."

Hastings jumped up. He had boundless enthusiasm and energy. "We can do that, but we will have to change the rear façade as well to keep the balance I was looking for."

Carrère turned to the second page of the letter. "Also, they want to omit the tall columns at the northeast and southeast corners of the terrace and substitute them with small sculpture groups." He wished the bureaucrats would leave architecture to the architects. "They should let us do the façade."

Miss Bough joined the partners in Hastings's office. Hastings glanced up at her and motioned for her to take a seat.

"There will be battles every step of the way." Carrère predicted the negotiations that lay ahead. "They are part of the business. We'll have to compromise, but most of the time they'll see our point and let it be."

"I know how persuasive you are," Miss Bough said. Her voice was quiet and soothing. "You will prevail most of the time."

"Sometimes it is a struggle, though," Hastings said. There was a moment of silence. "Now that our design has won," he added, "we don't have as much control over it."

Carrère glanced at Miss Bough—to see if she was thinking the same thing: *Who is Hastings to talk about control?*

Miss Bough added with respect now in her voice, "You'll have the control because you're capable and experienced."

Hastings regarded Miss Bough carefully, "How do you know?"

"She's very perceptive, you know," Carrère jumped in. Anyone who has assisted artists has to be."

Miss Bough shot Carrère a quick look. She didn't want to reveal anything about her assisting Horace Avery.

"Okay, but I don't want her commenting on my design work," Hastings warned.

"Oh I won't, you can be sure of that," Miss Bough said.

Toward the end of January Carrère informed the draftsmen, "We are moving our offices to 28 East 41st Street next month."

"That's almost next to the Library site," Ward said.

"That's right. We're adding more draftsmen to our staff in order to get this work done."

Hastings said, "The new office is very close to my house."

"That's the only problem," Carrère commented. "You won't ever have to stop to go home."

A couple of days later, Carrère realized he'd like to have one of the paintings of Miss Bough. He considered his options: What'll she think if I ask her? Where would I put it?

Interlude

At the Farms Library, a backhoe struck a gas main and there was a great explosion. No one had marked the location of the main. The backhoe was destroyed in the blast; its operator perished. I had become lead architect on the project—perfect because the Farms Library physically connected me with the New York Public Library—and I rushed to view the damage. The backhoe was utterly destroyed: it lay on its side, blackened and twisted from the heat. The tires had burned and were missing completely. One side of the Library building was charred. The windows were broken. Most ominously, there was a significant crater where the blast took place.

Several firefighters lingered, making unpleasant comments that the backhoe operator could be buried in the crater. I had the sudden impulse to fill the crater in to undo the damage. I found a spade shovel that had not been damaged and began furiously to shovel dirt into the gaping hole. I shoveled like a man possessed, as hard as I could. One man couldn't possibly fill in the crater, but I just hated the thought of burying a dead man in an accidental hole, and I wanted the hole to go away. So I shoveled for about twenty-five minutes. When I stopped, I was wet with sweat and my hands were red, about to break into blisters. I looked into the pit and saw that I had actually made some progress. But I stuck the shovel into the ground and walked away.

I found a sandwich shop a few blocks away and slumped into a booth. I ordered two glasses of ice water and a Michelob. A TV suspended on the other wall showed early rounds of Wimbledon tennis. I gazed absently at the tennis. I had never liked the sport. Then, as if someone had written it on a napkin and put it on my table, the idea presented itself to me. If the crater was accidental space, then what was every other hole in the ground? What about the hole in a donut? What about the cavities in my teeth when I was a kid? The drinks came and I drank the beer first in one long gulp. Then, reeling from the effects of the alcohol and this big idea, I put ten dollars on the table and left.

I had to tell someone about this idea of accidental holes. But who could possibly understand what I was talking about? Who was around? I went back to the crater. No one was around. I pissed in it. Oh boy, just one beer and I pissed in a man's grave? No, I didn't. Would never. But the hole was abhorrent to me, and its effect on me was as nefarious as the beer's should have been pleasant. I scuffed more dirt into the pit and ran to my car.

Peri sipped on a glass of water as she listened to my description of the crater and of me pissing in it. Her favored beverage was water, except after going for a run, when she liked lemonade. "You didn't do anything wrong, didn't harm anything," she said.

"The dead man who used the backhoe. I pissed in his grave," I said, become increasingly consumed with remorse.

"It isn't his grave," Peri said sensing my deepening despair. "You hate that a man died there working on your project."

I loved that Peri could quickly sense my mood and say the right thing. "You're right. I don't hate the crater. But I did try to fill it in. I wanted to hide it."

"The man died. That's what you want to hide." Peri finished her water, and set the empty glass on the counter in a spot of sunlight causing a weird half-lit shadow. I didn't like the shadow—it reminded me somehow of half-life and half-death, neither one nor the other—and I pushed the glass out of the sun. I didn't think Peri had even noticed, and if she hadn't, then there would have been be no reason for her to investigate further my thoughts on this matter. I didn't want her to know everything. "But you can't change that," she said.

She had made me feel worse. "I'm going back to the crater, and I'm going to fill it in," I said. I pulled on my yellow work boots, some old leather work gloves, and found a hard hat from a construction job I had worked on once when I was a college student.

"Why don't you find out who the worker was and send a note to his family?"

"I'll do that after I fill in the crater."

Back at the construction site I found the shovel exactly where I had left it, stuck in a pile of dirt. It was dark, but there was enough scattered light for me to estimate that the crater was two feet deep and about eight feet in diameter. In the darkness it was impossible to see the dirt I had shoveled earlier in the day. That didn't matter though. I started where I had left off and tossed shovelful after shovelful into that pit, one after another, minute after minute, hour after hour. I had left my watch at home, so was unaware of the passing time. I reached some level of delirium, caused by fatigue, hunger, and thirst but kept at it.

The dirt was soft and easy to shovel. Over time though, my shoulders began to ache. A little while after I noticed my shoulders, the sky began to brighten. Dawn! I had been shoveling all night. I could finally assess my progress. The crater was almost completely filled in. I had done it! I had erased the evidence that a man was killed at the Farms Library. I was groggy—tired but gratified that I had done it. I could go home, have breakfast, and then write the man's family a note explaining what I had done.

A gray gas company truck pulled up. It must have been seven am, but I didn't know. I leaned on the shovel. Two men hopped out of the cab and walked slowly toward me. Both wore yellow work boots, loose-fitting dungarees, reflective safety vests, and white hard hats. They studied me curiously but didn't say anything.

I was eager to show these grizzled gas company men the results of my labor. "Look, I filled in the crater for you."

The two men looked at each other and slowly shook their heads. "You've been busy," one of them said. "But we've got to look at the gas main Brenda hit."

"Brenda?" I was puzzled.

"Yeah, Brenda Fiore was operating the backhoe," he said. I didn't know his name. "She was pretty new on the job."

The other man said, "Another backhoe is coming. We've got to excavate the whole area. Hate to tell you."

I felt utterly defeated. They were going to undo all my hard work, which actually had been done out of respect for a woman backhoe operator. What did Brenda Fiore look like?"

Okay," I said. I stuck the shovel into a different pile of dirt and walked away slowly.

Carrère

During a morning meeting in February, Hastings opened a book with drawings of Ange-Jacques Gabriel's twin buildings in La Place de la Concorde in Paris.

"This is what I want."

"If I recall," Carrère said, "there's a plaster mold of those capitals at the Ecole des Beaux Arts. Maybe we can get it." Carrère suddenly envisioned a bold heist in broad daylight. Two swarthy men carried the plaster models out to a wagon. . . They had covered the models with a black tarpaulin and driven to a remote train station. The capitals were brought to Antwerp and transferred to a decrepit freighter bound for Philadelphia. . . Alas, unfortunately, one of the models was dropped and smashed on the pier. What a devilish fantasy! That was not how it really worked. It was not uncommon for architects to borrow models, operating within proper channels.

"I think the Corinthian order is correct for the portico as it sets the tone for the whole building," Hastings said.

Miss Bough entered with a tray of pastries from the bakery across the street. "Snacks for anybody?" she suggested. There was a gleam in her eye and Carrère wondered what it was all about.

Carrère couldn't stop thinking about the paintings. After that morning meeting he privately asked, "Miss Bough how did Horace. . . um, how did it happen that you posed for Horace?" Carrère felt very uncomfortable asking her this, but increasingly he had to find out. He had to know. As much as he tried, he could not put the idea away. Everytime Carrère saw her he thought of the paintings. It was midmorning, and it was quiet. Hastings left to meet with Billings at the Astor Library, Barber was with several draftsmen, and Brainard, the engineer, was at home with a cold.

"Oh," she said with a smile, "he didn't ask me, I just did it."

"You just—"

Miss Bough continued, "I could see that he needed new inspiration, for he was getting into a bit of a rut with the portraits. So one day I said, 'Look Horace, why don't I pose for you?' And that's how it started."

"You don't seem like the kind of person," Carrère said.

"What kind of a person would that be?" asked Miss Bough. She looked at him quite strongly, and he wasn't sure what to do. "I was just trying to help him."

"Did it help?"

"I wouldn't say so," Miss Bough said, having finished straightening some papers surrounding the typewriter.

"I'd like to see those paintings again."

"Anytime is fine," Miss Bough said.

She had said any time! Carrère knew he had to be careful. He didn't want anyone else to know about the paintings, least of all Hastings, who wasn't comfortable with a lady working for them. If people found out, Miss Bough would have to be fired, because people would think she was a whore. Carrère didn't want to hurt her. "I won't tell anyone."

Miss Bough came closer to him, close enough that he could feel her warmth. "I wanted you to see the paintings because I had a feeling that you'd like them, and—"

A door slammed shut and there were footfalls on the stairs. "Tell me the rest later," Carrère spun away from Miss Bough just as Hastings burst through the doorway.

"I forgot my reading glasses," Hastings stormed past Miss Bough. "Now I'm going to be late. I hate that!" He stormed past Miss Bough again going the other way, completely unaware of Carrère.

Interlude

After my all-nighter at the crater, Peri didn't speak to me for several days.

I could understand her behavior, although neither she nor I could understand mine. By filling in the crater that night, I had tried to make some kind of statement of regret for the incident that killed Brenda Fiore. There was something else though, or at least there must have been. But I had no idea what it was. When Peri finally ended her verbal embargo, I asked, "Were you on duty when the accident happened?"

Peri wasn't in much mood to talk and gave me a short monosyllabic answer, "I was."

"Did they bring her to your hospital?"

"Nope."

I wasn't going to get anywhere with Peri by talking about the victim or work or the hospital. It was going to be all about me. I should have seen it coming.

"What the *fuck* were you doing?" She never used that word, and yet as she did, she knew exactly how to modulate the word's intensity so as to give it meaning. That of course was impossible, and yet she did.

I stared at the tops of my shoes. I had come home from the office at the regular hour and still had my "business" clothes on. Peri was wearing her bathrobe again, though I strongly doubted she would let it fall open.

"I went crazy," I said, "had to fill in that hole so that so one would see it."

"What if someone did see it?" Peri was good at asking rhetorical questions.

"They would think it was part of our design, *my* design, for the Library, and I would be ruined." I didn't say it but I felt that I would be laughed out of town.

Peri turned and walked away from me. "Anyone could have seen that it wasn't part of the design. It was a hole in the ground, not part of the building!" She entered the bedroom, and I saw her lovely bottom disappear around the corner as she tossed her robe on the bed. She returned a minute later wearing sweatpants and a running bra.

"I'm going out for a run."

"Okay," I said. Maybe Jayne could understand. After all, she was an artist and an architect, too. I tried to imagine what she would say when I told her about spending all night filling in that crater. "Henry, you're too sensitive," or "You've gone off the deep end," or "You have to find out why." I decided that she would encourage me to find the answer, and then I realized I was swamped: my (and Jayne's) job, Carrère's book, and now some wacko personal odyssey. Peri was angry, too. Job Number One was to fix that; Job Number Two was to locate Jayne.

Carrère

The winter waned. Crocuses started popping up in various Fifth Avenue gardens. One morning in late March, Hastings announced while pointing at his new sketch of the façade, "We're going to double the columns."

"Why?" Magonigle asked. The lad was never shy, always asking questions.

"To give a stronger sense of purpose to them."

"What about the side flanks?" Magonigle pressed.

"By converting the pilasters into engaged half columns, we unify the whole façade." Hastings gestured grandly extending his arms across the large drawing, making eye contact with everyone around the table. "The façade is stronger and communicates the interior spaces more effectively."

Another question formed on Magonigle's face. "I thought the pilasters did the job pretty well."

"Engaged columns are just better," Hastings said, "and more monumental."

Spring in Manhattan advanced. Shirtsleeves were typical in the office. Outdoors, hats were common on most heads, but gone were coats and side curtains on the carriages. It was the season of picnics and parties.

"Yesterday was Dell's birthday, wasn't it?" Hastings asked Carrère one day. "How old is she now?"

"She's seven," Carrère said. "She had several friends over, and they had a nice time."

"Was there a big cake?" Hastings asked with genuine interest. He didn't have children—he was not even married yet—and often liked to hear about family life from Carrère.

"Yes, it was a wonderful cake, and all the girls sang *Happy Birthday*, and Dell opened some presents, and her older sister had fun, too."

"I remember my older brother Frank being jealous of my birthday parties. And I remember being jealous of my younger brother Henry's birthdays," Hastings said.

Miss Bough entered the room with the day's newspapers. Carrère thanked her politely. Hastings quietly avoided eye contact with her. When she had left the room, Carrère asked, "Why does Miss Bough bother you?"

"She doesn't," Hastings adopted a defensive posture and looked Carrère squarely in the eye.

"She's a good secretary and helps us in many ways," Carrère explained.

"I'm sure she does. I just don't want any Stanford White-like behavior here at our firm." Stanford was a known ladies man, which Hastings found quite distasteful. "She could upset the balance here."

"I wouldn't worry. She's not like anyone you know."

Hastings accepted Carrère's word. "I'm concerned that I won't be able to do my work if she's around all the time."

"She won't bother you."

Hastings displayed in the drafting room his new ideas for the 40th and 42nd Street façades. "I wanted these façades to be harmonious with the Fifth Avenue side." He turned his conceptual drawing rightside up for the men on the other side of the table. "In our competition elevations, the walls were too plain and too flat. So what I did was continue the colonnade motif along the two end façades," Hastings explained. "This provides a stabilizing grid for the two stories of windows."

"What made you think of this?" Ward asked.

Hastings furrowed his brow, "My concern was that the windows seemed to float in excessive expanses of marble." He held up the new drawing of the 42nd Street façade next to a competition drawing pinned to the wall.

"See what I mean?"

"You've added simple laurel swags, too," Barber commented.

"They break up the monotony of the wall," Hastings added.

"What are you going to do about the door?" Carrère asked.

"Well, we're going enhance its decorations," Hastings replied. Enhance the decorations. Carrère could tell his partner was already looking forward to the fun of making the entryway better.

"See, the doorway was subdued, with only a small pediment that breaks through the top basement course of stones." He winced a little, then his eyes flared, as if trying to emphasize something he couldn't articulate. "But that's a weakness in the strengthened façade."

This was one of those times that Hastings exhibited a crazed countenance, like a demon's, and Carrère wondered if he was out of control on a wild racing horse that couldn't stop. At first, Hastings would soberly explain dry architectural principles; then he became something else, even if only for a moment. Carrère asked him about it.

Hastings shook his head slowly. "It's the chattering monkey."

"What did you say?"

"A damn little monkey sits on my shoulder chattering in my ear," Hastings patted his left shoulder with his right hand, "egging me on."

"So I guess he's not your friend."

"No, he's not my friend," Hastings shrugged.

"Can you get rid of him?"

"Sometimes. But most of the time, he's there doing what he does."

"Do you ever get angry with him?" Carrère leaned forward.

"Oh, yes," Hastings nodded deliberately. "Sometimes he—I get confused."

"He confuses you?"

"Yeah, but sometimes it's my fault."

"So who's in charge, you or the monkey?" Carrère asked.

"It depends on what I'm working on and if I'm liking or enjoying it." Hastings appeared gray and weak, as if he had just made some personal revelation that could destroy him.

The next day, in the anteroom, Carrère told Miss Bough about Hastings's chattering monkey and asked, "Do you think Horace had one?"

Miss Bough, wearing a beige skirt and white blouse, thought for a minute and said, "When do you want to see the paintings? Maybe then we can determine if Horace had one."

"Well, I'd like to, but I don't think we'll find out anything new about Horace. All the paintings are the same."

"I'll bring one here," she volunteered, "and you won't have to come over."

Carrère took a step backward, "But how would you keep it private?"

"Oh, I'm not worried about that. Nobody would know I have it," Miss Bough shrugged. "You let me know."

"I'll come over," Carrère said.

A few weeks later, Miss Bough asked Hastings pleasantly, "Are you having a nice Bastille Day?" It was a sweaty day in July in New York. Hastings's head jerked up from his work.

"Is that today?" he asked with surprise.

"That is today," she said. "You must remember the celebrations, don't you?"

"How could I forget?' Hastings exclaimed, forgetting for a moment that it was Miss Bough who had started the conversation. "Those Bastille Days were wonderful in the middle of the summer in Paris. Weren't we there the year they made it a national holiday?"

"I think so," Carrère said, joining the conversation. "Eighteen-eighty. France was a republic again. The war with the Prussians was just a memory. So was the Communard uprising."

Miss Bough offered Hastings a croissant from the bakery. "It's not wine," she said, "but you can celebrate anyway."

"Oh, thank you," Hastings said. "There were parades and parties and everybody had a good time," he reminisced. "It was great fun." He leaned back in his chair, savoring the memories for a moment.

Carrère took a seat next to Hastings as Miss Bough retreated. "I want to know more. Do you ever design and create without your monkey?"

"We have to talk about that again?" Hastings's head snapped toward Carrère. "Is Miss Bough helping you?"

"A little bit," Carrère acknowledged. He rested his elbows on the table.

This revelation irritated Hastings. "How can I trust you two if you're constantly worrying about how I work and, and—" He stood and started to walk away. "We've got a library to build."

Carrère found Miss Bough later in the day, "I'm coming over to study those paintings. How about this afternoon?"

Miss Bough smiled, "That'll be wonderful. I'll get everything ready."

Miss Bough had set the paintings in sequential order around her living room, propped against the wall, chairs, lamps, and anything else she had. "How do you know which one was the first?" Carrère asked.

"Horace numbered them on the back."

Carrère turned one over and nodded, and set it on the floor again. "He was organized."

"He was." Miss Bough seemed oblivious to all the paintings of herself lining the room. "Meticulous."

"May I have one of them?" Carrère asked. "Maybe I can figure out why he was stuck if I study it."

"Oh, by all means," Miss Bough said easily. "I don't need it. Why don't you take two, the first one and the last one."

The unframed paintings were about seventeen by twelve inches on thick paper. They were really only studies but were practically identical. Carrère folded some brown paper around them and slipped them into his briefcase. When he arrived home, he slid them inside the cover of a thick book of Renaissance Italian paintings. "I'll study them later," he said to himself.

Carrère

Hastings decided to changed the windows of the stack room. "There are now twenty-eight vertical windows," he explained, "the full height of the stack room. I'm looking for simplicity."

"What did you emulate when you designed this frieze?" Magonigle asked.

"Well, I was thinking of the Place de la Concorde in Paris, but I didn't refer to any book. The oak leaves, bay leaves, rosettes, everything you see here, sort of emerged by themselves. The frieze was the last thing I drew. Actually, the false doorways between the reading room windows came last. I needed something to fill the space."

"What came first?" Magonigle persisted.

"The reading room windows were the first priority on this façade." Hastings had retrieved a book on the French monuments to Louis XV. It was an old book published in 1765. He carefully opened the large book and turned its thick pages to an example of a doorway with a segmented pediment. "I used this engraving here as the basis for the doorways. Take a look and you will see the similarities." Hastings rotated the book so the others could see.

Magonigle looked at the book's cover and asked, "Has this book always been here, sir?"

"In our library," Hastings replied.

"I bought it at a bookshop Jacques, my atelier, told me about," Carrère said.

The season advanced and the summer of 1898 disappeared. Carrère sat at a table with Miss Bough. There were several pencils on it.

"Have you begun to study those two paintings?" Miss Bough asked brightly. She adjusted the cuffs around her wrists.

"No," he said dully. "They're in a bookcase at home. I haven't forgotten about them." Carrère perked up, "The thing about Hastings is that he says he modifies in the direction of simplicity."

"Okay, I'm listening," Miss Bough said.

"But I'm wondering if the revision owns him," Carrère said. "He just can't stop tinkering."

"Hmmm," Miss Bough repeated the word *own*. "I can imagine a writer being more or less inexorably drawn into a plot direction, one not considered at first. In architecture you rely so much on the past, on precedent. . . it's hard to imagine. . ."

"When we apply the canon to our designs, are we really choosing that next construct or is it being *offered* to us?" Carrère wondered.

"It must go both ways, don't you think? What was it like for you at the Ecole?" Miss Bough suggested.

Many images flashed through Carrère's mind: the design competitions, long days and nights, the Grand Prix prize, artists painting the façade of the Notre Dame cathedral, the energy and desire of the young men at the Ecole de Beaux Arts. It was a busy place and a busy time. "I was just a student then," he said.

"Yes, you were. But weren't you freer to test ideas then?"

"Well yes and no. Most of my ideas came from the books. Some of us worked from the books, others relied on their—"

"—intuition, experience, imagination?"

"Yes, that's right." Carrère tapped a pencil. "But I think there's less to it than that. At some point, the work dictates to the artist what comes next, and the artist can do nothing about it.

"Barber once said that a design he did came in a dream. And when he got up and sketched it, did it *own* him or did he *own* it? I don't know." Carrère continued to tap the pencil. "At times, our work is the product of a subconscious activity—a dream. On the other hand, some artists are purely rational and calculating."

"Hastings can operate in both realms, I think," Miss Bough suggested. "He receives an idea, verifies it in the books, and then draws furiously. He can move back and forth."

"He probably gives no thought to where it came from and how he himself is involved in the design. Is he a conduit for the design that comes from *out there* somewhere or is he the actual creator?"

"I suspect he is both, and he's assisted by his chattering monkey," Miss Bough said.

Carrère checked his pocket watch. "It's time for me to go," he pulled on his suit jacket. "Agreed. Whether Hastings is a conduit or the creator, this Library is going to be one of the world's finest, he's convinced."

Interlude

I took a shower, trying to freshen up, my mind inert from fatigue. Peri didn't have to work that day, so I knew her run would be long. I used the time to clean the dirt off my work boots.

When Peri returned and had helped herself to a tall glass of lemonade, she said, "I think you should have left the crater. I ran past it and the gas company had already dug it out." She looked healthy and fit, in perfect contrast to how I felt. Her cheeks were pink, her arms and abdomen glistened with sweat. She sat at the kitchen table to remove her sneakers.

"They said they were going to do that," I said, stifling a yawn.

Peri stood to get another glass of lemonade. She always had two after a run. "You never saw what the backhoe hit. Maybe there was something else in there besides the gas main."

"There was nothing, Peri," I said. "It was a bomb crater, that's all, where someone died. It's my project, and I feeel terrible."

"Do you know anything about the man who was killed?" Peri put her empty glass in the sink.

"I do. It was a woman named Brenda—Brenda Fiore, I think. It still surprises me that a woman was operating the backhoe. I still haven't found out where she lived or anything about her family. I'm going into the office later and I'll find out."

"Are you going to visit the Farms Library today?" Peri asked.

"Haven't decided."

Later at the office, I contacted the general contractor, who provided me the name of the excavating subcontractor. Soon enough, I knew the victim's address. I found out the time and date of the memorial service. I didn't like funerals, wakes, or memorial services, and I planned not to attend.

Jayne came in. "I heard you spent all night filling in the pit at the Farms Library," she said. She wore pointy black leather shoes, low-top corduroy jeans, a white t-shirt with the iconic yellow smile-face on it, and her hair was done in a single thick braid.

I stood at my desk. "How did you know? Is that what brought you here today?"

"I saw Peri."

Oh God, were they ganging up on me? "Where? What did she say?" I stifled another yawn." I sensed suddenly in an almost automatic fashion that these two women were going to put "the squeeze" on me. I couldn't fathom why. I certainly fulfilled my responsibilities at the office, doing my job and most of Jayne's at the same time. For Peri, I was a good companion (not yet husband), and she respected my ambition and work ethic. So what were they after?

"She was at the cleaner picking up some things. She said you were tired." Jayne folded a stick of gum in her mouth and began to chew.

"I am tired. I don't know why I did that. Maybe I was burying the dead or something. I guess I shouldn't have bothered."

Jayne folded her arms and shook her head. "No you shouldn't have. There's quite a lot of beauty there. You never saw it because you went crazy and filled it in."

I had never thought of it: the beauty of an empty space! As an architect, I had thought about volume, that which is contained by a building, usually in the context of the number of cubic feet that needs to be heated or cooled. The volume was never beautiful though nor anything to regard in anything but a mathematical sense. I'll have to see it again, I thought, to see if there was any truth to what Jayne said.

"What did you see?"

"A hole in the ground," Jayne said enigmatically. She chewed her gum slowly turning it over again and again. She looked at me as if she knew something but was not telling.

Carrère

"It's hard to believe that two years have already passed since we were drawing for the competition," Carrère said to Miss Bough on the 41st Street sidewalk outside the office. It was a humid end-of-May day in 1899. His shirt clung to him like a second skin but it didn't really bother him. Forty-first Street was quiet with no traffic. It wasn't a thoroughfare like Broadway or Fifth Avenue.

Ever affable, Miss Bough said, stepping through the doorway into the brownstone building. "You have been busy, that's all."

"I need you to prepare this letter to Doctor Billings on the heating plan devised by Mister Woolf. Send Woolf a copy as well." He gave her a handwritten letter. Wolff was a consulting engineer.

The secretary, wearing a light cotton skirt, studied the letter briefly and nodded with approval. "I shall send these today." She placed the papers on the desk near her typewriter and looked up with apparent affection. "I know you're thinking about something else. What is it?"

Miss Bough's perceptiveness always amazed Carrère. She could unerringly detect when he was thinking about something. "How did you know?"

"It comes from having five sisters. They're always conniving, especially when you're the oldest. Now tell me what's on your mind," Miss Bough demanded. A fruit fly buzzed against a window.

"I'm thinking of writing a monograph on the Library building."

"It's about time," she said.

"Why do you say that?"

"Because you're building something that will last forever. People in the future will want to read about it," Miss Bough said.

"We rely on you every day Miss Bough. I had no idea you felt this way."

"I try to keep quiet," she said, "but I am always observing." She set her brown purse on the table beside a vase with daffodils. "What made you think of a book?"

"I've thought about it for a long time. I want to do this because the Library is becoming special to us." Carrère took a seat in the secretary's cramped space.

"Then you must do it."

"That's what I'm afraid of," Carrère said. He began to calculate the time it would take and all the other work he had to do.

"You'll need some help, I should think," Miss Bough said. "You have to keep accurate records. That way you will have the information available when you want to use it."

"The firm has records, Miss Bough." He always addressed her formally. "I spend most of my time here at 41st Street, and I'm not often enough at the library site. It's a problem. I never know what's going on over there." He gestured with his thumb over his shoulder.

Miss Bough agreed, "You are so busy with clients you have little time for architecture."

"That is very true." Carrère was resigned to the truth of the situation. It had been that way for far too long. He would have liked to draw some houses again. Maybe someday it would be his own house.

"You should have one of the men make notes for you, at least on a weekly basis. That way, you can be busy with the other business and yet even the smallest details will be recorded."

"That's an excellent idea. The job will be done even if I can't be on hand. I could write the book without being fully involved." He found Miss Bough's suggestions to be excellent and congratulated himself for hiring her. She had become indispensable. "Now it won't take over my whole life."

"It could take over your whole life?" Miss Bough arched her eyebrows.

"Only if I let it. But I like to be in control."

Interlude

I did my best to continue with Carrère's book, The Library Book. Although I spent hours in the evenings supposedly engrossed in Carrère's project, the book had not attained any discernable shape, and in truth was going nowhere. Still though, it had to be done!

Two days later, I returned to the crater. It had begun to rain softly. The roads were barely wet; I put the wipers on the slowest intermittent setting. Several gas company men were hanging around, leaning on shovels and trading opinions about what had happened. They had indeed excavated the crater, undoing all my hard work. A black dump truck with red cab idled nearby. I snuck around the edges, hoping not to be seen by the workers, and I wasn't. I stopped at the point nearest where I had urinated into the pit and tried to divine what Jayne had said was beautiful about the space. Instead of turning and dismissing the crater and Jayne's idea as folly, I gave myself some extra minutes. I stared. I tossed a pebble into the bottom of the crater. The workers got into the dump truck and left, leaving me in there in failing light. The crater became dark first, and once it had, there was nothing left for me to observe. Although I trusted Jayne's assertion, I didn't see the beauty. The crater was the site of an industrial accident, nothing more, nothing less.

Temporarily satisfied, I delved back into the book. I decided to concentrate on the details. Details, details! The problem was, I didn't have the facts; therefore, it was impossible to provide interesting, detailed information if the facts did not exist.

But the facts did exist! Right there on Fifth Avenue stood the New York Public Library with all its marble, bricks, mortar, and beauty for all to see. As Carrère's librettist, I would encourage—no require—everyone to visit the New York Public Library. On the dust jacket there would be a stern "black box" warning that the book would be difficult to follow if you did not first visit the Library. "Go to the New York Public Library and take a tour. You'll see the details for yourself and you won't have to read about them!"

What a bargain!

Carrère

It was a sticky day, June 6, 1899. Carrère dressed in a plain shirt, the usual dark trousers and jacket. Brainard, similarly dressed, joined him as they watched Mr. Lentilhon, the contractor, unlock the rusty, ivy-covered 42nd Street gate to the Croton Reservoir. The gate didn't want to swing on its hinges; it was scaly with rust. Two strong men pushed hard to force it open. Along with Lentilhon, an assembled gang of about seventy-five workmen with shovels, picks, and crowbars in hand swarmed through the opening.

Lentilhon beckoned Brainard and Carrère to follow him into the reservoir foundation. "This should be interesting," he called out. He was wearing rough work overalls. They stepped carefully through scattered wooden beams laying about the floor. The musty air inside the foundation must have been at least 20 degrees cooler than outside. They entered three small connecting square rooms about forty feet high. Brick arches separated the rooms. The roofs were arched domes. What marvelous construction—too bad it was hidden from view for all those years. Green mold covered the walls and mildew clung to the arches. It smelled too. The city's prisons were nicer than this place, Carrère thought.

The workers shuffled a bit, as if signaling impatience. "This place is coming down," Lentilhon boasted.

"I knew it was well built, but now that I see it, I suspect it'll take a long time," Brainard said.

"We calculate that there are one hundred and ten thousand cubic yards of masonry in this structure," Brainard said. "Once we are underway, we can remove a thousand cubic yards a day. About five hundred men will work on the site."

"A good amount of the stone will be saved to be used in the Library foundations," Brainard said.

As Brainard and Lentilhon spoke, Carrère closely examined the masonry inside the reservoir structure. He touched the wall carefully with his index finger, and then examined the finger to see if there was any slime. There was, and he wiped it on his trousers. The place was a hellhole. Good riddance, he thought. They were going to be replacing a hellhole with a library. How appropriate, Carrère thought.

"That's true," Lentilhon nodded, "but until we have access to the interior of the reservoir, we can't begin the foundation." The contractor unfurled sheets of drawings the architects had prepared and showed his foremen where to begin.

The workers, armed with pickaxes, crowbars, shovels, mauls, wedges, levers, wheelbarrows, wagons, sledges, rope, and horses, began to take apart the reservoir walls. Brute strength, cunning, and ingenuity were required to bring the ramparts down. Crumbling stone fell underfoot and was shoveled clear. Men and horses in each other's way; the incredible din created by the hammering and wrenching; the peculiar mix of the hot summer day; the unlimited dampness of the stone and earth; and the sweat and power of the hundreds of strong arms and strong backs, all gave validity to the scale of the enterprise. The slow and laborious job had begun.

Carrère

Tom Hastings decided it was time for the special day. He and Helen Benedict had been courting for many years. When his friends at the Meadowbrook Hunt Club suggested that he bring Helen to a hunt, Hastings evidently thought that would be just the thing and just the place. The hunt was to be in September, and he'd found the perfect ring to put an exclamation point on their ten-year-long romance. All he really had to worry about was the weather.

"I'm going to be away this weekend," Hastings mentioned.

"Where're you going?" Carrère asked innocently.

"I am bringing Helen to the Meadowbrook Hunt, and I'm going to ask her to marry me." Carrère could tell he was excited.

"Excellent! It's been a long time coming." Carrère quickly forgot about some demands the contractor had made. "Have you got a ring?"

"Of course. It's at home," Hastings said. Everything seemed to be just right, even though there were already problems with the Library.

"So you're going to a hunt. Have you ever seen one before?" Carrère asked him.

"Once a long time ago," Hastings said. "Helen likes the horses, and I thought it would be fun to get away."

"I watched a hunt at the Rockaway but was not very interested. I like the sound of the hooves pounding toward you, though."

"I know. You like tennis and cars. The hunt will be a good place because it will be elegant, outdoors, and although busy, it will be more-or-less private because we won't know anybody."

"A good thought. Helen will like it because it's the finest hunting club from the point of view of wealth and social prominence." Carrère glanced out the window. "I think it'll be a nice day tomorrow."

Interlude

I had known all along, almost since I met Peri at church in New York, that we'd get married someday. I always knew we would combine traditional aspects of the engagement and wedding with informal elements. But I actually had no plan for "popping the question;" in fact, I didn't even have a ring.

It was an ordinary Saturday in the early spring. The snow had melted but the buds on the trees hadn't yet opened. My all-nighter at the crater was well behind us. In fact, I had mostly forgotten about the unfortunate accident. It was a day for regular weekend chores: grocery shopping, the hardware store, gas station, and the like. I had never expected "the like" to include a jewelry store.

We had replaced Peri's Kia after it was wrecked. Peri wasn't hurt because she wasn't in it when a tree fell on it. The workers cutting the tree down paid for its replacement, which turned out to be a secondhand four-wheel-drive Subaru. It was a good car, and we used it for everything.

With lists in hand, we set out on our rounds. Groceries first, then gas. Gas in those days was only a dollar a gallon, but even then, I usually watched closely as the dollars mounted on the pump's display. Peri went into the little convenience mart to get something while I pumped the gas. She didn't immediately hop back into the car. And even in the early spring early morning shadows, her face radiated. She looked happy and healthy, and all of a sudden I said, "Hey, are we gonna get married or what?"

Her reaction indicated that the same thing had been on her mind. She raced around the car and hugged me around the neck. The nozzle was still in the fill tube, and I let go of the handle to embrace her. "Where's the ring?" Peri asked brightly.

I topped up the tank and shut the pump off. "We'll have to go get one," I said.

"I hope that's not why you wanted to go to the hardware store!"

Peri was all smiles, unconcerned by the lack of a ring.

"Hose clamp or lock washer?" I asked.

"A karat, please."

Carrère

"Tommy Hastings got engaged," Carrère reported when he came home on Monday.

"That's wonderful news," Marion smiled. "Do they know when and where it'll be?"

"Oh, I don't know," Carrère shrugged. "He didn't mention that." He emptied loose change from his pocket into a saucer on the front hall table.

"I think he'll have little to do with the wedding planning," Marion suggested.

"If I know Tommy, he won't do any at all. He's got other plans to work on," He kissed Marion gently on the cheek and headed for the parlor to examine the day's newspaper.

Marion asked, "Doesn't he want to? You helped with our wedding."

"That was so long ago and our wedding wasn't elaborate," Carrère said without looking up from the paper. "Tommy and Helen will have it all with a thousand guests, I'm sure. Helen will want it to be perfect."

"Ours was perfect," Marion said, standing before him.

"It was, couldn't have been better," Carrère really didn't like talking about or even remembering their wedding. It had been a frigid day—why they got married in January was anyone's guess—and the orchestra was missing several of its players, who were sick with the flu. He had hurt his back that day, and he therefore couldn't dance. "But I still wish it had been a better orchestra."

"You've been saying that for years," Marion chided.

"I mean it." He hated those conversations. "It was impossible to dance. The room was too small."

Marion grimaced. "You must remember some good things, don't you?"

He folded the newspaper and dropped it onto the floor. "I really wish you would let this go. Look, I loved you, but not the orchestra."

Marion picked up her husband's slip instantly. "You *loved* me? What about now?"

"Of course I love you, still do," he said. "Nothing has changed. Never," he stammered.

Marion stood before him with a hurtful look on her face. "Is there someone else?"

He stood and took her hands into his. "Of course not, my dear. Never in a thousand years." In his mind, though, something was different. He thought about how he used to draw and how he didn't anymore. He thought about how Stanford White used his power and prestige and always had a mistress. He made the practice seem acceptable in the profession. Am I suitably prestigious? Carrère wondered. No, all I do is back-office administrative work, negotiations and such. Hastings attracts all the glory because he is the chief designer and not married— at least not yet. Maybe if I still drew, I would have a different image and a different kind of life. "It was a perfect wedding. We're happily married."

"I hear Stanford White has a different mistress every year."

A punch to the stomach. Carrère said, "He does, but I don't." His voice rose, "Are you accusing me?"

Marion whirled around and stormed out of the room. "I am not, but I think there's trouble in your paradise!" She returned and added, "You've got some explaining to do!"

"I do not! There's nothing to explain. I love my job—and you. That's all there is to it."

Marion glared at him from the doorway. "You complain about our wedding as a way to complain about our marriage, don't you?"

"I don't know how you can say that. How dare you! I provide you and the girls with everything you need. And now this. I know, have you found a better man, a fabulous architect who is famous and wealthy?"

Marion began to weep. Her weeping never heightened, though, to become a torrent. She wept only a little, then she stopped. "There's no other man," she said. Her composure regained, she added, "I hope there's no other woman either."

Carrère

"Brainard tells us the test borings indicate that bedrock is only about ten feet below the proposed basement floor level." Carrère explained this particular problem in muted tones.

Hastings immediately said, "We either have to make the cellar the least possible height—"

"—or we will have to blast out a lot of rock," Brainard brushed job site dust off his trousers. He had been onsite all morning.

"That wouldn't please the neighbors," Hastings said, polishing his glasses.

"And it would cost more," Carrère added glumly. "We can't go to the City for money right now."

Miss Bough spoke up, "Why don't you conduct more tests? Maybe there's been an error."

Hastings threw the secretary a fierce glance. "The engineers have done their job well."

"Of course they have," Miss Bough brushed off Hastings's posture. "They should double-check."

"She's right. It can't hurt to double-check," Carrère defended Miss Bough. "It will cost a little extra but not as much as blasting, and if we don't have to reengineer the heating and plumbing—"

"Okay, okay. We should check again. It's not my problem." Hastings polished his glasses again and stormed out of the drafting room.

"I'll order more tests," Brainard said. "If it is bedrock, we'll have to raise the basement floor two feet."

"Good, good," Carrère said. "As soon as you can, I hope?"

Brainard collected several engineering studies, leaving Miss Bough and Carrère in the drafting room.

"Why does he get so testy around me?" Miss Bough asked.

"Oh, it's just him. He's never had a woman in the office. He's getting married soon. He's not sure, that's all."

"Getting married?" Miss Bough inquired.

"In April, I think."

"To anyone I know?"

"Do you know Miss Helen Benedict?" Carrère shrugged his shoulders. "Her father is a banker."

Miss Bough seemed disappointed and shook her head slowly. "I guess I won't be a bridesmaid."

Carrère wasn't truly sure how Miss Bough was feeling, but asked, "Wouldn't you rather be the bride?"

Miss Bough spun around, her skirt flaring wide. "I would have gone all the way with Horace," she revealed. "But he never did. I was only his secretary. I don't think he loved anybody."

What is she looking for? "You are our, or my, secretary. You didn't come here looking for a romance did you? Or did you?"

Miss Bough's eyes gleamed. All of a sudden Carrère sensed that perhaps she did seek something more. "There are a lot of fine gentlemen here. I can't help but notice that," she purred.

Carrère thought of his little tiff with Marion the other night and got panicky. No wonder she had posed for Horace. He had those two paintings. How could he stop this? Did he want to stop? Marion. . .Miss Bough?

"I have work to do, and I'd like not to know—Maybe I can introduce you, or—" He stammered, uncomfortable, sweat forming on his brow.

"Oh, come now," Miss Bough said. "You don't have to do anything you don't want to do."

A few weeks later, Hastings and Carrère visited the Reservoir with Brainard, who pointed excitedly at some test pits. "I have good news," Brainard exclaimed, his broad, wrinkled tanned face showing the effects of many hours spent in the sun. "The results of the borings were false."

"Miss Bough was right," Carrère said. He couldn't stop thinking about the secretary.

Brainard nodded rapidly. "We found large boulders strewn about the plot. Our drills hit the boulders, not bedrock as we thought. So—"

"—we can go back to our original plan," Hastings instantly figured.

"That's right. You don't have to compromise on the basement," Brainard said.

"I'm glad *we* decided to order more tests," Hastings glared at Carrère.

Carrère pretended not to notice Hastings's comment and said, "She'll get you another time."

Once Hastings proposed marriage, Carrère began to notice that it was as if Hastings had started an engine, and soon the machine had a life of its own and nothing could stop it. Carrère thought of his wedding—so long ago—and then Carrère began to think of wedding planning as a painting. A painting can have a life of its own. A wedding has a normal and natural conclusion, but a painting is never finished; it only stops at interesting places.

According to Hastings, Helen had already found a wedding gown she liked. The service was to be at the Second Congregational Church in Greenwich in April. The church would have an arch of white lilies. Carriages would bring the wedding party to the reception at the Great House. Hastings was content to have Helen's family—particularly the Commodore, Mr. Benedict—take charge of the event. Hastings, a creature of the present, stayed focused on the Library. He never concerned himself with either past events or future obligations. He was always focused on the immediate task at hand, whether it was an elevation or a cocktail party.

Interlude

We had to wait for the jewelry store to open. Peri knew just what she wanted, and once inside, she found it quickly. It had one diamond, about three-quarters of a karat. She tried it and it fit. Peri held out her hand for me to see. I nodded approvingly. The store clerk swiped my credit card and we were on our way.

A few days later, Jayne came into my office. I wondered if I should tell her. "Peri and I are getting married," I blurted.

"When?" asked Jayne, sipping a Diet Pepsi from a can she held.

"I don't know. We haven't told our families yet." I shoved my hands in my back pockets.

"Why don't you tell'm?" Jayne said. "You must be excited."

"We don't want them to know yet. It's no big deal really. Maybe we'll get married at the courthouse or city hall. We haven't decided anything, except that we're going to get married."

We went into her office and Jayne reached into her desk, producing a photograph of a smiling married couple. "You know who they are?"

I looked closely at the black and white photograph. The clothing appeared dated, nothing people would wear today. The groom wore a tuxedo and the bride a long-sleeved gown. "I have no idea."

"My parents in 1949," she said. "Don't you or doesn't Peri want a classy, elegant wedding?"

"I think she would vomit," I said. "You've met Peri. She has her own ideas, so I really have to go along with them. I like her ideas for the most part, though at times she has trouble with mine."

Jayne sat at her desk. "You've got some very odd ideas."

"Yeah, I still don't know what happened to me that night. I did go back there to look for that beauty you talked about, but I didn't see it."

"How many times have you been scuba diving in that quarry?" Jayne asked.

"Around ten."

"What is there to see?"

"I just like it," I explained. "It's deep, dark, and cold."

"Do you see fish?"

"I think I saw a fish once. I wondered how it got there." I started thinking about how beautiful it was. "You see, you don't dive there to see fish. I'm not a fish diver anyway. It's the light."

"Light?"

"Yup. I love the quality of the light filtering down from overhead." I backed away from Jayne's desk and illustrated the quarry's space with my hands in front of me. "See, the quarry gets wider and wider the deeper you go."

"How deep?" Jayne interjected with some concern.

"One hundred and twenty feet to the bottom." I shrugged that away. "But one side of it disappears into a big black cavern. What I love is swimming a few feet into the cavern, turning around and looking at the light in the open water. It's dark greenish, and it's beautiful."

"So you like dark spaces with green light?" Jayne said.

"That's an overgeneralization. You can't say that I'd want the inside of the Farms Library dark and green. Nor my house."

"I know that," Jayne said. "What you have to think about is the space."

"I have thought about it," I said. "The quarry is enclosed and limited or defined, not like the ocean, which is limitless. I like how the space was chiseled out of solid rock, and how it is just there. "Man," I looked around, "it used to be solid rock; now it's solid water. Pretty cool, isn't it?"

"It must be if you've dived there ten times. Would you dive in that crater if it were filled with water?"

Jayne's question stopped me. I had never thought of it. What if it *were* filled with water? Well, I knew what was in it already. But what if I didn't know? The crater was the byproduct of an accident, and someone had died. The quarry was deliberate. Maybe workers died in it. I could never know. What about the crater that had made me fill it in that night? If I could, would I want to fill in the quarry? No, it was much too interesting. But why wasn't the crater interesting or desirable when the quarry was? "I guess so," I said without conviction. "It'd be a muddy dive."

"I think you like spaces," Jayne said. "You just haven't figured that out yet."

Carrère

Carrère found Barber illustrating in the Beaux-Arts tradition a plan of the entry hall from the inside out. In his latest iteration, ten piers divided the sides into ten bays, and Doric columns framed the bays on the long sides (east and west). He colored in all the solid masses, the piers and walls to mold the interior space of the entry hall.

Ward leaned over Barber's shoulder for a closer look. Magonigle walked around the table to get out of the sunlight pouring in the window. Barber explained, "As I shape the stonework, I'm thinking about how the interior volume will look. We are striving for unity, balance, and symmetry in the composition."

"One way we can achieve that is to shape the space," Carrère said. "Beaux-Arts architecture is about mass and interior space, which become experiences as you walk through them." He paced about the room, its floor creaking.

"What kind of experience do you want people to have when they come into the library?" Ward asked.

"Calm. The composition will induce calm."

"He's exactly correct," Barber said. "And you know, the edge or face of the marble here in the entry hall," he tapped a pencil on the drawing, "is the boundary between the emptiness of the room and the solidity of the stone. It's splendid, isn't it?"

"Also, both the room and the stone have shape because we want them to," Carrère rubbed his hands together with delight.

Magonigle said, "So you shape two things at once, the stone and the room." The clock in the anteroom chimed eleven-thirty.

"Of course," Barber said. "It's funny, you can chip, carve, and smooth the stone but not the volume, except by working on the stone,"

"You really should be thinking about both, the solid and the void, as you give shape to the stone." Carrère stopped pacing, and sat on the edge of the table.

"You need to understand Beaux-Arts principles to make a mark in this business," Barber said flatly as Ward, a student intent on learning from a master, listened closely. "Carving out the space is just one part of the overall Beaux-Arts idea of composition." Barber pushed his chair away from the table, making the shape of a building with his hands in front of him. "We conceive whole buildings as three-dimensional entities seen in plan, section, and elevation, and the interior manifests itself on the exterior." He paused. "It's not so much the design of ornaments or of façades."

"Is that what Hastings thinks about when he works?" Ward asked.

"Sure it is," Carrère said. "Certainly as he develops the early ideas."

"But now?" Magonigle wondered.

"We're well beyond the initial concept, past the early revisions," Barber said. "And he's focused on details."

"He loves to try to make things better, even trying to make a room's space better," Carrère said. "He gets carried away with the details sometimes."

"When he can't stop revising." Barber chuckled at memories of his years at the Ecole des Beaux-Arts. "We'd be working on things *en charrette* running through the streets of Paris."

"Sounds familiar," Carrère said. "How long ago were you there anyway?"

"I finished four years ago in ninety-six," Barber said. Looking at the two younger men, Ward and Magonigle, he added, "It's a great experience and I recommend it."

"I was there twenty years ago, and we were running through the streets, too," Carrère shook his head. "Some things don't change."

"So why does Hastings get so carried away?" Magonigle asked.

"I think you'd have to ask him," Carrère declared. "I can't say what makes him tick or why, but I'm going to find out."

Carrère

"Barber and Magonigle told me that they noticed how Hastings sometimes goes too far and can't stop." Carrère mentioned the recent conversation to Miss Bough. "If the younger men notice it, it must be pretty noticeable." Miss Bough was half-seated on the end of his desk swinging one foot in the air. "You know that sometimes I hide a drawing he's worked on too much, but—"

"You need another assistant," Miss Bough suggested. "How are you going to do your job, write a book, and figure out Hastings at the same time? You know, this firm would be in as much trouble without you as without Hastings."

"Okay, I guess you're right. Maybe it's me not Hastings."

"You'll figure it out," Miss Bough assured him. She stood, thinking about leaving for the day. Her clothes fit well and she looked great.

"You always have answers, Miss Bough. Did you help Horace with his problems?"

She laughed, "I must have created them. The poor man, I didn't mean him to go mad."

"He was unstable at first, don't you think? But you were trying to help him, weren't you?"

"And it was fun for me. You see, when I was a girl, I loved skinny-dipping with my sisters. It was great fun going to the college pond in our town at night. I loved the feel of the warm summer breezes blowing across my bare skin, and the cool water—it felt like an envelope." Carrère's breath left him as she recalled those summers. "So I've never been shy about being nude, It was nice at Horace's to be able to take all this off." She lifed her skirt a few inches and let it fall back to the floor.

"How old were you?" Carrère stammered.

"We were teenagers. It was a nice pond. We never saw snapping turtles or anything. It would have been more fun with a lover than my sisters, but I didn't mind."

"I used to skinny dip too, but only when I was a little boy."

"We should, then, sometime," Miss Bough suggested openly.

"Oh, I couldn't."

"Why not?" Miss Bough, her voice suddenly stern."

I'm married, you know that. If Marion found out—I wouldn't," he insisted. It would be fun though, he admitted, and wondered what it would be like. Where would we? Maybe Miss Bough's college pond. "Where did you grow up, where was that pond?" he asked,

"I'm from Lancaster, Pennsylvania. The pond was at a college there. I never went to college, but I loved that pond. We skated on it in the winter."

Carrère explored a little deeper: "Who was your first love, first beaux?"

She looked sad and admitted, "I've never had one."

Carrère stood and walked slowly to the window, then turned to face Miss Bough. "You're a fun-loving girl, why not?"

Miss Bough said slowly, "I don't know. It never worked out." She sat in chair that Carrère had just vacated. "I just don't know. It's just luck, I guess."

"I've been lucky my whole life," Carrère said, now half-sitting on the end of his desk, where Miss Bough had been a minute ago. "Solid family with three brothers, school in Europe, my family, and this firm. You must be more fortunate than you realize."

"I'm not counting any misfortunes," she smiled. "It's just the way things are, and I do like to have fun."

Carrère asked, "So, if I asked you to take your clothes off here in my office, would you?"

"I'd like to be the one with that idea," Miss Bough said.

Carrère

"Hastings's wedding is April thirtieth," Carrère said. The century had turned; it was January 1900. He seldom talked about work or his colleagues at home, preferring to keep the rough-and-tumble business world where it belonged.

"Is it in Greenwich?" Marion inquired. Attired in a comfortable plaid day-dress, she welcomed him home.

"It is," Carrère hung his thick gray coat in the front-hall closet, his hat on a peg above the shelf. "To hear Tom describe it, it is going to be quite an affair."

"I can only imagine what it will be like with a thousand guests," Marion said. "Has Tom appointed his groomsmen yet?"

"He has, but I am not one of them."

"Are you sure you don't mind?"

He and Marion sat in facing upholstered chairs in a parlor with a piano and luxurious curtains. "Oh, I really could not care. We'll attend of course, but I would rather not have the attention. And I won't have to stand for the blasted photographer."

She accepted this and let it be. "You are home early today, dear."

"It was a quiet day. Nothing new on the Library, only one meeting with a prospective client. So I just came home. What are Anna and Dell doing?"

"They're still at school," Marion said. "Look at this book. I thought you'd be interested in it, so I brought it home. It's about the Impressionist painters in Paris during the time you were there in school."

"The funny thing is that I had no idea the Impressionists were there," he said, leafing though the book. "Even if I had known, I would have thought it was junk."

"But what do you think of it now, twenty years later?" Marion asked.

He didn't reply immediately, studying the images of some of the paintings. It was not a large book—more of a pamphlet, and he reached the back cover fairly quickly. "It puzzles me how we architects are still using the languages from antiquity, and yet painters seem to invent new languages as they go."

"Do you think the language of architecture will change?" Marion reached for the booklet and flipped through it. "I do love the colors and the light in these paintings."

"Not until some client demands or approves a change." Carrère walked to the windows. "In the library, we are using the Classical languages or elements, but we are also using some new materials, like steel beams. So I guess we are evolving, too."

Marion joined him at the window and massaged his trapezius muscles at the base of his neck. Her thumbs and fingers probed deeply but gently. He loved it when Marion did this. But he thought: Does Miss Bough give massages? He sighed and relaxed.

Anna and Dell returning from school were surprised to find their father home early. He hugged them both tightly. "I came home because I wanted to see Anna's school art project, and I wanted to hear about the play, Dell. Won't you tell me?"

Anna disappeared to get the art project from her school bag, while Dell told him what it was like to act as another person in front of an audience. Dell was excited and said that she loved it. Anna returned with a drawing that showed a quiet enclosed garden with large elm trees. He savored the idea that his two daughters might become artists of one kind or another.

Carrère

A week before the wedding, Hastings and Carrère crossed Fifth Avenue and stepped through a green fence at the Library site. It was mid-April, 1900. The spring mud had dried up, but the ground had not become so dry as to be dusty. Many pieces of cut granite lay about waiting to be moved and stacked against the far wall, as prescribed in the contract. Hastings noticed that the stone blocks were weathered and dirty, not fresh and clean as if they had just come from a stone-cutting shop. A faint odor of onion lingered. At the middle of the site, Hastings said, "Right above us will be the exhibition hall, and above that, the catalog room." He tilted his head back and looked into the azure sky. "Instead of sky, there's going to be a roof here," he said.

Many of the workers didn't speak English. They were wearing rough canvas overalls, the clothing worn by construction workers everywhere. The workers seemed to be moving awfully slowly. "Lentilhon usually has labor trouble," Carrère noted. "The men want more and Lentilhon doesn't want to pay. So the work goes slowly. But look around. The Reservoir is more than half gone."

"When are they going to start the foundation?" Hastings asked.

"In the next month or so. After your wedding." Carrère adjusted his hat.

"I would like to witness that," Hastings said. "Helen will understand that I want to be back from our trip in order to see the first foundation stones laid."

Later, back in the office, "Why don't you slow down, Tom," Carrère said. The day had turned gray and the light was fairly poor. The windows needed to be washed.

"I just keep noticing things that can be improved," Hastings said. "This building has to be perfect."

"Of course it does." Carrère avoided stepping on several discarded drawings lying on the floor about Hastings's desk.

"Watch your step," Hastings said. "Those drawings are still valid, you know."

"Are you going to bring a sketch pad on your wedding trip?" Carrère said.

"Of course. What if I have an idea? I have to be able to jot it down."

"Does Helen know?"

"Of course! She knows everything!"

"I don't want to sound like your old man," Carrère looked Hastings in the eye. "You haven't been married yet. No wife knows everything."

Hastings set his pencil down and leaned back in his chair. "I love what I do."

"I know you do," Carrère said. "And Helen is going to make it easy for you to do your best."

Interlude

A breakthrough, and the book started to write itself! I found some traction when watching the NewsHour on New Hampshire Public Television. I don't watch every night. And I often tune out the commentaries at the end. But one of Roger Rosenblatt's essays caught my attention. I wrote it down.

The writer's mind, when it works, is like Alice's rabbit, leading quickly—almost recklessly—to mysterious yet attractive places. The animal is fretful because it has to find and display something at the same time. A writer writes to discover what he or she thinks. Take a single sentence. Take a sentence of William Manchester's—this sentence about Churchill's funeral: "When his flag-draped coffin moved slowly across the old capital, drawn by naval ratings, and bare-headed Londoners stood trembling in the cold, they mourned, not only him and all he had meant, but all they had been and no longer were, and would never be again." Most likely, Manchester had only the scantiest idea where that sentence would end when he began it. Only when he caught up with it could he know. But then, there was another sentence running ahead of him. There was always another sentence. And now there isn't.

Carrère the writer, had he written the book, would have revealed Hastings to be Alice's rabbit. I was excited and moved and found little trouble writing the book because there was always another sentence.

Carrère

Hastings had worried for days that there weren't enough rail coaches to transport the thousand guests to Greenwich. He also fretted about there being enough carriages to bring everyone from the train station to the church.

Carrère and Marion rode in the first of the train's eighteen coaches. "This is the time to enjoy himself," Marion said. "Mister Benedict, I'm sure has arranged everything."

"He has indeed. Hastings has nothing to worry about." Small talk like this annoyed Carrère.

"He's about to marry a wonderful lady."

The minutes elapsed neither slowly nor quickly. Carrère wanted to get off the train. But he was not looking forward to Hastings's wedding either. Soon enough, predetermined events commenced and everybody, Hastings included, went about their tasks within the framework, the construct that was imagined and engineered for the purpose of marrying Miss Benedict to Mr. Hastings. It was just so grand and marvelous to see Hastings step off the carriage into the dream. Nothing was out of place.

"Here we are, old man," McKim announced at the front of the granite church. Hastings glanced up at the tall steeple reaching for the sky. He had longed to design a church. "There are few guests here now. We will slip inside and disappear. You won't have to talk with anybody now," McKim coached the groom.

"That's fine," Hastings said, suddenly not interested in socializing. He and the groomsmen wore lily-of-the-valley boutonnieres. The ushers escorted guests to their proper pews. Stanford White, whose creative ability Carrère so admired, was a groomsman. Time advanced, and more than ever, he sensed the wedding machinery pushing Hastings along.

Hastings waited for his bride on the platform specially erected for the wedding. McKim stood beside him looking pleased as punch.

Hastings surveyed the vast congregation, scanning it for his partner sitting beside Marion. Employees from Carrère & Hastings sat further back. Mr. and Mrs. Benedict sat next to Grover Cleveland. What a lavish, spectacular affair it was!

At three-thirty, the waiting was over. Helen Benedict entered, accompanied by her father and a processional written especially for the wedding, she elegantly traveled toward the front of the church. There were no bridesmaids nor a maid of honor. Helen's gown, trimmed with white satin, was lovely and her diamond necklace shimmered. Her bouquet of rare orchids was spectacular, too.

Time accelerated, and in a moment, Helen kissed her father on the cheek. Then there was the benediction, the vows, and it was ever-so-swiftly all over. Carrère doubted whether Hastings had even noticed the bell of white roses suspended over the platform or the arches of flowers over the aisle. But nothing could have been as beautiful as his bride, who beamed as Hastings took her arm and started down the aisle, the congregation's applause filling the church.

Outside the church, a gleaming coach drawn by a handsome four awaited the bride and groom. The coach was spotless; its upholstery plush. Horses groomed, their harnesses in excellent condition. Hastings then assisted his bride into the carriage holding her right hand, making sure her gown's train was collected and in place. The congregation streamed from the church to follow the bridal coach to Commodore Benedict's limestone mansion.

The reception was picking up steam when Marion and Carrère arrived. The orchestra was already playing, although no one was dancing yet. Many friends, past clients, and business associates were milling around—too many for Carrère to catch up with at one time. After pleasantries with Mrs. Deaver, a past client, he watched a photographer make images first of the bride and groom, then the groom with his groomsmen, and finally of the bride with her family. The great camera stood upon a wooden tripod; the photographer, from Byron of New York, crouched under a thick black cloth at the back of the camera. While Carrère enjoyed seeing photographers work, he always wondered if a photographic image distorted the mind's perfect image of the event. The problem with a photograph was that it captured the bride in a state of being at one instant.

"That's a good-sized camera," McKim said absently, cradling a drink in his hand.

"You know," Carrère said, "I was just thinking about photography. What do you think about this idea? The photograph forces upon later observers the condition of the subject person at one moment in time."

"That is what a photograph is for," McKim said.

"If you're documenting a life chronology, you would want a series of those momentary views." Carrère paused. "But if you simply want to recall what a person looks like, the photograph is not good."

"Why do you say that?" McKim asked.

"Because the photograph is an instantaneous representation," Carrère shrugged. The shutter clicked inaudibly. Then it was time for the bride to pose with her family.

"Here's Stanford," McKim said. "Let's find out what he thinks. Stanford White strode with his wife Bessie across the green lawn toward McKim and Carrère. White clearly enjoyed himself immensely, loving the party and the attention he attracted.

"Stanford," McKim said. "Come over here. Carrère has a big idea about photography. He says that a photograph distorts the mind's perfect image of somebody." McKim looked at Carrère. "Am I right?"

"That's what I was thinking," Carrère said. "The mind's perfect image is developed through numerous encounters over a period of time. And a variety of forces affect your perception of a particular person." Carrère sipped some wine.

"That could be my experience too," White said, his voice deep and clear. Carrère always liked Stanford's voice. "You might be onto something, John."

"The mind's perfect image may be altered after the momentary image of the photograph is created," Carrère added. "In this case, the photograph returns you forcefully to an image since replaced."

McKim beckoned Hastings away from the bridal party. "You've got to hear this. I think you will like it."

Hastings came over. "Are you talking about architecture?" he facetiously demanded.

Hastings the man, the groom, the husband, not the infinitely picky artist had showed up. "Hi groom! You late-blooming groom," Carrère kidded. "How does it feel?"

"They are talking about photography," McKim said. "Hear what John is saying."

Carrère had the audience of some of his best friends. "Your perfect image of the bride has been, um, shaped by numerous experiences before this instantaneous view is recorded." He gestured toward the photographer. "His image could replace all previous images you may have had of her."

"Hastings looked at me, then at White and McKim. "We are all artists," he said. He straightened his boutonniere, which had tipped slightly on his lapel. "Our inspiration comes from I-know-not-where. But I am not sure a photographer has to have any at all."

Carrère nodded and said, "I wonder what the photographer would say if he heard us?"

"Why should we care what he thinks," White said. "I still can't fully accept photography as art."

"I think I know why you say that," Carrère said. "Because a photograph is so easily reproduced." He thought of the forty-six Miss Bough paintings, then of Miss Bough herself. She would love this wedding, wouldn't she? She'd never seen anything like this.

"Imagine a machine," White said, "that could make identical copies of a building over and over again."

"None of us would have anything to do," McKim said.

Hastings, standing elbow to elbow with McKim, added, "Our creations are permanent too."

Carrère agreed, "I don't think there will ever be a machine that can reproduce buildings!"

"Missus Hastings my dear, please come over here," Hastings happily called out to his liberated bride—liberated from the photographer, who next wanted the groomsmen to pose.

"Have you been wasting your time with these gentlemen again," she gently teased out the word gentlemen. The train had been removed from her gown so it was fairly easy for her to walk. Her diamonds glittered in the bright sunlight. Her lustrous face radiated happiness. This marriage was going to work. Helen would nourish this artist and protect him, too. It was now up to Carrère to do the dirty work for the firm.

Hastings rocked back on his heels and laughed happily, "It's a great group. None better!"

The bride and groom were summoned away by Commodore Benedict for some reason, probably to dance. White saw someone he wanted to talk to and left Carrère with McKim.

"He married for love, Charley," Carrère said. "I am not sure Stanford did."

"I'd say you're right." McKim agreed. "When you worked for us, I could see that Tommy truly lived for the artist within him." McKim paused and ruminated. "Now he'll live for the artist and his wife. It is so perfect and so special. Your firm is into greatness because of him."

"Sometimes it's interesting to watch him draw and paint. He enters another realm. I don't think I'll ever be able to explain it." Carrère watched the groom sashay across the lawn with his bride toward the dance floor beneath a big white canvas tent. "But I'm trying."

The orchestra was in full swing. The guests eagerly awaited the chance to see the bride and groom dance, for Hastings had a reputation as a good dancer. The tuba pumped out wonderful bass notes. The clarinetist tapped his feet to the rhythm. Carrère noted that this orchestra was much better than the one at his own wedding.

The groom must have felt like an artist's paintbrush, compelled to do whatever the artist wanted it to do. As the brush controlled by the artist painting a picture, Hastings painted his own wedding. Carrère thought of the irony: how the artist was at least temporarily an instrument, or implement; his thoughts and agency didn't matter at that moment. It was his bride's wedding.

Hastings and Helen danced a graceful waltz, their feet laying down the three-step pattern as surely as the bristles on a brush laying down a wash, while the guests watched, approved, and applauded. Hastings threw a long look at Carrère, his best man, McKim, and then his father, Reverend Hastings, who presided over the ceremony at the church. He danced, letting the artist within him take control of his steps, and by extension, his wife. They flowed and became one with the music. Dancing was another kind of art, even dancing on one's own wedding day. Hastings gave his all—his intellect and vital forces. Nothing could deny this artist.

The party wound down, and just as Hastings and his new bride boarded the Commodore's yacht for a three-week-long wedding trip, the wind shifted and picked up. The bright spring day faded behind dark clouds, which made the white yacht more conspicuous at the pier. Hastings shook hands with his groomsmen as Helen embraced her father. As they turned to board the yacht, Carrère called out, "You'll return in time to see the beginning of the foundation work, won't you?" "If I'm not back, just postpone it," Hastings yelled back, grinning. "Billings won't mind." He and Helen turned and disappeared within the yacht.

Interlude

Peri and I had decided to get married one hundred years to the day after Hastings, on April 30, 2000. We thought it would be fun, as so many other things were aligned as well. I first dove in that quarry in October, 1997, exactly one hundred years after Messrs. Hastings and Carrère were preparing to submit their drawings in the design competition. And I was designing the expansion of a community public library. There was no question of when our wedding would be.

I had always thought that we would get married in a quaint little seaside chapel somewhere in Maine. For some reason, I could envision dogs running around and through the church. It would be a green-grass day with purple sunshine. Afterward, we would have a lobster picnic on the beach, where anyone who wanted could have some—

even if they hadn't been invited to the ceremony. It would be a community wedding reception.

Peri had other ideas, naturally. She wanted to elope. "A big wedding would be an inconvenience for everybody," she said.

"Not for family," I said. "They will want to come." I was from New Hampshire and my family was local, except for one brother who was away in the Peace Corp. Peri was from Virginia and had a large, extended family scattered around the country. Peri's father was estranged, and her sister was overseas in the U.S. Army. But she still had a great-grandmother who was alive and well enough to travel.

We hadn't ever talked about what our wedding would be, so I was a bit surprised. "No one in your family is going to like it," I said.

"I'm just being sensible. We can't bus everyone to Eastport, Maine for a quaint wedding."

"I wasn't thinking about Eastport," I said. Eastport was all the way down the coast, hard against New Brunswick—not particularly near anything of significance. "And I wasn't proposing to bus your family anywhere."

"You know what I mean," Peri said. "We should just have a small little thing, a party, instead of something that will cost a lot of money."

"Okay," I said, "what if we hire out a restaurant and have a Justice of the Peace marry us there. Then everyone is in the food-and-drink location and nobody has to go anywhere."

Peri hopped onto the balls of her feet. "That's a great idea. We'll invite a few people and send an announcement later."

The first thing we decided was not to invite colleagues from work. I didn't want to invite Jayne Verbridge, and I knew Peri wouldn't want her there either. We easily agreed that parents should be invited. We debated getting married at one of our favorite restaurants in New York —a Thai place we used to frequent. But we felt that the restaurant was too small for even our modest party. I also thought our guests might not like Thai food. Additionally, New York was expensive. So we selected an American steak house-like restaurant right in Manchester.

Peri and I met with the restaurant manager, a heavy Chinese man named Joey Chen. He assured us that couples had been married in the restaurant before and that we could reserve three rooms at the rear of the building. While I noticed that the inside seemed dark, I thought the rooms were well-positioned to accommodate the passage of people from buffet to tables. Peri examined the menu, and I the liquor list. It seemed perfectly acceptable to both of us, and we soon felt certain we had found the right place.

"April thirty," Joey Chen said. He looked at his calendar. "We're hosting a gathering of New Hampshire fly fishermen that day. Can you pick another day?"

"It has to be April thirtieth," I said. "What time are the fishermen coming?"

"Let me see," said Joey Chen. They're coming at eleven-thirty. They are usually gone by about two." He looked at Peri, then me.

"Six o'clock," Peri said.

"Ah, no problem. Everything will be set up for you. Have no worry." Joey Chen mopped sweat from his forehead with a napkin.

We went about our regular lives without the hyperbole that seems to accompany the run-up to most weddings. We sent invitations and received replies. The restaurant handled most of the preparation, and when the day arrived, everything was perfect. The fishermen were gone, and we had the three rooms to ourselves. Peri's mom decorated them with flowers. My mom brought in a cake she had made for the occasion. Peri wore a long white dress with a somewhat immodest neckline. (She had joked about wearing tennis whites.) I wore a suit with yellow tie and a yellow handkerchief in the breast pocket. After the JP wed us, we sat down to eat. My brother, the one not in the Peace Corp, issued an unsentimental toast, and we danced and drank until Joey Chen tapped me on the shoulder. It was quarter to twelve and he had to close. I told the deejay to play one more song, the bride's request. Her request was *Killing Me Softly* by Roberta Flack. It wasn't what I would have requested, but then I wasn't the bride. It was a perfect wedding, better than the one I had envisioned on the Maine coast with dogs running around and yapping.

We decided to save the honeymoon trip for later. Two things—which really were one thing—dominated my non-domestic life: the Farms Library and the New York Public Library, and they needed my full attention. The Carrère & Hastings masterpiece on Fifth Avenue increasingly influenced my work on the tiny Farms Library. I wanted my work on the Farms restoration to be equal to the work on the New York Public Library. I would put every ounce of my professional capabilities into it because by that effort, I would hope to vicariously understand what Carrère had envisioned for his book. The Farms Library would inform Carrère's book.

Carrère

Hastings was away for three weeks. In his absence, massive granite blocks were brought into position for lowering into the deep excavation. Carrère wondered with the engineer if the new stone building would sink or settle into the Manhattan soil.

"No, sir," answered the engineer, scuffing the ground with his foot. "This soil here is compacted glacial till. Very stable."

"Wouldn't bedrock be better?" Carrère adjusted his hat as they inspected the site.

"Sure, but the glacier here was five thousand feet thick, and it compressed the soil pretty good. Don't forget the weight of the reservoir too. This is good soil."

A few days after the wedding, Miss Bough and Carrère talked about it. "There really were a thousand guests," he said. "It was the biggest wedding I've ever attended."

"How was the orchestra?"

"Very good, there were some very good dance numbers. A lot better than the orchestra at our wedding."

Miss Bough said, "I love to dance. I'll dance with anybody." She pretended to waltz with an imaginary partner. He couldn't stand seeing her dance alone, so he took her hand and they danced together. At first he held her away, then he drew her in. He felt Miss Bough pressing against him, and then he stopped and let her go. Their little dance had lasted only a minute, but they knew. At least he thought she knew it was meant to be.

"The food was excellent and the flowers were perfect. I don't think even Hastings, if he knew anything about flower arranging, could have—" Before Carrère could finish, Miss Bough had fled the room.

"I have been thinking about the approach," Hastings announced when he returned from the wedding trip. "I propose two large marble lions, one at each side."

"I like that idea," Carrère said, "As the king of beasts, they'll ennoble the approach."

Hastings added, "I'll have a discussion with Augustus Saint-Gaudens about them." He described other changes he wanted. "There's a lot to do. I need to see the job captains."

A meeting was called, at which Hastings explained the details. Then the job captains distributed projects, and the draftsmen returned to their tables hunched over their drawings. Pencils flew across white paper and erasers rubbed out mistakes. Rulers and T-squares were alternately employed. Mental exertion and concentration filled the drafting room.

Miss Bough carefully approached Hastings and gently asked, "Please tell me about the flowers."

Hastings did his best to appear startled. Miss Bough had never asked him anything before. It had always been business. "What flowers?"

"At your wedding. Mister Carrère said they were perfect."

Hastings asked suspiciously, "Why do you want to know?" He adjusted his pocket watch.

"I'm just wondering if you felt the same way about them. That's all." Miss Bough clasped her hands behind her back and stood straight.

Hastings lets his guard down just a little. "I don't know too much about flower-arranging. Helen was in charge of them, I think. No, it was the gardeners. They were very nice."

"Just one more question, sir," Miss Bough said. Hastings nodded. "No, I won't ask if you could have made them look nicer, because you said you don't know too much."

"I barely remember them. The flowers were pretty, and I wouldn't know." Hastings admitted.

She thanked the architect and disappeared into another room. Hastings asked Carrère what that was all about, polished his glasses, and returned to the approach drawings. Carrère didn't give him an answer.

Marion brought Anna and Dell to the office a few days after Hastings's return. Anna, 13, had wanted to see the design for the Library. "Daddy, I want to see more of the drawings," Anna stood at the top of the stairs still in her coat. Her blue and white dress didn't quite reach the floor.

"Miss Bough will show you the drawings I set up for you. I'll be right there." He reminded Miss Bough, "Make sure she sees the landscape plan."

Marion asked, "Is Miss Bough always around like that?"

Carrère said, "She is indispensable. Makes everything here run smoothly." He thought of the two *Miss Boughs* at home. She had such a carefree sense of fun.

"Well, she seems like a nice lady," Marion said.

"She's a hard worker," Carrère nodded, "and makes things tick around here."

"I think I'll see what Anna and Dell are doing." The girls and Miss Bough were drawing and talking about the plans and elevations. The drawings were from a design competition that Carrère & Hastings had failed to win a few years back.

"May I paint? I should like to paint a house," Dell asked me. I glanced quickly at Marion, who nodded, "Only if she doesn't get too messy."

"I will have our best watercolorist show you what to do." Carrère summoned Magonigle.

Anna, engrossed in the landscape, said, "Daddy, shouldn't there be more trees?"

"More trees would be very nice." Carrère was happy in his favorite locus, the drafting room, bursting with inquisitive minds. "The problem is that we are to design only the Library and the little area around it. Someone else will design Bryant Park."

"More trees would make the city nicer," Anna said.

"Trees make sense. I love trees. I love beautiful cities, too. New York needs more trees," Carrère said. "I wish we could do something about the trees in New York."

Anna looked up him and said, "When you design a house for us in the country, please make sure there are a lot of trees."

"I will do that. Of course, there are more trees in the country than in the city," He smiled at Marion, who nodded approvingly.

Magonigle set up paints and a cup of water for Dell and explained the primary colors. Dell sat quietly on a stool waiting for Magonigle, who wore a peculiar purple bow tie and a jaunty cap, to stop talking. "Use some blue and some yellow, mix them together and you will get green," he said. "Wet the brush, stir the paint around and lay it on." Dell's face contorted with concentration. Eventually she produced a multi-hued house and smiles.

"I really like this," Miss Bough said, holding up the painting. Carrère wondered if Miss Bough had ever critiqued the forty-six of herself.

The next day, Carrère stopped Miss Bough. "I've been thinking about the monograph, now that the foundation has been started. You were going to suggest someone who could help me."

Miss Bough pushed her chair away from her desk and stood. "I've always thought Peres Polhemus should serve you well."

"Polhemus? He joined us two years ago. He's a quiet man and a good draftsman. How'd you think of him?"

"I know everybody's strengths and weaknesses around here," Miss Bough said. She really had become the central cog in the Carrère & Hastings machine. She knew everything and Carrère could trust her judgment. In fact, she knew more about this monograph than he did. He wanted it to be about the Library, not about people, or himself. It wasn't very important who did the research or made the records. It just had to be done, and done well. Miss Bough knew best, Carrère was sure. He turned to the secretary, "I'll speak with Polhemus."

Miss Bough asked, "Then what?" She folded her arms across her chest, waiting for him to produce an idea.

"Well, I just want the facts. That's all."

"May I remind you," Miss Bough said, "that you're also trying to figure out something special, the relationship Hastings has with his art, or Horace and his art."

"That's right, I'm glad you suggested it. I'm supposed to find someone to help me observe Hastings. I'll have to do it, because only I can understand."

"You're right about that," Miss Bough nodded.

"Horace is more of a problem because he's dead."

"But there is plenty of his work lying around," Miss Bough again nodded.

"How could I forget?"

Miss Bough, this time shaking her head, said, "I don't know how you could."

Interlude

Jayne's sense of color, space, and composition were very refined. She could achieve visual perfection without making any effort. She made it look so easy, the way a major league ball player could turn a double play. When someone makes whatever they do look that easy, you know the person is really, really good. Jayne could look at a rendering and begin at once to verbalize corrections that should be made and decoration that would be appropriate. I was at loss to explain it, and seeing what Carrère and Miss Bough were attempting to do, I thought I would ask Jayne about it.

"So Jayne, help me figure something out." I placed myself squarely in front of her desk and asked if she'd ever had a guru, and whether it sometimes felt as though she was doing the drawing of a long-dead architectural student.

Jayne took a drag from her Pepsi can but it was empty. She reached into her desk for another. How could she stand warm Pepsi? She cracked it open and inserted the same straw. She became surprisingly easy and open. "I've never thought about it. But since you ask me, I'd have to say, sometimes I'm ga-ga, sometimes truly royally pissed off, or sad, or fascinated. I don't know. I haven't really thought about it."

I liked Jayne's range of expression. I should have expected that from her. From ga-ga to truly royally pissed off (t.r.p.o.)... I liked it, and it was that way for me, too. I had been immensely satisfied with a particular design while I had crumpled others into a ball and thrown them across the room. At home that evening I asked Peri, "Have you ever seen me truly royally pissed off when I can't get something right?"

"Oh, of course," she said. "You're an emotional artist, and now that you're writing Carrère's book, I'd say even more so."

"Well, I know I get involved with my work but I wouldn't say I'm emotional."

"It's a good thing that you are," Peri said. "It's healthier for you if you let it all hang out, and it doesn't bother me." Peri was wearing one of those loose blue cotton dresses she liked so much. It was a summer day, and she liked how cool and comfortable they could be.

"Well, I've never thought I show my emotions."

"When you tear up a drawing, I'd say that's emotional. I've noticed that you have feelings about whatever you're working on." Peri poured a glass of lemonade from the jug in the refrigerator. "We nurses try not to form relationships with our patients. It must be impossible for you not to form a relationship with some of your creations."

"I guess you're right," I said. "One of the most amazing things with Carrère's book is not knowing what's next, and yet it comes out, and it's valid and authentic."

"Let me tell you what's happening to you," she said. "Carrère is the long-dead, frustrated writer for whom you are writing, and not even you can be sure who is doing the writing: Is it you or is it Carrère?"

Part Three

PROGRESSION

Carrère

Foundation stones from the Reservoir had been shuttled around the property, while in the east, a new wall went up; and in the west, what was left of an old wall came down. Hastings and Carrère watched as one of the derricks lowered granite blocks onto the new foundation wall. It was an unusually cool day in July 1900. It gave both men great satisfaction to watch the two related operations: destruction and renewal.

"We haven't talked about the exterior recently," Hastings said in a morning discussion with Brainard and Carrère. "We decided on marble. Now we need to know where it's going to come from." He cleaned his glasses with a handkerchief, studying a list of specifications Brainard had brought in.

"We've received a letter from Norcross Brothers." Carrère flipped through some correspondence the firm had received. He slid the letter across the table to Hastings, who took a minute to read it.

"Norcross could be our man," Hastings said after reading the letter. "He says that he's got a new quarry somewhere in Vermont, and he can get us what we need at a good price."

"There are other marble men," Carrère cautioned.

"I know," Hastings said. "But the Norcross brothers are successful, the largest construction company in the country. What are their names anyway?"

"Orlando and George," Brainard said.

"We can't give Norcross the order until the Board says it's okay," Carrère explained and pushed his chair back from the table.

A few weeks later, Orlando Norcross visited Carrère & Hastings. He arrived in a whirl, tossing his hat on the side table in the entry hall, his impressive square frame in constant motion as he tromped into the drafting room. He had come to talk about marble.

"You've convinced everyone to use marble—I've got good marble for you and you'll have to visit the quarry sometime to see how we cut it, and how we dress it, and how we ship it and everything else. It's wonderful there in Dorset, Vermont— this old quarry. Mister West and I bought all that marble that can be used in the New York Public Library—going to be perfect let me tell you—"

Carrère tried to say something but Norcross kept on, his arms and hands swirling in front of him.

"We have an advantage you know 'cause we own the quarry, and we own the machines, and it saves us money and you money, too—"

"You own—" Hastings tried to ask.

"That's right the Valley Quarry in Dorset is the oldest marble quarry in the country. See, it closed in 1876, but now Spafford and I are going to reopen it." Norcross slowed his pace a bit. "And we'll get you the marble you need."

"That's very good," Carrère rested his elbows on the desk, his chin in his palms.

Hastings mopped sweat from his brow and turned to Orlando, "Can you deliver eighty-five hundred tons of top quality dimension stones to the cutting yard at Port Morris?"

"Eighty-five hundred tons to the yard is no problem, guaranteed," said Norcross, who assured tolerable waste percentage. "We inspect all the marble before we ship it to you—unacceptable material is not shipped."

Hastings stood and walked to an elevation drawing pinned to the wall. "Orlando, this is going to be my masterpiece. I don't want any trouble."

Carrère made note of Hastings's unctuous pronouncement, *my masterpiece*.

"We've worked for many great architects. We'll do just fine for you." Orlando stood and rolled across the room to the drawing. "Those columns will be the best in America."

Hastings warned, "I think you can give us what we want, but the Board has the final say." He looked at Carrère.

""That's right," Carrère said.

"When's the Board going to decide?" Norcross asked.

"Miss Bough will type the specifications and distribute them," Carrère said. "We have to allow sufficient time for bids to come in. Then we decide which offer we like, and the Board will probably agree with us."

"They usually do, at least," Hastings said, returning to his chair.

"This sounds like a typical municipal job," Orlando commented, a bit disappointed that he couldn't get the job right then and there. He paused and rebounded to his excited cadence, "This is good. . . I'll be able to give you more details about our marble and what it'll cost and how long it will take and everything else." He positively bounced on the balls of his feet.

Hastings drew a deep breath of relief that Orlando would be leaving.

"Miss Bough will deliver a copy of the bid request personally to your Manhattan office just as soon as it's ready." Carrère hastened to conclude the meeting.

"I'll look for it and have a bid on your desk the next day." Orlando grinned as he made his exit.

Carrère

"The drawings and specifications for the contract are ready," Carrère said when he brought the details to Miss Bough's tidy office. He sometimes wished that the rest of the firm's offices could have been as neat as Miss Bough's. It was hopeless, though. Too many men were very busy, the firm was going full tilt, and no one ever really cleaned up. It was February 1901.

"Didn't we submit the estimate in October?" Miss Bough asked. She sat at her desk-table with a black Remington typewriter. She rolled a fresh sheet of paper into the carriage and was ready to begin.

"We did, and the City came back with a lower number."

"Will that affect the marble?" Miss Bough asked with concern on her face.

"Oh, I hope not. Hastings would be distraught if he had to compromise the marble." Carrère handed her three sheets with his and Brainard's handwriting. "This is what has to go into the bid request, Miss Bough." His thoughts suddenly shifted elsewhere. He rubbed his mustache and tugged at his tie. "Hastings has a lot of pride."

"Well, I'm not sure what you mean," Miss Bough said, puzzled. The steam radiator pumped heat. The autumn sunlight streaming through the window visibly quavered in the rising hot air. "Why do you mention it?"

Carrère sat on an uncomfortable black wood chair. "Last week, Norcross came to sell us marble from his quarry and Hastings said, 'this building is *my masterpiece.*' He is responsible for the design, and I don't mind that he said 'it is *my masterpiece.*' But that surprised me."

"I wasn't there but let me guess what happened," Miss Bough said.

"Okay." Carrère could rely on Miss Bough's instincts, her intuition.

"Norcross is a very confident man, and so is Hastings, right?"

"That is true. A large man, too."

"So when the two were together, Hastings was confronted with an equal." Miss Bough paused. "He said *my masterpiece* for his own benefit, not for yours or Norcross's—his own comfort."

Carrère nodded slowly. "That's his pride showing through."

Miss Bough looked him right in the eye and said with assurance. "He's here every day working as hard as he can, always devising a new answer to some problem."

Carrère pushed the chair away from the table and stood. "I think you're right on the money." He remembered the contract. "Please deliver one copy personally to Norcross's office. We promised that."

"That is an unusual promise."

"Oh, it is." Carrère thought of Norcross's sales call. "Mister Norcross really wants the business. He has invested in the quarry to make sure he gets the job. We can do him this favor."

Miss Bough, returning to the task, studied the three pages. "This won't take very long," she said.

"I didn't think it would. We want to advertise the contract in March. So you have plenty of time."

Interlude

At home, I took all of our glasses out of the cupboard and lined them up on the counter. There were eight matched cocktail tumblers, eight regular kitchen glasses for water, and four wine glasses. Then I took out our cereal bowls and lined them up. They were white china with a blue lip. I stood back to admire my han- diwork. I then put the glasses away, leaving the four cereal bowls out. I filled one of them with uncooked rice. The rice made a hissing sound when I poured it from the box into the empty bowl. It's darker whiteness contrasted with the pure white of the china. I filled the bowl so that the rice was perfectly level with the top. Then I filled another bowl but only about halfway. I left the other two empty. Again, I stood back and studied my work.

The full bowl represented the land next to the library, before the gas explosion. The empty bowls represented the crater. I only needed one, so I put the other away. The half-full bowl depicted the crater after I had spent all night filling it in. (In truth, I was not able to fill it completely. Now I could see that the crater was an interesting possibility, not just the result of a construction tragedy.)

Peri walked in, returning from a run. She immediately saw the three bowls on the counter. "What's this?"

"An experiment," I said. "The bowls are the crater, the rice is the earth within it."

Peri poured some lemonade. "You're still thinking about that?"

"Yes, but not the accident anymore. I'm trying to understand what Jayne was talking about when she told me to go back there and look at the crater again."

Peri shook her head. She had always been doubtful about this idea, or fantasy, as she called it. "What are you looking for?"

"I don't know, but I think something is there."

"It was a crater. You filled it in—"

"Only about halfway," I said.

"Okay, half, and then the gas company dug it out. Have you seen it since?" Peri finished her lemonade. "Does this have anything to do with the book?" She stood with all her weight on one leg, hand braced on corresponding hip.

"Something is going on here, and I want to find out what it is," I said.

Carrère

Hastings hurried breathlessly up the stairs on the morning of September 7 with a copy of the day's *Tribune*. MCKINLEY SHOT BY ANARCHIST, the paper blared. Carrère had already heard the news. An animated discussion among Carrère, Barber, and several others filled the office.

"The paper says he was shot twice," Carrère said, holding the paper for all to see.

"In Buffalo," added Barber, drumming his fingers on the table.

"Why was President McKinley in Buffalo?" asked Ward in a rising voice.

"He was visiting the Pan-American Exhibition," Carrère said. "We have a model of the Library there right now." The windows were open and fresh air swept into the drafting room.

"Why'd they shoot him?" Ward asked.

"An anarchist, they say," Carrère shook his head.

"Is he going to be okay?" Hastings said.

"His doctors say he's resting comfortably." Carrère was the one with all the information because he had read both the *Tribune* and the *Times* that morning.

"Who shot him?" Barber asked.

"Someone named Leon Czolgosz."

"Is that Polish? Aren't we glad we weren't there," Hastings said. "You could've been, John."

Carrère wagged his head. "My duties at the Expo are pretty much over. The only thing is the model." Carrère had been the Chairman of the Pan-American Exposition Board of Architects.

"How can you say that?" Ward asked.

"When the show's over, they're going to tear all the buildings down! We architects build things. We don't tear them down."

Ward looked surprised, "Tear the buildings down?"

"Oh, don't be alarmed," Carrère said. "They're just flimsy plaster shells never intended to be permanent."

"So much effort, wasn't it?" Ward said.

"It was, but we wanted to show all the good that's taking place in America and in architecture. But McKinley being shot isn't a good thing. I'd want to tear down any building in which the president was shot."

Barber pointed out, "The Ford Theater is still there."

"Where Lincoln was shot, you're right. But I didn't own the building," Carrère said. "What I mean is, I'm glad the fake Pan-Am buildings are being destroyed. Helps erase the spot where McKinley was shot."

"I hope he survives," Hastings said.

Eight days later the usually busy office was subdued. Late-edition copies of the *Tribune* with the news that McKinley had died lay strewn across the tables.

"Roosevelt is our president now," Hastings mumbled.

"The paper says McKinley's funeral will be on the nineteenth," Carrère said.

"That bastard who shot him," Hastings continued. "He'll fry."

"No doubt about that," Barber said. "He confessed in writing."

Carrère looked up. "How many presidents have been assassinated? Wasn't Lincoln the first?"

"Yep, then Garfield, now McKinley," said Barber. Carrère was always impressed with his knowledge and recall. Barber had a lot of interesting facts up his sleeve.

"The funeral's going to be in Buffalo on September nineteenth," Hastings said.

"Sad day for Buffalo, sad day for the United States," Carrère said. "It says here that there will be a national observance for five minutes in the afternoon during McKinley's funeral. "We'll observe it."

"We'll observe it," Hastings said.

Carrère

Hastings and Carrère began the day, September nineteenth, with a special mission to the Library site. Workers were already toiling. The Reservoir was long gone, but rubble still lay all around. They brought a large American flag, and Hastings hung it from a section of masonry wall. He admired what he'd done for a minute, then decided there was a better place for the flag. He moved it to a stack of marble blocks. Carrère just stood and watched. The flag's blue field was to the right, and the flag looked to be backward. So Hastings turned the flag around. "Much better," he remarked to no one. But then he apparently decided that the flag couldn't be easily seen the length of the Fifth Avenue block between 42nd and 41st Streets. "I wish it were bigger," he grumbled, and, "If only I had a pole." Not satisfied but nevertheless aware there was nothing else he could do, Hastings shrugged. "How's it look?" he asked.

A gentleman they had never seen before said, "I saw you hanging the flag over there. Thank you."

Hastings said, "I thought it would be nice for the president's funeral."

"It is nice. Now tell me," the man said, "what's the new building going to be? Do you happen to know?" The man wore workmanlike clothes, a scruffy hat, and had a scruffy beard. His shoes were in need of a polish.

The architects were astonished. How could anyone not know that there was going to be a new library? Carrère said, "It's going to be the New York Public Library, which anyone can use."

"I can't believe it," the man said. A library. I can go to it, you mean?"

"It's a public library," Hastings continued. "You'll be able to read books and newspapers there whenever you want."

"I love to read, and now I can't wait. When's it going to be done?" He looked toward the site, and seeing the foundation walls poking up from the Manhattan soil he guessed, "It'll be pretty soon."

"I wish I could say so, too," Carrère said. "These projects take a long time. We've only started."

Back at the office, Miss Bough had already begun to examine the pile of things next to her typewriter. Hastings said, "What brings you here at this hour?" It was only quarter past eight.

"You shouldn't be here either," Miss Bough replied. "You're not an early riser."

"Is anyone else here?"

"No, sir, I'm the only one. I thought I'd be able to get something done without the usual distractions. And what brings you here?" she lowered her voice.

"We put a flag up at the library and then came here. I haven't thought about what I'm working on yet. I know there's a lot to do."

Miss Bough stood and brushed off her plaid skirt. Her white blouse reached all the way up her neck. "Is that what makes you happy?" she asked.

Hastings backed away saying, "I don't know what you mean. I am always happy when I'm here at work, designing, drawing, painting, perfecting."

"I don't think that's true," Miss Bough said, finding a crack through which to enter into Hastings's mind.

Carrère, who paused as he walked past the secretary's office door, sensed that Hastings was fuming—that he didn't need a secretary talking to him like that. Carrère shrunk back, listening but not wanting to be noticed. "You can't say something like that," he barked. Hastings turned his back and looked out a window.

Miss Bough set the cavalry free. "Sometimes you're not happy with your work. Why is that?"

Hastings wheeled around to face Miss Bough, who stood by her typewriter. His face was red with anger. "It's none of your business. You don't know what it's like to be—be a creative man—never to know what's next nor how to get there."

"I do know," Miss Bough said. Her voice was quiet and soothing, "because I've been with creative men before."

"Oh, do you mean Horace, what's his last name? Horace, um, Avery?" Hastings asked. His words were drenched with derision. "He went insane. He couldn't stand his life anymore and hanged himself. I heard Mister Carrère talk about him."

"Yes, Horace Avery, and now you," Miss Bough said, taking a step toward Hastings.

"You and Mister Carrère have this nonsense idea that I'm out of control. I don't know you. You work for Mister Carrère. There's nothing to talk about." Hastings glared at Miss Bough, hoping she might go away.

"Okay, "Miss Bough conceded returning to her chair. "I didn't mean to surprise you. I just wanted to get some things done while the office is still quiet."

Hastings walked away bewildered. A couple of weeks ago, she had asked him about the flowers at his wedding. On this day, she ambushed him about being happy with his work. What would she do next? Ward arrived, followed by Barber. Hastings was glad they did.

Hastings later confronted his partner. "And another thing," Hastings snapped, out of Miss Bough's hearing, "never again is your secretary going to attack me like that."

It was a good thing Carrère had thought about what he would say. "I'm hoping that Miss Bough can work for all of us. I hired her after Horace Avery died, I mean, after he became ill, because I knew that she is good, and I knew we needed someone like her." Hastings glared at him. "She means no harm, Tom. She's just trying to help."

"Help you, that is. Not me. There's a conspiracy here! You can't worry about how I work because I'm not going to lose my mind!" Hastings stormed out of the room.

At two o'clock all the men at Carrère & Hastings stood at the window looking down. The cabs and drays suddenly halted. The men in the office set aside their pencils and T-squares. All across the land and at the library, workmen stood at rest. Even trains stopped, as the nation held a session of silent prayer for the slain president. Hastings decided to head home.

"Why did Hastings leave so early?" Carrère wondered aloud when things returned to normal.

Miss Bough said, "He placed a flag at the Library this morning." She beckoned him toward her office. "I think I pushed him a little far," she admitted.

"You know I'm interested in what motivates him. But I can't let him be scared by our secretary.

"He thinks I work for you," Miss Bough said.

"I'll have to talk with him. But your job isn't to hound or harass him, not anytime and not for me. Tommy's world has to be safe and orderly. He can't be fearful if he's going to do his best work."

Miss Bough dropped her head. "I'm sorry, sir. I was only hoping to collect information for you."

Carrère

Every day, skilled masons, dipping their trowels into large troughs of mortar, continued their work. They set thousands and thousands of bricks to build the foundation for the New York Public Library as it grew irresistibly like a well-rooted tree out of the ground. Norcross's staging, derricks, and other equipment had changed the feel of the site from a graveyard to a land full of promise.

A few weeks later, Carrère looked around the unimpressive interior of the temporary office building at the Library site. Although the wood frame building was only a week old, it was already filled with drawings and draftsmen. The fresh white paint on the walls still gave off the faint odor of linseed oil. "Now that we have an office building on site," he said, "we can move the Library project over here." The 23-foot by 80-foot building, designed to last only a few years, neighbored a slightly larger but equally temporary modeling building.

Brainard shrugged. He had already brought over some of his structural engineering studies. "I will be spending a lot of time here, probably more than you, John."

Outside, a heavy crash followed by shouting and cursing startled them, and they hurried to see what had happened. They found several German laborers laughing and cursing at once. The men had already begun examining a cart that had tipped over, dumping bricks on the rough ground. Carrère knew some German and learned that the load of bricks had been destined for the foundation at the 40th Street end of the building. The horse pulling the wagon was old and barely fit for work of this sort. The wagon's right wheel had sunk into some soft earth, and the wagon had gotten stuck. The old horse gave an extra pull, which shifted the bricks, tipping the cart over, bringing the horse with it. The horse could not rise because the harnesses kept it tightly attached to the capsized wagon. When the laborers released the frightened horse from the wagon, it promptly lurched to its feet and ran to the far end of the office building, where it stopped and warily eyed the men. The laborers ignored the horse and unloaded the bricks remaining in the wagon. They righted the wagon to its two wheels, and then retrieved the horse.

"I feel sorry for the horse," Carrère said to Brainard.

"That horse has been in this business for a long time," Brainard said, watching the nag. "It probably thinks we people are incompetent."

The workmen's laughter died, replaced by grunts and silent toil as they loaded the bricks back into the wagon. "These men have been doing a fine job," Carrère pointed to the foundation. "Look at the brick walls rising from the ground. Great, massive walls. They have laid two hundred sixty thousand bricks this month alone."

"I'm the engineer here, and I don't even know that number. How do you know?"

"Polhemus is keeping notes and records for me. He gave me this tidbit yesterday." Carrère started for the office leaving Brainard behind. He had to wait for several carriages to pass before crossing Fifth Avenue.

At the office, Miss Bough cheerily announced, "Good news. We've finally heard that the Board approved Norcross marble for the project. Here, look at this letter."

"Excellent," Carrère said. "We'll get the Vermont marble we want but not this year."

"Why so?" Miss Bough asked.

"We got the marble we wanted, the weather wins for now," he said. "It's winter in Vermont. That's right. Cold weather slows the quarrying. We're going to have to wait."

"I would never have guessed," Miss Bough said. "But it makes sense." She turned and went into her office.

Interlude

Peri and I started house-hunting. We wanted a place we could call our own, and I wanted to start building equity. The rationale was the easy part but actually finding the right house was arduous. Peri had long had dreams of a Georgian colonial, replete with period ornamentation. The problem was that there were few houses of that style in Manchester, and none that we could afford.

Once, when we looked at a green Garrison colonial with attached two-car garage, I could tell she cringed at the possibility. She had grown up in a Georgian colonial. The efficient realtor explained what she could about the thirty-year-old house on a quarter acre of land. I started talking about the interior. "We live inside the house, Peri, not outside. Think about how it's laid out."

"I think you're becoming too focused on interiors."

"Not really," I said. We stood in the colonial's kitchen, with its old Formica counters and dirty windows. The ceiling was low and had a single glass hemispherical light fixture, which accommodated two bulbs. One bulb was dead, and the light was correspondingly dim. The floor was tired linoleum that had not been waxed in many years, I thought. The kitchen's closeness pushed me into a brief, neurotic state about interior space. How the space affects the life led within it. The kitchen gave me the creeps. I snapped, and said, "We want good space, not ordinary or bad space!" The realtor cringed as I said that.

Peri asked, "What's bad space?"

"Look at this kitchen!"

"We could improve it," Peri said.

I suddenly realized that she was right. Some paint, a new floor, and a new light fixture—but there was more. I realized that there was such a thing as space that was intrinsically good and intrinsically bad. This idea was going to need some time—and now wasn't the right moment to figure it out. So I delayed the idea. "We could renovate the kitchen, but that's very expensive."

"I've seen enough," Peri said.

"We can do better. Just think Beaux-Arts," I said.

Carrère

Carrère brought Ward to regular weekly luncheon at the Century Club on a sparkling January day, 1902. The weak winter sun warmed anyone who was outside. They ran into Stanford White outside the Club. White commented on the scaffolding and derricks Norcross had brought to the Fifth Avenue site. "I see that things are under way at the Library,"

"Tommy and I are pleased so far."

"Is Hastings coming to luncheon, too?" asked White, a large redheaded man.

"I think he's already here." Turning to the Century façade, Carrère said to Ward, "There is no marble in this façade. The lower half is deeply channeled granite. The heavy iron over the lower windows announces that this is exclusive territory."

White took over, "Yes, but the upper half is smooth Roman brick, and all that ornament around the windows proclaims the joys of membership."

"Let's find Hastings," Carrère suggested. Hastings, already seated at a table, stood to receive the others. "I didn't know you were bringing Ward."

"I thought he should see the inside of the Club, and we ran into Stanford right outside. Ward gets to meet the architect and see the Club at the same time."

"What a treat," Hastings said agreeably, returning to his seat. He placed a napkin in his lap.

Stanford and Carrère showed Ward around the Club. They visited the reading room, the dining room, and living room before passing through the billiards room and East Room. Conversations typical of the Century were concerned with art, music, literature, world affairs, and Club trivia.

Ward asked Stanford about the artwork on the walls.

"I relied on members to supply the art," Stanford said. "People like Edwin Blashfield, the mural painter. He gave us the large painting over there," Stanford pointed.

"What's your favorite room?" Carrère asked White.

"Oh, I can't say," Stanford said. "I'm pretty satisfied with the whole thing." He looked around the room where they were standing.

"You're satisfied? Isn't there anything you would want to change?" Carrère saw an opportunity to get an answer.

Stanford White stuck his thumbs inside his suspenders. "No, Mister Carrère, it's perfect." Stanford squared his shoulders. "The Century is the best I've ever done," he boomed.

Stanford sure could be boastful, yet this was more than Carrère had ever expected to hear from his big mouth. Maybe this wasn't an opportunity after all. But Carrère didn't stop and tried a different approach, certain Stanford had no idea what he was after, "Where do your ideas come from?"

"Why are you asking me?" Stanford retorted sharply. "I don't think I'd tell anyway. I wouldn't want to give away my secrets."

Ward said, "Sir, did you attend the Ecole des Beaux Arts?"

More generously for the younger man, Stanford replied, "No, I learned architecture here in America. So you can see my work isn't as heavily European as some of the others."

"There's more than one place where you can learn this business," Carrère said. "Paris was the right place for me and for Tommy Hastings, too. Your training ground can give you the inspiration for later works." Carrère thought of McKim's Boston Public Library as an example.

"That's quite true," Stanford said, moving his large self toward the bar. "Almost all architecture is inspired by some other thing, from somewhere else."

Carrère saw another opportunity. "What if the somewhere else is in your head?" Ward had a puzzled expression on his face.

"I'm not sure what you mean," Stanford said. He asked the bartender for rum and water. "Would you like something?" Stanford asked Ward.

"The same thing you're having, sir," Ward replied.

Stanford was puzzled. "In your head? What I meant is that we refer to a building from antiquity, or the Gothic, or something like that. We rely on the past." The bartender slid the cocktails across the bar. Stanford stirred his with a finger; Ward didn't.

Carrère realized that Stanford had no idea what he was talking about and decided to let the issue be. He said to Ward, "Look around. Stanford designed this building. It's obvious. He's in love with beauty."

Ward nodded vigorously. A waiter rang a small handheld brass bell, which gave notice that luncheon was served. "It took a talented man to come up with this."

Stanford beamed, relishing the appreciation for his work, "What's there not to love? Beauty makes all the world happy. That's what I strive for—beauty and functionality, too. But beauty first."

Carrère

While New York broiled, August 11, 1902 was an important day. Hastings, Billings, and Carrère had a private cornerstone ceremony. The ground was dusty and dry amid scattered marble blocks. Billings brandished a well-used mason's trowel and spread heavy gray-white mortar on a section of the emerging exterior wall. Hastings dropped a 1902 ten-cent piece into the goop. Billings tapped it three times with a hammer and declared in a ceremonial voice, "May this building be all that the builders, the architects, the trustees, and the people of New York hope and expect."

The three men shook hands. Hastings noted, "It has been nearly three years since we won the commission. We're making good progress now."

The builders hoisted a marble block to be placed on the coin and swung it into position. With precision and care, the workers lowered the block into place. Another worker, short and fat, held a plumb line against the rising wall.

The next day was equally hot, and Barber suggested that he and Carrère leave work early and go out to his club, the Raritan Yacht Club, to escape the heat. Carrère had been there with Barber before and agreed, "A grand idea."

"I have a new boat, well, new to me." Barber stood with his hands stuck in his back pockets. "I want to give it another go."

Shortly after noon, they arrived at the Club. The hot white August sun blazed down on its black roof. Barber held a lightweight screen door open for Carrère. Barber looked inside for the tide chart. It was a small place—just a single dark room with an old potbelly stove, which the summer's heat rendered unnecessary. Several rowing shells and canoes hung in slings from the ceiling joists. "Why all these canoes and shells?" Carrère asked.

"The club used to be a rowing and canoeing club," Barber explained. "I've never been in a canoe, have you?"

"Oh yes," Carrère said, holding his arms out wide, "but bigger than these here, and red. It was a long time ago at a place in the Adirondacks."

A spacious front porch graced the east end of the building. It's where, as Barber pointed out, the "Rocking Chair Fleet" convened. "You can watch the races here," Barber pointed to Raritan Bay. There were several nondescript oyster skiffs out there harvesting the abundant oyster crop. "Sometimes the oyster men enter their skiffs in the races, and there is usually a contingent from Staten Island and Newark Bay, too."

"Oh, that explains it," Carrère said. "Horace Avery pointed the sailboats out to me one time on the ferry. I had never noticed them before that."

"What happened to him anyway?" Barber inquired. His manner was ever so delicate, as he knew he was treading in sensitive territory.

"Oh, that was several years ago. I didn't know you knew about him," Carrère looked at Barber.

"I heard you and Miss Bough talking about him one time," Barber squinted in the bright sunlight.

"He just stopped working, stopped talking, wasn't himself anymore. Then he killed himself."

"Did he ever see a doctor?"

"Yes, he did," Carrère nodded. "Miss Bough, as you know was his secretary, and she told me that the doctor prescribed bed rest in a calm, relaxed place." Carrère took out his pipe and packed it with an aromatic, bourbon-flavored tobacco. "I saw him once in the hospital."

"I didn't know Miss Bough used to be his secretary. What was his work like?" Barber asked, shifting his weight in this chair.

"Well, he was a portrait artist and he developed his own methods. He liked to make a sketch first on watercolor paper, followed by a watercolor cartoon."

"Large portraits?" Barber was intrigued.

Carrère explained, "The portraits were much larger than life-size. So detailed, I used to wonder if the details caused him to forget the larger work."

"Maybe it was Miss Bough," Barber suggested.

Carrère didn't want to admit that Miss Bough could have been his problem. But she could have been! He had painted her in the nude forty-six times. He shrugged. "Could've been. She didn't say anything about that though." They watched a small sailboat return to its mooring. A boy fetched the mooring pennant while his dad steered. In the next several minutes, the sails were furled and the two rowed a dinghy back to the club's dock. "I've never been sailing," Carrère said.

"I'll take you out sometime. My boat's right over there." He pointed to a blue day sailer. "Murmansk is its name."

"For the arctic Russian town?"

"Yes, but I didn't come up with that name. Someone else did," Barber said blandly.

"Didn't you want your own name?"

"It's bad luck to change the name of a boat," Barber said. "Plus, I would have had a hard time deciding. So I let it be."

Interlude

In my teens and twenties, I did a lot of overnight camping. I liked to go out in wilderness areas of Canada and travel large distances by canoe. I used to pore over the green topographical maps published by the Canadian government in search of lakes and rivers to paddle. There were many: Ontario and Quebec each have something like four hundred thousand lakes per province. It was easy to lose myself in my imagination, dreaming about the possibilities, concocting ever more remote and difficult routes. My dreaming seldom yielded an actual canoe trip. A couple of times, though, when I had few obligations and no other ambitions, I engineered a trip. One of these was on a remote, powerful river in northern Quebec. A courageous fellow named Patrick and I canoed for about a month through some lakes nobody had ever been on, and then descended the river all the way to the sea—Hudson Bay.

That particular year I kept a journal. Now that I'm an architect and curious about interior spaces, I refer to the July 23 entry in that yellow-ochre-colored journal:

> *This morning we passed an interesting feature. Out of the face of a cliff there was cut away a nearly perfect rectangle, 60 x 30 feet, and a uniform depth of five or six feet. Below, there was a jumbled rockslide. It looked man-made—but it wasn't. It was completely natural. I have never seen a perfect geometric shape in nature—but this was as close as I have come.*

I realized that spaces didn't have to be man-made to be noticeable. Maybe it was because the river was flat and slack that I saw that cutout. It was early in the morning, or because the sky was gray, or for any number of reasons—and I saw it. In the years since, I have never thought about how it got there or why. Now though, with the Beaux-Arts in mind, as well as the crater at the Farms Library, and that awful kitchen in the green colonial, I had to think that those spaces were related.

Carrère

The official cornerstone ceremony went ahead as scheduled on November 10, 1902, which turned out to be a lovely autumn day. Carrère squinted in the bright sunlight. A few weeks earlier, Hastings and the foreman had located among the hundreds of blocks on the building site a flawless white piece of marble for the cornerstone. The date MDCCCCII was inscribed. A boom derrick positioned itself to lower the seven-and-one-half-ton stone into place. Just in case the street current powering the derrick's electric motor failed, a hand windlass had been installed at the base of the derrick.

The Reverend Dr. W. R. Huntington gave an invocation, calling the Library "wisdom's house" and asking the Almighty to give sound discretion to those who would govern its affairs. Then, John Bigelow, President of the Board of Trustees. brought the thousand guests in attendance up to date on the events that had brought the new building to its present state. Hastings placed a relic box containing several documents pertaining to the Library, photographs of the old Reservoir, and current newspapers into a cavity beneath the stone. This box would never be seen again. Carrère couldn't imagine the calamity it would take to expose that box.

Hastings presented Mayor Low a thin silver trowel with which he spread the mortar. Then, the great piece of cut marble was lowered into place. The electric motor operated perfectly. The Mayor stepped aside to allow Archbishop Farley, attired in his robes, to close the ceremony with a brief prayer and benediction.

Interlude

I "witnessed" the calamity on New Hampshire Public Radio in my car. The New York Public Library was unaffected.

Carrère

Barber approached Hastings and Carrère one day. "I'm going to start my own firm," he announced. They were in the drafting room at 41st Street. It was unusual for both Hastings and Carrère to be there at the same time. Since the construction of the temporary office buildings on the Library site, Hastings spent more of his time there, while Carrère presided over the regular office.

"Why, that's great news," Carrère said. "We'll miss you, and we'll compete against you but you have a lot of ambition, and you'll do well." He recalled the heady days so many years ago when he and Hastings had told McKim and

Stanford that they were going out on their own. It was dangerous and exciting because of a market crash and depression. Six hundred banks had folded, thousands of businesses had collapsed. And there they were, young and bold, starting out. They had made it though and became well established, as were McKim, Mead & White when they left them.

"I'm going to need someone like Miss Bough as my assistant."

Hastings's head snapped around. "I know I wouldn't mind if you hired her. She's terribly bothersome to me."

Carrère stayed quiet, thinking of how they needed Miss Bough. If Barber took her, everything would change. What would he do?

Barber walked to the other side of the table, where some façade drawings were spread out. "She has made you angry a couple of times, hasn't she?" Barber turned to look at Carrère. "Perhaps I can relieve tension here if I hired her?"

"That's a good thought, Donn." Hastings said. "If I didn't have to see her as much—"

"—you're over there most of the time," Carrère said. It was hard to stay detached from the possibility that Barber might hire Miss Bough. "She shouldn't affect you."

Hastings said through narrowed teeth, "You're trying to protect her to protect yourself!"

"I don't know what you're talking about." Carrère felt like punching Hastings. But Hastings had forced him to admit, if only inwardly, that Miss Bough was more than a secretary to him.

Carrère

Even when things weren't going well, time rushed by. Carrère noted in mid-March, 1903, a full eighteen months after Norcross had won the marble contract, how little progress there had been. Everyone could see the utter lack of construction activity. "Look, no workers, no progress, nothing," Carrère remarked to nobody one day as he visited the site alone. He thrust his hands deeply in his pockets and hunched his shoulders. A solitary crow perched on a marble block about twenty feet from him, its black beady eyes reminding him of how far, or not, certain contractors had come in evolutionary terms. The crow, spooked by something, flew away.

Carrère later said to Miss Bough, "We're going to send a letter to Billings saying that if the contractor can't speed up the stone work, we'll have to make other arrangements."

"That's a fine idea," she agreed. "But I don't think it'll change anything."

"It'll at least encourage the Library board to investigate the causes. "Please get the letter out in the morning."

Carrère went home that evening and slid the two paintings of Miss Bough from the bookshelf. They were right where he had left them, undisturbed. It was the first time he had looked at them since he had brought them home. He dreamily set them up against the bookshelf and luxuriated in their presence. They illuminated the darkness of the books in the dark parlor. Then he moved them near a lamp so that they were under better light. How great it would be to dance with Miss Bough, to go swimming with her, to bring her home sometime. That would never happen, of course. Imagine if they were larger. Imagine if one was on display somewhere. Miss Bough would have nothing to be ashamed of. But Horace would not allow them to be considered art. It didn't matter to him. He just liked them and Miss Bough, too.

He heard Marion coming down the passageway to the parlor and quickly tucked the paintings back into the bookshelf. "Oh, hello dear," she said. "I didn't know you were here."

"I've been reading," Carrère fibbed, pointing to a biography of Thomas Jefferson lying on the end table near the sofa. He actually had been reading it, just not that particular evening.

Marion sat and resumed her journey in a recent novel. Carrère ddn't know its title. He wasn't very much a reader of fiction, and in a few moments, he settled down with Jefferson. But it was hard to think about the third president after the session with the *Miss Boughs.*

McKim told Hastings about his trip to Philadelphia to meet with Alexander Cassatt, and Hastings told Carrère all about it.

"Mister Cassatt is president of the Pennsylvania Railroad, and they're going to build a new station in New York," Hastings reported. "They want it to be the biggest in the world, and they're planning to construct a tunnel connection under the river so trains can come to New York."

Carrère considered tunneling under the Hudson River, but he couldn't envision what that would entail. Architects didn't do that kind of work. "That's a job and a half, boring tunnels beneath the Hudson River. What about the smoke from the locomotives?"

"Pennsy would switch to electric locomotives for the under-river part," Hastings said. "In this day and age, anything is possible. They're digging that canal in Panama again. These tunnels should be easy. No mosquitoes anyway."

"Where is the station going to be located?" Carrère asked.

"Pennsy has been buying land on Seventh Avenue between 32nd and 33rd Streets. A lot of row-houses are going to be torn down."

"That's a good-sized piece. The residents there can't be happy." Carrère said. They were at the Club. Carrère stirred his cocktail with an index finger.

"They're not. It's going to be an enormous station," Hastings emptied his cocktail.

"Who's designing it?"

"McKim said they are. There's not going to be a competition."

"I'm sure the Pennsy will be an easier client than the City of New York," Carrère noted, thinking of the myriad contractual issues that seemed to crop up every day and how he and Miss Bough dispatched them so efficiently.

Hastings said, "Mister Cassatt will be demanding, I'm sure."

"That makes it easier *and* harder for them." Carrère stood, ready to depart for the evening. He had not planned to meet Hastings at the Club, nor did he expect that McKim and White would get the Pennsy job without even facing competition. "They will be able to control the whole project," he said.

Carrère

Hastings revised the entry hall again and again. Some engineering changes required design changes. Not a bother to Hastings; he lived for his work. And once the big things were done, he tweaked small details, such as the shape of a baluster or cornice. "I've seen the model of the entry hall," Hastings explained. The modelers had constructed a 3/4-inch scale model of the entry hall in two halves, showing the entire room. Made of plaster, it was located in the modeler's building on the Library site. He mumbled about the myriad options he had discussed with the engineers and the modeling foreman. "It's a complex puzzle, one with no one clear, correct solution. "I'm going to spend more time on this tonight."

Carrère nodded. "How are you going to know when you have found the right answer?"

"It will be the same as always. You know. It's never really done. At least with the drawing." He paused and looked at his partner. "Why are you bothering me about this? When the building is up and complete and all the contractors have gone home, then it's done."

Carrère stole a quick glance out the darkening window and said nothing. Streetlights had been turned on.

"My drawings are like a painting," Hastings stood and puffed out his chest in a triumphant way. "They are never finished, you could say. They only stop at interesting places. You know, a drawing has a life of its own."

Carrère was skeptical. "Even drawings of stair soffits?"

"That won't be the only thing I draw tonight," Hastings replied, folding his arms across his chest.

"If I know you, it won't be. I recommend a cocktail at the club."

They hustled down the wooden stairs, pausing to look at the plainly visible construction as they crossed the Avenue. An enormous quantity of bricks, dozens of marble blocks, and a partially complete foundation marked the extent of the construction. Two derricks stood silently, awaiting orders. "This is our baby," Hastings remarked.

Several carriages passed by and continued down Fifth Avenue, which was still wet from an earlier shower. Few pedestrians were out and about. "Where does your inspiration come from?" Carrère asked as casually as he could, not wanting to intimidate him.

Hastings smiled fiendishly, "I wait until God walks through the room." They turned left off Fifth Avenue onto 43rd Street. A woman and her West Highland terrier on slack leash blocked the sidewalk. The dog was doing its business. They stepped around them. Jones, the doorman, held the door of the Club for the architects. They each ordered a drink and slid into deep, comfortable leather armchairs. Soon the warming, relaxing, lubricating alcohol took hold of them.

Carrère insisted, "I need to know, and no more facetious talk about God walking through the room."

"Maybe the God in the room is a Goddess. Maybe it's Miss Bough." Was Hastings, lubricated and comfortable deep in the chair, dreaming of a sultry goddess that guided his work?

"Better than some damn chattering monkey," he announced, turning serious. "Here's what really happens. Sometimes it comes from within me, but other times it comes from somewhere else."

"How do you know when it is coming from which source?" Carrère asked quickly before the moment evaporated.

"I can tell by a sense of control," Hastings stopped. "When I am in control of what I am doing, I know the drawing is coming from me. When I am not in control, you could say I am merely a conduit for the idea."

"You said you are a conduit," Carrère pressed.

"Sometimes I am. Especially when I have to wait for the inspiration to hit me."

"What happens when you get stuck on a problem?"

"I am patient," said Hastings as he sloshed his drink around in its glass.

"But how does the solution come?"

"It's hard to say," Hastings said. "I just sort of hope that it'll just keep on coming to me." Hastings took another sip, and continued. "I am in charge of the received elements once they land, because *I* can always decide to alter a line or a window placement or a door molding."

"I have seen you do this over and over," Carrère said.

"But it often works out that the *received* elements are better than what I invent—that I like them more and that they give me greater flexibility as to where to go next."

"Judging by what I have seen you do, most of the time you are receiving material. Your ideas keep pouring out."

Charley McKim, coming up the stairs, suddenly interrupted, "I hope you're not talking business." Hastings and Carrère stood to greet their former employer.

"We try not to," Carrère said.

"Will you be staying for dinner this evening?" McKim asked.

"Not tonight," Hastings said. "When I finish this drink I am going back to draw some ideas for the entry hall. John wants to go home."

"Did you hear the news? Frederick Olmstead died last night," McKim said.

Hastings was surprised and saddened. "The landscape architect who designed Central Park—"

"He must've been in his eighties," Carrère said. We need more people like him to beautify our cities."

"His designs are so perfect, the way they use natural topography and all to shape urban landscapes."

McKim remembered Olmstead as well. "I liked him. He had a good eye. He knew beauty. I'll miss him, especially here at the Club, where he illuminated so many conversations over the years."

"We all will," Hastings agreed.

Carrère

The next day, Carrère summoned Miss Bough to his office. He'd been unable to focus on preparations for the day's client meetings. The office was as cluttered as ever. Several books from the firm's library commanded prominent space on his desk, and an extra pair of shoes lay in kicked-off position near the door. Miss Bough looked at the mess and remarked, "What is it?" She sat in the only available chair.

"You heard that Frederick Olmstead died, didn't you?"

"I did hear," Miss Bough nodded. "Wasn't he much older than you?"

"He was eighty-one and I'm only forty-five. That monograph. How is it going?" The morning sun beamed in the window onto faded blueprints lying across the top of a bookcase.

Miss Bough smiled, "Peres is doing good work. I've typed many pages of notes."

"I'm just glad he's helping me. It's been so busy around here, I can't stand it."

"Are you thinking about Horace again?" Miss Bough asked.

"Well, yes. Hastings and I were talking, and I started to worry about him, and he says he's not going to go crazy and—"

"I don't think you need to worry about Hastings. He's solid and reliable."

"He said he waits for God to walk through the room."

"I think you should take some time away from here. To hear Hastings say things like that will only make you nervous."

"I'd love to." Polhemus himself appeared in the doorway. "The family is sailing to Europe in a month's time, and they will stay for the summer." Polhemus, was a small young man with dark hair combed straight back.

"We were just talking about you. Come in, have a seat. I have a proposal for you. This is too convenient." Carrère stood and clapped Polhemus on the back, motioning toward a chair stacked high with books.

"Where should I put the books?" Polhemus asked.

"Oh, just put 'em on the floor."

Miss Bough smiled affectionately toward Polhemus, as a mother would toward her grown son.

"I wanted to give you and Miss Bough this month's notes," Polhemus said. He reached into his briefcase and produced ten handwritten pages. "Everything I saw and heard is right here."

Carrère cleared some space on his desk and glanced at the notes. "How did you learn how many bricks there are?"

"The foreman. He speaks poor English, but I'm able to understand him."

Carrère gave the papers to Miss Bough. "Please type these and put them in the monograph file."

"I also wanted to tell you that I won't be able to help you anymore because I am leaving the firm," Polhemus said, his face grave.

Carrère was momentarily stunned. Other men had left the firm usually to start their own. Donn Barber. He certainly didn't think Polhemus had the vision or ability to go out on his own. "What are you going to be doing?"

"I am going to work for the *Tribune*," Polhemus said. "After you gave me the record-keeping task, I started to realize that I really like journalism."

Carrère moved books from one side of his desk to the other for no apparent reason. "The *Tribune*? How did you find them?"

"They found me, sir. I was at the Library site one day making notes in my notebook, when someone who said he was a reporter for the *Tribune* saw me and asked what I was doing and for whom."

"Did you tell him?"

"I did. There's nothing to worry about."

"What's his name?"

"Mister Oxford."

"So Mister Oxford offered you a job on the spot."

"Not exactly. I went to their headquarters last week, and he wanted someone to cover midtown Manhattan. He offered me a raise and I said 'Okay'."

"I'm going to miss you and your fine work," Carrère extended a hand across his overflowing desk. "I wish you well. Please come by anytime."

"You might wish you had not said that because I am a reporter now and I ask a lot of questions. I might be here too much!" Polhemus grinned and accepted the handshake.

Interlude

On our way back from the seacoast on a day trip, Peri asked me if I would go to New York to see some friends, and oh by the way, see the World Trade Center site. She knew the towers had been my favorite buildings in New York, and that I had been disconsolate about their destruction. I had thought about what sort of building should replace the towers. Skyscrapers though, were not my specialty. Also, I had never been interested in funereal monuments. Some memorials are good art, most are bad. In truth though, I didn't want to see the hole by the Hudson where the towers once stood.

"I really have had enough of craters," I said.

Peri knew instantly what I was talking about. "You can't equate the pit at the Farms Library with the World Trade Center site! They're not related!"

I said nothing for a minute. Then, "Yes they are related." I glanced at Peri. "To me they are related. Nothing useful came from them. No one led a life in them. They were or are destined to be filled in."

Peri raised her voice. "Then there's doubly nothing to think about. Those craters will be erased from the earth!"

She was right. They were not to be holes in the ground forever. Maybe therefore, I could accept them. Maybe I filled that crater in that night in order to return the earth to normalcy as soon as possible. I did not play golf, but I did know that the little hole in the green was moved from time to time. I wondered if the hole in a golf course would evoke the same response in me that the crater at the Library did.

"Peri," I said, "let's find a golf course and go for a walk."

"Golf course—around here?" She gestured out the car window at the forest on both sides of the road.

"I know where there is one," I said. About forty-five minutes later, I turned right and then right again. We were at a private golf club where I used to caddy when I was a kid. I stopped the car. The tee was to the right on the other side of a pond; and to the left, up a hill, was the green. No one was on the course.

Peri spotted the wooden suspension bridge spanning the pond. "How did you know this was here?"

"I used to caddy. Once in awhile one of the men would drive the ball straight down into the water. There must be a thousand balls in there." I remembered the sound the ball made as it cut through the leaves on its wayward path. *Whackwhackwhackthwacksplash*, followed by an expletive. It wasn't easy being a fifteen-year-old caddy: I took some of the blame more often than not. "I want to walk up to the green."

"How far is it?"

"Oh, just up that hill. This is a par three hole."

"What's that mean?"

"It means you should be able to sink the ball in the hole in three shots. Some holes are par four or par five." We got out of the car and walked up the fairway to the green.

"Haven't you ever seen golf before?"

"Only on TV," Peri said.

In a minute, we reached the green at the top of the hill. There was a white stick in the hole with a white flag bearing the golf club's emblem, a gray squirrel. The green remained exactly as I had remembered from caddying all those years ago. The shape of a kidney bean, a slight pitch toward the back, three bunkers, and tall oak trees all around. I also remembered the mosquitoes. I walked over to the pin, lifted it out and gave it to Peri.

"What am I supposed to do with this?" she asked.

"Stay right there." I walked back to the road. She must have been bewildered. I crossed the bridge to the tee, counted to ten, then returned to the green.

"What are you doing?"

I covered my eyes, counted to ten again, and then approached the hole. I looked into it and waited. At length I said, "Nothing. If I had a putter, I would knock in a putt." I took the pin from Peri and returned it to the hole. "Nothing at all," I said again. "This hole is no problem."

Peri caught on. "Why would it have been?"

"I didn't know and wanted to make sure. You were right. Not all these spaces are related. I was just testing."

"Can we go now?"

We started down the hill. "Yeah." I looked over my shoulder at a place where I had spent a little time in my youth. I remembered the overly large golf bags stuffed with heavy clubs. I had really disliked having to carry two bags especially over eighteen holes. They had paid me about eleven dollars, sometimes a two-dollar tip. At the car I said, "I'm happy I never took up golf."

"I am, too," Peri said.

Carrère

With each passing day, more marble accumulated on the site. While some blocks were hoisted into position right away, others languished for months. During one of his every-other-day visits, Carrère asked the foreman why it took so long before some blocks were used.

"Because we want to match grain," the foreman said in halting English.

"So a block waits until there is a perfect match," Carrère said.

The foreman brushed off his overalls and repositioned his cap. "That's right. It has to be perfect, you know."

Thick, wet, slippery snow one morning caused some of the men to be late for work and it was quiet at the office, even at ten o'clock. Miss Bough suddenly hurried in, "There has been an accident at the Library. One of the wagons hauling stone was overloaded and collapsed. I think someone may have been hurt."

Ward, who had replaced Polhemus as Carrère's fact collector, rushed out the door with a notepad. He was exceptionally faithful to his job as reporter and recorder for the book.

Carrère jumped to his feet. "Give me the details as soon as you can."

"Will do, sir," Ward hollered as the door at the bottom of the stairs banged shut.

Carrère, shaken by the prospect of a death on one of their projects, hoped the contractor or the foreman responsible had helped the victim. The thought of one's livelihood contributing to his demise just wasn't right or fair. For a man to lose everything while he's trying to get ahead.

"I've always dreaded an accident on one of our projects," he said.

"I didn't know you cared," said Miss Bough.

"It's a matter of fairness." Hastings arrived, knocking snow from his boots. "There aren't any laws to protect workers," Carrère continued. "I think there should be. I wish we could do something to prevent these things from happening."

Hastings appeared unconcerned, "Safety over there," he pointed toward Fifth Avenue, "that's not our problem. Norcross should protect his men."

"Norcross should, I agree," Carrère folded his arms across his chest. "I think some kind of law might help. That's all I was saying."

"I don't know what kind of law that would be," Hastings said. His skepticism sometimes irked Carrère. "Accidents happen."

Miss Bough left the room.

Hastings said, "Good, now that she's gone, something has been on my mind. If you are together with her, it'll make work here at the firm intolerable for me and everyone else—just the way it was with Stanford White when we were there."

"Stanford's ladies didn't bother me," Carrère said. "And Miss Bough and I are not—I repeat—are not! I don't know what gives you the idea anyway." Carrère knew inside that it was not the truth. "She does her job, and I do mine." The sweat on his brow belied the wintry day outside.

"Well, all I want to do is my job. But if my partner is cheating on his wife with the secretary, it'll be impossible."

"My problem is—and I keep asking you about who guides you—all that." Carrère clasped his hands behind his head. "I see you overwork your drawings, draw them to death, and I hide them from you just to get you to stop. It doesn't work. You're the opposite of Horace Avery. He got stuck on those Miss Bough paintings. You can't stop."

"What paintings?" Hastings said.

Carrère fumbled for words, not sure what to say. He had never meant the paintings to be a secret; on the other hand, he had no reason to tell Hastings about them. Hastings would be more suspicious than ever about Miss Bough and wouldn't be able to trust his partner. Carrère decided tell him the whole story, the exact truth. Maybe he'd change his opinion of Miss Bough and want to see the paintings. That was the best Carrère could hope for.

Hastings sat and listened, asking no questions. When Carrère was finished, Hastings said, "She must've been Avery's whore."

Carrère

Labor disputes, bad marble, and uncooperative weather caused delay after delay. To make matters worse, much of the work was being done absolutely wrong. "Everything is topsy-turvy," Carrère complained one morning.

"It will get better," Miss Bough said. "It seems you have been put through a sieve."

"I'm going to go to Vermont with Brainard for a couple of days. I've got to get out of here."

"What are you looking for?"

"Answers. Why the marble is so bad. And what's taking so long." Carrère paced around the room. "Another thing—you've got to stay out of Hastings's way. He thinks you were Avery's lady, only worse. Just stay away from him."

Miss Bough laughed. "No, I wasn't his lady. I was his secretary and model. You know what? While you're away, I'll show him one of the paintings, just to prove I wasn't. I'll tell him all the paintings are the same. Do you think he'll faint?"

"Be careful," Carrère advised. "He lives in a dream world with his wife and almost not a worry in the world. He's a private man who needs to be safe. I wouldn't do that if I were you."

"Well maybe the painting isn't such a great idea," Miss Bough said. "Maybe there's a way he can just find it instead."

"I'd like him to see that you're not a threat, that you can be a good worker. But I don't know how we can do that. It'll be better for the firm if he does." Carrère started to collect some papers for the trip.

"Don't forget the notebook," reminded Miss Bough. "I want you to tell me about Vermont. I've never been there."

Carrère

Spafford West was the man in Vermont to talk with. A Dorset native who knew marble as well as any man who had ever lifted it out of the ground, he had a keen sense of Vermont humor. He was a portly man with big hands and was wearing a straw hat with a black hatband, loose-fitting jacket, and dark trousers, when he greeted Brainard and Carrère at the Manchester train station. "Greetings, gentlemen from New York!" The locomotive, at idle after pulling up the long grades into Manchester, puffed sooty black coal smoke. He stuck out a great paw. Carrère felt his hand disappear in West's when they shook.

Carrère noticed in West and Brainard the difference between New York and Vermont. In standard business attire—white shirt, dark trousers and jacket, and a top hat—Carrère represented elegant New York. In West he saw rugged, rural Vermont. Mr. West invited the New Yorkers to ride up the valley to the quarry. "There are very few automobiles in Vermont," West said. "I hear there are more and more of 'em in New York."

"That's true," Carrère said, "but still not as many as carriages."

West continued, "When Orlando and I bought the quarry, Dorset was a declining town. The marble industry was nowhere. But we took a chance."

"You must've thought it was a good opportunity," Carrère said, looking about the countryside.

"Fits with our other businesses," West nodded.

Brainard asked, "This is a quiet place, isn't it?"

"Mostly agrarian."

The carriage passed a field where cows grazed. "Folks around here live on self-sufficient farms raising vegetables and livestock. Uh-huh. You city people are losing touch with the land. It's pretty quiet, except near the quarries, where we're always sawing stone."

"Do you have telephone service yet?" Carrère asked.

"Uh-huh. There is a single line shared by a few people. I don't need it."

"Electricity?"

"Nope, but I hear it's coming." Mr. West changed the subject. "The marble here in Dorset is close to the surface and easy to get out of the ground." He pointed to a mountain ahead and continued, "That is Mount Aeolus up there, site of the first marble quarry in the U.S." He paused before adding a bit of local history. "In 1785, Isaac Underhill started splitting out headstones, hearths, lintels, and chimney backs from a marble ledge up there on Reuben Bloomer's land."

"How did they get the marble down from the mountain?" Carrère asked.

"Well, there was a railway with wooden tracks. Horses hauled the blocks all the way to the Hudson Canal landings," West explained. "We're going to build a railroad into Manchester to haul the marble for the Library."

Brainard said, "That'll make it much easier."

"That's right, the Manchester, Dorset & Granville " Mr. West continued, "We need the railroad to carry the half a million cubic feet you need."

"When do you think the railroad will be in operation?" I asked.

"Next year."

"Why so long?"

"So many problems," West held out his hands palms up. "Not enough men and not enough coal." The carriage reached the Valley Quarry pit, and the driver called the chestnut mare to a stop. Looking at the quarry for the first time, Carrère wondered how marble ever was discovered there. Piles of dirt and broken rock lay everywhere, muddy ruts were filled with melting snow. Carrère preferred New York's paved streets.

"The railroad will end here," West pointed toward the quarry. "Let's look at that large block they just hoisted out of the pit." Spring thaws had turned much of the soil into mud. They stepped carefully to avoid the lurking mud holes and traps. Four feet tall, ten feet long, and five feet wide, the piece of marble was veined with dark streaks and was marred by fresh saw marks.

"This was brought out yesterday," West said.

"I can see that we would not use this one."

"Not all of it," West said.

Brainard said, "Our problem is jambs, angles, sills, projections."

"You want white marble only," said West, "and where two or three faces are exposed, a face could be at right angle to a dark vein. We have to sort through a lot of stone to find pieces without veins."

"Don't you quarry between veins?" asked Brainard.

"Of course we do, but we can't anticipate every vein."

"Wait a second," Carrère said. He had a sudden idea. "We need some marble with veins!" Brainard looked curiously at him while West said nothing. "The exhibition hall's columns." He walked to a pile of impure marble. The blocks were of irregular shapes and sizes. Carrère beckoned West to come look.

"What do you see?" West said.

"We're trying to find cheaper marble for the columns in the exhibition hall. Maybe we could use veined marble from here."

"What are you planning to use?" West inquired, holding his hands behind his back.

"Well, my partner at first wanted to use Connemara marble—"

"—ooh. Expensive," said West.

"So we thought about Cippolino marble," Carrère scuffed the ground.

"That's still expensive," West added. He knew his marble.

"I know. So we let it be figuring that we'd find something somewhere."

West, drawing on that vast knowledge of his, offered a suggestion. "If the horizontal graining is stood on its end. The veins will run the length of the upright column." West turned his forearm from a horizontal position to vertical to demonstrate how the veins could stand on end.

"We can use veined marble throughout the exhibition hall," Carrère announced. "The veins would be horizontal in the walls and vertical in the columns. A nice contrast." Carrère was immensely pleased with this brainstorm. "I think Hastings will like the idea, too."

They walked to the railing at the edge of the pit, still avoiding obvious mud. The quarry, with its vertical gray-and-white walls, was a rectangle several hundred yards long, about half as wide, and about 70 feet deep.

His mind wandered back to New York. What was Miss Bough doing? It was nice to be away from there for a few days.

He looked into the quarry: wooden stairs switched back and forth in their descent to the bottom. Several derricks reaching across the open space above the great pit were poised to snatch already-cut blocks. A few men moved hand tools and ladders, but the black, sooty steam-powered channeling machines lay quiet. He wondered why so little work had taken place when Norcross had a two million dollar contract for marble. "Why are the machines quiet? You said you were cutting as fast as you could."

Again on the defensive, West explained the labor situation. "See, this quarry was closed for twenty-five years before Orlando and I reopened it. In the twenty-five years, the men who worked here drifted or moved away to other jobs. So we've had to hire men who don't know how to cut marble."

Brainard listened skeptically. "What's so hard about that?"

"Nothing, really. It just has to be done," West explained.

"Are there other reasons?" Carrère asked.

"Okay, look," West pointed to a road running around the pit, "see that road?"

"I see it," Brainard said.

"That road is new. We had to build it to replace an old one that ran immediately above a very good vein. This entailed considerable work. We also had to get preliminary authorization from local officials."

"We've had plenty of trouble with local officials in New York," Carrère said.

"Right. They really could not have cared less about marble for a library two hundred miles away," West huffed. "It just took a long time."

Carrère thought, how could it be so difficult to build a road around a quarry? Nothing else is here. He leaned on the iron railing carelessly, looking into the great pit. Clouds and shifting light created interesting shapes and patterns on the floor of the quarry that spawned diagrammatic plans in the architect's imagination. He pressed his belly against the iron pipe railing, leaning forward to look straight down. The quarry's unnatural creation was of no particular beauty. Carrère saw a cavity with no useful purpose for the future. The sun reflected in standing water in the bottom of the pit.

He turned from the void and looked around. Cut marble blocks laying here and there used to be part of the solid earth until humans needed them. They weren't defined as cubic rectangles until men needed them. Before they were cut, there was only one mass of rock; now the one solid mass was reduced to smaller units. What a feat, Carrère marveled. To take something so singular and logical, cut it up at random, and move the pieces to another place to make something new.

He beckoned Brainard and West to the railing. "What is going to happen to this quarry when you're finished?"

"I don't know."

"You haven't thought about it?"

West appeared impatient. "My business is disassembling the marble so you men can use it somewhere else. I don't give a damn about the pit."

"That's it," Carrère said. "They are taking apart the rock in the ground so that we can put it back together again."

"I am not sure what you are talking about," said Brainard, with his hands in his overcoat pockets.

Carrère bounced on the balls of his feet, "Can't you see that the stone here in the ground has little purpose. Soon it will form the Library—an inverse quarry."

The sun emerged from the clouds. Carrère took off his coat. Chickadees and thrushes sang in the spruce trees. A red-and-white milk wagon creaked along the road in front of the quarry. Light wind carried aromas of horse manure and wood smoke from the nearby village.

"I've never thought about this, you know, how two places—I'm not sure how to explain it," Brainard hesitated.

"You said it, Owen," Carrère draped his coat over the rusted iron railing and looked into the quarry pit again. "Two places are made at the same time for one reason." He was thinking out loud. "To build the New York Public Library." He paused, adjusting his coat on the railing. "Library is positive and good. But what about this place, a result of the Library? This place will become a relic, a byproduct. The Library is to be monumental." He looked into the quarry again. "It takes creative men like Hastings to arrange the marble in such a way as to make something good and permanent and positive for all, to make a new space." His eyes watered with discovery and possibility. "Or two spaces, if you count the Library *and* the quarry."

"What are you going to do now?" Brainard mumbled.

"I don't know," Carrère shrugged. His thoughts galloped ahead though. I'll have to write this down in my notebook before I forget. They didn't teach good space and bad space at the Ecole de Beaux Arts. What is space, anyway?

After touring Norcross-West, they hopped north to West Rutland, another marble quarrying town. Carrère wanted to meet Mr. George Eastman to talk about ornamental marble. Hastings had sought imported marble for various locations in the Library. The stone dealer in New York had described Eastman Cream, but didn't actually know it. As Carrère enjoyed being away from New York, he decided to see more of Vermont. It only made sense to see Eastman Cream at the source.

Mr. Eastman met them at the train station. "Welcome to West Rutland," he said. "I think you'll like what I have to show you." Carrère had noticed coal smoke hanging in the valley coming from the many saws and machines in town.

Eastman, as much a marble man as West, had a greater understanding of art. He was about five and a half feet tall, not quite as tall as Carrère, wore a golden moustache and beard, and walked with an erect posture and a short stride. He led the visitors from New York to a carriage for the short ride up the hill to his quarry. "We produce many varieties of commercial marbles," Eastman explained as they reached the railing at the side of the pit. "Most of it is used for interior decorative work." The Eastman quarry was smaller than Norcross-West but much deeper. Carrère guessed that it must be over 100 feet deep.

"I'll take you in if you'd like," Eastman said. "You'll need different shoes because it's very wet down there."

"I didn't expect to go into a quarry," Brainard said. "Didn't bring any other shoes."

"No worry, I'll check in the mill building for some overboots." Eastman hustled inside and returned with one pair.

"You take them," Carrère said to Brainard. "I'll sacrifice my shoes to see *this*."

Brainard tugged on the black overboots and they started down a light wooden stair fastened to one of the quarry's walls. About thirty feet down, still one hundred feet from the bottom, the stair shook slightly. Carrère speculated how unlikely it was that a New York architect had ever gone into some deep quarry in Vermont. Egad! It was a journey to the center of the earth! He wondered if Jules Verne had ever been to a marble quarry. What if this was a dream and there was a gigantic ape in there? He wondered if Anna had read that book yet?

As they descended, the air became quite cool and damp. A wide tunnel disappeared into the hill. An unseen channeling machine pounded its chisel into the rock floor deep inside the tunnel. The noise made it almost impossible to talk. Carrère peered into the tunnel. Infrequent electric lights barely relieved the tunnel's blackness.

At last, as they reached the bottom of the stair, the channeling machine stopped its hammering. Carrère glanced up. A small square of blue sky and daylight far above was the only opening to the rest of the world. He stood on the damp quarry floor turning around and around, scanning the walls, which grew farther apart as the quarry deepened. "This is excellent," he blurted, turning toward Mr. Eastman.

"I think so, too. Let's go in."

Carrère admired the quarry. He wasn't so sure anymore that the quarry was a byproduct—it was like a cathedral. The tunnel beckoned him, gradually sloping downward as it disappeared in the hill.

"I think I'll wait here at the stair platform," Brainard obviously didn't want to enter the tunnel.

"This could be the best part," Carrère said.

"There's nothing to worry about," Eastman said. "You can't get lost."

Brainard found some courage and said he'd come, and Eastman led the way into the tunnel's gaping maw. We reached the channeling machine in about two minutes. Eastman signaled the workers to stop the machine. Suddenly it was blissfully quiet aside from a leaky steam hose. The solid rock ceiling vaulted sixty feet overhead and the walls stood seventy feet apart.

Eastman pointed, "The machine cuts into the marble at a constant depth, and when the block's dimension is cut, we use that machine over there—a gadding machine—to bore holes along the bottom."

"The same equipment that Norcross uses in Dorset," Brainard said.

"That's right, except we don't produce nearly as much stone. Our marble is mostly ornamental." Eastman handed Carrère a piece that he guessed weighed about two pounds. "This marble has much finer grain than the marble they're using for the exterior."

"I can feel the difference," Carrère said. He turned the chunk over in his hands.

"It polishes beautifully," Eastman added. "I hope you can find some use for high grade marble in the Library."

"Once Hastings sees and feels this, I think he'll find a use." Carrère's attention shifted from the micro to the macro, and once again he admired the dark cavity in which he stood. He let his gaze run up and down the walls, and he looked at the entrance. He could imagine that the inside of this quarry was as big as McKim's train station. They turned toward the light. Carrère scratched his head. "So a new space is made in the ground, even when it's ornamental marble."

"We talked about that at Norcross-West," Brainard said.

"I know—I'm just trying to figure it out," Carrère said. The space idea was going to dog him the whole way home.

Back topside, Carrère said, "Let's look at this in the light here. Does it carve well?" He was thinking of interior figureheads and medallions.

"It does," Eastman said. "An artist can do much more with this than he can with the stuff from Dorset."

"The façade columns will come from Dorset," Carrère said.

"Your columns will be bored from solid blocks using boring machines. That is far different from detailed ornamental carving."

"You're right. We've been looking at ornamental marble from Italy, which we wouldn't use for columns. I'll bring this piece back to my partner. I think he'll like it."

The train's whistle wailed in the valley below. Mr. Eastman examined his pocket watch and said, "That train is headed north to Middlebury. You don't have to hurry."

"Too bad we can't use this marble for the exterior," Carrère said. Brainard sat to remove the boots.

"That would be insane," Eastman said. "Too expensive."

"That's what I mean," Carrère said. "We'll use it somewhere though."

Eastman drove the architects back to the West Rutland depot. They thanked the quarryman for the introduction to his marble and for the visit and boarded a southbound train.

Once they were settled in leather-covered seats in the parlor car, Carrère said, "I think Eastman's marble would be a good choice for the chimneybreast and mantel in the Trustees' room."

Brainard said, "I think Tom will agree with you when he sees this stone."

Carrère held the piece close for detailed examination. "Eastman says his marble polishes very nicely and is free of discoloration and defects." The train swayed as it churned south, sloshing their drinks back and forth in their glasses.

"Then it'll be perfect," Brainard said. "That room must be impeccably appointed." After some silence, during which the clacking of the car's wheels across the tracks became quite noticeable, he asked Carrère, "What got you thinking about the two spaces, the quarry and the Library?"

"Well, I was just staring into the Norcross quarry, when you and Mister West were talking and the idea came to me. I was thinking about floor plans and noticing how the light and shadows created an interesting design on the quarry floor. We architects are plan oriented, you know." Carrère sipped his drink. "I remember studying drawing and painting before I went to the Ecole—at a school in Switzerland years ago—and there was something I liked about space and composition." He recalled his busy days as a student in Paris with great minds and great talent all around him. "I have no chance to think about art because of what I do. Tommy is the artist of our firm. He certainly thinks about composition all the time."

The train's whistle blew sharply at a grade crossing. From the parlor in which they sat, they saw thawing fields on the right and across the coach out to the left, wooded hills. He began to wonder what had happened at the office in his absence. Only three days—he had been away for much longer periods—but not when Hastings was so volatile and Miss Bough so aggressive. He prayed that Miss Bough had kept a low profile.

Interlude

I used a vacation day to go to Vermont to learn more about marble. I knew that marble came in different hues and colors. Carrère & Hastings had wanted only the finest white marble for the New York Public Library.

Marble, I had learned, runs in a continuous bed north-south from Connecticut through Massachusetts into New York, and all the way north through Vermont. The stone from South Dover, New York, and Dorset are pretty similar.

I had borrowed Peri's car for the day because my car was in the shop receiving a 50,000-mile maintenance checkup. It was an early spring day and all the snow was gone. Leaves hadn't yet burst from their buds. But early migrant birds had returned.

I started my exploration at the town hall, where the fifty-fiveish town clerk, Ellen Pratt, greeted me. I introduced myself and explained, "I'm looking for information about marble."

Ellen smiled easily. People in upcountry New England towns are very helpful. That couldn't always be said of bureaucrats in New York, or any other big city. "You've come to the right town, but not the right person."

"Someone knows everything?" I asked.

Town clerks knew everything about their towns, or at a minimum, knew who knew what I wanted to learn. "Try Leo Kulik. He lives on Gilson Street." Ellen probably saw that I didn't know where to find Gilson Street. "Go out the front door here and head up Marble Street. You'll pass a cemetery on the right and then turn right onto Gilson. Leo's retired. Why don't you knock on his door. He's probably there."

There was a white Buick sedan in the driveway. The mail protruded from a black letter box beside the tan storm door. I didn't see a doorbell button, so I rapped on the storm door six times. After a few minutes, a short, gray-haired woman with deep wrinkles and jowls opened the inner door. Her dull eyes expressed weariness. "Yes," she said, evidently without concern that I was a complete stranger.

"I'm looking for Leo Kulik. Does he live here? I'd like to ask him some questions about marble."

The woman spoke slowly and sloppily. "He's eating his chicken sandwich now. I'll tell him you're here." She reappeared a minute or two later. "You can come in," but she didn't open the door for me.

Inside, the smell of stale cigarette smoke hung pervasively. It made my eyes water. Leo Kulik sat at a round table with a thick, glossy acrylic finish. He hadn't finished his chicken sandwich. The uneaten portion rested on a paisley-pink plate he had pushed out of the way in favor of an ashtray. A lit cigarette smoldered in the ashtray.

"Excuse me for interrupting your lunch," I began.

"Sit yourself down," Leo Kulik said. "I can tell you everything you want to know about marble from our valley." Leo Kulik drew a puff from the cigarette. He had Parkinson's shakes in the hand holding the cigarette.

I spoke slowly knowing that the old man probably wouldn't last too long. "I'm looking for information about the marble used in the New York Public Library."

"That was Dorset A, coarse, creamy to very light," he pulled again from the cigarette, then cleared his throat. "Also, a faintly greenish-smoke color. There's a ton of it available."

"Is that so," I said, just to keep Leo Kulik going.

""Yes, sir. It runs in layers starting at the surface, running to great depths. The thickness of the layers can vary greatly." Leo Kulik appeared to have little energy. "From five or six feet thick to thirty or forty."

"Can you predict it?" I asked.

"No. No, sir." Leo Kulik shrugged weakly. "That is the nature of marble in Vermont." He said nothing while he finished his cigarette and lit another. "That's why the quarries are so deep." He mumbled something else, but I couldn't understand him.

"Well, thank you, sir, for your time," I said as I rose from my chair. "Your information is helpful to me." I reached to shake his hand.

"Don't go," he pleaded quietly. "You should, should, I say, you should—" The cigarette fell from Leo Kulik's fingers. His eyes locked into a frozen stare toward the kitchen, where the old woman was pushing some old newspapers across the table.

I stepped on the cigarette to make sure it was out, and then I said politely, "Ma'am, I think Mister Kulik needs some help."

"She turned slowly and said, "Oh, it's nothing. Just pinch or slap him and he'll come to."

"But, ma'am, I can't do that. I don't know the man." Where was Peri when I needed her?

"You're closest, just slap 'im on the face and he'll be fine." The old woman saw me hesitate. "Just do it," she commanded. I hesitated again and backed away from the stricken man.

"Why do I have to do it myself when you're standing right there?" she fumed. I edged closer to the door, thinking about escaping. Finally, she plowed toward Leo Kulik, put a dishtowel on the table, and slapped his gray cheek with the back of her hand. Leo Kulik didn't stir. The woman struck him again, and Leo Kulik slipped downward in his chair. The woman asked me to help slide Leo Kulik up in his chair and I obliged. "I don't think he's going to make it this time. It's too much for him. Too much. Too much." Her speech trailed off as she began to sob uncontrollably.

I stuck around until the ambulance came. The EMTs asked a few questions, lifted Leo Kulik into the ambulance, and sped for the hospital with lights flashing but no siren. There was no need to disturb the peace there in rural Vermont. A state police officer asked me a few questions and said I was free to go.

There was nothing left for me there except the quarry. I stopped to look at it before heading home. It was easy to find, with large white marble blocks along the road. Someone had made an effort to maintain a grassy parklike area between the road and the water. It was an attractive spot. Several other motorists had stopped to look. No doubt this spot was listed in AAA tour books as an historical site. I wondered if they had ever thought about what lies hidden under the water or the human enterprise that excavated the space. It was a secret except to divers.

Carrère

When he returned from Vermont, Carrère found Hastings as engrossed in his drawings and designs as ever. There were a dozen renderings of the rear façade to be studied and redrawn. Carrère knew that Hastings would have liked to do it all himself if he could. Of course, that wasn't possible, so he conferred with the job captains and delegated the work. Miss Bough was sitting across from Hastings when Carrère walked into his office. "So you met Carrère—" she was saying.

"Thanks to Charley McKim. I forget whom he hired first, John or me." Hastings looked at Carrère.

"I don't remember either," Carrère said.

Hastings continued. "We worked on some projects together and soon started talking about opening our own firm. That was in ninety-three or so, if I recall. Carrère probably has a better memory than I."

"But it wasn't long after you returned from Paris?" Miss Bough asked.

"No. Only a year or two."

"Did the firm have a good start?"

"Oh, I do think so. Our first commission was a hotel in Saint Augustine, Florida." Hastings found a picture of the hotel and held it up. "We have never had to wonder where our next commission was coming from. Then we won the Library competition and all kinds of doors have been opened. Since we started this firm, we've had around eighty commissions including the Library."

"Weren't we supposed to meet Billings today?" I asked.

"His secretary called and told us that he can't make it," Miss Bough said.

"Why, that's unusual for him to cancel an appointment," Hastings said. He retrieved his pocket watch from his suit coat. He flipped up the gold cover and examined the white dial with Roman numerals. As he did so, Hastings remembered that he hadn't wound the watch when getting dressed at home. He proceeded to rock his thumb and forefinger back and forth on each side of the knurled winding knob until the watch's mainspring was tight. He held the watch to his ear listening for the faint ticking. It was there, according to Hastings's nod. He flipped the cover closed and stowed the watch once again in his breast pocket.

"His secretary told me that there's a family emergency, so we'll see him the same day next week," Miss Bough said.

"I hope everything is all right," Carrère said.

"It gives us more time to make changes and to improve the drawings," Hastings was gleeful at the lengthened opportunity. He wanted to alter the door leading from the catalog room to the reading room.

Miss Bough stood to return to her office. As Miss Bough disappeared, Hastings turned to Carrère, "I have one of the paintings."

"Where is it now?" Carrère was dumbfounded, and rather quickly he began to feel like a male wolf with a need to protect his harem—a harem of one—Miss Bough. How could she? Miss Bough had said that she wouldn't. He thought she would have wanted to keep their little secret private.

"I brought it home." Hastings yawned.

"Did Helen see it?" It was hard for him to speak, and words came out as croaks. "She did."

"Anything else happen?" Carrère was by then frustrated by the lack of information coming from Hastings.

"I revised some things, sent others to draftsmen for final prints. It was pretty quiet around here," Hastings continued his evasiveness.

Carrère decided to play along with Hastings, not wanting to reveal to him any 'little secret.' He briefly described his travels in Vermont. "There's an inexpensive solution to the exhibition hall's columns. It's still going to be a few months before we get any marble."

Hastings leaned back in his chair and smiled. "We'll wait, I'm glad it's coming,"

"Was there any mail? Did Miss Bough mention anything?" Carrère made his way toward his office.

"She didn't mention anything," Hastings said blandly. "Nothing important."

Hastings returned his attention to matters on his desk.

Later, Carrère approached Miss Bough at her desk. "What's changed? I didn't think you were going to give him a painting. I thought it was our little secret."

"It was never our little secret. They're just little paintings, and they're not very good either."

Carrère looked around to make sure nobody was listening. He sat. "But it was our little secret."

Miss Bough leaned forward. "From Marion, I bet." Carrère's face stiffened because she spoke the truth. "

"Hastings is a good man, as you know. I told him some things I haven't told anyone else."

"What did you tell him?"

"I talked about my family a little bit."

Carrère didn't know much. "Tell me."

"You know about my sisters. I'm the only one who isn't married. My father is dead. My mother isn't well."

"I'm so sorry your mother isn't well. Is she recovering?"

"Oh, I doubt it," Miss Bough replied matter-of-factly. "She has cancer." She looked down sadly. "We haven't spoken in years. I only know about her from my sisters."

"And about your father. How long's he been gone?" Carrère felt a little uneasy about prying, but on the other hand she had always been quite frank.

"He died from Caisson's Disease when working on the Brooklyn Bridge. It was terribly painful. I remember the doctors couldn't figure out how to help him and he suffered terribly. He hated going to work excavating for the piers of that bridge. It hurt his joints every day, and then one day it was too much for him. He coughed up blood when he died. We all still miss him, for he was a warm and generous dad. He didn't live long enough to see my sisters get married."

"So you know personally about construction accidents, I'd say,"

"I do, and they should be avoidable. Such a waste. My father worked down there in the caisson to provide for his family, and he suffered and died. And the rest of us suffered without him." There was bitterness in the secretary's voice.

"What would you change?"

"I don't know," Miss Bough said. "I don't ever think about those things. There should be laws, I guess."

"You've always seemed to be a carefree spirit. I'm sorry about your tragedy."

Miss Bough smiled easily. "The most fun I've ever had was working for Horace Avery. I just can't tell you. It was adventurous, daring, bold, innovative."

Her voice faded with the fondness and the memory. "I loved posing for him."

She hid nothing and yet she was modest.

"What else?' Carrère asked.

"I asked if Mister Hastings wanted to see the paintings, and he said yes." Miss Bough rolled a new sheet of paper into the typewriter. "He came to my place to see the paintings, and I gave him one."

"Why'd you tell Hastings? What did he think of Horace's paintings?"

"Slow down," Miss Bough commanded gently. "He was as happy to take the painting as I was to give it to him. I've never thought they are magic, but maybe he thinks so, and maybe you do, too. Maybe Horace wasn't mad."

"He *was* mad."

"It's sad," Miss Bough said. "That's the way it is. I'm happy here working for you and Mister Hastings though. It's sort of like a family for me." She peered longingly into his eyes.

"Was there any mail?"

"Not too much. A letter from Billings and a notice from the City about something or other. It's on your desk."

Carrère found his desk organized and tidy—Miss Bough straightened it for him. Other things eluded him though and he wanted answers. *What about* Hastings and Miss Bough? And yes, the quarries in Vermont, what about them? What will they ever be good for? Maybe the town dump.

Interlude

I was late to the office one day. It was snowing, and even in Manchester where everyone knows how to drive in snow, people were having trouble. I saw one car in front of me spin out, and I almost did a mile ahead. I got stuck behind a snowplow. At least school had been canceled and there weren't any school buses on the road.

I swept the snow off my coat as I trudged up the stairs to the office. I generally didn't use the elevator, figuring that the exercise, what little it actually was, would do me some good.

"Good morning," I said.

Jayne didn't even notice that I was late. "Don't you love watching the new white snow fall? It's perfect and new out there."

"It's okay, but I have to clear the driveway."

"Don't you use a snow blower?" Jayne sipped her usual Pepsi. "No, I shovel."

There was an empty glass on her desk. In the afternoons Jayne drank water and preferred an actual glass to a paper cup. "Cleaner," she always insisted. I picked up the glass, which was spotless. I peered through its sides through the thick bottom. I rotated the glass, stirred an imaginary drink with my right index finger, and observed how the sides of the tumbler defined the volume within. I tried to explain. "Space is invisible but we can experience it."

"How so?" Jayne perked up.

"Are you claustrophobic?"

"No. I like to take my shower with the lights off in the dark."

"I'm thinking that claustrophobia is just one way to experience space—the most common way, I'd say." I paused. "But there must be other ways to experience it." I looked into the empty glass again. "You know that crater; it was a space. So is a hole in a putting green. Or the pit where the World Trade Center towers stood. I've got this interesting notion."

"Which is?"

"When I think about it now, I think I've become aware of surfaces— the walls, the floor, and the ceiling of a building, or an empty pit.

"Or the quarry where you guys go diving."

"Oh, definitely. It's a giant room carved from solid rock, with great tapered piers holding up the roof. It's full of water now. Never was a place to live." I put down the empty glass and spread my arms wide to demonstrate the size of the quarry. "It's awesome."

"What about the space you were talking about?" Jayne set me onto my thought-train.

"Oh yes—space has no mass. We can't touch, feel, or weigh it. But it still can have important qualities."

"In architecture?"

"Yes, in architecture, Beaux-Arts architecture, and in painting, music, and in our lives, too."

I sensed Jayne starting to follow my idea. "In paintings there is a sense of space extending beyond the picture plane."

"Well, yes," I said, "but that's not what I'm thinking of. I'm thinking not of implied volume but rather unused space."

"In a painting?" asked Jayne.

"Yes in a painting. See, unused space in a picture defines the illustrated objects. So the unused space in a picture acts like the walls and ceiling of the quarry." I was concentrating. "Except when the quarry is all used up, it would be unused, useless space."

"So the spaces in the Library are—"

"Positive space, because those spaces are so wonderful and useful and new with a purpose."

"That means the quarry must be negative space," Jayne said breezily.

"Why, of course, that's it!" I had been so close to it all along. Maybe that's why I had filled in that crater. The Library is positive space; and the quarry it came from, the leftover hole in the earth, the residue, is negative space. That's brilliant! I thought of the quarry. How could it be negative and 'awesome' at the same time? Just a matter of perception, I decided quickly. Different things for different people. Jayne's phone rang, if you can call the sound it made a ring. "I've always appreciated how in the New York Public Library's renderings I've seen, the white spaces give the effect of a line. I guess I've always known about spaces."

"I think there might be a problem," Jayne said, her voice tentative and cautious. "In paintings, sometimes the empty negative space that defines the illustrated objects is actually in its own right very interesting. Isn't it different from architectural space?"

"Not at all," I said, pacing the gray-and-black-striped carpet on the floor of Jayne's office, "because the space in architecture also shapes things, shapes objects." Jayne's look was quizzical. "Think of a column, with its taper, as being carved out of space."

"We don't use columns anymore, Mister Beaux-Arts Man, but I know what you mean."

"We can't have a column unless there is space in which it resides, and that space, so molded, gives the column its shape," I explained, brushing off Jayne's poke.

Jayne clarified, "That makes the space a negative and the column a positive, and it's the same for those piers in the quarry, isn't it?"

"Yes, it would," I agreed. "But it gets a little confusing here. Is the pier or column shaped by the space or the space shaped by the pier? Which is negative? Which is positive?"

"I say the volume is the negative," Jayne nodded, "because it molded a feature that was deliberately shaped by humans."

"That could make the quarry doubly negative because it is a volume formed by human endeavor, just like the spaces in the Library, and because it is a remainder, a hole in the ground. And when it was in business, no one would have imagined any future purpose for it."

"But you like it," Jayne said.

"Just because I dive there doesn't mean it isn't still negative space. I found something good about an empty used-up quarry. It's positive space now." I rose onto the balls of my feet with certainty, then came back down on my heels with a thump.

Carrère

Carrère and Barber met for dinner at the club one winter evening. They discussed the library, Barber's projects, and general minutiae regarding the business, New York, and their respective families. Carrère particularly enjoyed his pork and peas.

Afterward, they watched a chess game for a few minutes. Black was in great peril, with an enemy knight having forked its queen and king. Pool and billiards were underway in the next room. Carrère enjoyed the arrhythmic clicks of the balls making contact with each other.

"I like this club, Barber said. I enjoy tour tennis matches in the summer, too."

"I second that. Shall we retire for a cognac?"

"An excellent idea," Barber said as if this were the first and not the fortieth or hundredth time Carrère had suggested it.

The waiter, Mr. Potter, appeared a few moments later with a snifter of Courvoisier for Carrère and Hennessey for Barber. Their preferences and patterns seldom changed.

"Someone said that there is no separation between artist and art. What do you think of that?" Carrère asked.

Barber was incredulous. "That's impossible for me," he exclaimed. "There is always a voice telling me what to do. It's not possible to be your art."

"A voice?"

"Yes, and at those moments there is quite a separation, at least for me."

Carrère thought of Stanford White. "I think at times he is 'one with his art'." When he is, which is perhaps quite often, he produces his best work. Look anywhere in New York. The Century Club, right here." Carrère spoke slowly, trying those ideas for the first time. "If the artist is 'in the moment' without fear or preconceptions, creating should be natural and heavenly. In this state, the artist and his art are one. Don't you think it's a wonderful feeling to be *one* with your work or to *be* your art?"

"What happens when the piece is finished?" Barber asked, keeping pace with Carrère. He adjusted the suspender strap over his right shoulder.

"When it's finished, it's *back there* and you're no longer in it. Only then, as you are doing it, is there the possibility of being one with the art."

"So you can't be *one* with something that *was* but no longer *is?*"

"That's about the size of it," Carrère said.

"So what about this monograph you're putting together?" Barber asked. "Are you in it if you are not working on it right this moment?"

"Well, I frequently have to set it aside, sometimes for many months. And when I return, I feel like I am outside it. It takes a while to be one with it again."

"So what happens when you're away from it?" Barber probed.

"It can't be anything without me. So it sits there on a shelf in a box."

"Is this why you say there is no separation between an artist and his art?"

"Not until the artist lets go. It helps if the artist knows when to let it go. But that's another topic." He crossed his legs and gently sipped his cognac.

"I see your point," Barber said, "but I am not sure this is the case for everyone. Perhaps Stanford received the creative ideas from somewhere outside himself, and he is only the transfer vehicle to humanity." Barber leaned forward in his chair, coming closer to Carrère as he sat across a coffee table from him. "Some artists create from within, or internally, and others create with eternal stimulus or a preponderance of it."

"Does it matter what kind of work the artist does?" Carrère started to feel like a pupil.

"Wouldn't you think so? An architect receives different stimuli than a composer," Barber said. He arched his eyebrows, too.

"Architects mostly get static," Carrère said, "from clients."

Barber said, "I know the feeling. We architects are prone to interference from those who hire us, and our efforts are often polluted by what we might think to be superfluous ideas. But Beethoven, even as deaf as he became, created his symphony from within."

"Yes, that may be true," Carrère said. "Brahms said that the ideas flowed in to him directly from God."

Barber grunted. He grunted when he was baffled or outfoxed or just too tired to go on. "This is going around and around. What if we just say we're *immersed* in the project?"

"Well, let's look back at Hastings and his portico," Carrère said, again assuming the role of teacher. "If he were simply immersed in it, then the possibility is implied that he is separate and distinct from the portico." Carrère paused and drew a deep breath. The waiter picked up now empty snifters and moved away unobtrusively. "I think, though, when he drew the capitals, which he did with such commitment and energy, there was no separation between himself and his capitals. They were actually one being or one entity, and it was amazing to witness." Carrère was pleased with himself. They had not yet been executed in marble, but the plaster models were sufficient evidence for him to make this point.

"You have spoken of taking drawings away from Hastings or else he'll work them to death."

"That's very true. As Hastings approaches a mastery of something like the capitals, they cease being something he can *finish* and increasingly become a connected part of him. The good thing is that when he walks away from the drawing, he's not attached to it any longer. It's not wrenching for him. It really is *back there*." Carrère rose from the depths of the comfortable chair and walked to a window. It had snowed. On the street below, a mix of wheel tracks and hoof prints broke the snow.

Barber came to his side and said, "As we talk about it, I realize that I love creating something new. Sometimes I'm fully in it, sometimes fully outside; sometimes part way in, and sometimes that varies as the thing unfolds."

"It's different for different artists, and different at different times," Carrère agreed. "These days, I administer projects and critique the work of others." It was not a bad role to have at Carrère & Hastings, because it allowed him to watch how Hastings and other artists worked.

"I agree with this, John," Barber said, "and I can see how you can make your best stuff when you're, as you say, *fully in it*. This might explain to some extent why artists sometimes have a terrible time arriving at something they like."

"And why some artists go insane."

Barber nodded. "I think we should work on this theory again sometime."

Carrère endorsed the idea and they departed the Club, each hailing a taxi. As his taxi passed the Library on Fifth Avenue, even in the darkness of night, Carrère saw that there was no new stonework. Too cold for the mortar, he grumbled to himself.

Carrère

More and more Carrère thought about spending the summer in Europe, getting as much rest as possible.

"It would refresh you," Miss Bough said.

He looked at a chart on the wall outlining the progress of at least a dozen commercial and residential jobs. "I want to visit libraries in England, France, and Italy, but will do no more work nor sightseeing than will break the monotony of the trip."

"You haven't told me about Vermont yet," Miss Bough said.

"I liked the quarry," he said. "It was good to see where the marble comes from."

"Did you write anything down?" Miss Bough asked.

"I did, but I'm not sure yet what it is that is on my mind. I have to find some answers, but they're not here. Maybe in Europe." Carrère rubbed his hands together.

"Will the family travel with you?"

"Yes, of course. Marion enjoys Florence."

Miss Bough handed him the finished draft of the specifications of the stacks. It was June of 1903.

"This is it, all fourteen pages," she said. "And here is the covering letter addressed to Doctor Billings." The stacks had to be strong, neat, and symmetrical in appearance. It had taken Brainard and Cooper, the consulting engineer, some months to design the stacks.

"Thank you. Send it to Billings. Everything will be in order when I return, I'm sure," said Carrère.

"You won't even have to think about it," Miss Bough said. "It'll be done."

"I'm not sure where this firm would be without you," Carrère said. He was looking Miss Bough in the eye. "You keep everything going."

Miss Bough blushed faintly. "It's my job," she said. "You are so fully occupied—the Library, your family, the book, Hastings—you deserve a vacation."

"You forgot the American Academy of Arts and Letters. They just elected me to the Board." Carrère felt his shoulders sag.

"You are a busy man," Miss Bough purred. "Just go to Europe and forget about New York. Things will be fine, and I'll report how Hastings is doing when you get home."

"I won't miss the rat race, but I'll miss you," Carrère said. She wheeled out of his office. He stood, looking at the spot where Miss Bough had been a moment ago, assessing what he had just said, and what that would mean in the future. She had a talent for keeping the office running smoothly and for understanding the feelings of others. A woman's intuition, he reckoned.

Carrère

Marion and Carrère packed their steamer trunks in preparation for the voyage to Europe. Marion's was already nearly full, while his was empty, its lid up. He recalled purchasing the trunks at Crouch & Fitzgerald several years before. He remembered the cat and all the empty trunks. His thoughts drifted: Is a marble quarry ever empty? "Marion," he asked, "is your trunk large enough?"

"I think it will be," Marion replied, folding a sweater on top. "There's plenty of room."

Carrère shrugged, wondering why this notion of emptiness and space kept returning to him. "My trunk is still empty. You can put something in, if you need to." Still slowly, it came to him that when you fill space, you change it.

"There," Marion said. "All done. My trunk is ready."

"I guess my trunk will be half empty," Carrère said. "The porters will notice how light it is."

"The most important thing is that we have a nice time," Marion said. "The marble will start to arrive, and when we get home, there'll have been lots of progress." She tucked several handkerchiefs into the trunk.

"Oh, I hope so," Carrère said, while folding trousers and placing them in the bottom of his trunk. They sailed aboard the *George Washington* of the North German Lloyd line. As always, they traveled first class, which cost $112.50 each. First class fares kept going up and up. They were assigned State Room No. 62. They played a fair amount of shuffleboard. Carrère visited the barbershop. Marion spent time in the gymnasium. The food was quite good: haddock, roast pork, leg of mutton, roast hare, and pheasant. One evening, they had *tutti frutti* ice cream for dessert. Marion always preferred a dockside landing, but the *George Washington* was too large for dockside in Cherbourg. So they were brought to shore by a tender. They spent four weeks in Paris dining with some of his old school friends, attending the theater, and strolling the river.

One day Marion remarked, "You seem different when you're away from the office. I like it this way."

He may have been different because he felt different. Although he loved Paris—it brought back good memories—he missed the daily energy at the office. "This is the break I needed," he said. But he didn't mean it. In truth, he wanted to get back to find out about the situation with the stacks and to see how the secretary had fared with Hastings.

Carrère

On August 31, upon Carrère's return, the Park Department approved the specifications for the stacks and bids were advertised. But Carrère & Hastings hadn't made the final drawings. This revelation came in the mail, and it was Miss Bough who delivered the letter to Carrère.

"Who approved the specifications without telling us? How are we going to make final drawings in just a few weeks?" he whined. Carrère rested his head on his desk. "It seems like I never went on vacation."

The next day, he gathered several of the job captains to discuss what was needed and how quickly. The meeting took place in the cluttered temporary office building next to the Library. The place was stacked with drawings on one table, books on another, and jammed with stools around the ten other tables. Carrère hoped the new Library would never become such a God-awful mess. With

Brainard seated on a stool to his left, Carrère said, "We've got to make final drawings of the stacks as quickly as can be done. *En charrette.*"

Brainard looked up, "What's that?"

"It means we have to do it in a fearful hurry." Carrère explained, "In Paris we made drawings at the atelier, and then took them to the Ecole in a little handcart or charrette. Sometimes we made last minute changes to the drawings as we rolled the cart through the streets. Hence *en charrette.*"

Brainard regarded this for a minute and said, "It sounds like something Hastings would have done."

"Oh, we all did. Too much work, not enough time." Carrère said. "Someone in the Park Department put the stacks job out for bid. If we can publish drawings now, we will have saved everyone a lot of time and trouble."

Delano, one of the job captains, said, "I think we could give you the drawings fairly quickly."

Carrère glanced at him. "The deadline for the submission of bids is October twenty-ninth, so the drawings need to be ready within the next few weeks."

"I don't think that will be a problem," Delano grinned, obviously relishing the challenge.

They had received bids from four contractors. Miss Bough gave the bids to Carrère: he placed them in rank, from high bid to lowest, across his desk. It appeared that the framing decisions within the Snead proposal were the best. "I think we should recommend to the Board of Estimate that Snead & Company be awarded the contract," Carrère said.

"Snead's isn't the low bid," Miss Bough said.

"There could be trouble with this contract." Carrère tried to think the problem through. He tapped the squared end of his pencil lightly on the table and looked blankly into space. "You know, these bids are actually false, because they were made on specifications not originally intended."

"So what's going to happen?" Miss Bough said.

"The low bidders will sue, and we'll have to start over. Just watch." Carrère straightened in his chair. "Nothing is easy around here. Nothing changed while I was away."

Miss Bough disagreed. "Hastings invited me over to his house. Helen is wonderful."

"Where's the painting?"

"I didn't see it. I found a kitten and brought it to them. Helen adored it. I don't know what they named it though."

Carrère could never invite Miss Bough to his house. There would be no chance of that. It seemed to Carrère that Marion was glad to have him away from the office and away from Miss Bough over the summer. He became edgy. "You brought them a kitten?"

Miss Bough said, "I'll get something for you sometime. Only for you, not for Marion." She gave him a little smile that suggested something, and at once he felt a little relieved. She added, "The Board of Estimate said that they're going to throw out the whole contract and start over."

"Start over?" Brainard came into the room.

"That's right," Carrère said, shaking the paperwork in front of him. "The low bidders appealed."

By autumn 1903, Carrère was up to his neck again in contracts and negotiations, with little time to think about the summer vacation in Europe. He met with Brainard and Hastings yet again to review the stacks.

"We needn't have rushed those drawings after all," Hastings said.

"The plans were never formally approved last summer," Carrère shook his head.

Hastings leapt to his feet. "What do we do now? Do we have to start over, too?"

"We need to have better control," Brainard said. "We should make a model, but not until we study more carefully the framing requirements."

Carrère added, "We should clean up the language in the specifications. It should become impossible for irresponsible or incompetent contractors to misconstrue the information presented and send in a bogus bid. But let's start with revising the plans and specifications we made last summer."

"We'll get started right way," Brainard said cheerfully, bouncing toward his office.

"I wonder how he can be happy about doing it over again," Carrère wondered aloud.

"It's a tremendous pain," Hastings agreed, and it's their fault. "We have to do it again because they put the contract out before it was ready." Hastings shook his head slowly, and then stood up straight and folded his arms on his chest. "You know," he said in an even voice, "Miss Bough is the cause of a lot of problems around here. I've decided you should let her go."

"What makes you think that? She does excellent work, is very dependable. I can count on her when everything around here is crazy. Right now, for example— the bids for the stacks."

Hastings half-sat on a table. "It's the other things. I think she likes me and you, and that's trouble. No mistresses around here."

"You have one of the paintings!"

"Helen thinks Miss Bough is dangerous, and she thinks you should fire her."

"What does Helen mean by dangerous? Are you Helen's poodle?"

Hastings seethed. "How are we ever going to work together with this issue between us? I am not Helen's poodle!"

"We've been partners for many years, Thomas," Carrère assured Hastings. "I think you're up-in-arms over something that is very minor. You need to stay focused on design."

"And for Christ's sake, just manage the contracts," Hastings huffed.

"Miss Bough stays because she helps so much with the correspondence and all that. I need the expert assistance. I hired her, she stays. And you're not Helen's poodle, but keep her out of our business."

Hastings turned to leave for the day. "Okay John, Miss Bough stays. She's very unstable, you know."

"I think we're all unstable," Carrère called after Hastings. "You are. I am. Miss Bough is. This Library could break us all!" He propped his elbows on the table and rested his forehead in his hands. This is insane, he sighed. My partner attacks me over a secretary, even though he has one of her portraits in his house. The stacks have to be redrawn. What's next? What's next?

Carrère

By August 1904, they had finished a new plan for the stacks. "It's taken a long time, but the stack plan has now been formally approved by the Library, the Park Department, the Corporation Counsel, and the Board of Estimate," Carrère announced in a morning meeting. "Now we can put the job out to bid again."

The bidders erected models of their proposed stacks in the Central Park Arsenal. It was a dark, cavernous place where voices echoed and flies buzzed about in the thick, humid air. Carrère hated flies. Overhead, bare light bulbs hung from the roof trusses, causing shadows that dramatically lengthened or shortened as Carrère, Billings, Brainard, and Hastings moved about the models. "I hope we can make the correct decision and avoid all the troubles of last year."

The bids waited in their sealed envelopes on a desk near the models. Billings produced a pocketknife, and with some drama and deliberation, carefully slit open each envelope. He removed the contents of each, and with exaggerated ceremony placed them on the table around which they had gathered. He closed the pocketknife with a conspicuous *snap*, set it on the table, and folded his arms.

Several minutes passed as the men examined the bids. Carrère shook his head in wonder at what he saw. "How is it possible to produce something other than that which we specified? Some of these models aren't even close."

Brainard said, "The Snead model appears to be of the highest quality."

Carrère examined the paint on the Snead model, leaning close to the shelving and running his palm along a painted surface. "You're right. The Snead model is the best. Where's their bid in relation to the others?"

"Second highest," Billings called out as he checked the figures.

"I think we will have to recommend Snead to the Board of Estimate," Carrère said cautiously. He looked at each of the other men and each nodded in agreement. "Remember when we tried to award the contract to Snead last year, the lower bidders cried foul."

Hecla Iron Works secured an injunction to stop the award of the contract for the stacks. Hecla had not furnished a good enough design, and therefore did not win the contract. Carrère intended to fight.

Miss Bough assured him, "You're on the right side; they're wrong." She looked great in a new dress. But her voice was nasally.

"You have a cold," he observed. "When did you come down with it?"

"I visited my sister over Thanksgiving and her children are all sick. I must've caught it from them." She sneezed into a handkerchief and smiled wanly.

"If you're ill, you shouldn't be here. You'll pass along your cold to everyone else. Why don't you go home?"

She resisted the suggestion. "I like being here." She sneezed again.

"You really should stay home until you feel better," Carrère insisted. He started shifting some things about on his desk.

"I have a couple of things to do first. I'll go home early but not now," Miss Bough said, gathering her skirt and twirling out of the office.

He studied the legal notice further. If it wasn't bad marble, then it was litigation, Hastings, Miss Bough. Thinking that he'd had enough, Carrère left for home. It was only noon. He walked down Fourth Avenue purposely to avoid the Library. He gave a panhandler a dime, stopped in a furrier's shop to look at a mink coat for Marion, just avoiding being run over by a milk wagon while crossing Thirtieth Street. He liked the freedom of spending the day as he pleased. He knew he wouldn't miss anything at work and that they weren't going to miss him.

He reached home at two o'clock feeling pretty good about the day. He tossed his hat on the front hall table, hung up his coat, and brought Marion the afternoon edition of the *Tribune*,

Marion was surprised to see him, "What brings you home so early?" Her voice was frosty.

"I had enough of all the craziness at work. Wanted to come home, get away from it. I won't miss anything; nobody will miss me."

Marion accepted a kiss on the cheek and then led him into the parlor, where to his horror, the two Miss Bough paintings sat on the mantel leaning against the wall.

"I know that's Miss Bough in those paintings, I recognize her," Marion said coldly. "Why do you have them in our house?" Her face was white and her eyes nearly black. Her auburn hair was wrapped in a tight bun. She was the picture of upper class virtue, and she demanded answers.

He was too stunned even to stammer an explanation. His shoulders dropped. He felt that he must have shrunk from his normal stature into something rather pathetic and uncomfortable in the extreme. Why had he ever brought them home? What was he thinking? What would he ever do with them here? He tried to explain but couldn't even begin.

"Well?" Marion insisted.

His earlier inner calm had become a maelstrom. Nothing was right at the office. And now the trouble had come home. Did he even have a sanctuary anymore? Nothing like this had ever happened in Paris. It was his own stupid fault, and now Marion wanted answers right then and there. Where was he to begin this tale? She'd only met Miss Bough once. He glanced at the two paintings, but opened his mouth and nothing came out. He tried again, "It's a short story."

It was Marion's turn, "I was looking for a gardening book, and these two pictures fell out of one of your books. You must have been hiding them." She accused him, gesticulating dramatically.

"I had to put them somewhere."

"You had to bring them home? Why do you have two pictures of Miss Bough in the nude?" Marion's voice rose a notch. "Miss Bough must be a mistress, is she not?"

Carrère begged, "Marion my dear, she is not an adulteress nor is she conniving, and she doesn't want to be anyone's mistress. You must sit and listen to this." Carrère started to tell her what he knew about Miss Bough, and why he had those two identical paintings of the secretary. Marion listened attentively.

"Now I know what's happening to you —"

"No you don't," Carrère protested. "She's an assistant at the office and that's all. Don't misunderstand."

"No, it's quite clear to me," Marion beat her drum. "She covets you!"

"I don't think she does."

"—Because she never won your friend Horace, and I know even further because she let you have the pictures." Marion stomped her foot for emphasis.

"We all need help," Carrère said, his voice plaintive. He was sweating visibly, his armpits drenched. "Hastings is out of control, and I'm up to here," He held his hand above his head, "with all the legal business and Miss Bough needing something, but I don't know what."

"You three ought to sit down and figure out what the problem is, if as you say there is so much going wrong." Marion squared herself in the chair, absolutely sure of the correctness of her observation and insight.

"Oh, I don't know about that," Carrère sighed. "Thomas wouldn't like it, and who would moderate the meeting?"

"You'll have to figure that out for yourself."

"So, what do you think of the *Miss Boughs*?" Carrère said, attempting to lighten the conversation, to elevate it somehow.

Marion hissed, "I think they're unsightly and unnecessary. I won't allow them in the house! I'll have the maidservant remove them in the morning, or else you can do it yourself."

"I'll take care of them," Carrère said, rising slowly from his chair. Without looking at the *Miss Boughs* he removed them from the mantel. He had decided to fly them off the upper deck of the Staten Island ferry in the morning.

He took the early ferry, faced the Statue of Liberty, and backhanded them into New York's bustling harbor, watching them spin, tilt, and slice into the brown water below. *No one would ever see them again.*

Interlude

We looked at more houses, and the more I looked, the more I became unhappy with what I was seeing. Everyone had a bad kitchen or the bedroom was too small. If there was a greenhouse, it was in poor repair. Even if the house had some nice attributes, they would never outweigh the bad spaces.

"This is a really nice family room," Peri would say. "A large picture window, the deck outside. . ."

And I would say, "Yeah, but that closet off the upstairs hall, it's too spooky."

"You're not going to spend any time it!"

"I just can't have any negative spaces in my house."

This went on and on, every house we looked at seemed to have an unacceptable negative space. Peri was becoming exasperated. "Our apartment is full of negative spaces. You can live with *them*."

I leaned against a fence outside the ranch we had just looked at. "It does and I can, because I didn't know they were negative spaces until after we had lived there for a while."

Peri shook her head back and forth. "You mean we have to keep looking until we find a house that has no identifiable negative spaces?" I didn't want to say so, so I didn't. I let Peri continue. "I guess we'll have to live in a barn!"

"A barn is positive space because animals live there, so it's good. But you wouldn't want to live with cows or in a place that smelled like cow shit."

Peri began to cry with frustration. "I would consider a barn negative space because people can't or don't live in it."

I realized then and there that we were shopping for a definition—whether spaces within a house were negative or positive. Pity the realtor. "If we lived under the sky we'd have no problems with space," I suggested, facetiously of course.

"But the sky is really just part of space, outer space, where the astronauts go," she said, playing along. Suddenly she turned very serious. "You wouldn't really live outside?"

"No, I'm an architect."

Later, I found Jayne furiously crumpling paper cups and hurling them into the wastebasket in her office. "I can't stand it, can't stand it," she was wailing. She had crumpled and thrown eight or ten cups.

"What can't you stand?" I asked from outside her office.

"I can't stand the fact that you are letting a fixation on negative space—"

"It's not a fixation," I protested. How would she know anyway, except for that one conversation I had had with her? "It's not bothering you anyway."

"Yeah it is, because Peri sent me an email asking me if I knew anything about it." She crumpled another paper cup and fired it into the trash can. "See, I'm destroying negative spaces! And your wife can't bother me with this!"

I agreed with that. Peri shouldn't have done that. About the negative spaces, I said, "It's no problem really. I want to design a house without any negative spaces. It'll be grand."

Jayne stopped smashing the paper cups and said, "I don't know how you're going to do that. Is it going to have walls?"

"I haven't figured that out yet but it's going to be perfection, as if God himself—"

"—herself—"

"—no, himself, because the god in question is me." I jabbed my thumb into my chest. "It's going to be perfection because I know what negative space is now, and there isn't going to be any in my house!" I felt pretty good about myself after saying that.

"What's Peri going to say or think?"

"She doesn't know anything about it because I haven't told her yet. And don't you dare email her either!"

Jayne actually looked. She sat down and leaned away from me. "Whatever you say, sir. But we have to forward the Farms' electrical drawings to the electrical contractor. They called today. Have you done that?

I hated reality. One minute, the perfect, divinely designed house with no negative spaces, then a moment later, electrical drawings. Reality was no fun at all.

Carrère

The richly paneled courthouse chambers of Justice William Dickey turned out to be, ironically enough, very pleasing and comforting. They reminded Carrère of the family's house in Baltimore where he grew up. He had always loved to run his knuckles across the wainscotting. Now in court, he had to refrain from reengaging his old childhood habit. That was all right, though, for they were going to beat Hecla down. He was looking forward to telling Miss Bough that they had won.

McCord, a tall, angular attorney representing Hecla, argued that the court should nullify the awarding of the contract to Snead & Company. Justice Dickey, a small man dressed in black robes, asked Billings for his account of the bid selection procedure.

Billings stood. "Your honor, Mister McCord will claim that the contract was won by Snead through misrepresentation and suppression of fact. That is not true, as I will explain." He straightened his waistcoat. "The only people involved were myself, Messrs Carrère & Hastings, and Mister Brainard, the civil engineer employed by Carrère & Hastings."

"Do you know a Jacob Costuma?" the Justice asked.

Billings answered, "He is a general foreman for the Park Department who was working at the Arsenal, where the models were set up."

"What do you know about Mr. Costuma?" the Justice turned to McCord.

"Mr. Costuma talked about swinging the contract to a certain bidder, irrespective of the amount of the bid, if he were paid," McCord replied.

That was complete hooey, Carrère grumbled to himself.

Justice Dickey, examining documents, continued. "According to an affidavit submitted by the District Attorney's office, there is no evidence that Snead & Company received the contract otherwise than on the merits of its bid."

He peered at McCord, who sullenly looked down. "In addition, there is an affidavit here from Mr. Costuma's wife. It states that her husband had gone to

Florida about three weeks before, and that she did not know where he was and did not know his postal address."

He wasn't even here!

Justice Dickey issued his decision. "I see no reason to rule in the Hecla Company's favor, and therefore, refer the bid award back to the Board of Estimate."

Carrère checked his watch. The hearing had lasted only a half hour. But McCord was huddled with Niels Poulson, Hecla's president, no doubt developing another maneuver. It wasn't over yet.

Carrère

Carrère was reorganizing books in his office when Miss Bough presented him with the current issue of the *Brooklyn Taxpayer*. "Have you seen this?" she asked. "Poulson has a very long letter on page one."

Carrère quickly slid some books onto the shelf. "Poulson? What's he say?"

"I could read the whole thing out loud but it's very lengthy," Miss Bough explained. "Let me assure you the whole letter is sour grapes." Hastings and Ward appeared in the doorway to his office.

"That's right. His proposal was not as good as some of the others, even though his bid was lower. Carrère ran his hand across his thinning hair and straightened his tie as if someone important were about to enter the room.

"We're not going to compromise basic standards." Hastings, slapped his hand on Carrère's desk. "Hecla wasn't good enough."

"I hope this is the last we will hear from Hecla, and I think we'll finally be able to move ahead with the stacks contract," Carrère said.

The next Friday, March 23, one of the draftsmen gave Carrère a copy of the day's *Daily News*. "This is nonsense!" Carrère exploded. Hastings and Miss Bough hurried in. "Now the press is accusing Billings of nepotism !"

Carrère read the headline. *Easy graft in Library Contracts! Learned and ingenious rogues. One of the contracts in Connection with the New Library on Fifth Avenue the Channel of Thievery. High up New Yorkers and an honored U.S. Official at Washington Implicated.* "Where did they make this up?" Carrère said. Hastings rolled his eyes. What could be next? They had had bad marble, bad weather, and now these contracts. And the press was all over them!

Carrère

Carrère wanted to discuss the monograph with Miss Bough. It had come to mind again. "I'm thinking about the book more now. I want it to be more than just a dry monograph. I want to tell some of the stories."

"You want to write a novel?" asked Miss Bough. She was just as bright that morning as ever. "That certainly would be more interesting to more people than a dry account of the building itself." She adjusted the simple gold bracelet on her left wrist.

"A novel. I've never thought of writing fiction, and I have no idea how. But I can see that it makes sense. The Library was built by people *for* people. It was never just there, as the marble was. He thought of the quarries in Vermont and how the marble had been brought to New York by people to be made into something useful.

Miss Bough said, "A novel is a much bigger project than the monograph." She removed a dictionary with a brown leather cover from the bookshelf in Carrère's office and read, "*Monograph. Noun. A written account of a single thing.*" She looked over the top of the dictionary toward Carrère.

"I realize that. I am not afraid of challenges though." Carrère paused for a moment. "When Tommy and I started out, McKim, Mead, and White were the biggest and most powerful firm in the country. We wanted to be as successful as they were. We were driven."

"And ambitious," Miss Bough added, adjusting her blouse cuffs at her wrists. "Your goal has changed,"

"Yes, ambitious. But this book has little to do with ambition. Instead, it is personal." He stared at Miss Bough, noticing and enjoying the dimple in her left cheek. "I want it to be good."

"People will be more interested in knowing about the human beings in this story. It's through the people, not the facts, that the story of the Library's construction will come alive." Miss Bough smiled. She always made things seem easy. Carrère would have to thank her somehow, but just how eluded him at the moment.

"Now I want to get started."

"One detail: the Library's not finished yet," Miss Bough reminded him.

"That is a problem, isn't it?"

"I am not so sure it is," Miss Bough closed the dictionary. He briefly considered how to invent fictional characters in a novel. A pigeon alit upon the ledge outside the office window. "Well, I know this much," Carrère said, "Polhemus is gone. Now I've got Ward to help me."

Miss Bough asked, "How are you going to make sure you don't overwork the book the way Hastings—"

"I haven't thought about it. I guess it's my right to do as much, or little, as I please." He glanced at the pigeon.

"How can that be?" Miss Bough challenged.

"Because the book is mine, and that's the difference between the Library and the book. I'll never own the Library—none of us will—but the book is mine."

Miss Bough eagerly pressed ahead. "But you want to know what happens when the artist no longer has command of his art. You say it won't matter because it's yours." Carrère listened carefully though with some skepticism. "It only matters in the context of Carrère & Hastings and the costs, is that it?"

"Don't forget Horace Avery!"

"Ah, how can I ever forget Horace," Miss Bough smiled, a dreamy look washing over her face. "He was stuck, though—the opposite of your concern. You won't ever know Horace's frustration."

"That never happened to Hastings, or to me back when I used to draw and design." Carrère couldn't imagine being stuck, unable to work, to create. He'd always wondered what allows or causes artists to go overboard. And what happens when they do—is the artist still in control of his work? Suddenly he admitted, "Maybe the Library book is already stuck, and I haven't even started!"

"It *could* happen to you," Miss Bough said, her manner becoming quite serious, even severe. "You didn't believe me. What are you going to do? Aren't you scared?"

Carrère inhaled deeply and exhaled slowly. "I'm not scared. But I want you to help me. I don't think Marion can. She's still angry over the pictures. I don't want her help, and I don't want her to know—.

"But I haven't said that I will," Miss Bough said.

"It's a book. You won't have to take your clothes off to help me."

"Maybe I'd like to," said Miss Bough with gleaming eye.

Carrère's inner palpitations were hard to suppress. For a moment though, he did suppress them. "But his thoughts raced: What have I got myself into? No one can ever find out! I would be risking everything, and for what? But she is such a sweet thing. Maybe. I know she's here, at least for now. I've got to think and plan. Don't know. Don't know. "Let's do it," Carrère said, not really knowing what he meant by that.

"You never know," Miss Bough said, her eyes twinkling. "We'll try it sometime, but first you'll have to address this." Miss Bough explained that the builders were running out of the preferred Meiers cement being used in the Library construction. "They say no more can be found anywhere in the country."

Miss Bough gave the letter to Carrère. How could he think about cement knowing that she was going to "help" him with the book? The pigeon flew away and Carrère opened the window, letting in the fresh air and street noise. Miss Bough told him that the remaining Meiers cement would be reserved for marble work. Regular Kane's cement would be used on the brickwork, even if it were close to the marble. "Thank you Miss Bough. We'll talk again about the book, sometime soon. I must talk with Brainard about this."

Carrère

In the drafting room Hastings discussed the Fifth Avenue façade with George Barnard, a rotund sculptor who was going to create the figures in the pediments at the north and south ends of it.

"An excellent idea," Hastings was saying. "Whenever I see the façade I get new ideas " Ward walked in, placed a half-dozen façade elevation studies on the table, and looked around to see who was there. "Please join us, Ward. We're going to look at the façade."

The steps leading from the sidewalk to the portico were complete. Windows hadn't been glazed yet and the sculptures for the niches at either side of the portico were still absent. Neither pediment's sculpture had been started. They walked carefully through construction debris, lumber, marble, tipped-over sawhorses, and the like.

Hastings squinted into the morning sun pointing out the south pediment and the correctness of its dimensions. Below the pediment, the decorative acanthus leaves on the Corinthian capitals curved outward, casting shadows beneath.

"See that?" he pointed toward the capital at the top of a column. "I love the shadow cast by an acanthus leaf on a capital."

"Is that so?" Carrère said.

"And you know what? Those shadows help me identify who carved the capital."

"What do you mean?" Barnard asked hands on hips.

"You're a sculptor, you know what I mean. Every artist uses the same vocabulary a little differently. Labrouste in Paris is different from Saint-Gaudens in America. I like figuring out who did the capitals and other carvings, and the shadows help me." He looked up at the capital, framing it with his hands held at arm's length. Hastings continued, "That's the space, right there." He pointed to the empty pediment above the capitals.

Passersby on the sidewalk, giving a tour to their out-of-town guests, mentioned that 'this building was going to be the new library or something like that.' Ignorant? Carrère thought. Maybe. Wait until it's done!

Barnard too squinted in the bright sunlight, "I need to know the measurements."

Ward quickly said, "The drawings have them."

Hastings suggested, "We think one group should represent the arts, and the other should represent history, to be emblematic of this Library."

"Classical figures consistent with the rest of the building," Barnard said, more to himself than to the others. Then speaking to Hastings and Carrère, "I'll show you some sketches in a few days."

Later in the afternoon Carrère explained the pediments to Miss Bough and said, "I'll give the information to Ward when he comes back." Ward had gone out for a visit to the barber.

"He's been wishing to help you. He says he wants to be more than the keeper of the drawings. You have to get going on the book."

"The drawings, that's a large job," Carrère said. "We'll make more than nine hundred before the Library is done. So he spoke with you about it?"

"He did," Miss Bough said. At times she was perfectly radiant, at others, she could be enigmatic. This time it was the latter.

"What did he say?"

Miss Bough revealed little. "Just that he wants to help you."

"You must know more than that."

"Okay. I see and hear everything that goes on around here," Miss Bough acknowledged. "You men have blinders on, doing your work, but my eyes and ears are open."

"That could be a little embarrassing for some of the younger men."

"It could," Miss Bough smiled, "but I don't tell anyone what I have heard. There are loose lips around here."

"About the ladies?" Carrère wanted to know more.

"Oh yes," Miss Bough continued, fixing a steady gaze upon him.

"What kinds of things do they talk about?'

"Oh, I don't tell," Miss Bough said with a mischievous smile. But I do hear about girlfriends from time to time. Sometimes it is racy."

"It might make a good story."

"For some writers," Miss Bough cautioned, "but not you." Carrère was taken aback. "You are good at some things, but you would not do well with saucy stories in the drafting room. Actually, most of them are terribly dull. You know very well the major people involved with the Library. Billings, Tom, yourself, Norcross."

And Miss Bough, Carrère thought, adding her name to the list. "You're right, as always. Many people are involved with the Library. I'll have to think about what they are doing, who is friends with whom, who does this or does that, and record the story of the Library with Ward's help. And your help?"

"Yes, and my help, too," she said, reiterating her offer.

"What should I do next?"

"Go have a word with Ward," Miss Bough recommended. "Give him this notebook. I'm sure you will be happy." She paused for a second, then added, "And then let me know."

Interlude

"Have you thought about designing a house, our house?" Peri had become tired of house hunting and having me veto every single one because of some negative space I didn't like. We were out for a bike ride and had stopped to refill water bottles. It was a warm and humid day.

"Well, you know what a lawyer that represents himself has, don't you?" I looked at Peri through my sweaty sunglasses. "He has a fool for a client."

"Oh, don't pay any attention to that crap," Peri said. "You're not a lawyer, and there would be nothing to lose or be lost."

I tugged down on the legs of my tight bicycling shorts. "It would be harder than you realize, because I'd have to design a house *without any negative space.*"

Peri pulled down on the legs of her tight bicycling shorts. At least we didn't wear matching shirts or have matching helmets, as if we were on a cycling team. "What do you mean by that? 'Without negative space'?"

"Every space in the house will have a purpose; no part of the house will be expected to enhance or define any other. That's what I mean."

Peri was ready to get going again. "I'm glad I'm not an obsessed architect," she said.

"You think I'm obsessed? With what?" I clipped one foot onto a pedal. "Is that why you emailed Jayne?"

Peri was on her bike and did a tight three-sixty around me in the parking lot. "Yes, and you are obsessed, and I don't want it to get out of hand. So I thought if you designed our house, you'd get this thing out of your system."

I mounted my bike and rode beside her. "I'm not sure it will. We'll have to find some land."

"That should be easier," Peri said as she shifted gears. "No negative space in a field or some old forest."

"Unless there's an old cellar hole or a well on the property. You just never know, especially in these old New Hampshire towns." I shifted gears as we started to go downhill.

"What if you lived on the moon with all its craters, negative space at every turn?

"We don't live on the moon, and all we have to do is find the right property. That really shouldn't be too hard."

Peri accelerated in front of me but I caught up. "I hope you're right," she said. "I don't think your negative space obsession is healthy."

Interlude

A few days later, Jayne looked at me with a puzzled expression. "If you're going to design a house," she said sipping a Pepsi through a straw, "it can't be negative or have negative space. According to your reasoning, that would be impossible."

"Are you saying that I am too picky about the houses we've looked at?"

Jayne continued, "You are, and this negative space thing is crap—"

"That's what Peri called it!" I thrust my hands into my pockets. Uh oh, what if my pockets were negative space. I yanked my hands out again.

"There can't be such a thing as negative space in a building that was constructed by people for the use of people."

"What about a jail, a prison?"

"Oh, a prison. You might be right. It might be negative space." Jayne tapped a pencil on her desk and then leaned back in her chair. "A prison, negative spaces—that might be a place for someone who committed a crime."

"I've never seen the inside of a prison," I said. "Imagine if the quarry were converted into a prison. Real negative space would be put to use." She looked at me with a weak smile. I shook my head vigorously. "They'd have to pump out all the water and that would ruin a good dive!"

Carrère

"I knew this was going to be a problem," Hastings looked at the model of the periodical room in January 1906. "The steel beams supporting the floor overhead are lower than the tops of the windows." He rubbed his chin and then looked at the ceiling. He and Magonigle pondered the situation in the future periodical room on the first floor of the unfinished library. As construction advanced, the Library itself was used as a drafting studio and office. The room was large enough to be used by twenty men at once and house models of various sizes. Dust and construction debris littered the floor. A stepladder spattered with paint leaned against an interior wall. Someone had brought peanuts; Hastings cracked one open and chewed thoughtfully.

"Yes, sir," said Magonigle, who had made drawings of the room. "We have a problem." He walked to the 40th Street window, turned his back to it and studied the offending beams.

"We can't lower the ceiling. We can't get rid of the beams," Hastings said, standing with his hands on his hips. "The beams are too close to the windows if we do nothing. It's just awkward."

"What do you think, Mister Carrère?"

"Shorten the windows, but that obviously isn't acceptable." Carrère noted that the windows on the 40th Street side would have to be shortened, "If we shortened only these two, it would look bad. We would have to shorten all the windows. But then that would change the whole Library, and we'd have to start over. No, we have to find an answer in what we already have."

Hastings found a scrap of paper and sketched the plan of the ceiling. His marks were straight and sure, even without benefit of a ruler or straightedge. Then, on another scrap he drew a section showing the beam and the wall. He tapped his pencil on the second sketch. He stooped for a clearer view into the model and then looked up at the beams again. "I'm going to have to bring this back to our drafting room and tinker around with it," Hastings finally said. "I just have to find a solution. It might take a little while. Sometimes when I keep drawing something, it's just to find the answer to a problem."

Carrère told Miss Bough about this. "This is exactly what I'm trying to understand," he said. They were in the office, Miss Bough at her desk. Carrère stood a bit impatiently first on one foot then on the other

"Perhaps his greatness comes from his unwillingness to be satisfied," Miss Bough said.

"Perhaps so, but I still want to know whether and at what point the art controls the artist.

Miss Bough stood and came around her desk. She led Carrère to his office and required him to sit in his desk chair, which was new. "I'm not sure you'll ever know with certainty." She showed him the day's mail, which she'd already placed on his desk. "Make yourself busy and stop thinking about Mister Hastings."

Carrère

One chill January day, everything in the city—the sky, the buildings (even the brownstones), streets and avenues, parks, the harbor—was a dispiriting gray. Christmas and New Years had passed, as had their holiday cheer. It was the routine, and Carrère was again consumed by the day-to-day necessities of keeping the Library on track. Donn Barber dropped in just to say hello and to catch up with old friends.

"Hi there!" Carrère bellowed across the drafting room. What brings you here? Why, I haven't seen you in at least a year."

Barber, with his overcoat open and flowing behind him, strode around several tables and shook his hand. "I see your Library every day—it looks great—but catching up with you and Tommy is impossible. So I just had to stop in and tell you."

Carrère sized Barber up. He appeared a little heavier than last time and his mustache had grown out. "Someone's feeding you right," Carrère said.

"And you, too," Barber smiled. "Now where is everybody? I expected to find a drafting room full of draftsmen. I don't see any."

Carrère said in a low voice, "Come into my office." Carrère abandoned a cup of tea in the drafting room. "Hastings is at the Library. Most of the men are at the office building over there. Brainard is away for the week. Miss Bough's mother's funeral is today. You picked a good time to visit."

"Hastings is at the Library every day," Barber said.

"Pretty much. He bothers the hell out of the contractors, I know that much. He's always wanting them to fix or replace something even if it's not defective."

Barber sat, tied one shoe, and crossed his leg. "Sounds like he's in control of the project."

"It's getting better. Once the marble started to arrive, the Library began to take shape, and our firm became a happier place." Carrère looked at his fingernails then used a letter opener on his desk to clean underneath them. "The stacks are on order and will arrive soon. The roof is nearly done. We're getting there!"

Barber noticed new drawings pinned to the wall. "Whose house is this?"

"That'll be my summer place, when I get around to it. We need to be able to get out of the city. I just haven't had any free time."

Barber didn't accept it. "I don't like that excuse!"

"It's true. The Library has my hands full. I want to write a book. Thomas, and Miss Bough—there's no end in sight."

"Is there something wrong? I always thought this was a perfect place to work. Never any friction. You and Tommy operate so well together. And Miss Bough. I thought she was going to be perfect for you."

"She is, but things are different now. I just don't want to go into everything here. Maybe some night I'll come over or we can talk at the club." Carrère said, thinking about Miss Bough and how what Barber had said was true. She was perfect for him. "Look, maybe you can help me with something."

Barber arched one eyebrow, inviting more detail.

"I'm still trying to figure out what makes an artist stop working or what allows him to never stop. It's been bothering me lately. Think about it and I'll come over sometime."

Barber was perplexed. "Okay, I'm game. I'll think about it, but I'm not sure I'll have any answers."

"I'm not sure there are easy answers," Carrère said as Barber pulled on his coat. "If I can understand, though, perhaps I'll be able to write my book and design my summer place, and make sense of what Hastings is doing."

Barber nodded slowly. "Sounds like there's trouble in paradise, I mean at Carrère & Hastings."

Carrère tucked in a loose shirttail and shrugged. "It's the way it is. I'll give you more details sometime, just not now." Once Barber left—it had seemed like a short visit. Carrère wondered if he had scared him? He decided to head home. As he waited for a taxi on Fifth Avenue, three fire wagons surged uptown. The hooves of the great gray horses pounded the pavement, unerringly throwing any muddy puddle water onto unsuspecting pedestrians. He jumped back, hoping to avoid the spray, but wasn't lucky. He regarded the situation with disgust: the overcoat was new, and his shoes had been shined by the boy next door to the barbershop. He had even had a haircut and shave, too, and with Barber's visit, he had been feeling pretty good. Marion was at home, as always, when he arrived. She was reading some periodicals.

"What happened to you, dear?" she asked, seeing his splattered attire.

"A fire wagon went through a puddle. The horses, you know, they're like a ship trough the sea sometimes, splashing." He shook his head. "Just bad luck, the wrong place at the wrong time."

Marion suggested, brow crossed, eyes dark, "You ought to take those clothes to the cleaner. I don't want mud in the house."

"Barber stopped by today. Good to see him."

"That's nice," Marion said hastily. "You should change now," she added.

"How was your luncheon group today?" Carrère made conversation.

"Oh, it was cancelled because Mrs. Greenough became ill. No one else was ready to serve fourteen ladies." Marion crossed her legs with the obvious intent of returning to her magazines. Carrère heeded cue and turned to slink up the stairs. "I don't like this anymore," he grumbled. He thought about the Miss Bough. She'll be in tomorrow. "I don't need any pictures of her."

Miss Bough returned to the office the next day. She set her plaid purse on the window ledge and inspected the heap of mail on her desk. Carrère approached gently, walking softly, not wanting to appear in any particular way as someone with an urgent matter. "I'm sorry about your mother," he said softly.

"Oh thank you for your sympathy. It was much harder for my sisters than for me. I just wish she could have died peacefully and that the police would finish their investigation."

"Investigation?"

"I thought you knew," Miss Bough explained with her arms crossed. "She was struck by an automobile uptown. She was in the wrong place at the wrong time." Miss Bough lowered her chin and shook her head slowly and began to weep softly.

He dared not comfort her. "Would you like another day off?"

"No sir, I would rather be here among normal people who are doing their job. I've had enough of sad and crazed people for now. I just want to get back to normal, thank you."

Carrère gave her a white handkerchief. "You know what it's like here, don't you? How can you think this is a safer place?"

"I hadn't talked with my mother in years." Miss Bough's tears dried up. "That's the difference. Mother wasn't part of my life anymore, but you and the Library, and—" she swept her arms grandly about, "everything—everyone else here, it's my family now, I love being involved and part of it!"

Carrère leaned against the wall. She still needed someone to love. Who's it going to be? he wondered. "Miss Bough, I still need your help on my book. Please feel free to remind me—"

"Oh I haven't forgotten," she said, hands planted on her hips. "You need me more than you realize."

Carrère couldn't tell whether the secretary was actually bereaved. "I think I'll let you catch up with the... the stuff on your desk. It looks like a lot."

"It will be a pleasure," Miss Bough stomped her foot for emphasis.

Carrère

In the next six months, Hastings didn't even touch the periodical room ceiling—no tinkering whatsoever. One morning, Carrère awoke having had a vivid dream in which he hung up one of the *Miss Boughs* in his upstairs hall. Miss Bough, in the painting on the wall beckoned him, curling a long index finger with alizarin crimson nail. As he came closer, she stood, letting drop the white knit shawl she had decorously been wearing. Miss Bough, keeping a mischievous eye on him, eased toward an overloaded bookshelf and returned with a tiny plaster model of the periodical room and winked at me. "This is what Mr. Hastings really needs," Miss Bough said softly. Carrère accepted the model and promised to give it to him. He cast his eye all over Miss Bough's nudeness and said, "Please, my dear, would you like to dance?" She accepted. "Such a wonderful idea! And Carrère, wearing white tie and tails, placed his right hand gently on her bare back, took her right hand in his left, and they began. They twirled and whirled around and around on a dance floor in a deserted party-tent, after all the guests had left the wedding reception. His tails flipped and flew. Miss Bough, wearing modest heels followed his lead. He drew her close and swam dreamily, intoxicated by the luxury of her supple form pressed into his. Miss Bough cooed in his ear with warm lusty voice, "I am your muse, and you can count on me!" And she kissed him in full blossom on the lips. Startled, he sat up, rubbed his eyes, and exclaimed, "He's got the solution!"

In the morning, Hastings burst into Carrère'c office, thrusting drawings into his face. "This is it!"

"I knew you'd have it this morning," Carrère said.

"How'd you know?" Hastings said.

"I had a dream," I said. "You solved the corner rooms."

Brainard came into the office as Hastings explained. "The structural beams running east and west are lower than the tops of the windows. This means the ceiling would cover the top part of the window." He looked around. "But it's not acceptable and needs some kind of treatment." Hastings's sketches showed hollowed out quarter spheres in the ceiling at each window. "Each sphere is a sort of interior awning," Hastings continued. "With them light can enter through the window, and the main ceiling remains where it is."

Carrère pointed at the repeated spheres symmetrically placed along the interior walls. "See what this original idea has done," he announced with increasing excitement. He turned the drawing over to reveal a ceiling plan on the back. "With the quarter spheres on both sides of the room, he created a three dimensional emphasis here with the hollows." He pointed at them in the drawings. "And that called for more sculpture and carving on the ceiling and a central oval panel." Carrère studied Hastings. "Am I right?"

"That's what I was thinking, but of course I didn't know this would be the result when I first thought of the spherical hollows," Hastings shrugged. "Isn't it amazing what happens when the moment is right?"

"What do you mean by that?" Brainard asked.

Carrère bounced up and down on the balls of his feet, excited to hear Hastings's answer.

"I got the idea, but I don't know how, then I thought the hollows should balance each other. So I added the interior hollows, which have no purpose."

"What about the ceiling?" Carrère pressed. "The carvings and the oval?"

"Those items just became apparent to me as I went along. The decorative vocabulary we have—it was natural. One thing leads to another."

"I think there's more to it than just that," Carrère said.

"I don't think so," Hastings said. "The beams blocked the windows. The half-spheres solved that problem and opened up other opportunities. It was fun."

"All right, I admit it must have been fun. And it's going to be excellent."

The next day, Carrère telephoned Barber to announce that he was coming over. "I've got to talk to you about Hastings, right now."

"Okay, c'mon over," Barber said.

Carrère hustled past Barber's front door without even knocking. It was a Saturday. Summer was in full swing, and the air was filled with delicious scents. "Where are you?" Carrère called.

Barber had been constructing a trellis for the garden. He emerged from a back workroom. His sleeves were rolled up, his dungarees covered with sawdust. "What's so urgent?"

"Hastings just hit the jackpot," Carrère panted. "He was stuck on that periodical room problem, and now he's not. The dam broke and he's himself again. Let me tell you!" Carrère shoved his hands in his back pockets but with his thumbs sticking out.

Barber, brushing off sawdust said, "Slow down, mate. What's so exciting?"

"Oh, it's brilliant. He's made a good design."

"Well I'm glad to hear that he's solved that particular design problem," Barber said, articulating each syllable. "Are you going to write about it in your book?"

Carrère's excitement dissipated instantly. "I haven't thought about it. This book might be more than I can handle. I don't know how. Who's my muse?"

Barber remarked dryly, "Isn't Miss Bough?"

Interlude

Having said that I wanted to design a house with no negative space, I set my mind to it. I studied precedents from the Romans through the Bauhaus. I pored through texts, monographs, reviewed design schemes I had developed at Columbia. I daydreamed about what the perfect house for us would be. A square, in plan? A polygon? A circle? No, none of these. The Golden Section! That would be it. The ratio of length to width is 1:1.618. The Parthenon in Athens was built according to these proportions, and it had no negative space (or so I was ready to believe. I had never seen it). Our house would rely on the Parthenon for precedent—audacious! I couldn't wait to tell Jayne of this inspiration. What if the rooms inside adhered to the Golden Section too? It would be so perfect. And if the house had no basement and no attic, there could not possibly be any negative spaces.

Carrère

A stately procession of wagons brought the marble drums to make up the portico columns from the cutting yard at Port Morris, up at the northern tip of Manhattan, to the construction site. The wagons, each drawn by two muscular horses, came to a stop in front of the Library. In a certain way, the wagons reminded Carrère of the caissons used in military funerals. The difference, of course, was that these wagons carried marble drums, not flag-draped caskets, and there was no riderless horse following them.

A sinewy-strong job foreman, Antonio Ricardi, took charge of the drums when they arrived. He had come to New York from Italy in the 1880s and wore a mustache and goatee. His leathery hands proved he'd spent most of his forty-two years working with stone. In his own language, he directed a gantry to hoist the fluted marble cylinders off the wagons. After a plinth was set in place, and with no fanfare, mortar was spread and the lowermost marble drum was then set. And in rapid succession, the other drums were hoisted into position, until all that was left to be raised was the elaborate Corinthian capital.

As the months passed, the marble drums were delivered, sorted, and assembled. The daily progress intoxicated Hastings, and yet he could still be analytical. "We made the correct decision to use segmented columns," he said.

"You originally wanted monoliths," Billings said, standing next to the architect observing the progress. Billings was a frequent visitor, at least once a week. "What was your reason for changing?"

Carrère explained, "Cost was a major factor. The drums were easier to move, carve, and install. Look here," He pointed to the joint between two drums. See how it's at the same height as the joint in the wall? We didn't want to interrupt the horizontal line."

"So there was an aesthetic consideration as well," Billings said.

"That's right," Hastings answered. He caressed the smooth, flawless white portico column with both hands and then rubbed his cheek on it.

"What about the capitals?" Billings inquired. "Are you happy with them, too?" A sharp wind nearly carried his top hat off his head.

"Oh, definitely!" Hastings walked to the green fence to take in as much of the façade as he could. "I copied Gabriel's capitals, but altered the spaces between the leaves and the shape of the leaves themselves. I might have done more, but Carrère thought they were fine and told me to stop."

"I didn't know," Billings said. A light delivery wagon clattered along Fifth Avenue followed by a new gasoline-burning Cadillac.

Hastings tilted his head back and reached out with both arms as if to embrace the capitals atop the columns. "They are my own interpretation of the order. They are perfect for this building." He dropped his arms to his sides and added softly,

"Now that they're up there, I can't change them."

Interlude

"It'll look like the Parthenon!" Peri's expression plainly suggested her belief that I was nuts. "That's a ruined temple in Athens with a lot of columns. How can our house look like that?"

We were in our apartment. Peri wore shorts and a t-shirt. I also wore shorts but had a short-sleeve collared shirt on." It won't look like the Parthenon," I insisted. "How could it? I'm talking about its plan dimensions and their perfect ratio." I explained the Golden Section and how that ratio appears in nature, and how it is satisfying to the eye.

Peri wasn't sure. "That means the long sides of the building are 1.618 times as long as the short sides."

"Right," I said. "Just think about living inside a building with proportions like that. Every time you look around, you will know you're in a perfect space, the anti-negative space space. This is what I'm going to do."

"Can you show me an example?" Peri asked.

Using a ruler and an ordinary sheet of paper I drew a tiny rectangle, which had two sides one inch long and two sides that were one and five-eighths inches long. "That's it," I said. I slid the piece of paper to Peri. That's the proportional shape of the Golden Section; and if I design our house in that shape, there'll be no negative space."

"But I want a greenhouse."

Jesus, I thought. A greenhouse appendage would introduce the exact sort of negative space I was trying to avoid. Tactfulness departed me at this moment.

"I could add a greenhouse on the south side, but it would be very difficult, and I don't think I could live there. I just couldn't."

"I think you could," Peri said.

"Wait a second, you don't understand," I began to whine. "This negative space issue is not negotiable. If it's there, I can't be. Get it? It's like smallpox—gotta stay away.

"Don't be so silly," Peri said. She had become hostile. We just need a house of our own. We can buy some cheap place and fix it up."

"No we can't! If it has that bad space in the cellar, I won't be able to sleep at night. I don't even want to go there!"

"All right, if you must, design our house. All I care is that it's done by winter. Make it comfortable."

Carrère

Hastings, Carrère, and others were visiting what was to become the reading room. "This must be a grand room, the grandest room," Hastings gestured fiercely about the great space. "I won't settle for anything less."

Billings wanted a glass partition running from the floor to the ceiling in the middle of the room, with the idea of closing off half the room whenever the room was not full. He marched across the room, stirring up small clouds of dust as he went. Ladders and piles of lumber had been stacked in the center of the room. "Two hundred ninety-seven feet long, seventy-eight feet wide, and fifty-one feet high could be one of the great rooms of the world. Billings's idea would ruin it."

Hastings had a pained look on his face as if someone were sticking a knife into the small of his back. He all but cried, "He wants to divide it!" He coughed violently on the dust in the air, and then doubled over until his coughing subsided. "We can't allow it," he hollered, "not in my life. We can't allow it!" Hastings turned in a full circle surveying the room.

"Billings says the screen would save on heating expenses," Magonigle said, playing devil's advocate that January morning in 1906.

"I can see the point," Hastings spit. "But I cannot see using glass. Glass is such a will-o'-the-wisp, elusive material. No, no, absolutely no!"

"We have to convince him," Carrère said, trying to project calm. Although he was in full agreement with Hastings, he betrayed none of the emotion that plagued Hastings at the moment.

"Maybe we could add some feature to the room that *he* would hate and then take it out in exchange for no glass screen," Ward suggested.

Carrère detected fraud. "You mean we would trick Billings?"

Hastings ended his rant, considering the tactic. "A small deception. We're not selling anything for money. We'll make a trade, that's all. A trade,"

"But it's deceitful, not open and honest," Carrère said, wide-eyed with disbelief that Hastings would go along with such trickery.

Ignoring his partner's caution, Hastings plunged ahead, "Let's think of things he might veto." He picked his way through debris along the east wall of the room, which was bathed in winter light pouring in through the eleven large windows in the west wall. He studied the bare walls, admiring the shallow reveals where the arches met the piers. Hastings cast his gaze along the eastern wall. "What if there were a railing about three feet from the wall?" he said. "I wouldn't like it. Maybe Billings wouldn't like it either." Hastings returned to the middle of the reading room, where Carrère waited with Ward and Magonigle. As Ward made notes Hastings explained,

"A railing that would stand about four feet away from the walls."

"What about the cost of such a proposal. Why do you think there should be a railing?"

Hastings drew a square with his toe in the dust on the floor. "I am not sure there should. I looked down the length of the wall, and the idea just popped into my head. But what if we traded the railing for Billings's glass screen?"

"How can we be sure Billings won't like the railing? I don't like what is taking place here. It's a deceitful enterprise that's going to cost the firm money. I can't go along."

Ward, the originator of the idea, stayed conspicuously quiet. Hastings said after a few moments' thought, "I'll sketch the railing and see how it looks." He rubbed out the drawing in the dust with his foot.

"That means our draftsmen will have to draw a railing that we detest, is that right?" Magonigle asked.

"Not yet. I'll draw it first, and if we like it, then the draftsmen will finish it up," Hastings said.

Carrère shook his head slowly. "Instead of a ruse, we should make the case for the room without a screen." He swept his arm around the immense space. "We should bring Billings here and just persuade him. We're good at that."

"His mind is pretty made up," Hastings said, doubt etched all over his face. "We should be prepared with more than our usual argument about aesthetics and beauty."

"I'm not going along with the idea until I see what you are thinking of," Carrère said. He thrust his hands unhappily into his pockets and started to leave. He couldn't help but notice the way seemingly innocuous things could grow and grow and become anything but. This idea to trade with Billings something that hadn't existed ten minutes before had no owner. But it had quickly acquired a life of its own and was betting bigger and bigger by the minute. How did this ever happen? When was he going—to—know—when—to—stop—? Carrère stood for a moment wondering and looking for answers

Carrère snuck softly down the marble stairs to the foyer, which had already become his favorite part of the Library, and then down the broad marble steps to the Fifth Avenue sidewalk. He looked both ways, crossed the Avenue, and walked up 41st Street, passing a panhandler he had not seen before. Someone standing in the open doorway of the building next to their building argued loudly with an unseen person inside. The source of the conflict was apparent: a large overturned pot of coffee on the front step. Someone must have dropped it. Perhaps it was too hot and the person who dropped it wasn't using potholders. It was just one of the myriad daily life struggles in New York City.

Once inside, Carrère slumped into his chair and considered the possibilities. The worst would be if Billings called their bluff. The railing seemed so risky. Wouldn't it have been better to rely on sound argument? How could Hastings go along with such a questionable idea? Carrère leaned back in his chair and started to fantasize about not working, sitting in a forest of chestnut trees, in which a million robins sang their spring songs. Out of the forest emerged Miss Bough with his manuscript finished and bound, ready to be delivered to a publisher. He blinked and shook his head. Miss Bough stood in the doorway. "May I help you, or are you here to help me?" he said.

"You don't look well," Miss Bough said.

"More of the same, but with a different twist," Carrère said, words just barely falling from his mouth. "Ward and Hastings have concocted this idea to deceive Billings, to prevent Billings from installing a partition in the reading room. I don't like the partition anymore than Hastings does, but I don't like the tactic they're going to use."

Miss Bough perched on the front edge of a chair otherwise occupied by several books. "Is there something else?"

Carrère sat up. "Within minutes of Ward suggesting the idea, it was already established and had a life of its own. There it was, and no one owned it, and everyone wanted to use it. How could that be?"

"When Hastings can't stop drawing an idea, you take the drawing away. Same thing, isn't it?"

"I can hide his drawings, but I can't hide this monster. It's not a drawing. If Billings ever finds out, why—"

Miss Bough counseled, "Just let them do what they think will work. I think Billings will agree."

Carrère stretched his arms overhead and arched his back. "I don't know how you can be so sure. You haven't tried to work with Billings. And Hastings isn't good at making presentations."

"You'll have to do it," Miss Bough said. She had a way of explaining the simplest things so that they made sense. "You don't have to have anything to do with them making the plan—"

"It's going to cost us a fortune," Carrère whined. "And I can't, I just can't abide lying to get what we want."

"You won't be," Miss Bough assured him. "I hear them coming up the stairs now. Just let it happen, and then let it die when it's over." She slipped out of his office. He made myself busy with correspondence, but he could overhear Hastings explaining to Magonigle what was needed.

"The railing has to be authentic. Nothing phony or fake."

Carrère thought, "I didn't go to the Ecole des Beaux-Arts in Paris to learn to how to trick our client."

"I think we can do it," Magonigle said carefully. "The railing should be intrusive enough to make Billings not want it. About thirty-two inches high, mahogany capped, mahogany posts every four feet."

Carrère covered his ears, not wanting to hear anymore, fearing the worst of outcomes.

A couple of weeks later, Magonigle had finished the drawings for the railing. The drawings were carefully executed in pencil, dated, and initialed "H. van Buren Magonigle" in the lower right corner. Hastings thought they showed his idea very well. "I like the wash you have added." He leaned over them to inspect. "Billings will see that we're very sincere about this feature."

I still felt that the railing idea was not right. "I agree the drawings are well executed, but we should be honest."

"I thought you were on board," Hastings said. He wasn't worried about the danger that Billings would like the railing. "This is going to work, I know it."

"What would your wife think of the idea?" Carrère demanded. Carrère knew that Helen sometimes helped Hastings think through and sort out sticky problems. Magonigle hastened out of the room, not wanting to hear our little spat.

"Well, she's not sure it will work," Hastings said, his voice low. "But I am. Plus I want to take a risk. It's exciting." He rubbed his hands together back and forth. "Oh, and what does Miss Bough think of this plan?"

"What she thinks doesn't matter," Carrère said, his defenses up.

"So you talked with her about it, did you?" Hastings taunted. "Is she your pillow? Soft and safe, who makes you feel nice and warm when things aren't going the way you want them?"

"That's enough," Carrère hissed through clenched teeth. "Just so that you know, Miss Bough thinks your plan will work. I don't agree with her, and I think what you're going to do is reckless and dangerous. I can't stop you, though."

"You'd like to. You want to stop me most of the time, thinking what I've done is enough or good enough."

Miss Bough glided into the room, and hearing the arguing, ordered them to stop. "What are you arguing about?"

Carrère studied the tops of his shoes, "We want to stop Billings's glass partition idea. It would be terrible. I don't think Mister Hastings's deception ploy is good. What if Billings likes it?"

Miss Bough said, "There's not as much risk as you think. Billings trusts you.

He'd never insist on the screen if you don't approve."

"How do you know? Carrère asked.

"I don't know Billings, but I do know you two, and you can do anything you want," Miss Bough clasped her hands behind her back.

"That's what I want to avoid," Carrère said. "It's dangerous. Nobody will own the results—"

"What are you talking about?" Hastings interjected.

"Let me bloody finish. Nobody will own the results, and nobody will be able to stop it. Just the same as when *you* can't stop. I think we shouldn't start down this road. It's fraught with too much peril, for us, for the Library…" Carrère's words trailed off. He knew that it was no use trying to stop the idea. It already had a life of its own.

Hastings said quietly, apparently not wanting to rub in his new victory, "I've done some of my best work when I don't stop. Look at the façade or the ceilings in the periodical room."

"You're right," Carrère admitted. "You are the master. I'll help you with the railing. We'll just bluff and Billings won't know what hit him, even after it's all over."

"Excellent," Hastings clapped him on the back. "We'll bamboozle him and he'll drop his idea of some glass partition. Hah!" Hastings danced a little jig of excitement out of the room.

Later, after everyone had gone home, Carrère spoke privately with Miss Bough in his office. "Why does it happen, how can an idea have a life of its own, even though it was created in the minds of men?" Everything was quiet. "If the artist dies, can the idea go on, even in the minds of other men?"

"What happened when Horace Avery died?"

"So the answer is yes, because you're standing right here in front of me, and I want to kiss you." He nudged the door closed with his toe and they did.

When it was over, all was still quiet, except for the sound of rain hitting the windowpanes. Carrère got up and saw that papers were strewn across the floor among her stockings and dress. What an exquisite, dangerous time. The railing was nothing compared to this. Hastings liked taking risks, he thought, and here he was, John Merven Carrère, risking it all: his marriage, his profession. The rain increased, spattering more noisily against the window. But then panic seized him. "Miss Bough," he said with urgency. "You'd better leave through the back door. I'll stay for awhile. He cracked open his office door. Miss Bough fled, her clothes fluttering down the stairs. She went out the front door. He would exit the back door instead. He dressed hurriedly, forgetting to put on his socks. He waited five minutes, during which time he put on the socks and smoothed his hair. With a quick look in each direction, he slipped out the back door.

Magonigle and Carrère presented the idea to Billings in his Astor Library office. Hastings stayed away, not wanting to inject himself into this matter just yet. Magonigle removed the drawings from a black leather portfolio and spread them on Billings's desk. "This will be a nice feature to the room," Carrère said as earnestly as he could, struggling to convey enthusiasm for the idea. "The railing will separate the wall shelving from the seating area. It features the same Classical elements that define the rest of Library."

Billings paused. "This is an interesting idea, but I don't think it is necessary. It consumes valuable floor space." This was exactly the reaction Hastings wanted from Billings.

Magonigle added, with more conviction in his voice than Carrère, "You should think of it as an important addition, embellishing the Classical ideas we depend upon to make the room more usable." Carrère bit the insides of his cheeks to prevent himself from smirking. "The railing would enhance the room in ways that we can't yet imagine," Magonigle continued.

Billings became a bit frustrated, enunciating each word, "I just don't think it is a very good idea right now. Maybe if I think about it for a day or two, it'll make sense." He sharply rapped his pipe on a brass ashtray.

Carrère offered, "We'll leave the drawings here so you can study them. And we can talk about the railings the next time we meet."

Billings said, "Before we meet again, I'll visit the reading room."

"We'll be off now," Carrère said, and he and Magonigle slipped quickly down the Astor's main stairs. Once out of Billings's sight, they shook hands and shared a nervous laugh.

Two weeks later, Miss Bough handed Hastings and Carrère a typescript missive from Billings that completely rejected the idea of the railings. Hastings read the brief letter and said, "Good." He gave the letter back to Miss Bough.

"The letter says he still insists on the screen," Miss Bough said.

"That is good, too. We'll send a letter stating that we insist on the railings, and that we disapprove of the screen," Hastings reiterated.

"This is what I thought would happen," Miss Bough said. "It wasn't even much of a risk."

Hastings and Carrère conferred briefly and agreed that Miss Bough would compose and post a letter restating and emphasizing his opposition to the screen. *"To any such division of the reading room, we remain strongly opposed."* The letter would read.

The impasse lasted for many months, even while other work progressed. Miss

Bough and Carrère found time to be together about once a week. She was most discrete, to the extent that not even Carrère would have known that she was involved with anyone. Carrère, on the other hand, hoped to avoid all but essential contact with her in the office. He did become comfortable with the risks, though.

Over time he more or less forgot about their dispute with Billings. It always seemed to be something that would work itself out. He had just put the situation in a box and slipped it among several others onto a shelf in the back storeroom.

The winter faded, yielding to spring crocuses. There was a constant parade of contractors, artisans, officials, and architects at the Library, as interior work progressed. Plumbing was installed, castings were made and positioned, and lighting fixtures were designed and fabricated. As the spring bloomed and windows everywhere were thrown open, Hastings and Carrère slowly become aware that something had to be done about that box. A resolution to the situation became necessary and Hastings grew impatient.

"We have to end this," Hastings said during a brief encounter with Carrère at the Century Club. They seldom discussed business at the club, but the reading room became such an annoyance that the topic surfaced during cocktails.

"I am forever opposed to dividing the room, What if the Bibliotheque Ste. Genevieve had a glass screen in it? What would Billings have thought of it?"

"I think he'll come around," Carrère said. "We just need some help, a mediator." He stirred his cocktail and thought for a few minutes. "I shall contact George Rives, the Board president. Maybe he has a suggestion."

A few days later, Carrère had news, "I spoke with Rives on the telephone and he agreed to help broker a resolution."

"Did you mention the railing?" Hastings asks.

"I did not but he knows about it. We'll meet on Monday."

They arrived at Billings's office early for the 9:30 meeting. Hastings bounced agitatedly on the balls of his feet, as eager as a boxer entering the ring for a bout. Hastings threw a right into the air, then a left, then a rapid combination, finishing with an uppercut. His eyes were wild with anticipation. He spun on one foot, dancing, ducking to avoid the blows of an unseen opponent.

"I didn't know you liked boxing," Carrère said. "You look like Marvin Hart."

Hastings dropped his fists. "Who's that?"

"The Champ, silly," Carrère chided. "He won by a knockout in the twelfth round."

Hastings resumed his imaginary sparring. "I'm going to whip you. No screen. No screen, not ever," he growled.

Rives, an attorney, and Cadwalader, representing the Board, arrived a few minutes later followed by Billings. They all seated themselves around Billings's broad desk. Rives began, "Mister Billings, you want the glass screen in order to be able to shut down half of the reading room, am I correct?"

"That is correct," Billings replied.

"And as I understand it Mister Carrère, you and Mister Hastings believe a railing around the room would add to or enhance the room."

"That's also correct," Carrère said. As always, he handled the negotiations on behalf of the firm.

"So let me see," Rives said, at some length, after spending at least three minutes perusing copies of the letters that had gone back and forth between Billings and Carrère & Hastings on the matter. "The architects like or dislike the screen and railing for aesthetic reasons. Billings, you are concerned with heating costs, primarily."

Billings interjected, "The railing has nothing to do with heating costs." He leaned back in his chair, assuming a commanding position, as if the president of a business.

"I can see that," Rives said. "It appears that the architects are not thinking of the director's concerns about heating costs. And the director is not paying attention to what the architects most care about, the aesthetics." Billings tried to protest but Rives held up his hand. "Both sides need to give some ground." The cast iron radiators in the office hissed noisily.

Carrère nodded. He saw Hastings pump a fist underneath the table, where no one could see it. Billings spoke first. "I've never wanted to compromise the monumental character of the building." Hastings pumped his fist again.

"You should not be concerned with the heating expenses. We will take care of them," Cadwalader said. Billings seemed to understand. Hastings shook his fist, holding his thumb up. "If it costs a little more to keep the Library open, then the Board and the City will find a way to pay for it."

"Well then, I am willing to forgo the screen, but I still detest the railing. There is no need for it, and it detracts from the room."

Carrère protested gamely, but eventually yielded the railing. "Doctor," Carrère addressed Billings, "if you are willing to let go of the screen after all these years, we'll let go of the railing. I think it's a reasonable compromise."

Hastings tried to look blankly at his partner but his satisfaction overwhelmed him. "This will be grand! The reading room will be the greatest room in the world after all."

Hastings was ebullient all the way back to the office. Carrère hadn't seen him in such high spirits since they had won the commission, except perhaps at his wedding. Hastings floated on a cloud. "Thank God Billings gave in," Hastings said.

"It's not like you to use the Lord's name," Carrère said reprovingly.

"Oh, never mind. That awful screen is history."

Miss Bough lingered until after everyone had left. She had a way of remaining out of sight while informing Carrère, at the same time, that she was still there. When the place was quiet, she slid into his office. Not a stitch of her clothing was out of place.

Carrère said, "That screen that Billings wanted. He was the only one who owned it."

"And?"

"And no one owned that railing device. It suddenly got big and out of control and it became its own entity."

"Your hocus-pocus philosophy is enchanting," Miss Bough said. Her voice was smooth and seductive. "Does that mean the railing was a better idea than the screen?"

"Much better," Carrère said. "It was a deception that worked perfectly, even if it was never built. Now why are we talking about that?"

Interlude

"Peri agreed with me, or at least she accepted the fact that I could design a perfect house." I couldn't be sure that Jayne believed me, but I continued. "I'm gonna use the Golden Section as the template for the plan. I can't imagine a better way to get it!"

"So that you can avoid negative spaces?" Jayne looked at me over the tops of reading glasses. They weren't actual prescription reading glasses, rather the ten-dollar variety that you can get at drug stores. "You know, if you study art in general, negative spaces aren't a bad thing."

"That may be," I said. "I'm not gonna live in a negative space. There is too much possibility for misconduct."

"What—what are you talking about? Misconduct?" Jayne took off her reading glasses. "What do you know about misconduct anyway?" She was right. I didn't know anything. My life had been pretty smooth compared to hers. "You've got a nice wife and nothing to worry about."

"I'm not going to design negative spaces," I said. My voice there must have betrayed weakness because I could tell that Jayne still didn't take the idea very seriously.

"Your Beaux-Arts men *used* negative space. There's nothing to fear."

"I realize that, I know; but I'm not going to live in it."

"You just have to do good things in the space to make it positive. Think of it as neutral space, then make love in it, then it becomes positive."

That was enough for me. "I'm thinking of the Parthenon. Its plan refers to the Golden Section, and the house I design will be as perfect as that." I turned and left Jayne's office thinking of the Parthenon, Greek goddesses, and Venus, the goddess of love and beauty—except that she was Roman not Greek. In any case, I needed a Venus-type goddess to help me with our house, to make it beautiful and a place of love. Weren't the two interrelated? Peri trusted me.

Carrère

"He what?" Hastings stood across the room and had not heard the news. His face registered incomprehension, blankness, as the information settled within his brain. Hastings hung his suit jacket on a hook that late June morning, preparing for another day of attention to the decorative details of the Library.

"Stanford's dead, was shot last night," Miss Bough repeated. "Here's the morning's paper."

Hastings's face twitched, struggling to form itself into a façade of comprehension. His eyelids fluttered rapidly and he pushed his glasses up his nose. Then he leaned against his desk with one hand as if to support himself. "I'm still not sure I understand. You mean to say Stanford White was murdered?"

"Yes, sir," Miss Bough said, her voice even and unwavering. "According to the paper he was shot three times by a madman—"

Brainard burst in, having run up the stairs two steps at a time. "Have you heard the news?" He tossed another copy of the Tribune onto Hastings's desk. "Stanford's dead! Shot dead! Harry Thaw killed him."

Hastings, now visibly pale, asked, "How do they know it was Harry?"

Carrère snapped the paper in front of Hastings. "There were witnesses who saw him do it."

His expression hardened; his throat tightened. He began to sweat harder. "The treachery. Harry's a millionaire lunatic, and he's jealous that Stanford had Evelyn as his mistress for awhile." Carrère shook his fist seething with rage.

"How did you know that?" Miss Bough wondered.

Carrère snapped, "Everybody knows, everybody in this business knows, and Thaw is a dirty bastard."

"Where, where did it happen?" Hastings asked, his breathing short and labored. He leaned over and coughed loudly as if in some kind of agony.

Miss Bough slipped in more information, "At the Garden. Mad—"

"No, no, no, that can't be, it can't be true," Hastings screamed in a rising falsetto. "At the Madison Square Garden? The building he designed himself? It's an insult, an insult of the worst kind."

Hastings reared up, a rictus of anguish contorting his face. "Oh my aching head, this is awful," Miss Bough hurried over to help him into a seat. Hastings moaned, then slumped into a posture of grief. He cradled his head in his arms. Carrère brought him a glass of water. Hastings sipped gratefully. And after several minutes was able to compose himself somewhat. "Help me understand what happened."

Miss Bough read out loud from the paper. "They were at *Mamzelle Champagne*. Harry Thaw walked right over to Stanford White's table and shot him in the face with a pistol."

"Blam, Blam, Blam," Carrère cried out, making a gun with his thumb and forefinger. "Stanford had no chance, couldn't defend himself."

Hastings mumbled, "What about Bessie?"

Miss Bough added, "She wasn't hurt. There were some gunpowder burns on her clothes though."

Carrère asked about Harry Thaw, and then wondered if Miss Bough had a jilted lover somewhere who would come after him. No, the old lover was dead, so he knew he was safe.

"The police took him away. There's no doubt at all he did it," Miss Bough said. She folded the newspaper shut. "I think this will be in the news for a few days."

Hastings stood and straightened his trousers. "I've got to visit with Charley McKim as soon as I can. He's already overworked and in poor health. Charley's going to die." He rattled through some old papers behind his desk and found some faded, yellowed drawings showing the Villard House, which he had worked on with White in 1882. He slid the drawing to Carrère. "Do you remember this?"

"I remember it well. I drew all the windows."

"Well not all," Hastings injected some levity.

"That's right, I drew most of them. You drew—"

"—you remember who drew what all these years later?" Miss Bough asked.

"Of course." Hastings managed a smile. "We both were trying to impress Stanford White."

"What was Harry Thaw's problem with Stanford?" Miss Bough asked. Carrère thought that when Hastings provided the explanation she would wish she hadn't asked.

"Harry's wife is Stanford's old mistress," Hastings said.

Miss Bough's face didn't quiver, twitch, or change color. Carrère added, "I've known all along that Stanford always had a mistress, but I didn't ever think it would get him in trouble. Certainly not *this* much trouble."

"Bessie must've known," Hastings speculated.

But Marion will never find out, Carrère thought. "I don't know how much she knew. If she did, she probably looked the other way," Carrère said.

He looked at the Villard House drawing again. "I remember because I walk by these buildings all the time on Madison Avenue between 50th and 51st Streets. "They're brownstone from Connecticut. One of the last brownstone buildings in New York."

"That's right," Hastings said. "Nobody has used brownstone since."

"What was it like working with Mister White?" Brainard had entered the room. Hastings and Carrère looked at each other, wondering where to begin.

"Let me tell you a story," Hastings said. "I think this will illustrate for you what kind of a man and artist he was."

"Which story is it going to be?" Carrère asked.

"When he crashed through the doors," Hastings said, rubbing his palms together back and forth.

"Oh, yes. A good one." Carrère smiled at the memory.

"We were drawing the entrance hallway, which opens into a two-story music room at the eastern end. It was fairly ordinary work, drawing sections, and the like." Hastings looked at the ceiling and shook his head slowly. "I don't know what happened, but all of a sudden, there was some shouting and some coarse language coming from the next room."

"This was at McKim, Mead & White in '82 or so," Carrère said, adding extra detail.

"That's right," Hastings continued. Brainard and Miss Bough listened with rapt attention. "Suddenly, he bashed through the swinging door into our section of the drafting room, having started on-the-run, sliding the last couple of feet to a stop at our table."

"He's talking about the first time this happened," Carrère said.

"He was boiling mad for some reason, and when he saw what John and I were doing, he got madder still." Hastings mimed White, huffing and fuming. "He looked at what I'd done, then pushed me off my stool." Hastings pretended he'd just been knocked off a stool. Miss Bough's eyes were wide with astonishment. Brainard folded his arms across his chest. Carrère nodded to authenticate the story.

"Then he made a dozen quick sketches, slammed his fist on two of them and stormed off yelling, 'Do that!' "

"You know," Carrère said, "I checked the hinges on that swinging door and found that they were bent."

"I didn't know that," Hastings lit up. "You never told me that."

"Nothing like that here," Miss Bough looked first at Hastings, then at Carrère, then Hastings again.

"No one here is as volatile as Stanford White," Hastings sat again.

"Did you work on the Garden?" Brainard asked, referring to Madison Square Garden.

"No, We started our own firm in '85, and the Garden was begun in 1890," Carrère explained. "We were on our own by then."

Melancholy returned. Hastings's wan smile disappeared. Stanford was dead. Nobody felt like picking up a pencil or doing anything. "I don't know what is going to happen to the firm," Hastings said heavily, pushing the sketch of the Villard House away from him. "I just can't say, I just don't know."

As soon as White's funeral service was announced, New York's reporters and sensation seekers descended upon St. Bartholomew's, the church where the memorial service was to take place. Reporters from every news bureau and newspaper milled around the church sharing rumors and gossip. When all the innuendo had made its rounds two or tree times, the reporters would strike up casual conversations that were often overheard, misinterpreted, and then a new rush of excitement would ripple through the assembled media horde. The reporters whipped out their notebooks scribbling in shorthand any possible item that could help advance the story and sell newspapers. Because of the frenzy, the service was moved to St. James, close to Box Hill, Stanford White's country house.

On Thursday morning, June 28, 1906, Carrère and Marion and hundreds of White's friends, relatives, and colleagues took a ferry across the East River, and then a special train, to White's funeral in Long Island. Verdant countryside was visible through the train's sooty windows, and through sadness, sorrow, veils, and handkerchiefs, it beckoned the city dwellers.

"Lovely countryside," Marion remarked. Carrère thought of Red Oaks, the property he had bought and quietly said to Marion. "I hope to build a place for us someday." The train's steel wheels clickety-clacked rhythmically over the joints in the steel rails and the car swayed slightly. He thought the ride was especially smooth, perhaps because a funeral train needs to be easy on the senses. The ninety-minute journey ended at the St. James Episcopal Church. He had never been to St. James before and was curious to see the three stained-glass windows White had designed for the chapel. White's casket rested on an open horse-drawn hearse.

Carrère whispered to Marion after they entered, "The windows are very artful." He looked about the plain, simple chapel. Stanford had been obsessed with beauty. Everywhere, in every building he had worked on, Carrère could see it. "Look at the windows."

Marion, wearing a dark dress and a black hat without any plumage, said, "They are very nice."

Out in the countryside and away from the city, there was freshness in the early summer air and the vague smell of animals. Carrère noticed a farm nearby, where about a dozen cows grazed in a pasture. He slowly became aware of a low drone of whispers. As people waited to be ushered to the pews, the murmuring increased.

Mourners spoke in muted voices: "Wasn't the show *Mamzelle Champagne?*"

"It got terrible reviews."

He whispered in Marion's ear, "I am never seeing that show."

Marion agreed, "Never. I heard it is being held over, and the table where he and Bessie sat is selling at a premium."

Another murmur: "Tragedy."

"Even a lecherous man doesn't deserve this fate." Carrère recoiled, glaring at the obese woman who had made the remark. He wasn't lecherous, he was gifted. He had a mistress, that's all. Many businessmen do. Miss Bough flashed through his mind.

"The song was 'I Could Love a Million Girls.' "

"Such a big man."

"Radiant energy." Carrère knew Stanford well, as well as anyone in attendance and agreed with this assessment. No one could produce so much, so well as quickly as Stanford White.

"Stanford and Charley designed the Casino in Newport." An older bespectacled man said audibly.

"He used to work for Richardson in Boston."

"Boston? I didn't know he was in Boston."

"Neo-classicist." Carrère nodded. It was an erudite crowd. How many people have any idea of Classical architecture anyway? Must have read about it in the paper.

"Now what does this mean for McKim, Mead & White?"

"He used to be an advocate of the Gothic." The erudite crowd again. Carrère shrugged. White switched. The Gothic is medieval, the McKim, Mead & White influence was so wide and deep, nothing could bring it down. Now the firm's creative genius and powerhouse was dead.

Carrère made eye contact with Thomas Hastings, who was already at a pew.

"Poor man. He didn't deserve this."

The congregation was soon seated. The murmurs faded as the organist finished the Bach fugues. Marion pointed out the abundant flowers on the altar. Carrère commented on the simplicity of the chapel. Marion agreed and opened a hymnal. White's casket was borne by eight pallbearers, evidently men from St. James Church, but Carrère wasn't sure. The Reverend Leighton Parks from St. Bartholomew's began the traditional Episcopal service. Some years before, Carrère had joined an Episcopal church on Staten Island, so he paid close attention, sang the hymns, and rejoiced for the life of Stanford White. McKim delivered the eulogy, extolling White's contributions to the city of New York and American architecture, and showing how he had brightened the lives of all around him. The forty-five-minute service ended as it began, with the solemn organ filling the spaces. But in the several minutes it took the crowded church to empty, the murmurs began again.

"Lovely service." In an emotional fog, Carrère agreed.

"McKim spoke so well."

"So sad."

Marion caught her husband's ear and said, "Was he good for you, John?"

He looked at her and said, "Yes, he was. But I didn't realize how excellent he was until we started our own firm. I'm glad I don't have his problems with debt and all the other things."

"What other things?" Marion asked.

"He had to sell all his possessions in order to pay his bills," he explained. "And he always had a mistress. Everybody knew that."

There was an announcement that White would be buried at a later time and that the interment would be private. The announcement jolted Carrère into another reality. He convulsed at the thought of White's grave, another void space in the ground, just like the Vermont quarry, which will someday be a dead space that no one knows about. White's grave would be honored and respected for as long as anyone who cares is around.

"What's wrong," Marion saw her husband was in deep thought.

"I can't explain it," he said. "It's a good thing the burial is private. I wouldn't want to see that."

"I understand, dear." Marion hooked her arm under his. "Let's get on the train."

Interlude

One day, I knocked gently on Jayne's open office door. "I want to ask you about your creative spaces."

Jayne leaned back in her chair listening carefully. She tossed her brown hair back over a shoulder. I continued, "Please tell me what it's like when you have a good design day or a bad design day."

"I never have bad ones," she said. Sometimes she could be most unhelpful.

"A bad hair day?" I pressed.

"Sometimes I do," she admitted.

"I think the piece of paper on which I'm drawing is *my* space."

"That makes sense,' Jayne said, a smile tugging at her mouth. "Do you get mad when someone invades your space?"

"Of course, don't you? Editorial interference before I'm finished. I get angry when my space is violated." I sat on the forward edge of a chair.

"It's your territory," Jayne said. I wondered how she could know anything about being an alpha-male wolf. I kept that thought to myself though.

"See," I continued, "I think there's a difference between positive and negative spaces for artists, for architects. Related to but different from the quarry and Library."

"And your house."

"If I'm in a positive space, my art will be good. If negative, then not so good. See what I mean?"

"I can see that," Jayne said. "I would regard my space as something sacred."

"Spaces have different net effects in different situations. In other words, the negative space of the quarry is different from my, or your, negative space." I leaned forward with my elbows on my knees.

"You're admitting that your house's spaces might be all positive, but only for you."

"That's why I'm using the Golden Section—to be universal."

"I think the net effects of negative space are more varied, while effects of positive space are, as you said, more universal," Jayne said. "So I think you're on the right track to use the Golden Section, which everyone knows is perfection."

"If you have a bad day, it affects you and maybe a few people around you. Your quarry's void, if that's what you think it is, it affects everyone. But a library's positive space could affect everyone. That's what makes it democratic," Jayne smiled broadly.

"So I think that negative space is probably more selective and isolated. Positive space is everywhere for everybody's pleasure. Aren't I an optimist?"

"You are," Jayne said. "I like your ideas. I have to say, my good space is positive and I make good designs. When I have a bad day—"

"You said you never did," I scowled.

"Sometimes I do. I admit it." Jayne flipped her hair around again.

"When I have a bad day, using your theory, my space would be bad space, and then I would have to go do something else, because I wouldn't want to be in the bad space, or negative space, as you call it." Jayne paused and began doodling on a notepad. "Is the quarry's space bad, or as bad as my space is when I have an off-day?"

"I don't think of the quarry as bad or hostile. It's just the inverse of the Library. You know, inverse architecture. The marble comes out of the ground and then is rearranged in a new way, making another space somewhere else. And it so happens that the Library is positive architectural space, which is good."

Jayne swiveled her chair around to her computer and Googled "space." With her left hand on the mouse, she clicked and scrolled. After a few seconds, she said, "How 'bout this?" she read haltingly from the screen. "An important characteristic—I'm paraphrasing—of architectural space is man's involvement in its creation and his partaking of life in it."

"Perfect!" I shouted. "Stanford White designed Madison Square Garden. He went to plays there and his life ended there! And the play was a story, a narrative about a time in some people's lives."

"A theater is a great space, designed for stories to be enacted. Now I want to design a theater. Since the play's story unfolds in a theater, then so could everybody's ordinary lives unfold in designed space," I said. "Most people live their lives in architectural space, not in negative spaces—"

"—like quarries," Jayne interjected.

"Great, you do follow my thinking! Architectural space could be a period of time; as we move through the spaces in a building, we experience them across a span of time. Right?"

"I see your point," Jayne turned from the computer. "Does that make any space in which nobody lives in negative space?"

"I think so." I found myself getting quite serious. Jayne could be serious, too. "The real difference is that architectural space is a volume contained and shaped by the physical construction of a building. Humans live and events happen over time in it. Human needs and desires give shape and purpose to the space. In other words, space in a building is the stage upon which our lives take place." I paced around Jayne's office, her space.

"If Stanford White," Jayne added, "was attending that play at Madison Square Garden and was shot to death, two stories unfolded at once in one architectural space."

"Poor Stanford," I shook my head and looked down. "He didn't deserve that. But yes, you are right, two stories unfolded at once, all in one space."

Carrère

"Miss Bough climbed the stairs to the office with Carrère one warm spring morning in mid-April 1907. "It has been a long time since you mentioned the monograph," she said. "Not since Mister White's funeral anyway."

"I think about it every other day but I haven't really done much," Carrère said. "But in fact, the only truly important thing to occur at the Library was the roof, and that was finished in, let me think—in December." He paused and licked his lips. "I wonder why I ever thought I could do that and run this firm, too? What makes you ask about it, Miss Bough?" The wooden stairs creaked underfoot.

"Well I am not actually, " she said. "I am thinking about you all the time, of course. You have a lot of things in the air right now. You've also obtained contracts to do the interiors of the Library. You've bought property for a country house. I'm just wondering how you can do it all."

They reached the top of the stairs and entered the reception room. A framed elevation print of the New York Public Library's Fifth Avenue façade rested in a chair ready to hang beside other framed elevations. Several oriental rugs, as well as a leopard skin and a tiger skin, covered the floor. Carrère paused near a round table with a porcelain urn on it and turned to face Miss Bough. "Actually, I could do a little more. I'm excited about getting a new car. The Library is fine. The book? Well, it'll happen when it does, or wants to, or whenever I get 'round to it."

Miss Bough nodded carefully, understanding what he had just said. "So you're willing to let it be, hoping that it just takes off someday."

Carrère turned to face Miss Bough. "It's not going to be like that, because I'm not an artist anymore. This will be quite businesslike and it will get done."

"What about the railings?"

A feeling of powerlessness grew within him. He fidgeted with some change in his pockets and avoided looking Miss Bough in the eye. At length he asked, "Are you telling me that unless I do something on it, the book is not in my control?"

Miss Bough twisted the toes of one foot about on the floor. "I would venture that once you have the idea, and once the idea exists, it becomes its own thing until you do something about it."

Carrère added unhappily, "And once I start to work on it—" He rubbed his eyes shut. "It's a fine line that determines whether I control the idea or whether it controls me."

"I didn't say that. I just was wondering how your book was coming along."

He held out his hands at arms length, as if telling someone or something to halt, "Okay. I wish to announce that the book is not started, and yet at the same time, it is everywhere. It'll be that way until I get moving again. Speaking of moving. Did you know we are going to move our offices?"

Miss Bough shook her head. "When and where to?"

"The Brunswick Building at 225 Fifth Avenue on May the first. There will be a lot more space. I'll have the corner office overlooking Fifth Avenue. Hastings's will overlook Madison Square. Your office and Brainard's will be in between. It's going to be much nicer."

"You really are too busy to be thinking of the monograph," Miss Bough reiterated her impression.

"I don't really need to do anything right now," Carrère said. "Mister Ward is keeping notes, and the Library is not done."

"So you're not thinking about it because Ward is doing the work for you?" "Isn't that perilous? Don't you want to know?" she pressed.

Carrère squashed her concern. "That's why Ward is making the notes, so that I don't have to. I'll think about the book later."

Carrère

"You have to see this letter," Carrère called out to Hastings. "Miss Bough just gave it to me. It's from Norcross."

"Bring it in here," Hastings barked from his office. It was August 1907 and hot city air wafted in through the open windows. Carrère was oblivious of the general din—traffic and commerce—rising from Fifth Avenue. Rather, he was interested in the tasty-looking muffin on Hastings's desk. It smelled awfully good—fresh from a bakery.

He thrust the single sheet of paper over to Hastings. "Norcross has finished their work under contract!" He was exultant. "It took about three years longer than it should have. But their work was excellent."

"It's everything I knew it would be," Hastings said, pumping Carrère's hand. A big smile broke across his face. "It took a long time, nobody's fault. How can you blame marble? It's done, and we're well into other contracts."

They shared the moment, if only a moment, of satisfaction. The building was structurally complete. Now it had to be finished on the inside and made ready for books and people and their intellect.

Carrère

Hastings, Magonigle, and several draftsmen huddled to discuss the trustees' room. They had crowded around a table in the temporary drafting studio next to the Library, studying Hastings's idea for a concealed door. Hastings had brought in a plate of cinnamon buns. There was barely enough room for the red-and-white plate among all the drawings, tools, and photographs piled up on the table. Hastings said, "In fact, according to the design hierarchy, the trustees' room is not important at all. But it should be elegantly decorated out of respect for the trustees." He slipped a muffin to Magonigle.

"Thank you, sir," Magonigle said, nibbling off one side of the muffin. "This is a pretty good muffin. We should have 'em more often."

"I think the door from the trustees' room leading into the office next door should be hidden." The men studied Hastings's plan and the sectional drawings of each wall in the trustees' room.

The concealed door would pivot, Carrère noticed, and he quickly determined that the hardware for it would cost less than for a hinged door. There would be no need to decorate it. A pivoted door would reduce drafting labor by a little bit at least. "I like the concealed door," Carrère said.

"More than that," Hastings said. "The main lines of a room won't be disturbed." He tapped his pencil on the drawing. "Why would anybody but those who work here have to know about the door?"

"What if there was no door at all?" Carrère asked.

"The door's meant to be a convenience for the Trustees." Hastings said. "The door has to be hidden and not violate the equilibrium of the wall spaces."

Hastings fiddled with the design. A pile of discarded drawings had accumulated on the floor around his chair: each time he ejected a sheet of paper it slipped side to side downward, settling on top of the previous efforts.

Carrère loved the dry autumn air in New York. It usually energized him, readying him to tackle new challenges. He decided to walk the eighteen blocks or so to the Brunswick Building at East 26th Street in search of a birthday present for Miss Bough. He browsed in the many shop windows along Fifth Avenue—Strauss's oil painting gallery was a favorite of his. But he wasn't going to get her a painting. Reiman's had beautiful diamonds, but that was out of the question. Gunther's had very nice furs, but a new coat would be too conspicuous. He wound up in Crawford's antiques and found a nice vase. It was green and white, fluted, about thirteen inches tall. It would be perfect. He paid for it and returned to the crowded sidewalk. A few minutes later, he stopped in Brentano's Books to pick up the day's newspaper before entering the Brunswick's tall bronze doors. These great doors reminded him of Hastings's door. It takes an architect, *an artist,* to make a door as inconspicuous as possible.

Miss Bough had watered some plants on the window ledge. The watering can was empty and she was at the sink the refilling it.

"How often do you water?" Carrère asked.

"As often as they need it."

"Is anyone else here?"

"Only a couple of the younger draftsmen in the drafting room," Miss Bough said.

"Could you water the plants in my office next?" Carrère said. There were no plants in my office.

"But you don't have any plants."

He had planned to wrap the vase in nice paper, but he couldn't resist the impulse to give it to her right away. It was still in the brown paper bag. "I hope you have a happy birthday tomorrow," Carrère said.

Miss Bough put down the watering can and held the vase in the sunlight coming through the window. "This is so special," she said, her eyes gleaming. She looked to see if anyone was near Carrère's office, then gave him a quick peck on the cheek.

He wanted to embrace her, to feel her, but that was just impossible at that time. The door was open. It was the middle of the day. It would have to be another time, and he made a quick plan. "How would you feel about meeting me up at the Library after work?"

"That's a good idea," Miss Bough whispered and slipped out of his office. She left the vase, probably not wanting anyone to see it.

Then Hastings returned. He was clutching several dozen sketches of the trustees' room door. "I've got it," he said, "and it didn't take too long either. No one will ever know a door is there."

"Let's see what you've got," Carrère said pushing the vase aside. He lay out just one of his drawings, leaving the others on a different table. With a cursory glance, he recognized genius. "This is elegant. I can see that it took several tries to get here." He glanced at the extra drawings on the other table.

"It did, and it was worth it," Hastings said defensively.

"It gets expensive. Our men see you at work and want to do the same thing. Look, McKim studied and restudied the Boston Public Library. His firm made only twenty thousand dollars." Maybe Carrère worried excessively, but he had to because no one else watched expenses. "We can't afford to spend all our profit on restudying invisible pivots or details."

"I draw to satisfy my own urges, and I don't pass new work onto the job captains, who start to run up the costs. They cost extra but I don't." Hastings explained. He was very patient with his partner.

"To satisfy your urges?"

"I like what I do, and I'm tired of all the constraints on me," Hastings again spoke slowly and evenly. "You're telling me I'm going to bankrupt the firm. The Board of Estimate, the Executive Committee, the mayor—" Hastings then lost his temper and drove a fist onto his other palm. "The governor. I don't know, the president. Everybody wants a piece of me!"

"That's not true at all," Carrère lost his temper, too. 'I'm just trying to keep things in check." He glared at Hastings. "I know you can be reasonable."

"Don't try to control an artist."

"I'm not trying to control you. I'm trying to control costs."

"Just stay out of my space, okay?" Hastings suddenly gestured to the paper spread before him on the table. "This is where everything I do takes place. Even if my work is expensive, you have to stay out of my space."

"Space? Why do you call it space?"

"This is where magic happens," Hastings said. He leaned across the paper trying to cover it with his arms. "No one comes in and breaks the spell."

"Do you even know what kind of space it is?"

"What does it matter what kind of space it is?" Hastings's anger flared again.

"Every space is different," Carrère slapped the table. "But I never heard anyone say that it's *my space.*"

Hastings abruptly pushed a chair, slamming it into a table. "Nobody gets between me and my work. You should know that by now." His voice increased another notch.

"Why are you so hot about your space all of a sudden?" Carrère asked as calmly as he could. "When you say *my space,* what are you saying about it?"

"It is so special and personal. Only *I* can occupy it," Hastings looked toward the plain wood ceiling. There were no decorations or embellishments on the ceiling.

"So it is good?"

Hastings looks puzzled. "It is good. I just love being in it."

"What if it were not good?"

"It's never not good," Hastings said. "Well that's not true. Sometimes it's not good."

"What do you do then?"

"I walk away," Hastings said. "What are you getting at?"

"When Brainard and I went to Vermont I noticed the quarry's emptiness, its space, and I've been thinking about space since. Now you say this sheet of paper is your space." Carrère tapped an index finger on Hastings's sketch. "And you say it's good space. I think there's a relationship between the emptiness of the quarry, your sheet of paper, and the Library, but I'm not sure what it is."

"They never taught us about this at the Ecole," Hastings said.

"I think in a way they did, but not specifically." Carrère sat on a stool and ran his hands through his hair. "But they never saw the relationship between a quarry and a building that came out of it."

Hastings paused, needing time to think. "You only thought of it after going to Dorset?" Hastings asked, starting to see some cogency in Carrère's idea.

"I thought the quarries were fascinating,"

"My space on a bad day is hostile," Hastings acknowledged at length. "When I get into that way, and it almost never happens, I know that whatever I draw might be garbage. So I get away."

"As fast as you can?"

"Just about," Hastings ruefully shrugged. "But it almost never happens."

"But what about your space on a good day? A great day?" Carrère prodded.

"Great things come out. I just love drawing and designing. And I don't want people in that space because the interruption might slow me down or be fatal."

"Fatal? Even if you're interrupted, you can't start up again?"

"Okay. It's not fatal, but I don't like it."

Carrère rubbed his hands back and forth and leaned forward, "So when I asked you to cease your drawing for the health of the firm, I got into your space."

"I would say that is correct."

"Your space must have been really, really good, judging by all the paper flying off the table," Carrère said.

"It was good."

"I'm going to have to make the firm a personal loan."

"You are? Have you made a loan to the firm before?" Hastings appeared concerned.

"No. This will be the first time. I would've told you. But you are so oblivious to business matters, you would have forgotten."

"I would have remembered," Hastings's eyes flashed. "This is a serious matter. What else can we do?"

"We can't have our draftsmen draw and redraw so much," Carrère drummed the table with his fingers. "The details are essential, of course, but we must cut back on the slavish attention to them. Have the job captains reduce the amount of work and we can reduce our payroll expense."

Hastings pushed his latest drawing away. "I can see the point. But everything has to be perfect. I love this Library."

The Library had become a labor of love. Love and money are not always compatible. Hastings wanted the Library to be so ornate; it could bankrupt the firm if he kept going. Carrère nodded, "So your space contains love, too?"

"On good days," Hastings acknowledged. "Isn't it wonderful?"

Carrère slipped the vase into a canvas bag and swiftly walked the eighteen blocks or so to the Library. Miss Bough wasn't there, so he stood and waited for her. He looked both left and right, expecting her to appear among the masses at any moment. He put the bag down and clasped his hands behind his back. Several minutes went by and no Miss Bough. She was ordinarily very punctual, but he tried not to think about that. On the other hand, he felt very conspicuous standing there, right in front of the Library his firm had designed. He should have been looking at it, not away from it. What must everybody be saying? He wanted to look at his watch. It must have been a half-hour at least. But he resisted the urge. Another few minutes passed and still no Miss Bough.

How long should he wait? Didn't she know where to meet? He had meant *this* library not the Lenox. She surely would have known what he meant. He remained in one place, not wanting to pace or appear impatient. Someone would notice. What if they found out? His brow felt hot. Then, there she was waving at him from across Fifth Avenue, as if not to give away their little secret. He snatched the bag and walked to the corner of Fifth and 42nd, where he crossed.

"Good evening," Carrère bowed slightly.

"I think my place will be more comfortable than the Library. I mean—"

Miss Bough had already been to her place and had changed. That explained why she was delayed.

"I know what you mean. What a grand idea!"

Shortly thereafter, Carrère placed the vase on Miss Bough's kitchen table. Then, with the same beckoning finger that he had seen in his dream, she asked him to follow her. He did, and she brought him into her small parlor, where she had set up two candles. The curtains were drawn and the room was warm. She had also set out his favorite cocktail and for herself, straight gin in a tumbler. They sat side by side on a velvet sofa and forgot all about inhibition.

Carrère

Barber and Carrère toured the unfinished exhibition hall together. "These columns are simply Dorset marble with the grain stood on end," Carrère said, feeling their cool smoothness.

Barber, not surprised, said, "You did this out of economy." He rubbed the column with his cheek.

"Connemara marble and Cippolino marble were too expensive."

Carrère pointed upward, "We have talked with Maurice Grieve. He's going to carve the ceiling."

"One piece at a time," Barber said knowledgeably also looking up.

"He'll carve each panel in his studio and then bring them here for installation."

"Is he going to use walnut or mahogany?" Barber asked.

"I don't know. He hasn't mentioned it, and we're leaving it up to him. Hastings wants opulent panels." Carrère recalled the number of discarded drawings surrounding Hastings when he sketched his ideas. "Winged figures, cherubs, satyr masks, acanthus, fruit garlands." He shrugged. "He used the entire classical vocabulary."

"Do you think Grieve is up to the job?" Barber asked.

"Oh sure. He's good."

Interlude

Just a few miles outside of Manchester, a new subdivision was going in. The land was once nice pasture but had been sold to a developer. There were going to be forty-six new houses, cul-de-sacs, underground utilities, and the works. The houses were going to be of the generic variety you see in magazines at checkout lanes in supermarkets. I didn't like subdivisions because of how they irreversibly removed land from agricultural uses. I had an idea though. What if I approached the developer, bought a lot, and erected a house of my own design? Peri didn't mind the idea of a subdivision as much as I did. I conceded, however, that the subdivision was a fairly easy way to get a good, level lot with all the services—sewer, gas, electricity—and with the potential to build my own Parthenon.

The developer, Bob Broudo, received my idea openly, but with one provision. His builders would have to build the house. He didn't care who designed it. That was fine with me, and I told Peri.

"So you can have a perfect house," she said with a bit of excitement in her voice.

"Let's drive some stakes," I said. "I've got a compass, a shovel, a maul, and some stakes already in the car. Ours was Lot 4, the fourth one on the right. There was a sign that read, "Broudo Development Corporation, LLC." The sign had an 800 number on it. The roadway into the property had recently been paved. The asphalt was very black. New red hydrants poked out of the ground at City-specified intervals. None of the houses had been started. Our lot was perfectly level and treeless.

The first thing I did was determine which way was North. The section of the road in front of our lot ran approximately northwest to southeast. The entry would be to the south, I decided. The house wouldn't be exactly parallel to the road. I drove in a stake and then measured, using a contractor's tape, twenty-five feet, where I drove a second stake. Then I measured forty feet ninety degrees from the first line. I drove a third stake. Another twenty-five feet, the fourth stake. There was the plan in the correct proportion. "You're off to a good start," Peri said. "What are you going to do about the foundation hole? Won't that be negative space?"

"I'm going to prove to you that negative space doesn't matter anymore." I grabbed the shovel from the car. At one of the stakes, I jabbed it into the ground, then jumped on it. It went in about two inches and stopped. Must have hit a fieldstone. I groaned. Had to start over. I selected another spot and jumped on the shovel again. It went all the way in. I pried the handle back, lifted the dirt and tossed it aside. I did this again and again, all the while with Peri watching me until I had made a little crater in the middle of our lot. "See, I'm not against negative space. We're going to have a beautiful house."

"What about a garage?"

"It'll be separate," I waved my hand toward one corner of the lot. "Not part of the house." After a moment I added, "All the negative space will be out there."

"So it'll be kind of like a storage shed," Peri said.

"Well, not exactly, but you could think of it that way, if you want."

Carrère

"Two pairs of candelabra in the entry hall," Hastings said in the library at the Century Club one snowy night in January. He had recently been elaborating on many of the decorative features in the Library. The candelabra, he said, would "give greater Classical authenticity to the entry hall." Carrère loved it. Creative forces had been exploding in his head. He decided not to mention the cost overruns. Hastings elaborated on his Roman inspiration by sharing with Carrère a book on the collection at the Poi Clementine Museum at the Vatican.

Hastings said, "It's going to be a challenge, making a stanchion of such length stand on one end." Several other Centurions passed on their way to the bar.

"It's like making a pencil stand up," Carrère said.

Hastings said in his excited high-pitched voice, "We'll use a truncated pedestal on three feet to give the candelabrum support. Look at the precedent." He pointed at the engraving in the book, tapping on the page. "On this general form," he made a cylindrical shape with his hands, "there's a lot of room for your imagination to decorate and enrich it."

"Who is the artist you are thinking of?" Carrère asked with feigned suspicion.

"Oh, I don't know. I was thinking I would do it," Hastings chuckled.

Later, Carrère found Hastings and Ward fully involved with drawings of the candelabra. Hastings started with a preliminary idea on a sheet of white drafting paper. Working quickly, he overlaid the original with tracing paper and edited and expanded upon the concept. Then he overlaid another sheet of tracing paper on top of the previous sheet, drawing more and new ideas. And on and on it went. There were more than a dozen sheets in the pile.

Hastings waxed enthusiastic, "The Beaux-Arts approach to design emphasizes imitation, method, and tradition, Classical ornamentation is like the sea: one moment calm, the next storm tossed. It is always different, never repeats." He waved his arms up and down in front of him imitating waves in the ocean.

Carrère loudly asked Ward, who was nearby, "How long has he been working on this?"

Ward, wearing the typical white shirt and gray flannel trousers, said, "I really can't say, sir. I wanted to see what he was doing and he started to show me." Hastings looked up from his work, glared briefly at his partner, and then wordlessly returned to the candelabrum. Perhaps Carrère had got into his space again.

Hastings was looking for a candelabra drawing. "I can't find that detail drawing," he whined, shuffling through large sheets of paper. "Did you hide this one, too?"

"Looks like it might rain. Hope you remembered an umbrella." Carrère avoided the accusation.

"No, I'm sick of this interference in my work. I've told you before." Hastings erupted, chasing Carrère around the room. "Are you listening to me?" Hasting yelled.

"You're whole problem is that you overwork an idea. We have to take away your drawings for your health and the health of the firm." Carrère spit the words through clenched teeth.

"My health? I think you're the one who's sick, always thinking about this!" Hastings's face was red with anger. "You don't care about details. All you care about is money, money, money."

"Not true," Carrère countered, throwing a rubber eraser violently to the floor. "You have no control over your work, your work controls you." Carrère stalked toward his office.

"Oh," said Hastings. He became quiet and a bit sullen. "Detail is necessary, sir, and it takes a lot of time and effort. It's all about quality."

"Your work is the best, *sir*," Carrère returned the accolade.

"You have to see what he's done," Carrère said to Barber, a few days later at the Century. "It is spectacular! There are ribbons, ox hooves, rosettes, dolphins and on and on. The stack of tracing paper was twelve-to-fifteen-sheets deep. And he kept on going."

They stood shoulder-to-shoulder at a window in the parlor. "I have an idea," Barber said. "I think he's afraid to stop because if he did, he might lose the details of an idea before he has a chance to put it down on paper."

"You think so?" Carrère said. He noticed that the traffic on the street below consisted more of cars than horse-carriages.

Barber turned toward him. "Sometimes what I create is an obstruction to further ideas. And sometimes an idea comes at me so fast or hard that I can't capture it. I can't keep up with my impulses."

"So what do you do?"

"I have to work harder and harder just to keep up sometimes," Barber shook his head, "It's not easy."

"Are you talking about creative delay?" Carrère asked.

Barber leaned on the back of a big comfy chair, "Maybe."

"Could delay disrupt the flow or continuity or integrity of what comes after the delay hits? Would what comes after the delay have been possible if the delay had not occurred?"

"So you're questioning the validity of the idea after an artificial delay," Barber suggested, rubbing his bearded chin.

"That's it! And maybe that's why Hastings works so furiously, to keep pace with the original idea. I guess I'd better pray he never stops. Then the Library will never be finished and we'll really go insane."

The waiter's bell signaled that dinner was served, and the two turned for the dining room. Barber added, "I think you'd better keep him working."

"All I've wanted to know is whether the artist controls the art or whether it's the other way around. There's no correct answer, I'd say." Carrère held a door open for Barber. "I've decided I'm not going to worry about Hastings unless he stops drawing.

Carrère

"Carrère asked Miss Bough when several letters would be ready for his signature. She was seated at the typewriter apparently almost finished. "They must go out today."

Miss Bough removed a letter from the carriage and handed it along with five others to him. "All done, sir."

"I'd like to compare the paintings again," he said. That had become their little code for a rendezvous. "You still have them, don't you?" This question was sincere.

"Not anymore," Miss Bough explained. She rested her hands on the table beside the typewriter. "A couple of months ago I threw out all those paintings, I decided I didn't look very good, that the paintings weren't very good, and that I didn't need them to remember Horace anymore." She looked at her hands, then at Carrère again. "I knew I had *you*."

Carrère touched her thin white arm. "Shall we?"

Miss Bough looked past Carrère and saw Hastings approaching the office. "Not right now," she said not loudly enough for anyone else to hear. Again, it was code for, "Yes, I can't wait." And Carrère couldn't wait to enjoy the candles and cocktails at her place once again.

Hastings though had the façade and the approach on his mind. "I've been thinking about those steps up from Fifth Avenue. They need a limit, some defining end points." He gave Carrère a very preliminary drawing of the approach with two marble lions, one at each side. "I was thinking that a pair of lions would make the Library even more grand."

Carrère experimented with the idea. He covered the lions in Hastings's drawing with his thumbs, attempting to see the approach without them. Then he uncovered them, "They'll add so much." Hastings covered the lions with his thumbs, too. "They'll guard each flank," he added.

"I'm not very good at modeling animals," Hastings said. He seldom admitted weakness but he was correct. Because of that, he didn't draw and draw, but let the lions take over. It was a remarkably free, lucid drawing without any eraser marks on the sheet. "We'll hire someone like Ed Potter to model them, then give the carving job to someone like Piccirilli.

"He's the one with the family studio in the Bronx, isn't he?

"That's him," Hastings said. "The lions—I like it that you'll have to walk between the lions to enter the Library." He raised his eyebrows provocatively.

"I do, too. I think there's money in the budget for them. And they should be a different color marble so that they'll stand out." Carrère stood and tucked his shirt in.

Hastings nodded, his arms folded across his chest. "But I don't think anyone will miss the King of Beasts in front of the Library."

Carrère brought Miss Bough to the Library. She had never been inside. He wanted to inspect the progress of the floor in the reading room, and he needed Miss Bough.

"It looks finished," Miss Bough said.

Workers were laying red tiles into mortar. The men wore white overalls, working on their hands and knees. Carrère thought they worked quickly, reducing the large piles of tiles at one side of the reading room. In the half-hour he and Miss Bough were there, the masons had installed about thirty feet of tile.

"I think I know why you brought me here," Miss Bough said.

"I wanted you to see the Library," he said. They left the reading room and stood at the top of the stairs. No one was around.

"You're crazy for me," she said. "Hastings works hard, is never distracted. But, you—"

Before she could finish her thought he had his lips on hers, his hand inside her blouse. "Let's go into the trustees' room," he suggested.

She unfastened her lips from his. "Are there any candles?"

Carrère

"Mister McKim passed away this morning." Miss Bough softly brought the news to Carrère & Hastings on a gloomy September mid-afternoon in 1909. Thick clouds had enveloped New York, as if to prepare the city for the sad news. His passing was not unexpected. "I heard it by telephone from Mister Mead."

"He was sick for so long. The Pennsy project must have killed him," Hastings sighed from a half-seated position on a desk near a third-floor window overlooking Fifth Avenue. The gilt-lettered words *Carrère & Hastings* were painted on the inside of the glass.

Miss Bough slipped out of the room, leaving Hastings and Carrère to themselves. Carrère was glad she had left, because it had become more difficult for him to contain his affection and therefore the secret. "I'm not sure if it was the Pennsy project or if he was just sick," Carrère said. He leaned back in his desk chair, considering the possibility that McKim's art had overwhelmed him. No, he concluded, "He had been declining the last few years."

Hastings removed a handkerchief from his suit-jacket pocket and dabbed away a tear. "Now two-thirds of McKim, Mead & White are gone."

Carrère gestured through the window at the hodgepodge architecture across Fifth Avenue, "We have so much to thank them for. They brought the Beaux-Arts to America replacing this mess." A horse-drawn wagon delivered fresh fruit to the Café Martin across Fifth Avenue.

"To America," Hastings agreed, holding his arms wide. "They broke a lot of ground for us."

"They gave us our first jobs after Paris," Carrère recalled. "Charley was the perfect complement to Stanford. Now they're both gone."

Miss Bough returned with information on funeral arrangements. "Thank you, Miss Bough," Hastings said. He turned to Carrère. "Stanford died three years ago. Time does fly."

"I think you two are at the forefront of the profession now," Miss Bough said, quietly, sincerely. She always made them feel like they were the best.

"What do you mean by that?" Carrère asked, wanting to hear more.

"Without him that firm is just about gone," Miss Bough said. Her voice was grave. "Carrère and Hastings have the greatest living reputation. You are the ones still going forward."

"That's true to a degree," Hastings nodded. "We are still here." He gestured toward his partner. "That is, John and I are still living. But the Pennsy project isn't finished, and neither is the Library."

"There are other architects, too," Carrère said.

"You two set the standards now," Miss Bough said, nodding her head to affirm her statement.

"I think we have always been as good as McKim, Mead & White," Carrère said. He wasn't really being humble. He just wanted to hear Miss Bough sing their praises again. "But they were here earlier."

They had found themselves a good place. "New York," Hastings turned to the window and gestured to the street below. "Look at this city. New York is a better, booming place. Look at the number of automobiles. I count six right now. The buildings. The industries—coal, steel, railroads. Commerce. It's amazing to see. New buildings everywhere, it seems. The money. There's so much wealth now."

Miss Bough and Carrère joined him at the gritty and grimy window." McKim and White were right there for the revolution, and we've been able to ride it."

"But I'm not so sure there is an actual movement," Carrère said. "All I ever wanted to do is make buildings and the cities nicer places."

Hastings watched the Avenue from the window. "We're part of it!"

"Your art is part of it," Miss Bough added.

"It's not just us. Look at all the prospering architects, sculptors, and artists," Carrère added.

"There are so many reasons for this success," Hastings said. "I'd have to thank McKim for hiring us after Paris." He looked at Carrère, who looked at the floor. Miss Bough stood beside him and he could see her shoes. "We'll miss Charley McKim, won't we?"

"We'll miss him all right. It's too bad he'll never see his Penn Station."

Hastings withdrew a new handkerchief from his pocket, polished his glasses, and stanched a new tear at his left eye. "He'll never come into our Library either."

"I think it is *your* library, sir. But we'll be around to see it open." Carrère placed an arm on his grieving partner's shoulder.

Carrère

"What are your plans for Marion's birthday this year?" Miss Bough gently reminded Carrère. It was October. She reminded him every year.

Carrère rolled his knuckles gently on his desk. "Can't forget. Can't forget."

"You might go to a show that evening. It is a Friday," Miss Bough suggested, her hands folded in front of her skirt.

"An excellent idea. The New Theatre opens in a couple of weeks, and *Antony and Cleopatra* will be playing. I think *we'll* go to that." Carrère & Hastings had designed the New Theatre at Central Park West and 62nd Street.

"That's nice, but it's sort of business, don't you think? You should do something on her real birthday." Miss Bough was wearing a pearl necklace outside her collar.

"Where'd you get the necklace? I haven't seen it before." Carrère asked.

"It was my mother's. It was the only thing I got from her after she died," Miss Bough explained. A cloud crossed the sun suddenly, if momentarily, darkening the street outside. She held it in her right hand, the pearls dripping from her fingers. "It's nice," she added. "My sisters got all her other jewelry."

"I once got Marion a pearl necklace for her birthday, and she never wears it." He shook his head slowly. "I don't think she likes it."

Miss Bough's face saddened. "You are a lovely couple."

"I actually like it when she and the girls go to Europe for the summer. It gives me space." He stuck his hands in his pockets. "When she's home I just want to stay at work or go to the club or play tennis. . . or be with you." He looked at her with big round eyes.

"I think you and Marion need to spend a pleasant evening together," Miss Bough said, her voice soft. He thanked her. Marion's birthday was on Friday. He would go home early, pick her up. They'd have dinner at a restaurant somewhere and then attend the show. That would be fine, he decided.

Carrère

Carrère watched Francoise Tonnetti-Dozzi, the sculptor, on his hands and knees measuring the width of the fireplace's location with a folding measuring stick. Hastings stood back and out of the way. Carrère thought of the Eastman quarry and the excellent adventure there. He gave the small piece that he had brought back from it to the sculptor. He still had it after all these years.

The thin French sculptor picked it up and turned it over and over in his hand, just as Carrère had when Mr. Eastman gave it to him. "I like it. Did you ever consider it for the exterior?"

"Much too expensive," replied Carrère. "Eastman marble was about eleven dollars a cubic foot. The Valley Quarry marble was only two dollars a cubic foot."

Hastings said, "When Mister Carrère brought this piece back, I knew I wanted to find a special purpose for more of it." He polished his glasses with a handkerchief. "Once the trustees' room began to take shape, and I knew there was going to be a fireplace with a carved marble mantel chimneybreast, I realized that we had a place for your Eastman marble."

Hastings said to the sculptor. "I've sketched an idea of what it will look like, subject to your interpretation, of course."

Françoise laid the drawings on some boards, which rested on sawhorses. "The upper part is supported by two maidens," the sculptor pointed with a sharpened pencil. "You want scrollwork between the maidens and inscriptions beneath." Françoise paused to further examine the sketches. "The mantel has a frieze below it. To the left and right of the fireplace itself are heads of whom?"

"I was thinking of Minerva on the left and Hercules on the right," Hastings said.

Françoise, stroking his long beard, said, "I will need more detailed drawings."

"We've thought of those things and will have the marble delivered to your studio," Carrère assured the sculptor. "We want you to give us the most elaborate carving inside the library for this most elegant room."

"This will be possible," Françoise Tonetti-Dozzi said in his in French-inflected English. "I just need some time."

Interlude

It was a cloudy day with no precipitation, and I was feeling pretty good about my decision to quit my job at Simcoe & Verbridge. I wanted to spend more time on the Library Book, start my own firm, and I had agreed to teach a continuing education course at a local community college. When I told Jayne, she suggested we go across the street to Finagle a Bagel.

"What's the course going to be called?"

"Architecture and Space, or Architectural Space, or something like that."

Jayne nodded slowly almost imperceptibly. "You're going to teach a class about space. Negative space, too, I bet. What are you going to teach? Can I see the syllabus sometime?"

"Sign up for the course!"

"I've already listened to you rave on and on about the quarry, the crater at the Farms Library, and your Parthenon. What else is there?"

"I've got a lot more," I promised. "There's more, believe me."

"So you're going to pull it outta your ass, is that it?" She held up half of the bagel and peered at me through the hole. The flat side was toward her, the rounded side toward me.

"I am not. It's going to be a serious class with thoughtful discussions." I was definitely on the defensive.

"Would there be a course like yours at Columbia?"

"Oh, yes, nowadays," I loaded my voice with as much sarcasm as I could. "Architectural ideas have progressed significantly, and I think there would."

Jayne left the table to use the ladies room. While she was away, I browsed the front page of the *Manchester Union Leader*. There was news of a bank robbery, as well as articles about New Hampshire's upcoming election for the U.S. Senate. I hated politics, so I looked for the sports section. Then Jayne returned.

"You've worked for us for only three years. What does Peri think?"

"She's been worried about my mental state since the explosion at the Farms Library."

Jayne again looked at me through the hole in the bagel. She evidently wasn't going to eat that half. "Consider this a mirror." She had good reason. "You were an ass," she said.

"I might have been out of control that night," I acknowledged. "But I really think I learned something, and it's very important."

Jayne put the half bagel on the plate on the table and stood. We headed back to our offices. "It must be important if you're quitting your job."

"I'm going to do other things, too." My voice must have lacked conviction because Jayne seemed to dismiss what I said. So I continued gamely. "I've got to finish the Library Book, you know, and"—I was struggling—"oh yes, our house, too."

"Tell me," Jayne said as we left the bagel shop, "when did you decide this?"

"We talked about it when we went to Katahdin a few weeks ago." In fact, Peri and I had not climbed Katahdin. I had climbed it a long time ago.

"What's Katahdin?"

I felt stronger. "It's the highest mountain in Maine. Baxter State

Park. Haven't you seen it?"

"Never heard of it. You climbed it? You and Peri do a lot of hiking."

"You should get in shape and climb it. It's beautiful, the most dramatic mountain in the East."

"How can you say that?" Jayne didn't believe me.

We crossed the road and entered our building. "Let me explain. There are three peaks. The first one we reached, the Pamola Peak—you can look down all the way to Chimney Pond. It's a breathtaking, spectacular curving drop all the way down, maybe a couple thousand feet. There are no trees. We even saw a moose in the pond."

"I saw a moose once running across the road."

I wanted to freak her out, and I knew the next part would. "Then we took the Knife Edge trail to the South Peak."

She listened warily and asked, "What is the Knife Edge trail like?"

"A narrow trail across a ridge that drops away a thousand feet on either side. It's great. Great views." I held my hands about three feet apart to indicate how wide the trail was.

"I wouldn't like that," Jayne said. She sat at her desk and sipped her Pepsi, which must have been flat.

"No, you probably wouldn't," I agreed.

"So you and Peri were hiking on a trail thousands of feet in the air only three feet wide? It sounds like you both are out of your minds."

"We're not out of our minds. This seems like the natural course for me to follow right now. It just feels right." I said.

"You're leaving us before the Library is done," Jayne complained. "We'll be in a tough spot without you."

I walked around and around Jayne's office. She was pressuring me with guilt. How could I quit before the job was done? I had thought about it but briefly and in only vague conceptual terms. The Library was on autopilot. It didn't need me anymore. It was going to cruise to completion. "It has a life of its own," I said.

"Not in my experience," Jayne said. "You have to be there until the end or else contractors screw up and it turns into a disaster." She looked down the top of her v-neck sweater for some reason. I didn't want to know.

"You just gotta let it go," I said, "because it's not part of you anymore and it wants to be free. So the Farms Library will be just fine without me."

"Strictly bullshit," Jayne said. "You're not making sense, and I should make you stay here. So off you go, right into your frigging neuroses-induced fantasy world. All I can say is, Good Luck."

I half bowed toward Jayne and said, "Why, thank you ma'am. I'll look for you in my class."

Carrère

Carrère's favorite season always was the summer. He liked to spend as much time as he could at Red Oaks, the country house on Long Island. He loved the place. It was near the top of a hill on wooded rolling property traversed by streams, with enough land for stables, tennis courts, and farm buildings. The house was part of its surroundings. The summer of 1910 had been a cycle of houseful after houseful of guests, picnics, swimming that kept him occupied. When the last of the summer houseguests had departed, it seemed as though he hadn't seen Marion at all. "The summer is over," he noted. "Tomorrow is September. Back to work in the city. But at least we're sure the Library will be finished within a year."

They walked together in a trellised garden. The day was still quite warm, even though it was after six o'clock. Cicadas buzzed noisily from high in the surrounding oak trees. There had been little rain in the last month, and the earth seemed dusty and dry as they strolled slowly. The faint smells of the farm down the road occasionally reminded him that he was in the country, and unfortunately, not for too much longer. A red squirrel, its tail whipping about in circles, chased another around and around up one of the oaks. He turned to look at the house. It had been very satisfying for him to design his own house. There were few changes he'd made. One thing he'd like, though, would be to have a weekend with Miss Bough there.

Marion, her dress reaching below her ankles, stooped and picked up a single rose petal that had fallen off a blossom in the rose hedge surrounding the garden. She looked at it thoughtfully and kept it. She studied her husband pensively, unable to say what was on her mind. There were other petals lying around. The season had gone by. "I just love it here," Carrère said. "We were here every weekend and most of the month of August."

"I think I'll bring the girls to Europe this fall," Marion announced. "Six months would be nice. I want to be home by the time the Library is dedicated,"

"That should be in May. You'll have a nice time. London again?" Inside he was happy she was going to be away. It would give him more freedom to get things done—Miss Bough, the book. Maybe some good would come of it.

"Yes, our friends the Southwicks will have us for a while, then we'll be with the Beasleys," Marion explained quietly. She stooped to pick up another rose petal and held the two side by side. The first one was pink, the second yellow.

They turned a corner in the path through the garden and returned to the house. "When do you expect to depart?"

"Not until October or November, dear," Marion explained. "I did write to Jane Beasley, and I'm waiting for her reply. As soon as I hear from her, I think I can book passage."

Carrère nodded. A nice time of year to sail. The seas usually aren't too rough in the fall. London at Christmas, while dark, is festive. They reached the side door to the summer house. He held it for Marion as she stepped inside. Carrère stayed outside for a minute, looking at the tops of the oaks. The trees were quiet, no birds sang at that time of year. The late afternoon breeze rustled the leaves. Through a window he watched Marion add a little water to a saucer and set the two petals in it.

Carrère

Hastings and Carrère stood together in the vast, empty reading room one day, discussing the latest challenge, the delivery desk. After some deliberation with Billings, they had decided on a wooden structure at the center of the room. A problem, though, was that it would divide the room, and of course Hastings wanted to avoid that. The solution, Hastings thought, was to divert attention from it. He gestured upward. "The ceiling is the answer. We'll divide the ceiling into a Henri the Second-style triple-panel arrangement, each panel with a mural." He thought for a moment and continued, "Three panels, because three goes into nine and there are nine outside windows."

Carrère said, "We would want to divide the ceiling to reflect the circulation patterns that occur below."

"But in this room we want a visual climax. I want the men to get to work, to be excited."

"Why are you delegating all this preliminary drafting? Don't you want to be in control?"

Hastings replied confidently, his voice strong, "They are good men. They will do what we want. We'll need a mural painter for the center panel of each part of the ceiling. Do you know anyone who can do it?" They started down the stairs.

"Yes, in fact. James Finn."

"Isn't he a draftsman?" Hastings was puzzled. "I know the name."

"Of course you do. He painted two ceilings in McKim's Morgan Library."

"Of course, of course, East 36th Street," Hastings said. "Those ceilings were very skillfully done. I was very impressed. He'll do an excellent job in the reading room."

They paused at the mezzanine balcony overlooking the entry hall. Carrère said, "I've talked with him quite a few times. He knows about the Library of course, and is interested in contributing. I'll start a contract with him."

Interlude

I had not told Peri that I was going to quit my job. Mental health professionals say that most often when someone commits suicide, it is an impulsive act with little or no premeditation. Quitting was an impulsive act. I did want to write Carrère's book, I did want to build our house. But my claim to be teaching a college course was a fabrication, or as Jayne said, strictly bullshit. So I committed professional suicide, at least in the architectural community in New Hampshire. I could start over, I supposed, in New Mexico. Again, since my action was an impulse, I had never thought about what Peri would do when I told her. She was home when I walked in. "Guess what?" I said. I didn't wait for her to reply. "I quit my job today. I'm gonna write the book and build our house and, and, and—" I couldn't give Peri that line about teaching a college course.

Peri's voice was strong and loud. "Why didn't we talk about it?"

"I just did it," I said. "Told Jayne. Didn't think or plan."

"Why are we married?" Peri burst into tears. "I thought you were responsible, handsome, smart, and now this. New Hampshire, Manchester, and now nothing. You shouldn't've! You'll never get another job. We should have talked first. There would've been a better way." She slumped into the sofa and buried her face in her hands.

"You should be happy for me," I said. I actually felt really good about my action. "Look, I have more to offer the world than what I could as a slave at Simcoe +Verbridge. Think about it, Peri. Negative space will revolutionize architecture as we know it. Everyone's gonna want to see our house when it's done. And the book, there's a story waiting to be told. It's too important to be neglected! Have confidence."

"You were so full of promise and such a gentleman when we met," Peri sniffled. "Wow, I thought, Columbia, an architect. Now you're just another lunatic. Peri's eyes were red rimmed.

"Nope, you're—" I wanted to say 'wrong,' but I didn't want to blame Peri in any way. So I said, "Not me. I'm too good. My ideas too."

Peri studied me. Sadness was written all over her face. "No one is going to believe you."

"It will take some time. Think of me as an intellectual avatar, someone who is going to introduce the whole world to the notions of positive and negative space in architecture." I spread my arms as wide as I could. "I think this is my calling, my future."

Peri put on some sneakers. "So what are you going to do when the house is done, when you finish the book?"

Aha! Peri had accepted it!

"Start my own firm, and I've thought about trying to teach a college course. I'm not gonna sit around all day watching porno movies and stroking myself. I've got these big ideas, and ambition."

Peri looked exhausted. "I guess we'll be all right," she admitted. "I just wish we had talked about it first."

"When's your next weekend off? Let's go climb Katahdin," I suggested.

Carrère

A week later, Finn came to Carrère & Hastings to show eighteen small watercolor sketches of the murals. Carrère invited him to pin them to the wall. In a certain way, they reminded him of the *Miss Bough* paintings. What if the murals were actually of Miss Bough? Miss Bough nude on the ceiling! That would cause an uproar!

Hastings arrived, and Finn directed him to the sketches. The architect opened his eyes as wide as they would go. "Did you label which study you did first?"

"I did, on the back, but I'm not telling you which ones came first," Finn said.

"Will you use sketches as you work on the ceiling?" Hastings asked.

"Yes, sir. I will use them as I work on the scaffolding. A good part of my creative energy had already been passed into the preliminary sketches before I even started on the mural."

Carrère asked, "You said something about creative energy?" He strode to the studies mounted on the wall.

"I was saying that I will use the studies as guides when I am painting the ceiling. But the finished mural probably won't be exactly like the sketch."

"That's understandable," Hastings and Carrère said in unison. They looked at each other, surprised by their meeting of minds. Carrère thought about how even the most carefully described projects somehow mutated in the course of design and then execution.

"I think it is interesting how an artistic endeavor changes as it goes along. I'm trying to figure out how that happens," Carrère said.

"Well, for me, it just happens," Finn said. "Especially when I go from the very small sketches to very large murals." He shrugged to indicate that it was a regular occurrence for him.

Later in the day, Carrère told Miss Bough of his idea about the murals. "Would you pose again or would we have to use the old Horace Avery painting as a model?"

"I would pose, but I wouldn't do it. Not for any artist, for any old mural or any other reason." Miss Bough drew herself close to Carrère to let him know why.

"You, you said it was fun with Horace."

"That was a long time ago, so long ago," Miss Bough sighed. "It's different now."

"Well, then, who do you love?"

"I don't have to say because you should know by now. Artists are too unstable. I wouldn't take the risk. They couldn't make me look the way I do. It's too risky." Miss Bough folded a piece of paper on her table in half.

Carrère must have blushed, at least a little bit, because his ears felt warm. "Mister Hastings wouldn't agree with that. He can control the outcome."

"I'm not sure you believe that. You've never thought that." Miss Bough's eyes became hot. "You've always thought Mister Hastings is out of control half the time. You've talked about him." Miss Bough swept imaginary lint off her dress.

"Wait, wait," Carrère held his hand up, as would a policeman halting traffic. "You don't know. I think I've figured him out, and I—"

"—you've figured him out?" Miss Bough reacted skeptically.

"Well, what I mean to say is, I'm not worried about our expenses anymore, and I think he does his best work when he's not restrained." He shifted his weight from one foot to the other and back again.

"I think you say that because the Library's almost done and your attention is on other things," Miss Bough challenged him. "You haven't figured him out. You've just decided to stop fretting." Her face was strong, fearless.

"Do you still want to work for us?" Carrère asked. The question came from nowhere, surprising even himself.

Miss Bough reacted calmly, as though she'd been thinking about it for a long time. "My last day at Carrère & Hastings is the day the Library is dedicated. You have my word that I'll do everything I've always done for you and the firm until that day." Miss Bough held her head in her hands, then ran her fingers through her hair, which had gray streaks. She stood, waiting for him to say something.

"But what about me, what about us?"

Miss Bough smiled gently. "I didn't say anything about that, now did I?"

Interlude

On the first Monday after Simcoe +Verbridge, I tried to do everything. I wrote a letter to the college where I hoped to teach the course. I tried to write a syllabus, too. That proved to be more difficult than I had imagined, because I had never written anything about space. The idea was still entirely in my brain, and at times, spewing from my big mouth.

After some time trying to write, I gave up and went to our lot, soon to be the site of my Parthenon. It was a beautifully flat piece of land with nothing on it except for a small pile of dirt, the excavated material from the hole I had made with Peri. There was nothing, though. So I went to the park. No one was there. I let the wind whip my hair around, and right then and there I decided that I would grow a ponytail. After a while, feeling a little weak in my resolve, I came back to our apartment and looked at the ten or twelve books I had collected, but not read, in order to write Carrère's book. It had been a few weeks since I last looked at it and I couldn't remember where I had left off. Was the revision done yet? Did they have the marble? Couldn't remember. Feeling increasingly defeated and despondent, I turned on our TV. I seldom watched TV. And what should be on the news channel but a story that some robot had landed in a crater on Mars. I wondered whether the announcer or a scientist would characterize the crater as negative space. No mention of it. These people were idiots. How was I ever going to proselytize them or anyone else? I'd have to become a negative space evangelical. Maybe it would be better to start as a space evangelist or televangelist. But then people would think I was a lobbyist for the space agency. I shut off the TV. It had become too confusing. Why couldn't life and ambition be simple and ordinary like a porno movie?

Carrère

They met Finn again in the reading room a few weeks later. The elaborate wood delivery desk was almost complete. Carvers carefully used wooden mallets and sharp chisels to create shapes from solid blocks of oak. Chips formed small piles on the floor.

Workers installed the heavily ornamented cast plaster bands that surrounded the murals. The scaffoldings they stood on looked strong enough for an infantry platoon. In the middle of each ceiling segment was a rectangular white plaster surface on which Finn was to create his sky murals.

"This is what I want to do," Finn said, proffering a new sketch. "This will be just right. The cool blues of the sky and the white clouds will offset the heavily gilt ornamented bands on the perimeter."

Magonigle, who was particularly adept at watercolor rendering, leaned in for a closer look. Hastings asked him, "What do you think of these, Van?"

"Will you use oil paint on the ceiling?" Magonigle asked.

"I will," Finn said.

"Could you explain why watercolor for the studies and why oils for the ceiling?" Carrère asked.

"Watercolor is inexpensive and almost infinitely changeable. I can make unlimited mistakes and not worry."

"What kind of mistakes? Carrère asked. He noticed Hastings pacing about.

"Oh, simple things, like going over an edge or having to change a color."

"What if the mistake turns the painting into something you like better?"

Finn seemed puzzled, stroked his goatee. "Sometimes that happens. But I try not to let it."

Magonigle said, "I've seen your Morgan Library murals. Did you sketch those in watercolor?"

"Yes, I did," Finn said. "Do you think those murals look okay?"

"Excellent Fifteenth Century style. They'll fool people in the future," Hastings said.

Finn was ready. "I have my paints here and I'd like to begin," he said. He ascended the most northerly scaffolding, carefully placing his feet on the wooden structure and rails. Once standing on the uppermost level with his head almost touching the white plaster, Finn poured blue paint into a metal tray, dipped the brush, drained it on the side of the tray, and at first, tentatively stroked the ceiling blue. In time, the blues covered the plaster, followed by the whites and some pinks.

After a few days, Barber and Carrère checked Finn's progress. The carvers were still busy. Finn had finished one mural and was working on the second.

"He is a master up there," Barber noted Finn's steady brushwork. "He knows what he's doing."

Magonigle, who stopped in to see the progress, remarked, "You know," he looked at the murals overhead, "I think a painting can be its own being. These are amazing." Carrère's head swiveled sharply toward Magonigle. So did Barber's.

"How did you know we've been talking about this sort of thing for the last three years?" Carrère asked.

"I didn't," Magonigle shrugged. "It just came to me. Another thing, too—how do I say it? When it he reaches a *stopping place*, it is suddenly in the past, behind him."

Barber and Carrère looked at each other wide-eyed. "If we had known, he could have saved me a lot of work." Carrère's hands were planted on his hips.

"Yes, but I think we still have more to figure out," Barber shrugged.

Magonigle rolled along. "A creative endeavor can actually be a series of extremely short acts with short breaks in between. Just look at Finn up there. He paints, then he stops, then he paints, then he stops. Some of his breaks are longer than others, and each is for a different reason." Magonigle grinned with satisfaction. "It depends on the artist."

"You know what I have noticed about Hastings?" Carrère said. "He never takes breaks, or almost never. I guess he doesn't like to let something out of his grasp, not even for the shortest time. He never wants something to be behind him or *back there*, as you would say, Van."

Finn called out from the top of the scaffolding, "I'm going to take a break now. I am coming down."

Magonigle pointed out quickly, "He is comfortable with letting the painting become its own being. *He* will stop."

Carrère

Several automobiles motored along Fifth Avenue, some with gas headlamps that flickered. It was a dark evening, December 1910. The sidewalk was wet from an evening shower. Fallen leaves lined the edges of the sidewalks. It was a comfortable evening though, and Carrère walked with his coat unbuttoned, with John Mitchell and George Cable, members of the American Academy of Arts & Letters and the National Institute of Arts & Letters after a joint meeting at the New Theatre. He didn't know either man well nor did he know where they were going.

"It was a good meeting," Mitchell, a rotund man, said.

"It could've been better," Carrère said. "Much time was wasted. It's only a matter of time before the American Academy and the National Academy merge."

Mitchell turned onto 46th Street waving goodnight. Then as Cable and Carrère passed the darkened white Library, Cable pointed, "It's just glorious!"

Carrère wasn't sure what to say. Cable appeared to know and appreciate the quality of the Library. He fumbled for words. As humbly and politely as he could, he explained, "My partner and I are the architects."

Cable seemed not at first to understand. A horse drawing a carriage clip-clopped past. Carrère wondered if it were the last horse carriage in New York. An automobile noisily rattled past.

Suddenly when he realized what Carrère meant, Cable hugged him. "I can't believe it," Cable exclaimed, "This is an agreeable ending to a most memorable day."

Carrère

The calendar hanging on Carrère's office wall was a typical thing with pen-and-ink illustrations of bucolic country scenes. Carrère took it down and circled December ninth. "Please put this in the notebook," he told Ward, who was waiting in the doorway, "As of today, December 9, 1910, the Library is complete. All castings are done, woodwork, trim, flooring, the boiler, plumbing… everything."

"Victory, at last!" Ward exclaimed.

"Yes, but it won't be opened until May because there's no furniture. Cobb, the furniture contractor has until April twelfth to complete it."

"You still must be happy," Ward said as he recorded the date in his notes.

"It took fourteen years." Carrère signed correspondence, slipped his pen back into its holder. Then he meandered through the anteroom, where a full bearskin rug covered the floor, and an elevation of the Library hung on one wall. "We're all old now. Look at my hair—it's falling out. Hastings is gray now. My daughters are grown. I've wondered if I would be around to see it finished."

"But it's finished, isn't it? Worth the wait, I think," Ward said. Carrère could tell he was treading on eggshells.

""The people of New York will think so," Carrère said. He smiled a squinty smile. "It'll be nice when it opens and everyone can use it."

In less than a week, autumn made a sharp turn into winter. It was beastly cold, and the glass outside one morning registered only nineteen degrees. Marion and the girls were in Europe over Christmas. Carrère awoke one morning convinced that the world had come to an end, that the house was crumbling, that the paper on the walls had split, and that he was lying among rifts and cracks and debris. His only appointment of the day was to visit the Packard Company to determine the color and final details of his new car.

Later he found Barber at the Century. "I haven't seen you," he said.

Barber, who had a bourbon and water in hand, said, "I know. The last time, you were going to go to the air show at Belmont Park. Did you?"

"We did go! It was very sporty. I'll tell you about it."

"I would love to hear. It was a rainy day, wasn't it?"

"It was a drizzly, rainy, nasty day. Everyone was dressed for rainy weather. They weren't even sure the aviation meet could take place," Carrère looked down at his waistcoat and then at his friend again. "I'm going to get a cocktail, come with me."

Barber joined him at the bar. "Who went with you?"

"Scotch and water, please. My brother Harry, Mister and Missus Holden, and Mister and Missus Ingalls came. The whole thing was exceedingly picturesque. The flying was wonderful."

"It must have been splendid to see all those aeroplanes at once," Barber said, asking him for a better description.

The cocktail arrived. "The engines sputtered and roared," Carrère said. "There was a strong smell of gasoline and oil, much stronger than that coming from automobiles. The aeroplanes are—are wobbly wood-and-fabric contraptions. They hurtled along the ground and miraculously rose into the air." He demonstrated with his hand palm down, rising away from himself.

"How far did they fly?" Barber was fascinated.

"Oh, Moisant flew out of view from Belmont, rounded a balloon ten miles away in Hicksville, and returned in thirty-nine minutes. His prize was eight hundred fifty dollars."

"That's a lot of money! What sort of plane did he fly?" Barber asked.

Carrère didn't know. "I think it was French. Those aeroplanes are awfully frail."

"They are amazing, though," Barber said. "They could change the world."

Carrère shrugged, "They could. I don't know. They need to be a lot better before I'd ever fly on one." He thanked the waiter for his cocktail. They moved to the library, which was always the most peaceful room at the club.

You know," Carrère said, "those pilots are very ingenious making those aeroplanes. They have to try ideas, build a new plane, crash, and try again." Barber listened. "Trying a new color on a painting or a new construction technique in a building is a lot less risky."

"It's less risky because there is more knowledge of how buildings work," Barber suggested, sipping his cocktail before continuing, "Aeroplanes are experimental. Nobody knows much about them."

"So they have to test their ideas. Some ideas are bound to fail." Carrère grimaced. "No crashes at the air show when I was there."

Barber said, "Those men are at the edge. They don't know what is beyond. . . what the next step is. . ." He licked his lips. "You know, *after this failure, they would have to say, then what?* They have no idea!"

"It's the same for an artist," Carrère said. "An artist doesn't know what's after the next pencil mark or brush stroke."

"An artist doesn't have to crash a plane to discover failure," Barber said. His face was grave. "An artist doesn't have to risk his life in a rattletrap machine."

"No, he doesn't. But here's something to think about. I really believe that for Tommy Hastings creative work is play." Carrère stood and walked over to a large pedestal globe in the middle of the room. He gently spun the globe counterclockwise. "For him, creativity is free speculation, using the vocabulary of his choosing," Carrère wagged his head slowly. "He finds complete freedom in using the familiar elements of our art, and he finds such joy in creating new objects. His imagination seems limitless."

Barber interjected, "Stanford White was like that, too."

"I noticed that when I worked at McKim, Mead & White back in the eighties. Especially when he started to work with decorative elements."

"You mean when he draws a plan, he is not playing." Barber gestured at the floor, a floor Stanford White had planned.

Carrère looked about the library in the Century Club. The plan was simple enough but Stanford had combined several other elements to create a special place. "Well, not exactly, not the way he does when he decorates a space. To distinguish one space from another Stanford, and Hastings, and other great artists rely on decoration."

Barber joined Carrère at the globe. The room had a high cove ceiling, gold leaf, a balustrade, sconces, several decorated fireplaces, and other details. "I really think Stanford was playing when he created this space, and I think Tommy has fun when he is designing something like the candelabra."

Carrère could picture those drawings flying off Hastings's table when he drew the candelabra. "He seems to have the most fun when he is experimenting with the elements he wants to use and deciding where to place them."

"That was easy to see," Barber said. They returned to their chairs.

"Tommy still prefers to draw every commission. He's not one to delegate and never see the product. He is involved. He will draw and draw and draw all night long if he can. Sometimes I will remove a drawing from his table, and he seems not to notice that the drawing is missing. He draws for fun."

"It could be play, but maybe something else impels him," Barber said.

"Last Christmas, I noticed how the children played."

"I haven't met your family," Barber said.

"I gave Willie a set of blocks made of marble. I thought the children could have fun with them."

"Where did you get the blocks?" Barber asked with mock suspicion.

"I got a call from Norcross about another project, and I mentioned the blocks to him. He said he could have them cut. A couple of months later, he delivered six-dozen two-inch cubes to me." Carrère leaned back, smiling at the memory. "You should have seen the boys, Donn. They built an entire town, even the library." He tried to illustrate with his hands, making an imaginary city plan on the floor. "It looked like a nice town, and the library was unmistakably the largest building. Thom found some horses somewhere and they organized a parade of toys. At one point, Willie scrambled to his feet and overturned all they had built. Thom wasn't upset in the least. He cried happily, 'We'll build it again!' I could hardly contain my surprise. I wished to question them in detail, but I decided to watch. But you can see my point—creative work *is* play."

"Or is play creative work?" Barber asked. "It sounds like it could be either way."

"Either way, my friend, creative work need not be drudgery. It can be fun. It is for Hastings, especially when he gets carried away. I haven't actually heard him squealing with delight but I know he is happy when he is just designing."

"And you get all the crap with the city and clients," Barber finished his cocktail. "I don't mind, really," Carrère leaned back and laughed. "We're doing okay."

Interlude

I started to keep the shades down during the day. I liked the quiet, dim solitude because it allowed me to concentrate on the book and the syllabus. I'll admit here, for all to witness, that it was easier to write the book than to write the syllabus. In the book, there was plenty of history to work with, and when the New York Public Library was constructed, New York was booming. Even back then, there was a lot of money flying around. The syllabus was a vexing challenge for me. When I had quit, I thought I knew everything and couldn't wait to get going. In the weeks after Simcoe &Verbridge, I felt the idea slip away.

My house, it was becoming increasingly clear to me, was going to be an odd monument to Greek Classicism in a modern subdivision. "Why that house there?" people would ask. The realtor would explain that the previous owner was a madman with unspecified ideas about modern architecture, and that the best example of how buildings should be built was actually the Parthenon. So he built himself a replica. . .

Alas, nothing was happening. The bank wouldn't give us a construction loan because I was not employed. Peri accepted that, and we gave up on the idea of building a home. Our apartment was just fine for the time being. So two-thirds of my ambition was stalled. No Modern Parthenon exemplifying perfection and beauty and reintroducing the masses to the Golden Section; *and* no syllabus, no college course. I felt two-thirds defeated. With the shades down all day long, my world shrank. I thought about trying new things. Computer games were stultifying. Internet porn was too raunchy. I was going crazy. Could negative space be a state of mind?

To find out, I went out one day, just to be outside. I had not done anything outside in three weeks. It wasn't raining as I thought it had been. There was daylight and hope. But I retreated to my lair. (My office was separate from the rest of the apartment.) I found a desk lamp with a spring-loaded adjustable arm and set it on the toilet tank with the light aiming into the bowl. We had a digital camcorder. I made a video of the toilet flushing the water down, down. And I did it again and again. Flushing, flushing the waste. What a waste.

Part Four

The Library

Carrère

Carrère skipped around his gleaming new Packard, giving it a loving inspection. He ran his palm over the shiny black fender; it was smooth and cool to the touch. He bent over to inspect the hubs, spokes, and tires. He lifted the hood to appreciate the iron engine and the several wires around it. Everything looked great. He then started the engine with the familiar crank, climbed aboard, released the hand brake, and in the mud and rain drove up Fifth Avenue past the Library. At Central Park, he turned around and motored past the great white building again. He stopped at Hastings's house, where Mrs. Hastings baptized the new car the *Hoodoo* on account of it being on Friday the 13th that Carrère had taken delivery. The new car was black; his mood was anything but. He felt like a child with a new toy.

Later he stopped at the Library to see Billings in his new office. He used the 42nd Street entrance, walked along the main north-south gallery and climbed the stairs to the second floor, where the Director's office was located. As he walked along the second floor gallery, he stopped to marvel at the entry hall's space and at the purity of the marble covering every surface. It reminded him of the quarry in Vermont from which the marble had come, except that this space was so great and majestic. This was where the people would come for reading, enlightenment, and learning. So very different from the quarry.

As he climbed the stairs, something caught his eye. For a clearer view of the whole foyer, he moved to the center of the balustrade. But he didn't see anything in the half-lit space, so he started to move on. Then he saw it again. It was a bird! A self-possessed bird perched upon the cornice near the Fifth Avenue door, looking about calmly as if he owned the place. "How did a bird get in here?" Carrère exclaimed out loud. The roof was complete. The doors were shut. How long had this bird been here?

He didn't recognize it, but then he knew little about birds. He knew the robins and blue jays at Red Oaks, but that was about all. Something about the bird in the entry hall made him stay to watch for a few minutes. It took wing and magically flew through the air toward him. Rust red with a yellow breast, the bird was bigger than a robin. It looked at Carrère, then flew in a sweeping arc back across the empty space toward Fifth Avenue; it banked sharply with a single beat of its broad wings, feathers spread, and then floated effortlessly like a condor riding thermals over desolate canyon country. The bird looked above and below and from side to side, as if surveying the enclosed entry hall. At length, it veered toward the exhibition hall and disappeared from Carrère's view below the balustrade where he stood rooted to the spot. He appreciated the effortlessness with which the bird flew—it wasn't simple or easy at the air show—and how perfectly liberated it was, even in such an enclosed space. The bird reappeared. With curiosity and wonder, Carrère put down his brief case and descended the south stairs. No workers were around to break the peace, and he had the place to himself. The bird rested on the north stair railing. The heavy bronze door to the exhibition hall was closed. But if a bird flew in there or down the gallery, it might get lost, Carrère observed.

He returned to the center of the entry hall looking up into the vaulted marble ceiling. This was his favorite part of the Library. The bird gracefully lifted off its perch and effortlessly ascended, contributing its beauty to that of the entry hall authenticating the space, and settled upon the balustrade where he had previously perched.

"There is a bird in the Library," Billings announced from the balustrade, startling Carrère.

He wheeled around to look at Billings. "He's been here for a half hour, but now I don't see him," Carrère replied.

"We should get it out of here," Billings said, his voice as pointed as a pencil.

"A good idea, but it seems like a smart bird. If it found its way in, it'll leave on its own." Carrère held his palms up and climbed the stairs to the second floor gallery. He gathered his brief case and joined Billings. "I would like to say one more thing about that bird." They walked slowly to Billings's office.

"Yes?" Billings seemed tentative.

"This Library, especially the entry hall, is the great inverse of the quarry. The bird made me realize it," Carrère said. "I don't think it's an important point really, except that this Library came out of that hole. I doubt anybody will care in the future where the marble came from."

Billings had a suggestion for him. "You should write the information down just in case some one in the future *does* want to know."

Carrère groaned. "I'm supposed to be writing a monograph on the construction of the Library, but—"

"But what?" Billings demanded. "I didn't know you wanted to. You should've told me. I'd help or do it myself."

Carrère peered at Billings. "What do you know about writing a book? Anything you know is more than I do. Frank Ward has been making notes for me, but—"

"*But*, again. You've never made excuses before. Why now?" Billings adjusted his gold pocket watch chain absently.

"I've been busy but I will get to it. With the family in Europe, I have some quiet time." He fumbled around for a reason to explain the delay. "Also, I just don't know how to begin."

Billings stood in front of him and offered grandfatherly advice. "You just have to start. Just begin tonight and keep at it, and eventually you'll have a monograph. I don't think it's much harder than that."

"If you say so, sir. I'll try to start when I get home tonight."

A couple of days later, on January 15th, Hastings told Carrère that the Library would be dedicated on May twenty-third.

"Why'd the Board select the twenty-third?"

"Don't you know?" Hastings asked. "That day is the anniversary of the date the Lenox and Astor Libraries and the Tilden Trust were combined to create the New York Public Library."

"That date makes sense."

"What about the furniture?" Hastings asked.

"It'll be ready," Carrère assured Hastings. "I will personally make certain Cobb has finished and installed it by then."

The same evening, Carrère started to fulfill his promise to Billings. He sat at his desk at home with the notes, records, and observations accumulated by Ward and his predecessor Polhemus. He cleared the desk of all extraneous papers—bills, architectural drawings, books, candy, and tobacco wrappers. He decided not to try to type. He would write longhand, and Miss Bough could type what he had written. But he knew he would have to make arrangements for Miss Bough to continue to work for him after she left the firm.

He pulled his chair forward and adjusted it so that each arm was the same distance from the desk as the other. No, wait! He needed extra paper in case he had to start over. He pushed out the chair, got the paper from a file drawer and returned to the chair, adjusting it all over again.

Next he prepared the pen. He inspected the tip for imperfections. He poured the ink from its bottle into the inkwell, using care not to spill any of the permanent black liquid onto the blotter. He slowly replaced the cap and nudged the bottle to the side of his desk. With multitudinous pages of notes, a pen, and several sheets of blank lined paper, he was ready.

In his mind, he heard Billings telling him to begin—but to begin was exactly the problem. Begin with what? Billings said, or was it Miss Bough long ago who said it? "Begin at the beginning." So he dipped his pen in the ink, slowly brought it to the paper, and began a pen and ink drawing of the Library from memory. The pen scratched and hissed across the page. Columns appeared, cornices, the roofline, pilasters, and windows, He bent over in furious concentration and drew what he'd seen Hastings draw over and over for these oh-so-many years. He felt a dam burst, an ejaculation, release from years spent minding the business of Carrère & Hastings. He tossed aside the drawing of the Fifth Avenue façade, slipped a clean sheet on his desk and drew from memory the rear façade. The vertical windows, emblematic of the stacks, appeared, as did the nine big reading room windows. After a few minutes, he tossed aside the rear façade and drew the detail of a Corinthian capital. Faster and faster, lost in the force, the beauty and the excitement of what he had missed, he drew the Library and its details. The lions, the entry hall, the fireplace in the trustees' room, the reading room decorations, the columns in the exhibition hall, Hastings's candelabra. The drawings accumulated on the floor beside his chair, until at length he lay his head on a half-finished drawing of a balustrade. He didn't notice that his cheek had rested in wet ink. His eyelids dropped; he was exhausted. His arms dangled straight down outside the armrests. The pen dropped to the floor with a clatter.

After some time, he didn't know how long, he lifted his head. The ink had dried on his cheek. He rose from his chair and inspected the new artwork on his skin in a mirror. He was grateful no one was around to see it. He surveyed the drawings piled upon the floor, picked up one. Shaking his head slowly, he said aloud to no one, "I don't think I'll be writing the book. I'd better find someone else to do it."

Interlude

Peri all but shackled me when she found me videotaping water swirling down the toilet. She snapped up the shades and flipped on the lights. I was naked. She threw one of her robes on me. It was much too small, so she wrapped me in a beach towel instead. I hadn't shaved in a few days and had not slept my regular hours. So I must have looked like hell. Then she called a hospital friend, who recommended that she bring me to the Emergency Room for evaluation. I put on my own clothes and didn't resist. A psychiatric nurse asked me questions, and

Peri answered them. I was dead tired and asked to go to sleep. When I woke up, I saw that I was in a semi-private hospital room. There was an IV in my right arm. The roommate's television was blaring. I had no idea what time it was, but I had to pee. I buzzed the nurse with the call-button device on my chest. One came. She was a large, older woman, and she told me to use the 'urinal,' a plastic piss pot that had been placed conveniently on a rolling tray table. I took care of that business and went back to sleep.

Later, I was awakened by the overhead lights and by Peri who was in her nursing whites, at my bedside.

"You're okay," she said. "All vital signs are normal."

"What time is it?" I asked.

"Seven o'clock. I've already ordered your breakfast. It'll be here in a few minutes. I've just come off duty."

"Were you my nurse?" I had forgotten about the large nurse I saw earlier. "How long am I going to be here?"

"You'll be released this afternoon. But we're not going home." Peri spoke in quiet but authoritative tones. I nodded, realizing that I had no say in the matter. "Where are we going?"

"You'll find out, Henry. You'll see. But it's going to be different. This can't happen again."

"What about the book?"

"I have packed all your research and notes, and books, and laptop into a carton, no, two cartons, which are in the car. They're coming with us, and that's what you'll do when we're not doing anything else. Trust me."

Carrère

"We need a ceremonial key at the opening," Billings said in a brief conversation with Carrère in the Director's Office. It was the last week in January 1911. "I envision a conspicuous thing that everyone can see. It'll be entirely useless, of course."

"I should have thought of it." Carrère felt a little embarrassed at the oversight.

"How about the lions? They are going to be very important to the Fifth Avenue approach. They must be done in time."

"We're going to see them soon," Carrère explained. "I'm told they'll be ready."

The next day, Ed Potter, the lions' sculptor, and Carrère went to see Attilio Piccarilli and the lions. Piccarilli, the stone carver, was hewing the large marble cats of Tennessee marble following Potter's models.

"They look fine," Potter announced.

Carrère ran his hand across an area near one of the cats' haunches and remarked, "The marble will have to be patched here." He tapped on a slight flaw in the stone.

"I know about that," Attilio acknowledged. "But, overall, I am pleased."

Potter said. "I like the color of the stone," commenting on the lions' faint pink coloration. "I think we selected the right color for contrast to the rest of the Fifth Avenue approach.

The lions, both nearly finished, took up most of the floor space in the shop. Dust coated everything. At least a window was open. Carrère drew a heart in the dust with his toe, then quickly rubbed it out. He didn't want anyone to see it.

Potter regarded his models impassively, as almost any artist would regard his work after it has left his control. When he looked again at the actual carving, he said, "It's out of my hands and in his," he pointed toward Piccarilli with an elbow. "He's the artist now."

Attilio, as quick as the cats he was carving, said with a twinkle, "I'm in control, but I don't think you ever were." In an instant though, his humor vanished and he turned serious. "Maybe I'm not either. Maybe I never was. Maybe nobody ever was. Whose idea were these lions anyway?"

Potter ruefully said, "I never was in charge of these lions, even though I'm the one who modeled them." He looked at Attilio, then at Carrère, then to the lions. "Right from the beginning when I first drew the studies, the lions took their own form. I could not change them after I started."

Carrère sensed Potter would yield an important idea. "Why did it happen?"

"No one controls a cat, and that was true for these lions," Potter said. His resignation appeared complete. No one said anything. They seemed to accept it as fact—fate, even—that the lions controlled the artists.

Carrère

"I have to visit the family overseas, I sail on the 25th, Miss Bough," Carrère said. "Could you take care of these matters for me before then." He gave her a list of the jobs in progress, another list with the jobs out for bid, and a list of personal matters. I'll bring them home for the Library's dedication."

Miss Bough, always calm, reacted a little. "Nothing else will change, will it?"

"Of course not." Carrère touched the back of her hand. "Why should we change anything?"

Miss Bough seemed a bit relieved. He had become the most significant person in her life, and he didn't want to hurt her. She sat in the chair beside her desk, crossed her legs, and examined the lists. "Your personal affairs? Do these include the book?"

"I have to say, the book is dead. I don't think I can do it. I have to find some-one who can. Do you know anyone? I thought I was going to ask you to stay with me to type the manuscript, but—"

"You're not?" Miss Bough looked up at him.

"The other day I sat down to start writing. I cleared off my desk, made myself comfortable in my chair, collected all the notes, and when I put the pen to paper, out came this drawing." He thrust the pen-and-ink of the Fifth Avenue façade at her. "It just happened, and nothing could stop me; and I didn't stop until I crashed, and my cheek landed in wet ink, and I was an inky mess." Miss Bough listened spellbound. "It was glorious. Nothing has felt so good in such a long time as drawing from my memory. No limitation! It was utopia, euphoria!" He leaned down, kissed Miss Bough on the cheek. "Will you write the book for me?"

Miss Bough rose and gently wrapped her arms around his shoulders and drew him close. She was almost as tall as he was. Her fingers were limp, without ten-sion. She said, "It's been many years I've been working here. I've done everything you asked. I love you, too." Her gaze was steady, her speech soft. "But you have to write your own book, sir." She released her arms and backed away a half step. "You have to be in control, or not, of its and your own future."

Her eyes became misty, her face dreamy. Miss Bough waited patiently, waited for Carrère to say or do something. He fidgeted with his pocket watch to make sure it was fully wound and then sighed deeply. "I will be home at the end of March." He studied her face. He was in love, too.

"I'll be here when you return." Miss Bough smiled weakly. "Everything will be just fine. The Library is finished and work is pouring in. And you'll be writing your book." Her voice had an edge. "You can't say there isn't much to write about. There is a great building over there."

"I know there is," Carrère said.

"I think you are still afraid of what the book will become," she said, "especial-ly if you had some time to think about it."

"I'm afraid that what happened to Horace Avery will happen to Hastings or to me. What if someone has to take my book away from me because I'm writing to death."

"You will never write it or yourself to death," Miss Bough assured him. "You will always be in control."

"How can you be so sure?" Carrère always respected her intuition.

"You are going to write what you know," Miss Bough said. "You know the Library every step of the way. You just have to do it; I'm not going to do it for you."

Then Carrère realized something and said, "All these years, Tom Hastings has been creating and I have been administrating. I designed Red Oaks but nothing else. This book will be a creative outlet for me. I could make it whatever I want it to be."

Miss Bough agreed. "It's not a bad thing to be like Hastings. You'll be wandering into the danger area he always occupies and you'll love it."

"And you'll be—" he shook his head.

"Anywhere and everywhere, like that guru or muse, beside you, with you, inhabiting your imagination, urging you on. If it sounds like love, it is."

Carrère

With his family in Europe, Carrère frequently dined with friends. One evening, February 11, Donn and Elsie Barber had him over. Barber's house was at East 74th Street. Carrère had much to talk about after the visit to see the lions. It was a chilly winter evening.

Dinner was London broil and beets. On the side was a béarnaise sauce, which Carrère always enjoyed. "What Potter said knocked my socks off," he said. "We all recognized that the lions controlled the artists. It'll be interesting to see what happens with the key."

"Tell me about it," Barber said. After the dessert of chocolate mousse, they retired to Barber's study, where Barber filled two snifters with brandy.

"It'll be an exaggerated key," I explained. "Brenner's designing it. Big and ceremonial, useless."

"I thought so," Barber nodded. He sniffed, swirled and sipped his cognac.

Carrère set his snifter on a mahogany end table and explained, "The key will feature a shield on a flat medallion, not quite round, attached at four points, one at each corner. Minerva and the Owls of Wisdom will rest on both sides, the obverse and reverse, as Brenner said."

"Is he a numismatist?"

"Well, I would say so," Carrère shrugged. "He designed the Lincoln-head penny—the face side—and his studio is full of different medallions and coins. I guess that makes him a numismatist."

Barber removed a penny from his pocket and studied it. "He designed the head but not the reverse?"

"That's right. He'll do a nice job on our key," Carrère sipped his cognac again. "He took a tour of the building with Billings and Hastings."

"Do you feel the key will be a reflection of the Beaux-Artsiness of the building?" Barber asked.

"Oh, most certainly."

"So Brenner did find inspiration in the building?"

"Must've, but he could have been inspired by other things, too," Carrère sat forward sensing prey in the forest. He wasn't going to let it get away.

"So where did those elements come from?" Barber asked the big question.

"I have spent so much time thinking and writing about this. I used to think it was something very complex. But now I'm not so sure."

"Not writing in the library book?" Barber was momentarily confused.

"No, no. In my journals." Carrère shook his head. "When *new stuff* comes to artists, it truly happens in the moment, I believe. It may not be finalized, glued into place, or in its ultimate location just then." Carrère stood and thrust his hands deep into his pockets. He had to pause to collect his words. "I suspect all great long works—the library is an example—are assemblages from over the years. Something as fluid, deep, and only as semi-conscious, as true creating really can't be achieved in short bursts."

"But the key didn't take Brenner years," Barber interrupted.

"Scale and time are relative," Carrère said, recalling how Finn had painted the murals in short bursts. Was this a contradiction? Only maybe, for the murals were a relatively short undertaking, and Finn had made those watercolor sketches first.

"But why?"

"Hastings, a minister's son who turned away from his religious background, might—just might—be the recipient of divine gifts." Carrère said, "There have been times I've been convinced that his ideas were being fed to him by God. "

"God?" Barber looked surprised.

"I think so. There's no other source for the quality of work he produces," Carrère said, but he was unsure of his reasoning. He swirled the snifter again.

"But what happens when he modifies his original intention?" Barber leaned against a bookcase.

"Well, the new idea could defeat it. But I think it's more likely that new ideas could suppress the artist, not the intention, because in Hastings's case, the intention comes from God." Carrère steepled his fingers and held them beneath his chin.

"That means the artist and art are separate from one another," Barber said.

"I think so." Carrère stared into the snifter.

"You said once that Hastings said there's a chattering monkey, the spirit of some dead architectural student—"

"I remember him saying that. But I think he underestimates the source."

"Could you say that creativity, a special power, is proof that God exists? Mathematics and physics are that way—"

"Maybe. But I am not sure," Carrère sighed. It was a challenging discussion.

"You've seen Hastings draw and paint. He seems to be a conduit sometimes, instrumental in putting the ideas on paper and communicating them to the public. I don't think we can ever truly know how an artist modifies what he's working on. Maybe it comes from God. Maybe one thing just leads to the next. It is probably different for every artist."

"But if God gives Hastings his ideas," Barber asked, "could He be the giver of creative powers?"

"He could be. But if we use the dictionary definition of creation," Carrère continued, "which is to 'bring into being or form out of nothing,' creativity would be strictly impossible." Carrère studied Barber's face for a response. "No draftsman, artist, or engineer ever made an artifact from nothing. It has to come from somewhere."

"That is logically correct," Barber agreed.

Carrère continued, "The Library was Billings's vision and dream. It was born of his study of libraries in Europe." He waited for his thoughts to reach equilibrium. "And yet, before we built the Library, there was only empty space, actually a reservoir, along Fifth Avenue."

Barber said nothing for a minute, obviously needing time to sort out the next idea. "Creativity is too beautiful, intimate, and special to be subject to hard, cold reasoning."

Carrère nodded in agreement, then checked his pocket watch. It was starting to get late. Time had flown in the comfortable surrounds of Barber's house. Carrère felt warm all over, his brain especially so, from the effects of the cognac. Where would this go next, he wondered. "I sail to France in a few weeks. Marion and the girls have been there since November."

"Have a safe passage, and please wish your family our best," Barber said.

"I don't enjoy Atlantic crossings in the winter," Carrère wrinkled his nose. "But I miss the family, and I'd like to see my old playground, Paris. Maybe Dieppe, where I spent that wonderful summer with my grandmother so many years ago." He pulled on his overcoat just as the taxicab pulled up to the curb. "I'll find you at the club upon my return in March."

"That sounds perfect."

"Very well. Thank you for the wonderful evening. We should talk about Finn's ceilings next time. You may want to hire him for your Justice Department building. And by the way, Elsie's pie was as good as always."

Barber held the door and cold air whipped into the entryway. Faintly white exhaust rose from the taxi's tailpipe as the four-cylinder motor idled quietly.

"Your Library is a good situation for Thomas as an artist. The project involved much controversy and legal maneuvering, but you were able to include almost all the details you wanted. It's a masterpiece."

Carrère was noncommittal. "It's taken fourteen years, but Tom and I are happy." They shook hands warmly and parted.

Sequence

That afternoon, when I got out of the hospital, we stopped at one of my favorite restaurants, a steak house that had outdoor seating. I ate heartily and drank a big glass of milk. I felt better. Then we went to New York. Peri chose the most active, frenetic location in America for me to recover. We visited with friends every day. Her old friends from NYU, mine from Columbia. We took a cruise around Manhattan. We went to the Central Park Zoo and the Bronx Zoo. We went to a Rangers game at Madison Square Garden. She kept me busy busy busy, but not once did we go to an art museum or gallery. She wanted to keep me away from art and its concomitant spaces. She did a masterful job over the ten days we were there. On the last day, she brought me to the New York Public Library and said, "I think you can write Carrère's book now. Why don't you?"

I had forgotten about it. "But I don't know enough," I protested. "I haven't done enough research."

"But you're here. You can do it. You have to. Nobody else did. Now you're the one."

And so I went to the third floor reading room, plugged in my laptop, and started to write. Not a great surprise, I later realized, but I didn't start writing at the beginning of the story. Rather it was as Barber watched from the top step as Carrère slowly lifted his frame into the rear seat. "Where to, tonight?" the driver asked.

"West 3st Street," Carrère said, waving to Barber.

Barber returned the wave and watched the taxi gather speed heading along 74th Street in the late evening winter hush toward Madison Avenue.

A patrolman stood at the intersection of Madison Avenue and 74th. A trolley from uptown entered the intersection. The black Studebaker taxi, with driver and single occupant did too, but the trolley didn't slow down. There was a huge, jarring crash—trolley and the taxi collided! The policeman jumped back. Glass shattered and fell to the pavement. Carrère was ejected from the back of the taxi, landing on the pavement with a sickening thud, his head snapping back and hitting the curb. Barber jumped with fright, shock, and urgency and ran as fast as he could toward the scene, slipping and nearly falling on an icy patch.

By the time Barber reached the corner of Madison and 74th Street, all the passengers had filed off the undamaged trolley car. The taxi, its rear end rent and torn open, and utterly demolished, lay on its right side. The driver stood stunned beside his taxi. Carrère lay unconscious some thirty feet from the taxicab. There was heavy bleeding from a deep wound above his right ear, and his breathing was labored. His coat, though still buttoned, was heavily torn by the abrasion with the pavement. His left shoe had come off.

The patrolman was the first person to say anything. "We need to call for an ambulance. Mister, Mister—," he said to Barber.

"—Barber," Barber said breathlessly.

"Can you call for an ambulance? Do you have a telephone?"

The patrolman looked at Carrère and then at the crowd that had gathered. "We have to get this man to the hospital," Patrolman Monaghan shouted. More quietly he said moments later, "Haven't I seen this well-dressed man before? Where is his family?"

"That is John Carrère," Barber said, as if reading the patrolman's thoughts. "He lives on West Thirty-first Street. I have a telephone."

"I thought I recognized him. But he's badly hurt. We have to bring him inside. We can bring him to your home, Mister, Mister—"

"—Barber."

"That's right. Excuse me, Mister Barber."

"It's just up 74th Street." You can see my door from here," Barber said.

As the crowd stood aside and two other men assisted, Patrolman Monaghan and Barber lifted and carried the injured architect to Barber's home. In the excitement of the crash, Barber had left his front door wide open and was not wearing a coat.

Within minutes, the four men had carried the heavy and limp, though not lifeless, form up the four steps into Barber's opulent home and laid him on a sofa. Barber disappeared briefly and returned with three hand towels, which the patrolman pressed against Carrère's head wound. Carrère still bled profusely.

Barber again disappeared to call for an ambulance. It arrived after fifteen minutes, and a Dr. Morgan set his black satchel on the floor, took out a stethoscope, and then gave Carrère a fairly thorough physical examination. He listened to Carrère's pulse and breathing with the stethoscope, checked the architect's limbs to see if any were broken. He felt the internal organs, and holding open the eyelids, peered into Carrère's eyes with a bright light. "Does he have a weak heart?" the doctor asked.

"I have no way of knowing," Barber replied. Patrolman Monaghan quietly left Barber's house, returning to the accident scene.

The doctor straightened up after placing a cotton bandage on the wound and a warm cloth over Carrère's forehead. "He's suffered massive head trauma," Dr. Morgan said. "We've got to get him to the hospital."

"Is that ambulance still outside?" Barber asked.

"It is," Dr. Morgan said. "I'll have the drivers bring a litter in, and we'll move the patient as gently as we can. How well do you know him?"

"He's a good friend," Barber explained as the ambulance driver bought in the litter. "We just had dinner together and Mister Carrère's taxi was rammed by the trolley out there."

"Did you say Carrère?" the doctor asked brightly. "Do you mean the architect?" Barber assisted moving Carrère onto the litter and watched as two strong men bore it out the door to the ambulance.

"That's who it is," Barber said quietly in shock. "I hope he'll be okay."

"The doctors at the Presbyterian are very good," the balding Dr. Morgan said. "They are the best doctors in New York."

Hastings was still numb. It had been a full week since Carrère's accident and the horrifying phone call from Barber in the middle of the night. Carrère was still at the hospital in critical condition. Hastings visited his partner, and seeing Carrère's pale white complexion, realized that he was not well at all. Carrère lay on an iron-framed bed, covered with a white sheet, his head bandaged. Nurses wearing white caps brought water and clean linens. A doctor periodically monitored Carrère's pulse. Henri Carrère, the stricken architect's brother, arrived.

"I'm Thomas Hastings, your brother's partner." Hastings offered his hand. "The doctors say his condition is grave."

"That's what I was told, and now I see why," Henri said. "Let's pray he makes it."

In a telephone conversation, Billings inquired, "When is Marion due from Europe?"

"She's on her way. She cabled from Cherbourg on Monday and expects to be here Saturday," Hastings fidgeted in his chair while leaning forward to speak into the mouthpiece. "She and the girls will be aboard the *Kronprinz*, which happened to be sailing at the right time."

"I hope things turn around for him. I must say that it is not likely," Billings said, relying on his training as a medical doctor.

"I hope you're not correct, doctor."

Silence gripped the line as the two men thought for a minute about John Carrère. Hastings admired his friend and partner: how Carrère through his persistence and diplomatic skill with myriad bureaucrats had made the Library reality.

"I owe him a lot," Billings finally said. "He's become my friend and guide. He has educated me on the beauty of Beaux-Arts architecture and talked once about which controls what, the artist and the art. We shouldn't speak of him as in past tense yet."

Hastings agreed, silently running his fingers around the mouthpiece. He added, "He's not dead yet. We should say a prayer for him. I hope. . . oh, I pray for him. . . and Marion and the girls. . ."

Hastings met Marion, Anna, and Dell when they arrived in New York after their passage from Europe. "I'm sorry, Missus Carrère, We've been praying for his recovery. I think that's all we can do."

"We have been praying the entire passage from Cherbourg," Mrs. Carrère nodded gravely. "We spent a lot of time with the chaplain on board. The hardest part is not knowing while we were at sea." Anna stood motionless; Dell slowly swung a purse by its handle. "I think we'd like to visit him at the hospital."

Hastings escorted Mrs. Carrère to Carrère's bedside. She leaned over and kissed her husband on the cheek. The prostrate architect didn't stir. She dabbed a tear from her eye and turned to Hastings, "The doctors don't think —" She choked on a sob, then quickly stood up straight, as if to force her composure to return. Hastings offered her a seat on the only chair in the room, a straight-backed oak number. She refused.

"I need to go home," Mrs. Carrère announced stiffly. She again kissed her motionless husband and stroked his warm hand. "Could you bring me, please? It's been a long time. I'll visit my husband again tomorrow."

"I'll do anything for you, ma'am." Hastings bowed slightly to honor his fallen partner's wife.

The often chatty, even boisterous drafting room had been subdued since Carrère's accident. A pall had been cast upon the men. The general pleasure with which they worked had been sucked way. The atmosphere was a vacuum. No one speculated. No one mentioned McKim, Mead & White and how they had fared after Stanford, and after McKim. The drafting room was dead: humorless and unfathomably empty. All prayed for Carrère's recovery, hoping that he would recover in time to see the great Library on Fifth Avenue open in May. Alas, it was not to be.

Hastings delivered the sad news with all the composure he could muster on Thursday morning, March second, "My partner and our friend, John Carrère, died last night at the Presbyterian." He slumped over at his desk, his face buried in his arms.

Miss Bough, ashen, sagged into a chair beside Hastings. "What awful news." She reached for an empty coffee mug on the table next to the chair. She made sure it was empty, and with precise aim, threw it as hard as she could against the wall. She didn't throw it hard enough to shatter the mug, so only the handle broke. "Why do the great men I've known have to die tragically?

Hastings, astonished at Miss Bough's violent reaction, sat up sharply. His own eyes were red and swollen. "I was going to ask you to help me tell the men. I think I'll do it myself." He rose, seeing that Miss Bough was angry, and wondered why architectural firms were stricken with tragedy. It seemed to be an epidemic.

"I will help you," Miss Bough promised. "I need some details."

"Marion called me at about eight last night to tell me. We know Carrère never regained consciousness after the accident."

"Wasn't the accident on February 13th?" Miss Bough checked her facts.

"About two weeks ago. Nobody ever truly expected him to recover." Hastings used a handkerchief to pat away tears and to stifle his runny nose. "She said she and Anna and Dell were at his side when he passed." He used the handkerchief again, struggling to contain his emotions. "He died at seven-forty last night."

"He didn't see the Library to completion," Miss Bough said. "That's rotten and unfair. I hope Billings can do something in his honor."

"Billings has already suggested that Carrère lie in state in the entry hall," Hastings said. The entry hall was Carrère's favorite space in the Library. It would be so fitting for him to lie in state there."

Miss Bough said, straightening herself. "It's the correct thing to do."

"That's what I think. I assured Billings that the steps to Fifth Avenue and the entry hall are complete and safe," Hastings said.

"If he's going to lie in state, are there funeral plans yet?" Miss Bough asked, dry-eyed.

"The funeral is planned for tomorrow at Trinity Chapel, West 23rd Street. It was planned before he died. "Billings and I are to visit with Missus Carrère this afternoon."

Mrs. Carrère greeted Billings and Hastings in the parlor with a wan smile and an embrace. There were surprisingly few reminders of her husband. A model of the country house, Red Oaks took up part of a shelf in his study. A small, framed pen-and-ink sketch of the first Carrère & Hastings commission, the Ponce de Leon Hotel in St. Petersburg, Florida, hung on a wall. She directed the visitors to a parlor off the front hall.

Mrs. Carrère, with veil covering her face and a floor-length black dress, addressed Billings first, "My husband spoke of you often and how much you contributed to the Library design," Mrs. Carrère said. "I do believe you were one of his best clients."

"Your husband and his partner deserve all the credit for the Library, not I."

Hastings directed his gaze to the floor, not wishing any recognition at that moment. It was time to remember John Carrère.

"Missus Carrère," Billings formally asked with as much tenderness as he could, "We would like your husband to lie in state at the Library for one day."

The widow kept a handkerchief in her lap even though she was dry-eyed. The last few weeks had been overwhelming; there was little emotion left for public display. She had contacted Edward Meyer, the minister at Trinity Chapel explaining that she would like the funeral service to take place as soon as practicable after the passing. He said he could arrange that. In spite of herself, Mrs. Carrère was overcome by Billings's suggestion and began to weep softly. She hastily brought the handkerchief to her nose. "Excuse me," she said. "He would not have wanted the recognition."

"I am sure not," Billings said with care, "but that building is his monument. Nobody should ever forget."

"Let me think," Mrs. Carrère rebounded after a few moments. "The funeral is planned for tomorrow at Trinity Chapel." She inhaled deeply and then exhaled sharply a heavy sigh.

"We want to do him an honor."

"Plainly so. We can change the funeral arrangements." She held the back of a white-gloved hand in front of her mouth.

"Missus Carrère how gracious of you in your time of grieving," Dr. Billings bowed to the widow.

"It's my husband's honor, Doctor Billings. Please just tell me what you would like to do, and I'll see to it."

"Mister Stover has said that we could have your husband lie in state on Sunday, March 5th. We need a day to clear construction debris and sweep the entry hall."

"The entry hall was his favorite part of the Library," Mrs. Carrère said. "It's proper that he lie in state in a space so important to him." Mrs. Carrère agreed.

By Order of Park Commissioner Stover

March 5, 1911

That our City's feelings of admiration and gratitude toward the departed architect of the great Public Library may find fitting expression on the occasion of his funeral, I, the Park Commissioner, whose official relations ever filled me with the warmest regard, have directed that tomorrow at 10 A.M., for the first and only time before its completion, the doors of the library be opened to all the people, that they may enter and behold him lying in state there.

Later that month, the City of New York was shaken by the terrible fire at the Triangle Shirtwaist factory. Over a hundred young women perished. In April, its owners were indicted. Also, the Library's furniture began to arrive. Preparations were made to move books from the Lenox and the Astor to the new library. Hastings and Miss Bough discussed current events and the Library.

"Mister Carrère wouldn't have locked the exits," Miss Bough said. "He cared about workers."

"I didn't know that side of him," Hastings said. He sucked on a hard candy that was stuck in his cheek. He flipped the candy to the other cheek. "What did he ever tell you about why he used to bug me about, you know, overworking my drawings?" He tapped a pencil against his desk.

"He was really worried," Miss Bough explained, "about the firm's finances a few years ago, but then he stopped thinking about it, I think." Miss Bough inspected her bracelet. "He turned to other things. Maybe he was satisfied with everything he had learned. I don't know."

Hastings, still sucking on the candy, asked, "What else was there?"

"I know he was thinking about his book," Miss Bough said.

"Book? I didn't know he was going to write a book," Hastings said, perplexed.

"He called it the Library Book, because it was going to be a monograph about the Library. He wanted there to be a record of how the Library was built, the architecture, and so forth." Miss Bough fluffed her skirt slightly and crossed her legs.

"Did he finish?" Hastings asked.

"Oh, no! He barely started. In fact, the one time he sat down to write, he ended up drawing the façades. All he could do was draw. He couldn't write. So he never started, except for having Polhemus—remember him—and later, Ward keep notes for him."

"Hmmm, I never knew. He never said anything to me about it. Or if he did, I forgot." Hastings scratched his chin. The candy was completely dissolved. "I wonder why he couldn't get started?"

"The real reason is that he was afraid," Miss Bough said. "He was afraid of it becoming something he couldn't control, or of it becoming something he didn't want it to be, and not being able to change it. He even asked me to write it, but I said no." Miss Bough looked at Hastings and was sad.

"Why didn't you agree to do it?" Hastings asked.

"I just said that I couldn't write his book, besides I'm leaving the firm the day the Library is dedicated."

"You are? I didn't know that. Carrère never told me. Where are you going—what are you, what are *we* going to do?" Hastings rubbed his hands on the sides of his head.

"I've been here over fourteen years, and I need to go. That's all I can say." Miss Bough's eyes were as evasive as her words.

"Oh, Miss Bough, we're going to miss you. My partner died, and now our secretary is going to leave us." Hastings was distraught. He ran his fingers though his hair. "What's going to happen to us? How are we going to carry on?" Miss Bough shifted a bit uncomfortably. Hastings had never been one to show her his emotions. "Why do you have to go?"

Miss Bough had decided not to reveal her secret. Her lover, like the previous one, had died tragically, and it was to remain a private matter forever. She waited stoically for Hastings to continue.

"We all had our jobs to do, and you did yours very well." Hastings polished his glasses. "I thank you. Thank you for helping us, and helping John Carrère in all the ways you did." He replaced his glasses.

"I'll be here until May twenty-third." Then she slipped out of the room.

Invitations to the dedication of the New York Public Library were sent to officials at many levels of government, including President Taft and Vice President Sherman. Heads of industry and higher education, members of the judiciary and the clergy were invited. Widows and offspring of departed trustees were sent invitations. Hastings made doubly certain that Mrs. Carrère, Anna, and Dell received preferential seating at the ceremony. In all, about six hundred people were present at two o'clock the afternoon of May 23, 1911.

On a small, temporary platform under the central arch of the entrance portico facing Fifth Avenue, The Right Reverend David Greer, Bishop of New York, opened the ceremony with a prayer. "Here within these walls," he intoned, "may we hold communion with whatsoever things are just and right and true and of good report…"

George Rives, standing erect and tall, recounted the Library's history in a lengthy address. He began with the arrival in New York of an immigrant named John Jacob Astor in 1783; he spoke of the generosity of James Lenox, and of the life of Samuel Tilden. Finally, as the sun crept toward the western façade of the great new Library, it was Hastings's turn. "Mister President, Ladies and Gentlemen: In presenting Commissioner Stover the key of the New York Public Library," his emotions started to congeal, "I desire to remind you of how closely associated with the occasion is the memory of my late partner, John Merven Carrère, whose executive and administrative ability have so largely contributed to the architecture of this building." He looked at Mrs. Carrère and continued, "He, too, would wish to have expressed our appreciation of the intelligent cooperation of all the contractors, and the genuine interest that so many working men have shown in their part of the undertaking, an interest and enthusiasm stimulated by the love of doing their work, and in many cases by their interest in the welfare of this institution." Mrs. Carrère was remarkably dry eyed, though the older daughter, Anna, privately wept.

Hastings set the brown box on the podium, opened the smoothly-hinged lid, and with an exaggerated, ceremonious gesture, handed the key to Commissioner Stover. With the gesture, the Library forever passed out of the control of the artist and into the public domain. The Library was his child, and it was bittersweet to see it grow up and move on. At that moment, it was *back there*.

Commissioner Stover, wearing dark suit and black shoes, followed Hastings to the podium, and called Carrère's untimely death a personal loss. His voice rang:
"He could not perish! He but sank from sight.
As sinks the sun, effulgent in its sphere,
Which knows its heirship to the morning's light.
He died to live, —the marble acclaims him here."

Carrère's widow wept, joining her daughters. "No, he could not perish!" the Commissioner boomed, "Nor will his living mate, whom we all honor this day, perish, while stands this monument of their genius." Not a person who knew John Carrère was dry. The building was as much the headstone as the one to be placed at the Silver Mount Cemetery, where Carrère was buried on Staten Island. Only this one will be seen and loved by everyone for all time.

Stover concluded by presenting Brenner's key to William Gaynor, the new Mayor of New York, the fifth man to hold that title during the construction of the New York Public Library. After a brief remark, Mayor Gaynor handed the key to John Bigelow, the President of the Board of Trustees, who spoke of the palatial structure as a work of art consecrated chiefly to the edification of readers. Bigelow then recognized the Governor of New York, John A. Dix, and President Taft, each of whom spoke for several minutes in generalities on learning, libraries, and philanthropy. When the ceremony concluded, Hastings located Mrs. Carrère. They exchanged an embrace and then greeted well-wishers.

One of the well wishers was Miss Bough. She wore her finest dress and colorful parasol. "I must offer my congratulations and my condolences," she said. She was withdrawn and shy.

"Why thank you, Miss Bough," Marion Carrère said. "We appreciate it. And we will be all right."

"Miss Bough departs the firm today," Hastings looked at Miss Bough. "Am I right?"

"You are sir," Miss Bough nodded.

Mrs. Carrère curiously inquired, "To another firm?" A queue had formed. Several others want a chance to speak with the architect, who said he would be there in a minute.

"No, I'm going to take a trip to I know not where," Miss Bough admitted. "I won't know where I'm going until I get there."

Hastings excused himself to speak with the others. The building had been thrown open for inspection by the invited guests. Hastings confidently strolled beneath the arches through the open door and into the great marble entry hall. He and Billings became the masters of ceremony. Hastings in his element as host, relished explaining the building to the delighted visitors.

Hastings greeted the guests, many of whom said nothing as their eyes followed the curves of the arches and the vault; as they embraced the columns and their meticulously carved capitals; as they observed the strength and beauty of the railings and balustrades on the stairs. Mostly though, the hush was due to the simple fact that there was so much to see.

President Taft made a point of speaking with Hastings: "This is a magnificent building. It's a place for the people of New York for all time."

"Thank you sir. Great credit goes to the City of New York."

"Yes, they have done as wisely as you have done well," said Roosevelt's successor. "I think I'll spend some time here myself after my time in office."

"Thank you again, sir," Hastings said, noting the President's candor. "Thank you for coming."

Hastings answered questions and accepted congratulations. "Thank you ma'am," he said with his easy smile, when one lady remarked on the triumphal character of the entry hall. "We wanted everyone to feel important."

A tall gentleman mentioned the rear façade, "Why is it so much different from the front and sides of the building?"

Hastings was delighted that someone had noticed. "I was looking for an original solution within the bounds of architectural canons," he explained. "The rear façade actually is not all that much different from the front. It's just treated with restraint and simplicity. It's my favorite."

Another gentleman inquired about the marble. "Where did it come from?"

"It came from the Valley Quarry in Dorset, Vermont."

"I say, why marble?" the gentleman asked.

"We wanted a monumental building," Hastings said, "and only marble conveys that." A small crowd gathered around him as he stood, hands behind his back, on the bottom step of the north stair. "This room is completely marble—the walls, the floor, and the ceiling."

"I didn't know Vermont had marble," said a silver-haired man.

"Yes it does, more than you can imagine," Hastings said. His patience was so durable. "We got the best price for marble in the U.S."

"How much was that?" the silver-haired gentleman asked again.

"I don't know. I never concerned myself with those details. My partner, Mister Carrère, would have known. Mister Billings here might remember."

Billings, in a voice loud enough for many people to hear, called out, "I think it was around a dollar a cubic foot, but I don't remember exactly."

Someone else said, "That was so tragic what happened to your partner."

"We miss him a great deal." Hastings's voice was appropriately reverential. He pressed his palms together in front of him as if in prayer. "This building is as much his creation as anyone else's."

The questions for Hastings and Billings continued for awhile. People explored the exhibition hall and the main reading room, where again, they were respectfully quiet. Hastings moved easily, the gracious host, through the building, pointing out details and offering explanations until the last visitor had left. The next day, the Library would open to the general public. It was the day and the future for which the Library was built.

Carrère

Hastings and Brainard, wearing their overcoats, hats in hand, toured the finished building in December, 1911. All details met their satisfaction. "I will send a letter to Billings confirming our opinion that the building is complete," Hastings said. He stopped at the balustrade where Carrère saw the bird and said, "Miss Bough left the firm for who-knows-where." He looked all around the marble hall. A few library patrons were on their way through. Voices echoed; hard soles hitting the marble floor did, too. "I miss her now. She helped us build this place. She was here the whole fourteen years." They descended the south stairs to the entry hall of the New York Public Library on their way out.

"That's right," Brainard said. "Barber, Delano, Aldrich, and Magonigle, have all started their own firms. Polhemus left. Only Ward is still here."

"Our partner is the greatest loss. If he could only have been at the opening," Hastings sighed.

"He was there, Tom. We didn't see him, but he's keeping an eye on you."

"I am sure he is!" Hastings laughed out loud, standing in the center arch of the portico, "I have been thinking of how I would like to improve the Fifth Avenue façade."

Fugue

I checked my gauge: *20 feet.*
Again, *40 feet.*
95 feet.
I finished writing Carrère's book in 2006. It didn't take me as long to write the book as it had taken to build the New York Public Library. I was busy, though.

I knew I should never see the quarry again. We moved to Salem, Massachusetts. Our apartment was a short walk from Salem's famed McIntire District with its fabulous architecture. Peri easily found a job at Salem Hospital and began to think about becoming a physical therapist. When I finished the manuscript, I found a new job with an architectural firm in Cambridge. There was no one like Jayne at my new firm. After things settled down, we finally decided it was time for our honeymoon trip. Peri had always been interested in the Scottish countryside, its history and castles. I wanted to dive the German fleet wrecks at Scapa Flow in Orkney.

We caught a connecting flight from Glasgow to Kirkwall one July day. In a certain way, when we arrived I thought we were still in rural New Hampshire: a faint, distant aroma of cow manure greeted us. *110 feet.*

During World War One, the British Royal Navy interned the German High Seas Fleet at Scapa Flow. There were dozens of ships at anchorage. When the War ended, instead of allowing the British to take possession of the ships, the German skeleton crews on board one morning opened the seacocks and scuttled all the ships. The Flow was defiled beyond belief: oil and debris covered the water for years afterwards. In the ensuing years, the enterprising British salvaged most of them, as the steel was a valuable commodity. Seven of the ships were not recovered, and today these wrecks are the only German warships from the First World War within recreational dive limits, and I wanted to dive them. My friend Tom was to be my guide because he was making detailed, large-format underwater photographs of the wrecks.

110 feet.

Tom used a four-inch by five-inch large-format camera in a home-made underwater housing that withstood the water pressure. He demonstrated how he could clamp the camera to some piece of the wreckage, compose the image through a viewfinder, and open the shutter.

"You're not going to use flash," I remarked.

"No, I'll use a time exposure about seven minutes long," Tom explained. "I swim around and shine my torch on the subject."

"Won't you appear in the image? Shouldn't you stay out of the way?"

"No," Tom began to pull on his drysuit. "You won't see me in the picture. Just what I illuminate."

This should be interesting to see, I decided. A few minutes later we were fully "kitted up" and over the side of John Thornton's converted North Sea trawler. The ocean water in the Flow was warmer than the water in the quarry. We descended along a "shot line" down to the wreck, which appeared out of the gloom at about one hundred feet. It was an immense thing: steel plates, propellers, large-bore guns, and all. The *Dresden* lies on her side.

110 feet.

I followed Tom. He knew just exactly what he wanted to photograph: a small antiaircraft-type gun. I was not familiar with First World War armaments, so I couldn't verify what Tom was going to photograph, except to say that it was a small gun. Anyway, as Tom had said he would, he clamped the camera to a protruding steel beam. His bubbles rose and disappeared into the poor light. He moved efficiently, a man who had performed these maneuvers many times over. He looked at his timepiece, then swam easily toward the small gun. He turned on his light and, like an artist with a paintbrush, swept the beam back and forth across the areas he wanted to highlight. He gave shorter attention to other areas, then returned again to his main interest. He swam back to the camera to check something. He looked toward me and gave me the universal "OK" sign—thumb and forefinger forming a circle, the other three held aloft. I returned the sign. Everything was okay, indeed. *110 feet.*

Tom returned to the subject with his light and brightened it a little more. He touched up other areas, then switched the light off. He took care not to aim the light into the camera's lens—that would have spoiled the image instantly. Tom manipulated some controls on the camera, detached it from the protruding beam, and then clipped it to himself. He didn't want to drop it on the way up.

On John's boat after the dive, I asked Tom, "How did you know where to shine the light?"

"That was a perfect dive," he smiled broadly, still clad in his drysuit. "I could just let the picture take itself. Didn't have to think."

Sources

Blake, Curtis Channing. "The Architecture of Carrère & Hastings," (Columbia University, 1976).

Cameron, Julia. *The Artist's Way* (Penguin Putnam, Inc., 1992).

Carlhian, Jean Paul. "Beaux Arts or 'Bozarts,' " The Architectural Record, January 1976.

Carlhian, Jean Paul. *The Ecole des Beaux-Arts: Modes and Manners*, (Publication and date unknown)

Carrère, John Merven. Typescript diary.

Carrère & Hastings. Correspondence.

Clute, Eugene. *Drafting Room Practice* (Pencil Point Press, 1928).

Dain, Phyllis. *The New York Public Library* (The New York Public Library, 1972).

Dale, T. Nelson. *The Commercial Marbles of Western Vermont* (U.S. Geological Survey, 1912).

Drexler, Arthur. *The Architecture of the Ecole des Beaux-Arts* (The Museum of Modern Art, 197?).

Dunn, Charles. *Conversations in Paint* (Workman Publishing, 1995). Reed, Henry Hope. *The New York Public Library* (Norton, 1986).

Edminster, C.F. *Architectural Drawing,* (Published by the Author, 1905).

Gardner, Howard. *Creating Minds* (Basic Books 1993).

Gray, Christopher, ed. *Fifth Avenue from Start to Finish* (Dover Publications, 1994).

Gray, David. *Thomas Hastings, Architect* (Houghton Mifflin, 1933).

Hitchcock, Henry-Russell. *Architecture, Nineteenth and Twentieth Centuries* (Penguin Books, 1958).

Hooper, Parker Morse. "Office Procedure 1," The Architectural Record, February 1931.

Isbouts, Jean-Pierre. "Carrère & Hastings, Architects to an Era," Rijksuniversiteit Leiden, 1980.

Lowe, David Garrard. *Beaux-Arts New York* (Watson-Guptill Publications, 1998).

Lowe, David Garrard. *Stanford White's New York* (Watson-Guptill Publications, 1999).

Lydenberg, Harry M. *History of the New York Public Library* (The New York Public Library, 1923).

Magonigle, H. Van Buren. *Architectural Rendering in Wash* (Charles Scribner's Sons, 1929).

Mayer, Grace M. *Once Upon a City* (Macmillan, 1958).

Monograph of the Work of McKim, Mead & White (Architectural Book Publishing Co., 1981).

Polhemus, P.B. Manuscript diary.

Resch, Tyler. *Dorset* (Dorset Historical Society, 1989).

Ware, William R. *The American Vignola* (Dover Publications, 1994).

The Century, (The Century Association, 1947).

Van Diver, Bradford B. *Roadside Geology of Vermont and New Hampshire* (Mountain Press Publishing Co., 1987).

Ward, Franklin J. Manuscript diary.

About the Author

John Fiske studied history at Trinity College in Connecticut, where he started to write. A PADI Divemaster, he dives whenever he can.